LUSIGNAN,

OR

THE ABBAYE

OF

LA TRAPPE.

A NOVEL.

Friendship and love, by Heaven seem'd design'd,
That to ennoble, this debase the mind;
Friendship's pure joys in life's last hours remain,
By love, that cheating lottery, we gain,
A moment's bliss, bought with an age of pain!

EDITED WITH A NEW INTRODUCTION AND NOTES BY
JACQUELINE HOWARD

VALANCOURT BOOKS

First published London: William Lane, 1801
First Valancourt Books edition 2015

Introduction and notes © 2015 by Jacqueline Howard
This edition © 2015 by Valancourt Books

Published by Valancourt Books, Richmond, Virginia
Publisher & Editor: JAMES D. JENKINS
http://www.valancourtbooks.com

All Valancourt Books publications are printed on acid free
paper that meets all ANSI standards for archival quality paper.

ISBN 978-1-941147-73-3 (HARDCOVER)
ISBN 978-1-941147-74-0 (TRADE PAPERBACK)
Set in Adobe Caslon 10.5/12.8

LUSIGNAN

CONTENTS

INTRODUCTION

In his *Notes* of 1817, the traveller William Dorset Fellowes declared that the monastery of La Trappe, in the *forêt du Perche* in Normandy, "had dwelt among the earliest impressions of his youth, with something like the force of a romantic tale", and had stirred him "to become an eye-witness of what had so long been one of the most powerful objects of [his] imagination". The source of these youthful impressions is revealed in his later admission that he had also wished to satisfy himself regarding "the truth of those austerities which [he] had read of in the *Memoirs of the Count de Comminge*".[1] This sentimental short novel about thwarted lovers by Claudine Alexandine Guérin de Tencin, which features La Trappe as the setting for its surprising denouement, also provided the signal inspiration for the anonymous author of the present volume.

Having enjoyed considerable success when first published anonymously in Paris in 1735, de Tencin's novel had crossed the Channel with Charlotte Lennox's serializing of her own translation of it in her short-lived British magazine, *The Lady's Museum* of 1760-1.[2] Given that Fellowes was born in 1769, however, it seems more likely that he had read the later translation of 1774, published in London by G. Kearsly who had falsely attributed the work to "Monsieur d'Arnaud".[3] Ten years earlier this gentleman, François-Thomas Marie Baculard d'Arnaud, a former protégé of Voltaire, had frankly appropriated the story's details, building on the denouement and melancholy ending at La Trappe, to create his first, sublimely funereal *drame sombre* which he had called *Les Amans Malheureux, ou Le Comte de Comminge*.[4] While abridged translations of d'Arnaud's sentimental short stories and novels were popular in England in the late 1770s, through the '80s and into the '90s, translations of this play and others by him were not in circulation.[5] In Paris, on the other hand, amidst the fervour for revolutionary drama, *Les Amans Malheureux* was performed twenty times in 1790, twice in 1792, and six times in 1793.[6] Thus it is not impossible that, in his early twenties, Fellowes had had his youthful impressions reinforced by attending a performance there, in which he would have found La Trappe's "austerities", in particular its devotional interior and monastic Rule, morbidly sensationalised.

Lusignan, or, The Abbaye of La Trappe, published by Lane's Minerva Press in June 1801—after a decade in which adaptations and translations for the stage of popular novels and romances had burgeoned—is remarkable in being a four-volume Gothic novel based on both Madame de Tencin's first-person novella, and Baculard D'Arnaud's three act, heroic verse play. However, while canonical Gothic novels and romances such as those of Horace Walpole, Ann Radcliffe and Matthew Lewis come to us with a sizeable history of commentary, exegesis, discussion and debate, *Lusignan* is a neglected work, unassimilated, and virtually unread. One obvious reason for this is that very few copies of the first and only edition of the novel have survived. A second is its imprimatur, which I will discuss later in closing. A third is its anonymity. This in 1801 was nothing unusual; anonymous publication had long been prevalent, and if anything was on the rise in England in the late eighteenth century. The reasons for anonymity among authors, new and established, male and female, undoubtedly varied, but important considerations in the troubled political, economic, and cultural climate of the late 1790s were protection of one's identity from censorious and carping critics, and the freedom to experiment.[7] According to Dorothy Blakey, almost half of the novels published in 1800 by the Minerva Press were anonymous.[8] But although anonymity could stimulate curiosity and interest, and *Lusignan* made its way into twelve out of nineteen possible circulating libraries,[9] it did not receive any attention at all from reviewers at the time of its publication. In contrast, *The Orphans of Llangloed* by the same unknown author, and published in September 1802 by Lane and Newman, was received warmly by the *Critical Review*.[10] Given the strength of anti-French feeling at this time in Britain—the protracted war against revolutionary France begun in early 1793 was an increasing drain, and the uneasy peace negotiated at Amiens in March 1802 lasted only a year—it is most likely that *Lusignan* was deemed too francophile and gloomily sentimental. It may also have been simply ignored as just another Minerva production with "abbey" in its title. However, the "abbaye" of *Lusignan*'s alternative title is not a "fancied abbey" at which late-eighteenth-century literary critics of romances and novels, like the Rev. James Mathias, might sneer.[11] Rather, the novel gives a largely accurate, if anachronistic, representation of the late-seventeenth-century reformed Cistercian monastery which is still located, though rebuilt, and with a practising Trappist community, in an isolated valley in Normandy about eighty-four miles north-west of Paris. Moreover, as Fellowes' traveller's notes bear witness, in the eighteenth century La Trappe was something of a legend in its own right.

Founded in 1140, La Trappe had become an abbey of the Cistercians of the (enclosed) Order of Citeaux, in 1147, but after a long period of prosperity, over the following centuries it had suffered times of ruin and neglect. Its celebrity in the late seventeenth century was due to the reforming zeal of Armand Jean le Bouthillier de Rancé (1626-1700) who by inheritance had been installed as the fourteenth commendatory abbot, and who had experienced a conversion following a tragic love affair, itself the subject of scandal and writing by his contemporaries. As regular abbot, in 1663 Rancé had restored the severe traditions of the self-supporting monastery's holy founders, whose Rule included the divine offices, prayer, meditation, penance, manual labour, sleep on a straw-filled mattress, two daily meals of the most frugal kind, no medical care, and adherence to virtually total silence. This strict monastic observance at La Trappe had then continued until 1790, when, pursuant to the February revolutionary decree against religious orders in France, the monastery was suppressed, abandoned, damaged, sold by the French government as national property, and by 1814 once more reduced to ruins.

In addition to this real life monastery, *Lusignan* does feature two entirely fictional Catholic institutions, and like La Trappe, these function in the plot as places of sanctuary and respite for the protagonists. After the mode of depiction in Ann Radcliffe's romances, they are also strikingly in contrast with each other in terms of their local governance. The first, the Convent of St. Clair, welcomes pensioners as well as housing the nuns of the order. But its corrupt and hypocritical abbess not only happily complies with the demands of a tyrannical parent for the forced monachization of his daughter, but also, on her own authority, later cruelly punishes and incarcerates the young woman as a disobedient nun. The second institution, the monastery of St. Benedict, near St. Jago in Spain on the confines of France, is overseen by a resident abbot of true piety, wisdom and compassion, one who is prepared to risk the disapproval of the Inquisition; but even here we have the narrator's qualification that he was a man who "had been much in the world, and one of the few who retire to a cloister from a pure, though mistaken motive of religion" (Vol. IV, Ch. IV). With this critical focus on monasticism as a system of unnatural, private enclosure where fear and force could be utilised to achieve conformity of belief and behaviour, *Lusignan* taps into the momentous revolutionary changes that, after 1789, had overtaken not just the Abbey of La Trappe and its numerous religious, but the status of the Roman Catholic Church and monasticism in France, with their subsequent ramifications for Britain. By the time of Fellowes' visit, La Trappe had been repurchased, the monastery rebuilt, and its austere Rule restored by its former abbot, Dom Augustin de Lestrange. This only added to its potency for the Englishman as a symbol of vestigial practices from the medieval or Gothic past, practices that, from his descriptions, obviously both fascinated and appalled him.

Despite *Lusignan*'s alternative title and the prominence of monasticism in its plot and themes, however, it is not only a convent story. The barrier to marriage which produces so much anxiety, grief and woe for the novel's protagonists, the eponymous Marquis of Lusignan and his beloved Emily de Montalte, has its provenance in another Gothic vestige. This is *patria potestas*, an ancient European law, entrenched in France, that historically gave virtually unlimited authority to a father over his children and their property until they were married, established in a separate household, or emancipated by some other legality. The lack of freedom to marry for love is also the basis of the lovers' problems in de Tencin's classically structured *Comminge*. But within the broad and baggy compass of *Lusignan*, a hybrid, self-styled "novel", with a primary tragic plot of cruel persecution, a secondary romance plot, and three intercalated stories, the author has scope to exploit much more extensively the feudal laws and customs which had persisted virtually unchanged in France from the period of the novel's setting, the early seventeenth century, to the time of the revolution. In particular, the stories of three of the pairs of lovers—Lusignan and Emily, Eugenia de Foix and the Chevalier d'Aubignac, and Julia d'Ermancy and Marsillac—draw on certain similarities in the way fathers could use civil law and abuse canon law to force their children into marriage or monastic/

conventual life, and also prevent a particular marriage, if the proposed union did not suit a parent's desires or ambitions regarding property and alliance. The early fortunes of the fourth pair, Caroline de Montfort and Dorville, the main characters of the romance plot, are also affected by past unscrupulous use of an aspect of civil family law, primogeniture, in relation to Caroline's parents. As *Lusignan*'s omniscient narrator comments on yet another character's hopeless aspirations to love, this was "an age when even reciprocal attachment was ever sacrificed and made subservient to aggrandizement and sordid considerations of wealth" (Vol. II, Ch. VIII).

Seventeenth-Century French Civil and Canon Law regarding Marriage

In the realm of law in early seventeenth century France, we find an incipient move towards secularism in that the ancient legal doctrine of *patria potestas*, giving the male head of the family complete control over his wife, sons, daughters and servants, was increasingly upheld by the French monarchy against the Catholic Church's Tridentine rulings on marriage made at the Council of Trent in November 1563. French marriage and family law had long been under the canon of the Church, which had stipulated that, while parents had authority to find spouses for their children, and were required to agree to a proposed union, marriage was a sacrament, and therefore the unforced consent of both parties entering into it was essential to its validity. At the Council of Trent, the canon known as *Tametsi* affirmed more strongly this necessity for free spousal consent as the sole requirement for the validity of a marriage, thus upholding the validity of clandestine marriages. Furthermore, the Council fathers "proclaimed anathema (excommunication) against those 'who falsely assert that marriages contracted by [minor] children without the consent of families are invalid'".[12] Likewise, the Council ruled that women could not be thrust into conventual life without their consent, and again proclaimed anathema against all who compelled them to vest and profess. These Tridentine rulings on marriage and monachization thus "flew in the face of *patria postestas*, which was thoroughly ingrained in civil law and parental practice".[13]

Subsequently, the French monarchy did not ratify the Council's Tridentine reforms regarding marriage as French canon law. Instead, in a series of edicts, it made modifications and additions to them in what was effectively its own royal legislation. Henry II's Edict of 1556 had already attempted to prevent clandestine marriages by forbidding men under the age of thirty and women under twenty-five from marrying without the consent of their parents or relatives. While his edict could not attack the validity of secret marriages directly, it introduced severe penalties for disobedience, such as disinheritance and revocation of any gifts and marriage benefits. Without any precedent for royal legislation regarding marriage, the edict could only point strongly to the Christian duty of obedience to parents, and rely on the authority of the king as "the executor of the will and commandments of God".[14] King Henry III, with his Edict of Blois of 1580 went further. *Curés* and vicars were expected to check carefully the ages of persons seeking to marry, and, if they were minors, refuse to celebrate the sacrament without the prior consent of their parents or guardians. A man who married a minor against family wishes was now guilty of rape—this being defined as seduction of a minor under twenty-five years of age, notwithstanding the consent of the minor—and the crime carried the death penalty.[15] Not surprisingly, in practice these laws frequently brought the monarchy into conflict with the church about whether disputes involving marriage and family law should be heard in church or secular courts.

With the growth in the early- to mid-eighteenth century of ideas about love, sentiment, or mutual affection and esteem as the basis of marriage and family life, strict adherence to civil law by parents in disposing of their children also led increasingly to family strife, and intense emotional conflicts of "duty", both familial and religious, with "inclination". In this respect, royal involvement in the enactments of civil law had long enabled parents to request and make use of a *lettre de cachet* to discipline wayward children in relation to marriage or monachization.[16] Husbands also could make use of this method to punish and restrain their wives for supposedly serious breaches of the marriage contract.[17] Moreover, despite its Tridentine rulings on parental use of force and fear, the Catholic Church still emphasised the peace and happiness of a good conscience attendant on the faithful performance of duty, whatever the calamitous circumstances. Regional variations in the way laws were implemented in France, and loopholes for corruption further exacerbated the situation. As shown by Anne Jacobsen Schutte's fascinating historical research on the taking and breaking of monastic vows in early modern Europe, in which Schutte studied nearly one thousand cases,[18] the intrigues and machinations of unfeeling parents and relatives, together with either duped or unscrupulous monastic superiors, were not merely the inventions of eighteenth-century Gothic novelists.

The negative effects of conflicts of love or sentiment with the pressure of filial duty and parental use of force and fear for economic and social advantage are registered in many French literary works and philosophical treatises of the eighteenth century, from Denis Diderot's play, *Père de famille* (1758), his novel, *La Religieuse* (1796), and Jean-Jacques Rousseau's *La Nouvelle Héloïse* (1761) to Holbach's *La Morale Universelle* (1776). Such conflicts are also integral, but with different emphases, to the two works of this period on which *Lusignan* is closely based. As both de Tencin's *Comminge* and d'Arnaud's dramatic adaptation of it are so little read today, I propose now to examine each more closely, with a view to their "Gothic" potentialities. As this will inevitably reveal aspects of the plot of *Lusignan*, readers may like to skip the sections that follow until they have read the novel.

Madame de Tencin's *Mémoire du Comte de Comminge*

The author of *Lusignan* did not find in de Tencin's sentimental *Mémoire* a ready-made romance/novel of the 1790s mystery and terror variety we nowadays label "Gothic". However, the denouement at gloomy La Trappe, the tyranny of Comminge's "ever haughty and malicious" father, and Comminge's extremes of grief and anxiety obviously provide some materials for one, as does Adélaïde's choice of husband, the Marquis de Benavides, whose odious person, rendered more "despicable" by his "meanness of spirit and capricious humour" leads Comminge's mother to "dread the consequences". These features, along with the novella's emphases on mood and theme, are therefore worth considering in detail.

De Tencin's Comminge is first confined by his angry father after he has confessed to burning important legal papers which, many weeks previously, he had been sent to fetch from an abbey in Rouillon in north-western France where they had been lodged for safety two generations earlier during "the confusion of the civil wars". At that time his great-grandfather had disrupted primogeniture in the family by making his younger son his heir "in prejudice to his brother". On the advice of the family's steward, Comminge's father had known since his youth that certain title deeds would provide evidence of entailment that could be used for restoration of estates that had been denied him by his grandfather's will. However, he had had to await the death of his own father before taking action. The purpose of his legal suit is to strip his cousin, the Marquis de Lussan, whom he detests, of virtually all his estates and also avenge what he perceives to be past humiliations by this noble and more able man. Hence his anger escalates to the point of violence and oppression when he learns not only that the papers have been "committed to the flames" by his only son, but that his son's motive is his avowed passionate love for his second cousin, Adélaïde, the hated Lussan's daughter and, again, an only child.

However, in terms of narrative atmosphere, the ominous paternal requirements that Comminge immediately go into exile at one of his father's castles in the country, and that he marry someone else lead initially to romantic episodes highlighting the lovers' sentiments and sensibility, rather than Gothic ones involving fear. On the high road to the castle, Comminge fortuitously rescues Adélaïde and her mother, both injured, from an overturned carriage, and experiences rapturous heights while carrying the lame Adélaïde to a nearby inn, her arms folded around his neck, her hand gently pressing on his lips. Although confessing her love, Adelaide is resigned to waiting for "the smiles of fortune", and she stands firm on the need for filial duty, virtue and constancy, chastising her lover for his unrestrained views that they should not "submit to the tyranny of [their] parents", but simply "fly to the extremist corner of the earth, and enjoy in retirement the sweets of mutual love".[19] The occasion nevertheless has given Comminge the opportunity to renew his pledge, and after a day on the road consumed by the misery of his departure, he at length begins "to taste the tranquillity which results from a consciousness of being loved" (pp. 60-61). Moreover, although the castle is "remote and silent", he does not find his "retreat" threatening. Situated at "the bottom of the Pyrenees", where it is surrounded only by "groves of cypress and barren rocks", croaking ravens, and "the thunder of the cataracts which [fall] from the mountains", it romantically complements his melancholy state of mind:

> This situation, all savage as it was, gave me much satisfaction. For the gloominess of the prospect fed the melancholy of my mind. I spent whole days in the woods, writing the effusions of my love; this was my only pleasure, this was my sole employ. (62)

Even later, when he is closely confined in a dimly lit dungeon of the castle for refusing to marry Mademoiselle de Foix, he is not "wholly devoid of satisfaction", and pays "no regard to the inconveniences of a prison". Only as time goes on, does he become subject to "agonies of grief" and "apprehension" regarding the possible use of force against Adélaïde (68-69). The letter he then receives from her, informing him of her imminent marriage as the price his father has demanded for his liberty, constitutes a deft and swift use of parental force against them both.

Subsequently, the source of continuing threat for the lovers becomes the gloomy, capricious, and implacably jealous Marquis de Benavides, whom Adélaïde, as a mark of her fidelity to Comminge, has chosen to marry as the most repugnant of her suitors. Suspense builds when the grief-stricken but still passionate Comminge, with the aid of his ever faithful manservant, St. Laurent, rashly inveigles himself into Benavides' country estate in Biscay disguised as a painter so that he may observe his melancholy Adélaïde without her knowledge. His own extremely labile emotions soon erode his resolve, this instability not helped by the marked kindness and protectiveness extended to Adélaïde by Benavides' young, "universally esteemed" and amicable brother, the Chevalier d'Orfanne. When the inevitable confrontation occurs, and the Marquis confronts the lovers just as the distressed Adélaïde, having discovered Comminge's presence, is urging him to leave, both men are wounded, Benavides more seriously. Comminge is confined to a dungeon, and having compromised his virtuous Adélaïde's safety, wishes to die. But as the Marquis still does not know his true identity, he eventually heeds the injunctions of the devoted Chevalier, who tells him that the Marquis's wound is not mortal, that Benavides has already confined his wife to her room, and that it is her wish that

Comminge leave immediately because his continued presence will only make her situation "more dreadful". The Gothic overtones of this situation are palpable. Comminge's refuge in a "convent of religious at some small distance" will enable him to elude the search the Chevalier will be necessitated to make, as the Abbot is one in whom he may "most implicitly confide".

Thus do French religious institutions enter the tale as places of succour, despite de Tencin's obvious reservations in her preface about the psychological and physical deprivations of the cloistered existence. The Abbot is "a man of address, well acquainted with the world" and has "much philanthropy in his disposition". Only "a variety of accidents had at length fixed him in a cloister" (124). He not only has a surgeon dress Comminge's wound, but takes pity on his mental affliction and gains Comminge's friendship and confidence "by his sensibility". Prepared to listen attentively again and again to Comminge's misfortunes as he repeats his story "a thousand times", the Abbot enters with compassion into all his sorrows, and gives him news of both the Marquis's gradual recovery and Madame Benavides' withdrawn condition, with a view to preparing him for departure. But after two months, with his wound still not properly healed, Comminge's agitation on discovering that Adélaïde has died reduces him once more to a state close to death, and then, when he rallies, to renewed indulgence in self torment. To this end, he begs to see the Chevalier d'Orfanne, himself now in the depths of misery at the loss of the woman he had come to adore. D'Orfanne relates the circumstances of Adélaïde's sudden death, which had occurred only three days after he had left for Angers on business at Benavides' request. Though suspicious of a number of circumstances, d'Orfanne, on the evidence of a letter, had perceived his brother to be so affected by the loss of his wife that it was difficult to believe him guilty of contributing to her death. While the truth of this matter is thus left in question for the reader, both men prepare to move on.

D'Orfanne determines to immerse himself in "the perils of war" in Hungary, and "either recover [his] long-lost tranquillity, or find in an honourable death a period to [his] woes". Comminge resolves to re-acquire the physical strength for the fatigues of a journey which will enable him "to secrete [himself] where melancholy reign[s] alone" (158-159). After sending St. Laurent to deliver a letter to his

mother, he disposes of his effects apart from sufficiency for his journey. His only significant possessions are Adélaïde's letter and the
picture of her he had acquired in a duel early in their relationship,
and which he always carries close to his heart. Preoccupied with
thoughts only of her, he farewells the honest Abbot without the
heartfelt gratitude and affection that is his due, and proceeds without interruption to La Trappe. There he requests the habit, under-
takes the novitiate, and is professed.

   In her brief preface about the severe practices of the founder's
Rule for the institution, de Tencin describes the approach to La
Trappe romantically. It is seemingly "designed by nature the retreat
of penitence; it being invironed (*sic*) with with woods, lakes, and
mountains, which render it almost inaccessible":

> In this solitude silence ever reigns: language can but faintly paint
> the melancholy scene; a scene teeming with the most noble traits
> for the gloomy imagination of a painter or a poet. (3)

With her usual commendable brevity, she has Comminge neither
augment this, nor dwell on the monastery's "prescribed austerities".
To these he merely conforms with "indifference", confirming the
desired effect the place has for him:

> The solitude, the silence of this seat of misery, together with their
> melancholy which was stampt on every face, contributed not a
> little to the nourishing of my grief. (162)

The real centre of his devotion and ritual becomes apparent in his
revelation that every day "he secreted [himself] in the bosom of the
woods" where he read his Adélaïde's letter, dwelling on every word,
and examining her picture "till imagination gave it life". Having
bathed one and then the other with his tears, he would return to
the convent "more ineffably miserable" (163). In this manner, he had
lingered for three long years in "a life of misery without the least
alloy, when the bell summoned [him] to assist at the last moments
of a brother," who was lying on a plank strewn with ashes, and
receiving extreme unction.

   For the next thirteen pages, this brother, who has begged permission from the Abbot to break the rule of silence, and has startlingly

confessed to being "a wretched, sinful woman whom love, unholy love, conducted thither", speaks in her woman's voice. As she begins to relate her story to the Abbot and assembled community, we recognise her as Adélaïde. She had not died, but been immured in a dungeon by her cruel husband, and released by a domestic only after his death. Having found all enquiries after the only person for whom she wished to live fruitless, she had determined on retirement. Dressed as a man, she had stolen away from her home with the design of entering a convent near Paris, but drawn to the chapel at La Trappe on impulse, she had heard in "the fulness of the anthem" a voice she recognised, the voice of her lover. Despite harbouring blasphemous thoughts towards God for "seducing" him from her, she had found that she could not tear herself away, and earnestly praying for admittance had been accepted. But her heart had then throbbed "with guilty passion", as her soul remained "wrapped up in him [she] loved", and suffered her "to taste the empoisoned joys of breathing the same air, and of being under the same roof" (170).

Most amazingly for the reader—and this reveals the extent of Comminge's self-absorption and indifference to externals—she had "haunted [her] lover as his shadow", assisting his labours with what little strength she had. Such was her infatuation that she would even have revealed herself but for the dread of interrupting his tranquillity. The zeal with which he dug his grave according to the Rule of the order at one point had induced in her such sorrow that she had been forced to retire, but the idea of losing him had then preyed on her imagination to such a degree that she had become loath to let him out of her sight. It was on one occasion when he had eluded her, that she had discovered him in the maze of the wood, and found that his object of contemplation was her own picture, and that, far from enjoying spiritual repose, he was, like herself "an unhappy victim to a more unhappy passion". At this point, in the full realisation of their sacrilege, Adélaïde had prostrated herself at the holy altar, praying for her conversion, that she might obtain it also for her lover. By God's grace, she had found peace of mind and was prepared to die. Without revealing his name, or addressing Comminge directly, Adélaïde finally prays that, "if the companion of [her] infatuation still labours under the oppression of iniquity, let him reflect on the object of his foolish passion," and also on the death that awaits him (176). She dies after requesting the pardon of the community, and acknowledging herself unworthy of partaking of their sepulchre.

That de Tencin's primary focus is unfulfilled romantic love as an anarchic passion, not subject to reason or social conventions, is reinforced when Comminge does not heed Adélaïde's prayer, but "delirious with grief", springs from the religious who have crowded to his assistance. He seizes her lifeless hand, and bathes it with a torrent of tears, bewailing this final loss of her, especially as she had been with him and "[his] heart ungrateful knew her not." Removed forcibly to his cell, he is treated with pity by the father Abbot, who agrees that the same tomb shall unite the lovers' ashes, in return for his promise not to take his own life. Comminge, confident that his Adélaïde "will intercede with the Almighty for a remission of [his] sins", is also granted permission to remove to a hermitage where he can continue to nurture his grief. Again, the father Abbot's toler-ance and compassion, especially in such a strict order, makes of him all that Comminge's own despotic father was not. Duplication of parental despotism by church authority, such as we often find in late eighteenth and early nineteenth-century British Gothic fiction, is not a feature of de Tencin's *Comminge*.

Baculard d'Arnaud's *Les Amans Malheureux*

D'Arnaud's sublimely gloomy adaptation of de Tencin's tale in turn gives far less prominence to the parental tyranny that ruins the lovers' happiness. Highly emotional and declamatory, the play instead capitalises on the anguished conflict between worldly love and religious vows, and the nascent sensuality, of de Tencin's final scene. Frère Arsene (Comminge) is acutely aware of his sacrilege from the start, and also inexplicably drawn to another brother, the frail and ailing Frère Euthime (Adélaïde), who is often close by. However, in its use of the supernatural, *Les Amans Malheureux* does anticipate more directly the terror and suspense of later eighteenth century Gothic romances and novels, although not the sort of evil-associated horror depicted in Matthew Lewis's monastic scenes in *The Monk*. Rather, the play evokes intentionally a specifically reli-gious awe and terror.

To this end the sole *mise en scène* is a vast and deep *souterrain* or underground vault, with solemn inscriptions on its walls. At the back is a tall cross surmounted on the tomb of Rancé and surrounded by inscribed skulls, to the sides, newly dug, unfilled graves, and in the two wings, at distant intervals and on slightly higher ground, an "infinity of little crosses" which mark the sepulchres of La Trappe's profoundly religious. In this macabre place, with its rule of silence, the play's cowled protagonists, the professed Frère Arsene and Frère Euthime (her identity unknown to all, and revealed by her only at the end of the play) dig their graves. A high point of this action occurs in the sixth scene of Act II, in which Euthime discovers Arsene contemplating Adélaïde's portrait, speaking her name, and covering the miniature with kisses and tears. Involuntarily breaking silence, Eutheme cries out his name, unknown in the fraternity—*"Ah! Comte de Comminge!"*—and he is riveted by the *"accents"* of her voice—*"cette voix . . . cruel. . . ."* He follows her as she quickly retires, repulsing his attempts to speak to her. His uncanny attraction to the brother has grown incrementally, and he now thinks of him as *"cher Euthime"*. However, the subtle markers which could prompt his recognition remain subliminal until the end.

They are blocked by the central anxiety which arises from his emotional enthralment to his pledge and feelings of love in contradiction of his monastic vows. This obsession erupts in his every thought, and frames his perceptions of his surroundings—*"ce lieu de terreur"*—as he calls it at the outset of the play. In this scene, alone on stage, anguished and prostrate before the crucifix and the tomb of Rancé, Arsene prays aloud to Rancé, as *"maître des passions"*, about his inability to conquer his passionate love for Adélaïde. When the much concerned Père Abbé later allows him to break silence, it is with Arsene still at the tomb of Rancé that the former hears his confessional story. The tomb and characters' positioning are important for the atmosphere of the *sombre* and the moral and spiritual reflection d'Arnaud wished to evoke in his audience, and which he explicates in the play's *discours préliminaire*.

It must be remembered that for centuries the Roman Catholic practice of keeping saints' relics and tombs near the church altar had been an important aspect of devotions. Western Catholicism's Doctrines of Merits, Works of Supererogation, Purgatory, Intercession of Saints, and Invocation of Saints tended not only to the belief that departed saints loved those adhering to Counsels of Perfection (such as vows of poverty, chastity and obedience), prayed for the conversion of sinners, and interceded for both groups; it also gave rise to the commonly held and comforting notion that the saints' bones and ashes had the same virtuous efficacy for the prayerful living and the buried dead positioned near them in the church or monastery.

It is in the context of such rapprochement between the living and the dead that we need to situate our understanding not only of the prominence given to the tomb of the revered Rancé, but also of d'Arnaud's use of the supernatural. Near the end of his guilt-ridden prayer about his worldly love at the beginning of Act I, Arsene reveals his uncanny sense that the dead brothers, reassembled, are rising from the ground and calling him near as one of themselves, and chastising him with the assertion that a just God will avenge his profanation.[20] Again, in another vision early in Act II, the conflicted Arsene sees these shades once more—"*ces Spectres ténébreux ... toutes ces pâles Ombres*"—and then the rising ghost of Rancé, who he anticipates will cover him with the flames of his anger, and whose voice he hears addressing him. Why is he straying from the arms of a God to whose bosom he wished to retire? He wants to break those bonds which have attached him to Him? Rancé continues to chastise him, warning him that Heaven has rejected him, and to tremble before the roaring fires of hell that await their prey.[21] This vision comes at a climactic point when Arsene is strongly tempted to break his vows and leave the monastery to rejoin Adélaïde, who he has learnt from a visitor did not die, but was imprisoned by her now deceased husband, the Comte d'Ermansay. Not only is she still alive and at liberty, but she still loves him and awaits him at the Comte's chateau. Finally, early in Act III, a tomb is once more the location of terrifying supernatural events which involve both Adélaïde and Euthime, and constitute the climax of a symbolically prophetic dream. This he describes to his lingering visitor, bearer of news and fellow sufferer, the Chevalier d'Orvigni (d'Orfanne), who has earlier confessed to Arsene the circumstances of his own adulterous passion for his sister-in-law, and is now also grief-stricken. Formerly d'Orvigni had urged Arsene to leave and make his yearning Adélaïde happy. But the Chevalier's late receipt of a letter informing him that Adélaïde, in the despair of her loss and continued suffering, had terminated her own life a year previously, has confirmed his resolve to remain at La Trappe. In consequence, d'Orvigni is present with Arsene at Euthime's dying, confessional address to le Père Abbé and the assembled fraternity.

Because Arsene's supernatural visions are products of his conflicted state of mind and emotions, they could not be dismissed by the play's audience as a gratuitous indulgence in superstition on the part of the author. In his preface to his play, d'Arnaud claimed that, executed well, the impact of such visions on characters and audience alike would be striking and profound, "a source . . . of delicious horrors for the soul", and conducive to self-reflection and moral improvement.[22] Melodramatic though his play undoubtedly is, the intensities of his realisation of the *sombre*—the proximity of death, the sense of a supreme power beyond the grave, and the conflict of worldly love, melancholy, grief, with religious vows and enthusiasm—could not be better evoked than in a drama played out amidst Rancé's Rule of silence and mortifications at La Trappe.

It remains now to examine *Lusignan*'s expropriations of d'Arnaud's play, and also of de Tencin's *Comminge*, bearing in mind that the changes made to prior works in the process of their appropriation and reworking frequently lay bare not only the extent of the author's skill and style in bringing together overlapping and disparate elements to create a new, apparently unified text. They also reveal ideological positions. Omissions, additions, nuances, distortions and conflations can be most telling in terms of the author's own views and social, cultural and political milieu.

Gothic transformations: *Lusignan, or, The Abbaye of La Trappe*

The importance of the anonymous author's decision to set the novel a century earlier than de Tencin's *Comminge* cannot be underestimated. Historical allusions at the beginning of *Lusignan* to the late-sixteenth-century religious wars in France between Catholic and Protestant or Huguenot factions, which had split "the illustrious house of Meronville", firmly place the novel's main action in the relatively more peaceful and enlightened decades following Henry IV's 1598 Edict of Nantes. This royal decree, which remained in force with varying implementation by his successors until its revocation in 1685, granted substantial civil rights and freedom of conscience to French Protestants, who were no longer to be treated as heretics. However, the Edict still affirmed Catholicism as the established religion, and all citizens had to respect Catholic restrictions and rituals regarding marriage. Much intolerance also remained in various quarters from the time of the wars, and it is against this tension that the plot of *Lusignan* is played out over a period of about twelve years.[23]

An allusion to Catholic massacres of Huguenots "at the shrine of ambition and bigotry" as "an excess of barbarity at which humanity shudders" makes clear the author-narrator's allegiance to the Protestant cause. When the Marquis of Lusignan and his second cousin, Emily de Montalte, fall in love and hope to marry, given the past Protestant affiliations of some members of Emily's family, the lovers are positioned to suffer the legacy of religious bigotry of Lusignan's Catholic great-grandfather. A bitter and self-serving hatred of her family has been nurtured in Lusignan's gloomy and vindictive father, the Duke of Meronville, by the Duke's former tutor, now his elderly steward and spiritual adviser, the Abbé La Haye. An evil character entirely absent from both de Tencin's novella and d'Arnaud's play, he is essential to the Gothic transformation effected by the novel.

Seemingly an *abbé de cour*, that is, an ordained man who has taken the vows of chastity, poverty and obedience, but is not attached to a parish, abbey, or any regular exercise of priesthood, La Haye has achieved an oppressive power over the beliefs and actions of his patron. He thus displaces the hero's father in the Comminge story as the chief perpetrator of the lovers' persecution. His manipulation of the civil laws of the land for his own ends includes the procurement of a *lettre de cachet* on the Duke's behalf in order to confine Lusignan legally, while his exercise of his clerical authority enables him to obtain information and cooperation from the superiors of religious institutions, such as the Abbess of St. Clair. Both the novel's initial Protestant, historical perspective, and La Haye's malevolence and abuse of his position render him a Gothic villain in the tradition of Ann Radcliffe's *The Italian* (1797). Moreover, in contrast to his unfeeling trickery and cruelty and the Duke's ferocity, Lusignan and Emily, like the virtuous hero and heroine of *The Italian*, are anachronistically endowed with appropriate eighteenth-century sensibilities, including British liberal principles that highlight the full significance of the delusions and iniquities of the *ancien* political and religious regime with which they must contend.[24]

As the primary source of evil, La Haye is less sympathetically developed than Schedoni in *The Italian*. While Schedoni is memorable for his sublimely austere and gloomy appearance, his loftiness of spirit, and his complexity of character, the degenerate La Haye, without such mystique, is more like a stage villain, relegated to the wings for much of the novel. At a point well into the first volume, the narrator asserts that he possesses "every quality that can constitute the finished villain", but description of his physical appearance seems to have been deliberately eschewed. Indeed, at the service of suspense (and at times with bad faith), the narrator proceeds by often holding something back, so that the full extent of La Haye's deceit, religious hypocrisy, ambition, and disloyalty to his patron are revealed only incrementally. Nevertheless, it is soon made evident to the reader that the Duke's dependence on his confessor and tutor is misplaced, as the cleric's chief characteristic is "dissimulation". His frequent resort to verbal bullying, with its attendant casuistry and blatant hypocrisy, positions him as an object of detestation and contempt rather than of fear for the lovers, though his intrigues are throughout a source of apprehension for the reader.

A representative example of La Haye's spuriously pious and casuistical manner is his persistent counsel to the Duke against consenting to the obviously advantageous marriage of Lusignan and Emily on the grounds that the latter's grandparent, the Comte de Clarival was "a heretic". When Meronville reminds him that his late cousin and Emily were admitted into the pale of the Church, La Haye asserts that Madame de Clarival has remained a Protestant, and that "the blood of heresy is mingled in the veins of her daughter with that of true believers". He thus "dread[s] to sanction [. . .] an union which might pollute [their] holy religion":

> As a minister of Heaven, I must carefully guard the interests of the Catholic faith. . . . Heaven avenges the heterogeneous union of true believers with infamous apostates; and the sins of disobedience, if not punished on earth, will be recorded in Heaven and eternal perdition waits on successful villany!" (Vol. II, Ch. VI)[25]

In fact, the cleric has secretly fathered two illegitimate sons, known only as his nephews, the Chevalier St. Amand and Chevalier d'Aubignac, for whom he has his own dark ambitions of advancement by marital alliance; hence his intention of "occasioning a breach" between Lusignan and his father. Apart from intrigue, La Haye uses opportunistic lies, theft, and forged letters and signatures to gain his desired ends, all the while playing on his patron's desires and emotions:

> La Haye . . . opened his batteries by degrees; his projects were not formed on system, but always adapted to existing circumstances; and the versatility of his attempts rendered them less suspicious, but more to be dreaded. (Vol. II, Ch. I)

Ironically encapsulating the narrative strategy critics perceived in Radcliffe's novels, the narrator further comments that "La Haye knew the effect of suspense; he tried it, till his patron was wrought to the highest pitch of impatience and curiosity."[26]

Exemplification of his ploy occurs when La Haye forges, and then shows to the Duke, a letter supposedly from Emily, which implicates both her and Lusignan in the disappearance and concealment of Eugenia de Foix, the Duke's chosen bride for Lusignan. When the enraged Duke solemnly swears by his God and all his future hopes of mercy "never to forgive [his] degenerate son", La Haye feigns piety and intercessional prayer:

> With profound hypocrisy La Haye lifted his eyes to Heaven, and falling on his knees, with a deep sigh pronounced these words:— "Recording spirits, that note the words of man, blot from thine eternal register this sacred oath! And all ye sainted spirits, that intercede for sinful mortals, pour repentance into the deluded heart of Lusignan!" (Vol. II, Ch. I)

But once the Duke has grown calmer and more rational, and requests to see the letter again, La Haye withholds it, claiming that he is "not permitted" to divulge any details of how it came into his possession. Moreover, when the Duke later experiences a crisis of conscience, La Haye uses the supposed "inviolability" and "immutability" of his patron's former oath against him, denying that, as a priest, he has any power to absolve Meronville from the "obligation an oath imposes". This assertion is, of course, obfuscatory and dishonest. In Catholic theology, to swear falsely does constitute a (mortal) sin of perjury, but Meronville's promissory oath would not be considered an act of virtue in religion in the first place, and would not entail the obligation of fulfilling it. Here again one is reminded of Radcliffe: this time of her narratorial remark regarding the monks of the Abbey of St. Augustin in *A Sicilian Romance*, that "scholastic learning, mysterious philosophy, and crafty sanctity supplied the place of wisdom, simplicity, and pure devotion".[27] As *Lusignan* highlights problems and hypocrisies in regard to Catholic oaths and vows in a number of different contexts, her comment seems particularly apposite.

The author also uses La Haye's malignity towards Lusignan and his mother to evoke a sense of supernatural fear at Luneville Castle. La Haye bears "an inveterate hatred" towards the gentle and wise Madame de Meronville simply because she also shares the Duke's confidence, and has devoted her life to soothing the ferocity of his nature, as well as caring for Lusignan, whom she loves dearly, and for whose interests and well-being she often mediates. Notably, on her arrival at Luneville Castle, La Haye subjects her to supernatural terror when, late at night, she attempts to traverse the long gallery leading from her apartment to that of her son. The uncertainties and fear resulting from the introduction of a possible ghostly presence immediately inject a further Gothic element into *Lusignan*.

The narration of this first supernatural episode is brisk and compelling. At intervals along the dark gallery, arched cavities house white marble statues of distinguished persons. When one of these inexplicably moves twice, and "a hollow voice" from seemingly nowhere, and then from the end of the gallery, says "Beware!" Madame de Meronville, who has absolutely "no propensity to superstition", stands in "motionless terror, debating on the best course to take". The sudden appearance of a dark figure crossing the end of the gallery, and carrying a small lantern, she mistakes for Lusignan, and rushing towards it, finds herself "forcibly detained by her robe":

> Unused ... to every species of alarm, her gentle frame could no longer sustain itself; she sunk lifeless on the floor. When she recovered, to her infinite surprise she found herself in her own apartment, without the least appearance of having quitted it. (Vol. I, Ch. VII)

She soon discovers, however, that the letter from Emily, which she had held in her hand to give to Lusignan, has disappeared. Next morning, in the manner of Radcliffe's Emily St. Aubert in *The Mysteries of Udolpho*, she reproves the too garrulous maid, Gabriella, for her credulity in believing another servant's report of a similar ghostly figure. However, while affecting "to disbelieve the whole", Madame de Meronville privately (and most plausibly) thinks it "not improbable that some plot was carrying on that required the aid of supernatural appearances", a view with which Lusignan concurs when Emily's letter, with its seal broken, subsequently turns up in his room.

If this provides an instance of Radcliffe's "explained supernatural", three further episodes introduce a real ghost which, at its second appearance, proves to be that of Emily's father, returned to warn her to flee the castle. However, the strange amnesia experienced by the anxious Emily in response to this warning—like a dim awareness of a bad dream which had been eclipsed on waking but which has left an indefinable dread in its wake—continues to trouble her days. She becomes increasingly apprehensive about her approaching wedding at the same time as her beloved Lusignan rises in her esteem. When, just as the clock strikes 2 a.m. on what is supposed to be the day of their nuptials, the phantom, in "spotless white garments" and with "haggard countenance", again appears before her, it is to give her dread news. As "the east already glows with orient red", he bids her farewell, requesting, like the ghost in Shakespeare's *Hamlet*, that she remember her father. The anxieties raised in her by this episode, coupled with the dreaded news only a few hours later, of Lusignan's mysterious disappearance during the night, reduce Emily to a state of pathological stupor which progresses to a complete mental breakdown and life-threatening fever.

With such dramatic events, *Lusignan* departs markedly from *Comminge* while subsuming its plot in outline for the atmosphere of the Gothic romance-novel. Emily de Montalte's subsequent marriage to the loathsome Bentivoglio certainly parallels that of de Tencin's Adélaïde to Benavides in terms of motivations, events, and consequences. But in contrast to Adélaïde, Emily exists as a character in her own right from the second chapter of the novel. Moreover, as in the case of Lusignan, her mental and emotional states, such as those mentioned above, her conflicts of "duty" with "inclination", and her grief on the death of her mother, are all closely tracked in the manner of Radcliffe, providing stages in her spiritual journey as she refuses to give in to despair. The author also invents many details to exploit the melancholy and apprehension of threat in Emily's situation at Luneville Castle, and later, at the Castle of St. Jago, not least by emotive descriptions of the sublimely sombre locations and architecture of these Gothic piles.

This scene painting is again strongly reminiscent of Ann Radcliffe's descriptive style, with its penchant for the terrific. Take, for example, the travelling Emily's first impressions of Bentivoglio's St. Jago, which cause her to exclaim in wonder at "the luxuriance of the prospect":

> In a valley beneath stood the Castle, in the construction of which the architect had exhausted his utmost powers, and one side of it, through the lapse of ages, had defied the wreck of time. The magnificent ruins of the other side, which was not equally sheltered by the haughty Pyrenees, formed a contrast at once terrific and astonishing; its base was laved by the encroaching waves of the Mediterranean, and the eye, at one view, seemed to compass the vast expanse and the immeasurable Pyrenees; extensive woods and plains of boundless width, appeared objects in miniature before these gigantic features of nature [. . .]. (Vol. IV, Ch. II)

But on the steep descent down a hewn path, the mansion is revealed to be "melancholy and cheerless". Its dark stones, and antique windows, mostly "obscured by strong iron bars, through which they presented a picture of sublime ancientry", hold no promise of enjoyment, raising only a wonder "unmingled with a softer sensation". Likewise, the "gloomy and spacious halls", exhibit "an awful solitude", while the "traces of magnificence", the "grotesque figures on the tapestry, the roof of mosaic fretwork", and the huge mirrored panels, all reflect "the various vestiges of antiquity", only to produce "a concatenation of differing ideas". Following the practice of Radcliffe still further, the author-narrator here, as elsewhere, is at pains to point out the accordance of the heroine's feelings with her environment:

> At a moment when the susceptible mind attunes itself to impres-

sions of sorrow, the most common incidents convey importance, and are construed into presages of woe.

Earlier, in marked contrast with both this forbidding location and that of Luneville Castle, Emily's home, Montalte Abbey, is invitingly situated on the Norman Coast, "nearly at the entrance of St. Michael's Bay". This "monument of antiquity", first possessed by "the celebrated Rollo", and which in part has been "somewhat modernized" for the family, commands "a vast diversity of prospect":

> . . . nature seemed here to have combined those various beauties which are usually scattered with a frugal hand.
>
> To the eastward a beautiful ridge of rocks, called the Casquets, which, at low tide formed a delightful seat, whence the inhabitants had an extensive view of Old Ocean; the small island of Alderney was completely traversed at a glance; and to the west the ports of Cherbourg and St. Maloes were distinctly seen. . . .
>
> At the back of [the Abbey] some small eminences rose perpendicularly, to shelter the fertile dales from the detrimental north winds; and these, by the regularity of their position, formed a kind of natural amphitheatre, covered with brushwood of various tints.
>
> A small rivulet ran at the bottom, whose gentle course was sometimes interrupted by enormous stones, which appeared at a short distance to form beautiful cascades and waterfalls.
>
> From the Abbey windows the eye soared many leagues beyond this, and on a clear day the distant towers of Paris might be discerned.
>
> Wild and terrific scenery sometimes interrupted this mild prospect. Ships were frequently wrecked, or in imminent danger, in that narrow channel which separates the island from the coast, and called the Race of Alderney. (Vol. I, Ch. VIII)

Described with Radcliffe's balance of picturesque, beautiful and sublime vistas,[28] this domain offers Emily and Caroline many opportunities, not only for happy, leisurely walks along the coast, where they become "lost in admiration of the vast expanse, which no eye could compass", but also for interaction with, and reflection about, the Abbey's idyllically hospitable and harmonious peasant community.

Lusignan further participates in the Gothic by virtue of the double time scale in the secondary romance plot concerning the name of the orphaned Caroline de Montfort, and the mysterious disappearance of her mother when she was an infant. The providential revelation of her real identity, and subsequent restoration of both her mother and her inheritance, are familiar Radcliffean plot elements. The extension of the novel to four volumes with inset and intertwining stories is yet another feature common to Gothic fiction. We have Dorville's tale of his and Marsillac's adventures in Northern Africa and their providentially sited rescue from shipwreck, the satirically-edged and threaded story of the romance-reading Eugenia de Foix who fancies herself a romantic heroine, and the sad, cautionary tale of Julia d'Ermancy, who had been betrothed to Marsillac, but was forced to profess by her tyrannical father, and later persuaded to escape from the convent. Moreover, Julia has been deceived, seduced and abandoned by the same libertine whom Emily discovers duping the foolish Eugenia at St. Clair. With their coincidental intersections of lives, these sub-plots seem designed to reveal, through a complex of destinies, the underlying moral process of the world.[29] Such frequent reliance on the workings of Providence, as in Radcliffe's Gothic romances, foregrounds "a strange fatality" also not found in de Tencin's *Comminge*.

One of the most far-fetched of the novel's providential ironies occurs in the ante-penultimate chapter, and is foreshadowed in the description of Meronville's entry to La Trappe. Here de Tencin's steep, woody, fog-enveloped approach to the monastery[30] is aestheticized after the style of Radcliffe, the timelessness of its "profound and solemn silence" causing "a religious awe" to take possession of Lusignan/Meronville's soul:

> [He] felt his heart in perfect unison with the scene; a sort of pious terror penetrated his soul; he stood for a moment in the attitude of contemplation; the mournful cypress and the weeping willow, their leaves agitated by the breeze, to which terrified imagination and his ill-boding mind ascribed a horrid murmur and a prophetic sound, covered the valley beneath. (Vol. IV, Ch. V)

The presaged horror occurs after he has completed his year's novitiate and taken his vows. Meronville is sent by the Abbot "to attend the last moments of a poor sinner, just expiring in a neighbouring cottage". Heavily cowled on entry, he recognises La Haye's "hated voice" immediately, and struggles to speak, but the unsuspecting La Haye takes the proffered crucifix from him, and joins with him in "devout prayer" as prelude to confessing the full extent of his shocking crimes, which include the murder of the Duke, as well as the ruining of the lovers' lives. The session becomes even more ironic when La Haye verbalises a wish that his victim could "see his injuries avenged by the agonies of parting life—of a soul on the verge of eternity—that dreadful eternity to the unpardoned sinner", and, despite his own ever-mounting sorrows, the "dreadfully shocked" and trembling Meronville still manages to fulfil his priestly office within the household with goodness and generosity.

With further uncanny portents and coincidences, the penultimate chapter, which focuses on Dorimond's activities after he leaves St. Jago, effectively winds up the restorative romance plot elements of *Lusignan* by providing some further happy outcomes for the now long wedded Caroline and Dorville. In contrast, the final chapter based on *Les Amans Malheureux* provides anything but a joyful romance ending. The author deftly connects the two chapters and plots by making the main instrument of resolution the ever honourable and truth-seeking Dorimond, and by inventing the unfinished legal business he is required by his brother to address. Introduced late in Volume Two as Emily's chance acquaintance and discreet admirer, not only is he later given the pre-programmed role of her and Lusignan's generous friend and helper at St. Jago in the main plot based on *Comminge*; he also discovers the name of Caroline's parents, reintroduces himself in her life as her amiable young uncle, and assists in the restoration of her mother and inheritance. His friendship and generosity are then further attested in the final chapter where, following d'Arnaud's d'Orvigni, he offers to take Meronville's place at La Trappe so that the latter may return to Emily. Here Meronville's refusal is marked by reciprocal generous wishes that Dorimond return to Emily, and that she transfer her affections to him, who has the capacity to make her happy. Meronville's resolution to die worthy of Emily thus effectively terminates the role in the novel of his more chivalrous rival helper and friend:

Dorimond himself felt awed; the tenebrose gloom of the place, and the lugubrious sound vibrating in his ear, struck to his soul, and taking a melancholy farewell of Meronville, he retired with a determination of instantly returning to Emily. (Vol. IV, Ch. VI)

Unlike de Tencin's d'Orfanne and d'Arnaud's d'Orvigni, Dorimond has struggled, and to some extent succeeded, in transforming his own intense love for Emily into what Radcliffe, in commenting on Louis de la Motte's love for Adeline at the end of *The Romance of the Forest*, calls "the placid tenderness of friendship . . . unalloyed by any emotions of envy". At St. Jago, "the fervor" of his love gradually subsides into "the purest sentiments of esteem and friendship", prompting the narrator to remark:

> Oh, love, how different are thy effects from those of friendship; thy ardent fire consumes the heart, and destroys the senses: while friendship's pure flame emits that genial heat, ever equal, which vivifies without consuming! (Vol. IV, Ch. II)

Even when he realises that he has not overcome what he conceives as an "excess of passion", he still manages to acquit himself in the best interests of others. In all, the more fully developed role for Dorimond exemplifies *Lusignan*'s overarching theme announced on its title page in the epigraph from Henry Fielding's play, *The Wedding Day*: that friendship seems "designed by Heaven" to bring joy and "ennoble" the mind, while love debases it, and brings only endless pain for a "moment's bliss." By the end of the novel this "moment" in the lives of Lusignan and Emily—their joyful reunion at Montalte Abbey—has occurred well over a decade earlier.

The transition to the unrelentingly melancholy drama of *Lusignan*'s final chapter is effected by an untranslated epigraph that signals its close dependence on d'Arnaud's play for the tragic outcome of Meronville's obsessive preoccupation with thoughts of his Emily. Indeed, both the play's actions and its imagery of the lover's tortured souls, their hearts constantly consumed by the undying flame of their passion as they commit daily to the austere life of the religious, are appropriated throughout. However, d'Arnaud's grim sensationalism regarding the monastery is for the most part abjured. La Trappe continues to be depicted, more nearly after de Tencin, as the "abode of modest devotion" and "majestic austerity", with a solemn chapel containing a lamp, crucifix, images of saints, and a consecrated shrine, and d'Arnaud's climactic grave-digging incident occurs in the surrounding forest.

Nevertheless, the author-narrator has earlier weighed in more heavily than de Tencin in regard to the deleterious effects of La Trappe:

> The air is damp and unwholesome, thickened by perpetual and impenetrable fogs; a profound and solemn silence reigns, which seems to have existed from the creation of time! What a field is here presented to the hypochondriac! what food for melancholy! (Vol. IV, Ch. V)

This comment complements several others in this chapter and throughout the novel, including epigraphs, regarding favourable geographical locations, sociable activities and treatments for the preservation and restoration of physical and mental health.[31] The motif concerning unnatural isolation from society occurs most prominently in Emily's grave doubts about the motivations and true piety of monastic retirement, and her conviction that it is not "the will of Heaven". For her, and by extension the author-narrator, there is no merit "in wasting in criminal supineness" a life that could be dedicated to "active discharge of our duty" in society. Worse, "in the contracted sphere of monastic society, amongst the professors of conciliating Christianity, every evil passion existed" (Vol. III, Ch. V). In retrospect, such comments gather force over the four volumes from the fact that melancholic and non-pious monastic retirement is the very situation to which the tyrannous persecution of Lusignan and Emily, and their own obsessive longing, has finally brought them.

To maintain an atmosphere of religious awe and dread in this situation, the author adapts the two supernatural visions of d'Arnaud's play, but these, too, are altered and toned down. Meronville's crisis of decision about leaving La Trappe is dramatically resolved by similar warnings from what appears to be a real ghostly presence, though not the ghost of Rancé. Like d'Arnaud's Arsene, Meronville finds himself uncannily attracted to an ailing brother who is often close by, and who discovers his secret ritual at the grave he is digging, the shocked exclamation of his name by Brother Ambrose also adding to his anxieties. But Meronville's subsequent dream vision varies in a number of details from that of Arsene. For example, the author eschews d'Arnaud's doom-laden references to "celestial vengeance" and "bellowing inferno" by having the tomb close around the vanished spectre of Emily/Ambrose "with a sound so hollow" that it shakes the concave of heaven, and convulses the earth. The added reiteration of an earlier image concerning "two souls united in one error", now contextualised in terms of their religious redemption, also serves *Lusignan*'s thematic purposes, as does the perplexity and suspense of the melancholic Meronville when, on waking to hear groans and a "deep lament" seemingly in the voice of Ambrose from an adjoining cell, he wonders if he still dreams.

Relevant here is a further important difference from de Tencin's and d'Arnaud's depictions of Adélaïde, in that Ambrose is vested but not professed, and dies so on the day fixed for this rite. Moreover, in consonance with Emily's reflections at St. Clair on monastic retirement, Ambrose views the taking of monastic vows with repugnance:

> "Ah, that sound announces the return of morn!—but daylight to me is as the darkest night! When next the sun's refulgent orb shall rise to bless the universe, I shall be—oh God! Let me not think how much more closely I shall be united to misery! Supreme Creator, ah deign to listen to my prayer, ere I pronounce those vows my heart rejects take my immortal soul to thee, and let my perishable body unite with its parent dust! (Vol. IV, Ch. VII)

Her prayer granted, after her long, impassioned confession of her sacrilege to the assembled brothers, Emily, like d'Arnaud's Adélaïde in the certitude of imminent death, still opts for love over rectitude in her request to the accommodating Abbot: that her ashes be united with those of Meronville, "when the lifeless form of him I love shall be inanimate as mine". Apart from the narrator's silence regarding the ultimate fate of Meronville, the difference of *Lusignan*'s finale lies in Emily's last words, spoken directly to him. With their material images of "remembrance"—a recurring motif in the novel—they reiterate her preoccupation with her lover, and her unassuaged longing for association,[32] building to her promise of eventual spiritual union:

"Alas! is this my last wish? and do my dying accents speak of love?
is my latest breath exerted to pronounce thy name? my parting
sigh heaved to thy remembrance? thy idea mingled in the last
vibration of my heart? Farewell! no more shall I return to thee!
But oh, remember my spirit, even after death, shall linger on the
verge of eternity, and wait to unite with thine!" (ibid.)

While the framing of these images in rhetorical questions may be
viewed as a lament, and an attempt by the author to wring the last
drop of pathos from the chapter's theme, a more sympathetic and
consistent reading can see them as Emily's delicate paean of deliverance from monastic regulation of her body and beliefs. Her words
echo Lusignan's subversive insight that the sanctity of his lover's
vow is present in the very nature of his love ("the dear idea"of his
Emily "mingle[s] in the fondest vibrations of [his] heart"), and that
it precedes his institutionalised vow or sacrament with its attendant
hypocrisies.[33]

Further Ideological Considerations: the Novel's Rejection of Monasticism and Endorsement of the Gothic Pastoral Ideal

Published after a decade of upheavals in France during which
Britain had provided compassionate refuge and economic relief
for some 12,500 French émigrés per annum, including over 5,000
Roman Catholic clergy,[34] *Lusignan* treats the regulatory aspects of
Roman Catholicism with consciously ideological intent. Certain
passages of narratorial comment and the novel's depictions of the
Abbé La Haye's casuistic manipulativeness and abuse of clerical
authority, Julia d'Ermancy's forced monachization and incarceration, monasticism's unhealthy and unnatural rules of conformity,
and the hypocrisies and immoralities of promissory oaths and vows,
all conduce to a negative view of Catholicism's modes of regulating
belief and behaviour. As additions gothicizing the *Comminge* story,
they can be said to register a number of British religious and political concerns and anxieties of the late 1790s concerning monasticism
and the activities of the French clergy working in England.[35]

The French revolutionary government's Civil Constitution of
the Clergy of July 1790, condemned by Pope Pius VI in April 1791 as
schismatic, had prompted large numbers of French clergy to choose

exile over acceptance of the new church order which required them to swear an oath of allegiance to the Constitution. What began as an independent flow of emigration to Britain increased dramatically in the wake of the September Massacres of 1792, when large numbers of non-juring priests, some of whom had retracted their former oaths to the Constitution, arrived on British soil with virtually no possessions, and in need of political and religious asylum. Members of the Established and English Catholic Churches and the British Government responded admirably to their distress, quickly establishing a jointly organised, successful relief fund and mode of distribution. For charity's sake, and not a small degree of political expediency, the papal connection of the French clergy was consciously overlooked by the fund-raising and organising committees in stressing to the public the clergy's persecution by the revolutionary government, their Christian suffering, and their fidelity to a legal throne/altar alliance. Every effort was made to accommodate the needs of the French priests and nuns, and the quick passage of the Aliens Act[36] of January 1793, which required all foreigners to carry passports, enabled the government to monitor the numbers, details and movements of people entering the country, and deal with any suspected of being undercover Jacobin agents or harbouring revolutionary principles. The large number of French "Grand Vicars" in London, who had personal knowledge of their clergy, and through whom it later became the accepted practice to grant faculties and impose disciplines, also made oversight of the clergy's activities somewhat easier for all parties involved in their relief.[37] During the middle years of the decade a number of *ad clericum* documents stipulated codes of conduct regarding the clergy's social behaviour and clerical life, and, with very few exceptions, there was little complaint about improper behaviour.[38]

However, most of the clergy still needed to supplement their incomes by assisting in pastoral duties in English Catholic parishes or by teaching, and as the war with revolutionary France dragged on with no apparent end in sight, their protracted sojourn became a cause for alarm. Initially this seems to have been fuelled in the main by Establishment concerns in early 1796 about the proselytising of the Abbé Couvet, a member of the largest community of self-sufficient priests, numbering several hundred, who lived in the King's House at Winchester. On the orders of the Bishop of Saint-

Pol-de-Léon, the leader of the exiled clergy, Couvet was removed from Winchester and "ultimately from the country for what was regarded an infringement of the Alien Bill".[39] By early 1798 when an amendment was made to the Aliens Act to improve documentation and close existing loopholes, however, general paranoia and anxiety were more widespread. With the Continent lost to Bonaparte, and Ireland on the verge of rebellion, much anti-French feeling related to the threat of invasion. But another issue was the perceived and possible effects of the continuing presence on English soil of the French clergy, in particular their ongoing accommodation in convents and monastery-like institutions, and their opening of schools and access to the teaching of children. In all of this it was the privacy and closed nature of Roman Catholic religious institutions, the unnaturalness of monastic retirement, and the threats posed by proselytising priests and nuns, however unfounded, that were uppermost.

This is attested by the debates in parliament, in May to July 1800, of the Monastic Institutions Bill, which was passed with a large majority in the Commons and then rejected in the Lords. Put forward initially by Sir Henry Paulet St. John Mildmay to remedy what were perceived by him and others as inadequacies in the Aliens Act, it was entitled "An Act to prevent any addition to the number of Persons belonging to certain foreign Religious Orders, or Communities, lately settled in this Kingdom, and to regulate the Education of Youth by such Persons." While affirming the British "spirit of toleration" and compassion that had "admitted the Catholic emigrants to the free exercise of their religious duties", Mildmay believed that the government, by contributing money for relief of the clergy, had "in some degree been made a party to the revival of what seems to us the most unnatural part of the Romish faith". This was "the immuring, in useless inactivity and seclusion, young persons of both sexes, subjects of this country", and it was essential to prevent the admission of any new members to convents and monasteries. The recent foundation of a great variety of Catholic schools, many of which were "engrafted on, and under the immediate superintendance of their monastic establishments" made this all too possible:

I think we may reasonably apprehend, that the intention is not merely to educate children in the common tenets of the Romish faith, but to give a total ascendancy to the minds of their pupils, to familiarize and attach them to the superior duties and seclusion of a monastic life, so as hereafter to secure a supply to fill those vacancies which may happen to arise in these monastic establishments.[40]

It was therefore the duty of the parliament to prevent any offence or harm to the Protestant church established by law and to British subjects. Given "the arts and address which priests bred up in convents have possessed at all times" and the dispersal of the émigré clergy throughout the country for what seemed an indefinite period, it would be easy for them "to insinuate themselves into private families, to gain ascendancy over weakminded parents", as well as those parents drawn in by the prospect of free education for their children.

In swaying the Lords to vote against the bill, Samuel Horsley, Bishop of Rochester was at pains to make clear that he opposed the proposed legislation not because "the apprehensions" of the dangers it foresaw by members and those "without doors" were "altogether groundless". Rather, he felt that the security of the Established church and the country were already provided by existing statutes, and the new powers which the bill would give to the Crown would be unconstitutional. While the number of regular French clergy was admittedly high, his statistics revealed that the actual numbers of French monks were few, no more than twenty-six, including "five miserable Cistercians of the order of La Trappe settled near Wareham". In regard to the nuns, there were twenty-two convents, of which eighteen were in fact English convents previously located in France, only four were French, with very few inmates, and in total there were not more than three hundred and sixty nuns. Moreover, he argued, the existing laws made it "completely unlawful" on the nuns' part to attempt to profess new sisters in Britain. They would be "guilty in every such instance of a gross overt act of popery; and the whole artillery of the penal code points at them its dreadful thunders". Far more threatening to the interests of the State and the Protestant religion was any measure that might conduce, such as the proposed act, to "a revival of the rancour between Protestant and Roman Catholics" which he believed to be "dying away".[41]

The whole strain of Horsley's long speech is on the necessity for protection. While approving of expanded provisions for Catholic children to be educated in Britain rather than their being sent to the Continent, he signals the need for the monitoring of Catholic schools "as part of a general bill to regulate all schools". He enumerates many clauses protective of public safety from the 1791 Catholic Relief Act and earlier statutes. His rejection of the "Romish" private right of superiors of religious houses to direct rites and observances contrary to British law, and which might lead to the maltreatment of his majesty's subjects, such as the administration of Catholic penance by "imprisonment for any length of time" and "other corporal severities", is also made with rhetorical force.[42] All of this demonstrates a full appreciation by the parliament of the day of widespread concerns, and the perceived need to keep monastic institutions and any spread of Roman Catholicism subject to close government regulation.

In addition to registering these political and religious anxieties, *Lusignan*'s quasi-feudal world is also anachronistically infiltrated by a significant amount of eighteenth-century moral and political philosophy which hails the progressive nature of British Protestant constitutional liberty in contradistinction to the French Catholic feudal past. Like Radcliffe, the author-narrator imbues the protagonists with an eighteenth-century aesthetic idealism, which is not simply a matter of taste, but also of virtue, and which flows into their moral, political and religious positions. The narratorial comment that Lusignan's countenance expresses "the feelings of a benevolent, generous and susceptible heart" (Vol. I., Ch. II), together with his receptiveness to the natural environment, places him with Radcliffe's enlightened Valancourt in *The Mysteries of Udolpho*. Inspiring Lusignan on his way to Montpellier, vistas of picturesque beauty also soothe his mind just before he leaves the resort for Paris, to face his enraged father. Here, as Lusignan traverses the countryside, the narrator also underlines his rejection of aggrandisement, and his envy of the cheerful peasants who hasten to begin their morning labours, greeting him with "rustic grace":

How little, thought he, is that happiness which reigns in courts, and is so much valued in the haunts of luxury, compared with this; here nature limits our desires to our possessions; here no

consideration of interest disturbs the rural lovers. Ah! why was
not Lusignan placed here? (Vol. I, Ch.V)

He is given similar sentiments in a two-page reflection at the outset
of Volume IV. Having succeeded to his "brilliant inheritance" which
he will subsequently reject, Lusignan is discomfited by the gaze of
the surrounding villagers "fixed on him, his splendid castle and rich
equipage". He envies "their more fortunate lot", his morose conviction being that, if "these poor rustics" but knew his misery, they
would give thanks to "that Almighty Power, which has placed them
in a happier sphere". In a veiled reference to the turbulence of revolution, this idea is expanded in a series of metaphors regarding the
tempests that assail grandeur, and ends with a further observation
that for "the happy villager" whose wants are bounded by the subsistence supplied by his lord, "the plagues that haunt the rich man's
door ... the snares of ambition, the maze of politics are unknown".

Lusignan's yearnings for the simple, pastoral life have more buoy-
ancy in another, much earlier passage in the novel that is remarkably evocative of Ann Radcliffe's well-known delight in the sea and
sea-going vessels of all kinds, as recorded both in her posthumously
published poetry and in her journal written during her many trips
to the south coast of England. This passage occurs during Lusignan's first confinement at Luneville Castle on the coast of Normandy, when he surveys the vast prospect of "the Albion coast"
from the parapet wall and sees "the vessels majestically sailing from
its numerous ports":

> Lusignan envied the perils they must encounter ere they returned;
> he melted at the happiness they would enjoy when, after long
> roving on foreign shores and seas unknown, tossed by rude winds
> and faithless billows, their dear native isle should rise to greet
> their longing eyes. He sighed for England's chalky cliffs, and
> would willingly have resigned all his prospects of gilded slavery
> to share with Emily liberty and a cottage in that happy land. (Vol
> I, Ch. VII)[43]

A little later, after he has read a second letter from Emily urging
him to forget her, and to comply with his father's command that
he marry Eugenia, he considers again the prospect of emigration

to Britain as a country offering constitutionally assured rights of freedom:

> It was possible, he thought, to escape to the opposite shore, where liberty is the right of the meanest subject; there, in some obscure corner, he might with his beloved Emily forget the splendour he had left behind. He almost fancied himself there. (ibid.)

Thus is his retirement ideal, like Radcliffe's own, commensurate with British liberty, a modest income, and a cottage with a rural or ocean aspect. By the time *Lusignan* was published, British liberties in fact had been not a little eroded by a number of repressive measures to stamp out radicalism. War weariness, high food prices and economic depression were also causing widespread discontent. But the Terror and internal disorder in France, along with conservative propaganda at home, had persuaded many British subjects to cherish the stability enjoyed under the British constitution, and the war with France had aroused deep-seated nationalistic sentiments more powerful and more widespread than any desire for immediate and radical political reform.[44]

The contrast of Lusignan's enlightened opinions with the feudal bigotry of his father is again emphasised in the narrator's lengthy description of Lusignan's disgust at the Duke's initial ceremonious arrival at Luneville:

> Lusignan approached to welcome his father, but a frown of displeasure warned him to retire, till the numerous vassals dependent on his domain had paid homage to their imperious lord. Each bowed the knee as he approached, while he received their submission as a debt they justly owed to his exalted state. [...] [S]lavery was in every way abhorrent to [Lusignan's] nature; he felt convinced, that although a subordinate class was necessary to preserve order in the system of nature, yet it was the duty of those in whom chance, rather than merit, had given power, to exert it only with a view to render all happy who were subject to them; and if he ever desired to possess that power, it was with design to lighten the yoke of servitude, which was a component part of the feudal system. (Vol. I, Ch. IV)

Here, as in Radcliffe's romances, we find the advocacy of benevolence in the feudal relation of noble master or mistress and faithful tenants and servants. On settling down on their respective estates, the blissful heroes and heroines of *The Romance of the Forest*, *The Mysteries of Udolpho*, and *The Italian* all look to "the situation of all [their] poor tenants, that [they] might relieve [their] wants, or confirm their comforts", while their indigent tenants in turn rejoice in their benevolence.[45] Underpinning those endings is an optimistic belief that social inequality can be combined with recognition of equal human rights, distribution of wealth by the upper classes, and a sociability between classes so that universal affection will prevail. What is different in the passage quoted above is the author's choice of a more critical, politically attuned discourse, particularly in phrases such as "slavery", "subordinate class", "imperious lord", and "yoke of servitude". In so far as this questions the social and political system of the novel, its tone and sentiment is commensurate with the reformist views regarding slavery and "*civilized Barbarians*" expressed by Edward Dorville, in the story he tells to Caroline and Emily at Montalte Abbey, following his rescue from shipwreck.

In Dorville's interpolated traveller's tale, which makes a claim for realism by its cynical, prefacing comment regarding its lack of the genre's usual "embellishments", the author has Dorville make a number of observations regarding the African slave trade to which he and Marsillac had fallen victim. For example, in describing their wealthy Mahometan master's overseer, himself a slave, who had treated them so brutally, Dorville reflects on the way in which slavery perpetuates the worst in humans:

> Cruelty and the abuse of power are inherent in the breast of man. This vile slave, subordinate himself to some rigid taskmaster, who exercised every species of inhumanity on him, avenged his sufferings on us, and seemed happy in his wretched state of servitude, since it enabled him to gratify his propensity on two helpless beings. (Vol. II, Ch. II)

Later, having described their escape and re-capture by cannibalistic natives who spoke "the Moorish tongue", Dorville condemns the perpetration by European nations of atrocities in Africa:

> Europeans were known here, and white men held in abhorrence; they had taught these harmless savages the barbarous policy of

destroying their fellow-creatures; some of our most polished nations have here exercised such cruelties as the most ferocious barbarians would blush to commit. (Ibid.)

His subsequent account is further informed by the Enlightenment sentimental view that "savages", uncorrupted by European influence, are noble children of Nature. He relates how two members of this ferocious tribe, Yaratilda and her brother, Yaramanza, had been so driven by a "compassion bordering on Christian charity" that, at risk of death to themselves, they had acted successfully to save him and Marsillac. Yaratilda in fact exhibits the sort of expansive love for the planets and universe that philosophers such as Shaftesbury in his *Moralists* (1709), and David Hartley in his *Observations on Man* (1749), had held to be "a reasonable enthusiasm" and at the heart of "natural religion".[46] As a stand against slavery, Dorville's tale can be said to support the need for reform voiced in the 1790s by, among others, the Unitarians Thomas Bentley and Josiah Wedgewood, the Deist Erasmus Darwin, and the Evangelicals William Wilberforce and Hannah More. Thomas Bentley's niece, Ann Radcliffe, had also denounced the slave trade in her *Journey Made in the Summer of 1794*. *Lusignan* shares with her denunciation an expressed belief in a divinely ordered world in which God's justice will be meted out to the wicked, or all those who negate the well being and happiness of others in the universal system of which they are part.[47] While this may seem a conservative position, it is well to remember that the raising of the slavery question in any form at this time could be said to raise necessarily the whole question of the limits of authority over other humans.[48]

A further denunciation of self-interested and criminal practices occurs in Emily's ideal of retirement, verbalised forcefully to Caroline at Montalte Abbey, when she gives Caroline the gift of her small estate in the Valais. Given the exposure by the younger David Hartley and others of the injustices of the *ancien régime* in response to Edmund Burke's whitewashed account, Emily's depiction of a tyrannous and grasping French nobility and their stewards would have been familiar to many British readers:[49]

My possessions in France are so large, and so infinitely exceed my wants or wishes, that I would willingly relinquish them all, and retire with you to Ivy Cottage; but there are duties which superior rank imposes, and we should be criminal to neglect them. These duties compel us to reside on our estates, that we may know the real condition of our vassals and tenantry and apply our superfluous wealth to the relief of their indigence. I have seen too much of the selfish policy of intendants and stewards . . . careful only to enrich themselves, and obliged to supply the inordinate extravagance of their masters, who lavish with criminal profusion in the great metropolis that affluence earned by the sweat of many a sufferer's brow, they deprive these poor peasants of the common comforts heaven designed for all, and, by their practice, imply the belief that a subordinate class of beings was created only to administer to the artificial cravings of intemperate luxury. (Vol. II, Ch. IV)

Although there is strong reference here to the disproportionate wealth and "criminal" extravagance of the nobility, and the poverty and suffering of "the subordinate class" from which such riches are derived, Emily does not suggest the possibility of peasant discontent and rebellion. Rather, she insists, as a matter of their "duty", on the nobility's redistribution of their "superfluous wealth". The existence of the class system itself is again simply accepted, in a conservative eighteenth-century way, as "the system of nature",[50] albeit without any sign of Shaftesburian optimism about the capacity of "the superior rank" in general to cultivate virtue, and work for the good of all.

An exception, of course, is Emily herself, whose rectitude has compassion and benevolence as defining components. She befriends and assists not only the orphaned Caroline, but also the foolishly vulnerable Eugenia, and the victimised and guilt-stricken Julia, not to mention the incarcerated Lusignan, for whose freedom and happiness she ineffectually sacrifices her own. Moreover, the author portrays her as conscious of the satisfaction she gains from this active ministry, and of its role in helping to assuage her grief and melancholy. The needs of others also customarily govern Emily's oversight of those servants and tenants living on her own estate, and a mutually supportive friendship exists there between members of the different classes. Much is made of this when Caroline and Emily discover that some cottagers have courageously plucked Dorville from the sea, taken him in, and cared for him until his recovery. Subsequently the cottagers' wedding festivities are attended by the

entire party from Montalte Abbey, Emily having purchased garments for the bride and the children attending her. The detailed
care with which the narrator describes these festive garments also
recalls Radcliffe's delineation, in *Udolpho*, of "the Arcadian air" of
a group of Tuscan peasant girls, also dressed for a festival.[51] In the
description of the wedding festivities themselves, the emphasis is
again on the romantically idyllic nature of the scene: "rural choristers fill the air with ineffable melody", and "no less harmonious the
shepherd's pipe", as happy peasants "danc[e], with rustic grace, the
merry Lavolta". Described as quite spontaneous, their sharing of
their joy with their superiors in rank inspires in Lusignan, Emily,
Caroline and Dorville a yearning for "the liberty and happiness" of
rustic life.

The occasion also becomes one in which Lusignan concurs with
Emily's views on "the tutelage of mercenary tutors, fertile in their
inventions to distort Nature", and he again laments the experience
of simple and pure delights that his rank has withheld from him.
With the sudden arrival at Montalte Abbey of his austere father,
the Duke, whose magnificent and splendid retinue has brought out
en route "crowds of admiring villagers", this contrast is clinched for
the reflective Emily:

> Riches and honour still left a vacuum in the generous mind.
> Virtue, thought she, elevates its possessor, however humble may
> be his lot, to the highest dignities of man. Vice, though gilded by
> splendour and independence, reduces us below the level of the
> poorest subjects. (Vol. II, Ch. IV)

As signalled in the chapter's epigraph from Edward Young's "Love of
Fame" and closing four lines from James Graeme's "Elegy XLIII", it
is the ostentatious display, greed and self-interest of the rich, rather
than the actual existence of social inequality, which most disturb
Emily and Lusignan.

Later in the novel, the country of Emily's childhood home, the
"Elysian" Valais, is again lauded not only for its incomparable,
"diversified beauties", but also for its freedom from "despotism",
and the happiness and hospitality of its peasant inhabitants. The
idealised harmony of *Lusignan*'s early-seventeenth-century pastoral
communities is thus consistently constituted through eighteenth-
century discourses about nature, virtue, duty, and benevolence,

generalised from Rousseau, Shaftesbury, David Hartley and others. The portrayal of this sentimental ideal nevertheless gains a reformist edge through a variety of contrasts in which Britain is named as the locus of liberty, and threads of a politically loaded discourse are woven judiciously.

Reception and authorship

Without doubt, an important reason for *Lusignan*'s neglect has been the persistence through two centuries of the stereotyping of Minerva Press fiction as formulaic, mindless and badly written. Often referred to as the "trash" from "the Leadenhall manufactory", the prolific output of Lane's press was a continuing butt of derision for late-eighteenth and early-nineteenth-century critics, satirists and conduct book writers, who in any case often treated novels and romances as inferior genres, particularly those penned and read predominantly by women. Only in the last twenty-five years or so have the derogatory comments about both the Minerva Press and popular Gothic fiction made by authoritative contemporaneous writers such as Wordsworth, Coleridge, Charles Lamb and Thomas Love Peacock been challenged as distorting, testifying to their own elitist interests, and not truly representative of what was in fact a far more complex cultural situation.[52] Using quantitative analyses, social historians have begun to evaluate the impact of the wide range of circulating library fare, fiction and non-fiction, on the development of reading practices and the fabric of British society. Scholars of the Romantic era and women's writing have also uncovered the reach and importance of this neglected output for canonical writers, such as Jane Austen, the Shelleys and Byron, as well as for others, such as Eliza Parsons and Charlotte Smith, who were forced to take advantage of the popularity of sentimental romances and "horrid" or Gothic tales to support themselves and their families.[53]

Although blanket assumptions still persist about the lack of any literary value in Minerva publications, the response is somewhat more nuanced amongst scholars who have begun to read and research the many writers for Lane's press more closely. The pickings may remain slim, but other names have begun to take their place alongside those of Ann Radcliffe and Matthew Lewis as authors of worthwhile sentimental and Gothic fiction. For example, in the early 1980s, Natalie Schroeder's articles on *Children of the Abbey* (1796) and *Clermont* (1798) drew attention to the achievement of Regina Maria Roche as a minor popular novelist; and more recently Dale Townshend has revealed T. J. Horsley Curties's early-nineteenth-century Gothic novels to be a "welcome exception" to common critical assumptions.[54]

So what can we say about *Lusignan* in this respect? Undoubtedly its author not only shared Ann Radcliffe's close knowledge of, and admiration for, the works of Shakespeare and a wide range of other English and French writers, but also the keen interest in France evidenced in Radcliffe's journals, *The Romance of the Forest*, and *The Mysteries of Udolpho*. As a reworking of prior texts, *Lusignan* may well be viewed as pastiche and *hommage*, and its use of chapter epigraphs and occasional interpolated fragments of poetry as "literary kleptomania";[55] yet it is not a mean feat. For all its faults—its unedited length, multiple far-fetched coincidences, occasional inconsistencies and *longueurs*, abrupt changes of viewpoint—in generic and stylistic terms it is still the work of an accomplished writer. The depictions of Lusignan's obsession with the duty-bound Emily, a manic love that overrides social constraints and religious duties, evinces considerable insight into the pathology of extreme anxiety and melancholic depression. The author can also create moments of riveting drama. Consider, for example, the dramatic scene in Volume I, Chapter IV when Lusignan reveals his true identity to Emily and her mother, and pleads that his father's enmity, softened by his own adoring mother, will yield to his entreaties. The warm but firm tone of Madame de Clarival's "maternal" response, with its even tempo, carefully selected diction, and balanced phrasing, is an impressive example of the author's skill in handling dramatic dialogue:

> "Listen," continued Madame de Clarival, "to maternal solicitude; believe that it is the voice of Reason that addresses you, and that I am not a cold or insensible observer of your sorrow. Unions formed on the basis of filial disobedience are ever baneful in their effects. Return to Paris, and let no recollection of Montpelier disturb the exercise of your duty. Remember that paternal commands are sacred; that Nature has made this one of her most inviolable laws, which no fortuitous tie can weaken. Should you succeed in obtaining his consent, mine will not be withheld; but

as the chances are so unequal, let us part as we do after every casual connection, without regret, and endeavour to feel indifferent whether chance may favour any future meeting."[56]

In another example, the narrative impetus of the short, paratactic sentences that constitute the climactic ending of Volume II—Lusignan's abduction by La Haye's thugs who are brandishing not only pistols but, more chillingly, a *lettre de cachet*—surpasses in suspense and terror Matthew Lewis's description of Don Raymond's preternaturally fast carriage ride in *The Monk*. Lusignan's dazed state, and the extreme rapidity of the exit and drive are conveyed with a vividness that anticipates the visual immediacy of filmic juxtapositions of shots in medium, long, and close range:

> Lusignan, almost annihilated, obeyed. They led him down staircases, passages, and gloomy recesses, of which he had not the least knowledge, to a postern gate. Here a carriage was waiting. They hurried him into it. Benedoit seated by his side, and his companion on the box, it drove off with the rapidity of lightning.
>
> Lusignan was bewildered,—lost in a maze of conjectural doubts. The clock struck three as he entered the chaise. In six hours he was to have been for ever united to Emily. Distraction followed the recollection. The velocity of the motion almost precluded reflection. He thought it was a dream. Relays of horses they found at every stage. They stopped not. Every turn of the wheel removed him from Emily. He sighed, and resigned himself to despair!

Who would not have reached for Volume III?

Nevertheless, scholarly attention to *Lusignan* has been minimal. In 1946 Muriel Mary Tarr criticised the accuracy of some of its representations of Catholicism in her *Catholicism in Gothic Fiction*, John Foster gave it a glancing sentence in his *The History of the Pre-Romantic Novel in England* of 1949, Montague Summers in *The Gothic Quest* (1964) was effusive in his praise for the novel, noted its French sources, and gave a brief outline of its plot, and Frederick Frank, in his earliest critical guide to the first Gothics (1987), listed it as "high Gothic" and also provided a plot summary.[57] In the present century, the novel's publication details have been made available in the invaluable online research resource, *British Fiction*,

1800-1829: A Database of Production, Circulation & Reception (2004) by P. D. Garside, J. E. Belanger, S. A Ragaz and A. A. Mandal. More recently (2009), Maria Purves has drawn attention to *Lusignan*'s French sentimental pre-texts and representations of Catholic devotion in her polemical *The Gothic and Catholicism: Religion, Cultural Exchange and the Popular Novel, 1785-1829*. My own research, a distillation of which was published in the digital journal *Romantic Textualities* by the Centre for Editorial and Intertextual Research at Cardiff University in 2013, points to the distinct possibility that *Lusignan* and its successor, *The Orphans of Llangloed*, were written by Ann Radcliffe.[58]

While I have not pursued the question of attribution specifically in this introduction, preferring to situate the novel in its broader, historical contexts, I have extended the commentary to discuss some of the ways in which *Lusignan* participates in the particular structure, themes, style and ideology of Radcliffe's Gothic romances. Other marked similarities of imagery, diction and intertextual reference between *Lusignan* and Radcliffe's writings are mentioned in the notes that accompany the text. What we know of Radcliffe's personal life, the reception of her work, and the political and cultural climate of England at the turn of the century, are also not inconsistent with the possibility of her return to her earlier anonymity in order to follow her strong impulse to write and publish. However, in the absence of archival evidence, whether *Lusignan* can be said to be actually Radcliffe's, or just uncannily Radcliffean, is for its readers to decide.

JACQUELINE HOWARD

Jacqueline Howard's previous publications on the Gothic include an edition of Ann Radcliffe's *The Mysteries of Udolpho* for Penguin Classics (2001), and *Reading Gothic Fiction: A Bakhtinian Approach* (Oxford: Clarendon Press, 1994). Formerly Coordinator of English and Languages at St. Mary's College, Adelaide, and now retired from teaching, Dr. Howard has also published widely on the use and interpretation of a variety of literary and visual texts in the classroom. An independent scholar with a primary interest in the long eighteenth century, she is currently at work on a study of eighteenth-century British elegiac and romantic poetry in the context of both attitudes to death and the development of a Protestant culture of memoria.

NOTES

1 W. D. Fellowes, *A Visit to the Monastery of La Trappe, in 1817: with Notes Taken During a Tour Through Le Perche, Normandy, Bretagne, Poitou, Anjou, Le Bocage, Touraine, Orleanois, and the Environs of Paris.*, 2nd ed. (London: printed for William Stockdale, 1818), pp. viii, 1-2. Fellowes (1769-1852) also wrote about the loss of his ship, the *Lady Hobart*, when it hit an iceberg in 1803. A man of liberal ideas, and a fan of Napoléon, he abandoned his wife for a woman he had met in Paris in 1815, and whom he married on the death of his wife.

2 Claudine Alexandine Guérin de Tencin, *Mémoires du Comte de Comminge* (La Haye: J. Neaulme, 1735); [Charlotte Lennox], *The Lady's Museum. By the author of The Female Quixote*, 2 vols. (London: Printed for J. Newbery [. . .] and J. Coote [. . .], 1760-61), vol. I, pp. 122-28, 190-92, 298-305, 379-87; vol. II, pp. 449-55, 538-51, 609-26, 673-85, cited in Marianna D'Ezio, *Claudine Alexandine Guérin de Tencin, The History of the Count de Comminge, translated by Charlotte Lennox* (Newcastle upon Tyne: Cambridge Scholars Publishing, 2011) pp. 2-3. D'Ezio here explains the complicated history of Lennox's English translations of de Tencin's *Comminge*, which date back to 1756, when her first translation appeared as "a sort of 'insertion'" within another work translated and adapted from the French by her.

3 *Memoirs of the Count of Comminge. From the French of Monsieur D'Arnaud* (London: G. Kearsly, 1774). D'Arnaud is a misattribution. See Josephine Grieder, "The Prose Fiction of Baculard D'Arnaud in Late Eighteenth-Century England," *French Studies*, vol. XXIV, no. 2 (April 1970), p. 125. Certain English phrases from this translation which also appear in *Lusignan* point to this edition as its most likely source.

4 François-Thomas-Marie de Baculard D'Arnaud, *Les Amans malheureux, ou Le Comte de Comminge, Drame en trois Actes et en Vers, précédé d'un Discours préliminaire, suivi de la Lettre & des Mémoires du Comte de Comminge* (La Haye, L'Esclapart, 1764). "*Amants*" in later editions published by Le Jay.

5 See Grieder, op. cit., p. 125.

6 Bertan de la Villehervé, *François-Thomas-Marie de Baculard D'Arnaud, Son Théâtre et ses Théories Dramatiques* (Paris: Librairie Edouard Champion, 1920) p. 111.

7 See K. L. Dawes, "Anonymity and the Pressures of Publication in the Early Nineteenth Century," *Romantic Textualities*, 4 (May 2000).

8 Dorothy Blakey, *The Minerva Press* (London: Oxford University Press, 1939), p. 48.

9 P. D. Garside, J. E. Belanger, and S. A. Ragaz, *British Fiction, 1800-1829: A Database of Production, Circulation & Reception,* designer A. A. Mandal, http://www.british.fiction.cf.ac.uk [12th June 2008] DBF Record No: 1801A007 & 1802A011. The title page of *The Orphans of Llangloed* has "BY THE AUTHOR OF LUSIGNAN".

10 *Critical Review,* 2nd ser. 37 (Feb 1803): pp. 237-238.

11 Thomas James Mathias, *The Pursuits of Literature. A Satirical Poem in Four Dialogues. With Notes.* 7th ed., revised (London: Printed for T. Becket, 1798), p. 58. Well over two dozen novels published by Minerva in the 1790s had "abbey" in the title. In providing "A sketch of the Abbey of La Trappe" as a brief preface to her tale, Madame de Tencin herself had anticipated "minds which are dissatisfied with fictitious scenes of misery", and claimed that "the most striking incidents" in the subsequent Memoirs had been "unhappily realized" (*Memoirs,* op. cit., p. 8).

12 Anne Jacobsen Schutte, *By Force and Fear: Taking and Breaking Monastic Vows in Early Modern Europe* (Ithaca and London: Cornell University Press, 2011), p. 53. Schutte is quoting here from the *Conciliorum Oecumenicorum Decreta,* Decrees of the Ecumenical Councils, 755. "Monachization" is Schutte's term.

13 Ibid., pp. 5, 54.

14 James F. Traer, *Marriage and the Family in Eighteenth-Century France* (Ithaca and London: Cornell University Press, 1980), p. 33. Traer is quoting from a complilation of old French laws prior to 1789 by François André Isambert.

15 Ibid., p. 34.

16 Ibid., p. 140; Schutte, op. cit., pp 54-55.

17 Mary Trouille, "Buried Alive: Genlis's Gothic Tale of Marital Violence in 'Histoire de la duchesse de C***'", *Studies on Voltaire and the Eighteenth Century,* (December) 2005, 12:77-114, p. 78, n. 5. Trouille notes here that "a vindictive husband could have an unfaithful wife confined to a convent for two years".

18 Schutte, op. cit., p.12.

19 De Tencin, G. Kearsly edition of 1774, op, cit., p. 59. Future extended references will appear in the text

20 D'Arnaud, op. cit., p. 19: "Tous les morts rassemblés dans ces funestes lieux,/Se levent de la terre & m'appellent près d'eux./Je vous suis … je l'éprouve, un Dieu juste se venge./Quels coups! quel châtiment!"

21 Ibid., p. 51.

22 Ibid., p. 8.

23 Calculated from the time of Lusignan's introduction to Emily at Montpellier.

24 For an exposition of this ideological pattern in early Gothic fiction, see Robert Mighall, *A Geography of Victorian Gothic Fiction: Mapping History's Nightmares* (Oxford: Oxford University Press, 1999), pp. xvi-xix; 1-26.

25 In the 17th century, Calvinist theologians had argued for, and recognised, only two sacraments (thereby excluding marriage as a sacrament), a doctrine considered heretical by Catholic theologians, who continued to uphold all seven sacraments. However, as both Lusignan and Emily had no doubt both been baptised as Christians, and were maintaining their Catholic faith, any problem seems unlikely. Even had there been one, it could have been removed by a dispensation (with conditions about the raising of children, etc.), from a presiding authority which would have enabled them to marry in the Catholic church as was required by the law of the land.

26 One reviewer (on evidence, not Coleridge) in 1794 wrote of Radcliffe's *The Mysteries of Udolpho* that "curiosity is kept upon the stretch from page to page, and from volume to volume, and the secret, which the reader thinks himself every instant on the point of penetrating, flies like a phantom before him, and eludes his eagerness till the very last moment of protracted expectation". *Coleridge's Miscellaneous Criticism*, edited by Thomas Middleton Raysor (London: Constable & Co. Ltd., 1936), p. 356.

27 Ann Radcliffe, *A Sicilian Romance*, edited with an introduction and notes by Alison Milbank (Oxford: Oxford University Press, 1993), p. 117.

28 Cf. the description of Chateau Le Blanc in *The Mysteries of Udolpho*, edited with an introduction and notes by Jacqueline Howard (Harmondsworth: Penguin, 2001), Vol. III, Ch. X pp. 439-42. Like those living near Montalte Abbey, the peasants in the vicinity of the Chateau are similarly hospitable and caring.

29 The author-narrator frequently makes explicit the ironic workings of Divine agency, for example:

> His [d'Aubignac's] last attempt on Emily had crowned his guilt, and he expiated it on a scaffold. Thus, by one of those ordinations of Providence, concealed from prudence till the hour of completion, Emily, who had been the victim of La Haye, became the executioner of his son, and inflicted on his pride and ambition a pang no suffering could exceed. (Vol. III, Ch. VII).

30 Confirming de Tencin, Fellowes (op. cit., pp. 8-9) found La Trappe situated in a valley of "total solitude ... undisturbed and chilling silence", and approached through almost impenetrable woods, with an intricately winding path hollowed into the hillside leading down to it.

31 See, for example, the epigraph to Vol. II, Ch. III of *Lusignan*, from John Armstrong's *The Art of Preserving Health*.

32 For use of the phrase "longing for association" as a definition of Romantic love in the Western tradition, see William M. Reddy, *The Making of Romantic Love: Longing and Sexuality in Europe, South-East Asia and Japan, 900-1200 CE* (Chicago: Chicago University Press, 2012), pp. 6, 17

33 See Vol. IV, Ch. VII: "Alas! the dear idea of her my soul worships will, till my latest hour, mingle in the fondest vibrations of my heart!" and "Shall I break these sacred vows? or, can I erase them from the register of heaven? Yet were not my oaths of tenderness, of fidelity to Emily, first enrolled there?"

34 These per annum figures are averages. For further details, see Dominic Bellenger, "'Fearless Resting Place': The Exiled Clergy in Great Britain, 1789-1815," in *The French Émigrés in Europe and the Struggle against Revolution, 1789-1814,* edited by Kirsty Carpenter and Philip Mansel (Basingstoke: Palgrave Macmillan, 1999), pp. 214-216. Also Kirsty Carpenter, *Refugees of the French Revolution: Émigrés in London, 1789-1802* (Basingstoke: Macmillan, 1999), pp. 39-44.

35 For a different, neo-Foucauldian slant on monasticism in the Gothic, see Mark Canuel, *Religion, Toleration, and British Writing, 1790-1830* (Cambridge: Cambridge University Press, 2002), pp. 55-81. Canuel argues that negative images of monasticism in Ann Radcliffe's romances do not simply register concerns about a set of beliefs, or even about the presence of monastic orders in Britain. Rather they are more fluidly representative of a broader concern with a "confessional" mode of governing the beliefs of political subjects in Britain by oaths, tests and regulation on speech, and an Established Church. For Canuel, "Gothics used the imagery of monastic terror in order to distinguish a confessional rule by belief from their own alliance with a more secular rule *over* belief: a practice of government that exposed religion itself to new techniques of observation, analysis, and manipulation."

36 This Aliens Act "laid down that when the king, by proclamation, order in council, or under his sign manual, required any alien to leave the realm, and the alien disobeyed, he should be liable to arrest; and one of the secretaries of state might put him in charge of one of His Majesty's messengers, to be conducted out of the kingdom." During the 1790s over fifty aliens a year were deported. J. R. Dinwiddy, "The Use of the Crown's Power of Deportation Under the Aliens Act, 1793-1836", *Historical Research*, 41; 104 (Nov. 1968), 193-211, pp. 194, 207.

37 Dominic Bellenger, "The English Catholics and the French Exiled Clergy", *Recusant History* 15 (1983) 433-52, p. 436; Carpenter, op. cit., pp. 34-35.

38 Bellenger, ibid., p. 436.

39 Dominic Bellenger, "The Émigré Clergy and the English Church,

1769-1815", *Journal of Ecclesiastical History*, 34:3 (July 1989), 392-410, pp. 405-6.

40 *The Parliamentary History*, XXXV (1800-1), 341.

41 Ibid., 374, 384-5.

42 Ibid., 381.

43 His vision is remarkably similar in content, sentiment and diction to that in Ann Radcliffe's poem, "Written in the Isle of Wight", in *Gaston de Blondeville*, half title, *The Posthumous Works of Mrs. Radcliffe*, 4 vols. (London: Henry Colburn, 1826), IV, pp. 221-2, possibly written during her visit in 1798:

> Oh! for a cottage on the shady brow
> Of this green Island, where the Channel flows
> With less tumultuous wave, and sends abroad
> The many sails of England to the world,
> And beareth to his home the mariner
> Who shouts to see the light blue hills, that rise [. . .]
> Oh! for a cottage on the breezy cliff,
> That points the crescent of thy harbour, Cowes!
> And bears the raptured glance o'er seas and shores—
> A boundless prospect. . . .

44 The period after 1797, when *Lusignan* is likely to have been written, was a particularly repressive one in Britain, with hasty Parliamentary legislation, committees of secrecy, and constant surveillance by government spies and informers throughout the land. The Government again suspended *habeas corpus* from April 1798 to March 1801, allowing the imprisonment of subjects without trial, a drastic infringement of civil liberties. Following the naval mutinies of 1797, a Bill was enacted making it a capital offence to encourage mutiny in the armed forces, and in 1799, Parliament banned by law the leading radical societies of the decade, even though their already collapsed state made such legislation virtually unnecessary. Again, in 1800, legislation made illegal all combinations of workers or trade unions. Even though not frequently implemented, all of these laws constituted a serious threat to trade unionists, radical reformers and propagandists, and their rank and file. As such, they were a grave challenge to civil freedom—that 'liberty' the author of *Lusignan* undoubtedly cherished. Food was also drastically short, as the blockade by Napoleon had restricted imports, contributing to the high anti-French sentiment. See H.T. Dickson, *British Radicalism and the French Revolution, 1789-1815* (Oxford: Blackwell, 1985), pp. 25-42, 53, 63

45 See *The Romance of the Forest*, edited with an introduction and notes by Chloe Chard (Oxford: Oxford University Press, 1999), p. 363; *The Mysteries of Udolpho*, edited with an introduction and notes by Jacqueline Howard (London: Penguin, 2001), Vol. IV, Ch. X, p. 549; Ch. XIX, p. 631; *The Italian*, (London: Penguin, 2000), Vol. III, Ch. XIII, p. 476.

46 The idea of the essential virtue of "savages" is usually attributed to Rousseau's *Discourse on the Moral Effects of the Arts and Sciences* (1750) and *The Discourse on Inequality* (1754), but by 1800 it had permeated much eighteenth-century writing. On "reasonable enthusiasm" and "natural religion", see the dialogue between Theocles and Philocles in Lord Shaftesbury, *The Moralists; A Philosophical Rhapsody* (London, 1709). David Hartley also argued that humans could "infer the existence and attributes of God", along with "their relation and duty to him, from the mere consideration of natural phenomena" in his *Observations on Man, his Frame, his Duty, and Expectations,* 2 vols. (Bath and London: S. Richardson, 1749), Vol. II, pp. 10-11, 49.

47 Ann Radcliffe, *A Journey Made in the Summer of 1794* (Dublin: P. Wogan et al., 1795), p. 377: "And not only for itself may Manchester be an object of admiration, but for the contrast of useful profits to the wealth of a neighbouring place, immersed in the dreadful guilt of the Slave Trade, with the continuance of which to believe national prosperity incompatible, is to hope, that the actions of nations pass unseen before the Almighty, or to suppose extenuation of crimes by increase of criminality, and that the eternal laws of right and truth, which smite the wickedness of individuals, are too weak to struggle with the accumulated and comprehensive guilt of a national participation in robbery, cruelty and murder." This belief in divine justice is also evident in Radcliffe's romances.

48 Roger Anstey, *The Atlantic Slave Trade and British Abolition, 1760-1810* (London: Macmillan, 1975), pp. 403-13.

49 David Hartley (son of the philosopher of the same name), *Argument on the French Revolution* (Bath: Crutwell, 1794), pp. 10-15, reproduced in *Gothic Documents: A Sourcebook, 1700-1820*, edited by E. J. Clery and Robert Miles (Manchester and New York: Manchester University Press, 2000), pp. 247-249. Cf. Edmund Burke, *Reflections on the Revolution in France*, edited with an introduction by Leslie Mitchell, (Oxford and New York: Oxford University Press, 1993), pp. 137-140.

50 For example, Edmund Burke's acceptance of a divine purpose immanent in the existing order of things:

> The Awful author of our being is the author of our place in the order of existence; and ... having disposed and marshalled us by a divine tactic, not according to our will, but according to His, he has, in and by that disposition, virtually subjected us to act the part which belongs to the place assigned to us.

Quoted by Alfred Cobban in *Edmund Burke and the Revolt against the Eighteenth Century: A Study of the Social Thinking of Burke, Wordsworth, Coleridge and Southey* (London: Allen & Unwin, 1960), p. 94.

51 Cf. *The Mysteries of Udolpho*, op. cit., Vol. III, Ch. VII, p. 397.

52 Wordsworth's preface to the 1800 edition of *The Lyrical Ballads* inveighed against "frantic novels" that degraded all taste, and in 1817 in his *Biographia Literaria*, Coleridge was still berating circulating libraries for furnishing the minds of readers with nothing but "laziness and a little mawkish sensibility". Dorothy Blakey (op. cit., p. 2) quotes and endorses Peacock's view of Minerva Press productions as "completely expurgated of all the higher qualities of mind".

53 See, for example, William St. Clair, *The Reading Nation in the Romantic Period* (Cambridge: Cambridge University Press, 2004), and Deborah Ann Macleod, *The Minerva Press*, Ph.D. dissertation, University of Alberta, 1997. Also Anne K. Mellor, *Mothers of the Nation: Women's Political Writing in England, 1780-1830* (Bloomington: Indiana University Press, 2000); Susan J. Wolfson, *Romantic Interactions: Social Being and the Turns of Literary Action* (Baltimore: Johns Hopkins University Press, 2010); Robert Miles, *Romantic Misfits* (New York: Palgrave Macmillan, 2008); *Fellow Romantics: Male and Female British Writers*, edited by Beth Lau (Aldershot: Ashgate, 2009); Jacqueline Labbe, *Writing Romanticism: Charlotte Smith and William Wordsworth, 1784-1807* (Palgrave Macmillan, 2011); Karen Morton, *A Life Marketed as Fiction: An Analysis of the Works of Eliza Parsons* (Kansas City: Valancourt Books, 2011).

54 Natalie Schroeder, "*The Mysteries of Udolpho* and *Clermont*: The Radcliffean Encroachment on the Art of Regina Maria Roche", *Studies in the Novel* 12:2 (Summer 1980), pp. 131-143; "The Anti-Feminist Reception of Regina Maria Roche", *Essays in Literature* 9:1 (Spring 1982), pp. 55-65; Dale Townshend, "T. J. Horsley Curties and Royalist Gothic: The Case of *The Monk of Udolpho* (1807)", *The Irish Journal of Gothic and Horror Studies*, 4 (June 2008), online: http://irishgothichorrorjournal.homestead.com.

55 The phrase is used by E. J. Clery in her discussion of Ann Radcliffe's use of epigraphs in *Women's Gothic From Clara Reeve to Mary Shelley* (Tavistock: Northcote House, 2000), p. 57.

56 In terms of appropriate register, this address is comparable with Radcliffe's handling of Emily St. Aubert's response to her would-be suitor, Count Morano, in *The Mysteries of Udolpho*, on the occasion of Morano's nighttime entry by stealth into Emily's bedroom while she is resting, fully clothed on her bed. His purpose is not to harm, but to persuade Emily, formerly promised to him as his bride by Montoni, to escape with him from Udolpho:

> "Count Morano," said Emily, at length recovering her voice, "calm, I entreat you, these transports, and listen to reason, if you will not to pity. You have equally misplaced your love, and your hatred.—I never could have returned the affection, with which you honour me, and certainly have never encouraged it; neither has Signor Montoni injured you, for you must have known, that he had no right to dispose of my hand, had he even

possessed the power to do so. Leave, then, leave the castle while you may with safety. Spare yourself the dreadful consequences of an unjust revenge, and the remorse of having prolonged to me these moments of suffering." (*The Mysteries of Udolpho*, op. cit., Vol. II, Ch. VI, p. 250)

57 Muriel Mary Tarr, *Catholicism in Gothic Fiction: A Study of the Nature and Function of Gothic Materials in Gothic Fiction in England (1762-1820)* (Washington: Catholic University of America Press, 1946); James R. Foster, *The History of the Pre-Romantic Novel in England* (New York: Modern Language Association, 1949), p. 197; Montague Summers, *The Gothic Quest* (New York: Russell & Russell, 1964), pp. 194-95; Frederick S. Frank, *The First Gothics: A Critical Guide to the English Gothic Novel* (New York & London: Garland, 1987), p. 218.

58 Maria Purves, *The Gothic and Catholicism: Religion, Cultural Exchange and the Popular Novel, 1785-1829* (Cardiff: University of Wales Press, 2009) pp. 68, 141-143, 148. Jacqueline Howard, "Merely an Imitator? The Preponderance of 'Radcliffe' in *Lusignan, or The Abbaye of La Trappe* and *The Orphans of Llangloed*", *Romantic Textualities*, 20 (Winter 2011). Online: http://www.romtext.org.uk.

A NOTE ON THE TEXT

The text used here is that of the first and only edition published by William Lane's Minerva Press in Leadenhall Street, London, in June 1801. For the sake of authenticity, the original punctuation and spellings (such as "develope", "apostacy", "befal" and "farewel") have been retained. However, a few obvious printer's errors have been silently corrected. The chapter numbers in Volume III have been emended to make them sequential.

Notes have been provided on matters of textual interest as well as on words and passages which assume some knowledge of French history and eighteenth-century literature and society. The notes are signified by an asterisk in the text and can be found at the end of the volume.

LUSIGNAN,

OR

THE ABBAYE

OF

LA TRAPPE.

A NOVEL.

IN FOUR VOLUMES.

" Friendship and love, by Heaven feem'd defign'd,
" That to ennoble, this debafe the mind;
" Friendfhip's pure joys in life's laft hours remain,
" By love, that cheating lotter, we gain,
" A moment's blifs, bought with an age of pain !"

VOL. I.

LONDON:
PRINTED AT THE
Minerva-Prefs,
FOR WILLIAM LANE, LEADENHALL-STREET.

1801.

LUSIGNAN.

CHAP. I.

"The boast of heraldry, the pomp of pow'r,
  "And all that beauty, all that wealth e'er gave,
"Await, alike, th' inevitable hour;
  "The paths of glory lead but to the grave."

The illustrious house of Meronville, was one of the most ancient in
France; its founders had been ennobled by some of the first Kings
of the Carlovingian race;* and the honours it then received were
increased by many succeeding Princes, and descended in lineal suc-
cession to the times of those civil wars, in the reign of Charles the
Ninth,* in which religious zeal obliterated all traces of social affection—arming father against son, animating the dearest friends to
persecute and destroy each other, and deluging France with the
blood of its best subjects. The dissentions which this created, were
not, like many, buried in the graves of the contenders, but were per-
petuated by hereditary prejudices, to many succeeding generations.

The house of Meronville, from its great possessions, and authority in the state, was deeply concerned, and warmly engaged in these
pious broils; and its different branches, according to their several
persuasions, engaged ardently in the cause of one or the other party.

The Duke of Meronville, the head of the family, had two sons,
the eldest of whom, in contracting a strict friendship with the celebrated Admiral Coligni,* attached himself for ever to the faction
he headed, and made it his chief glory to attend that great man,
whose virtues excited his warmest admiration; and it need scarcely
be added, that he acquired a proportionate aversion for the opposing party, guided as it was by leaders who sacrificed every thing to a
mistaken zeal for religion, and with an excess of barbarity, at which
humanity shudders, immolated each day innumerable victims at the
shrine of ambition and bigotry. The Duke himself, with his younger
son, a minor, adhered firmly to the Guises, from whose party he

had the best hopes of succeeding to some great office in the state, an event he passionately desired. His frequent and warm solicitations on this subject, had at length obtained for him a promise of the Grand Constableship, in reversion, whenever a vacancy should occur.*

Elated with these hopes, Meronville wasted days and nights in revolving the various honours to which this new dignity would give birth; a love of pageantry and show, with every pursuit of ambition, were the predominant features in his character; to the gratification of this, nothing could so much conduce as the death of the Grand Constable, which would lay open the road to preferment; and his prayers to every tutelar Saint, were not wanting to accelerate the wished event.

The Constable was seized with a mortal distemper; Meronville wrote a pressing letter to the Duke of Guise, claiming the promised boon; a favourable answer crowned him with joy; his hopes were on the eve of fruition, when an event, as unexpected as fatal, destroyed them all, and left Meronville to deplore the insufficiency of human wisdom, whose best connected plans are in a moment reversed, by a single decree of that all-seeing Providence, who at one view discovers our most secret actions, and their motives, directs events, and ensures their accomplishment.

At this critical period, considered by Meronville as an epoch in his life, Poltrot,* actuated by revenge or inspiration, assassinated the Duke of Guise, at the memorable siege of Orleans. With his patron expired Meronville's elevated hopes of aggrandizement; previous to this event he had neglected neither promises nor threats, to detach his son from a communication with heretics, whose very name he abhorred; but as it was then admitted as an undoubted fact, that Coligni instigated the perpetrator of this murder, the feelings of a friend and a bigot, were rendered more poignant by the stings of disappointed ambition; and he informed him by a peremptory mandate, that he had now nothing to depend on, with respect to him; that his estate should be the reward of his younger brother who had never disobeyed him; that he might seek support in the party he espoused; and that he only lamented his inability to deprive him of the title with the property—a title which, till now, had never been possessed by any but the zealous adherents of the Holy Roman Church, and the infallible Pontiffs who govern it;

that his apostacy gave him claim to no patrimony but his malediction, which he bestowed in the most unqualified manner on all the
favourers of heresy; and concluded by advising him to recollect his
immortal soul, brought to the brink of perdition, whence nothing
but repentance could preserve it.

Meronville had now in some degree tasted the sweets of revenge;
but his vengeance had been wreaked only on one member of the
hated communion, and he ardently desired the extinction of the
whole race.—But in vain he revolved vast purposes in his capacious
mind; they failed of execution, and chagrin at his circumscribed
powers, preyed on his mind, and brought him to the grave; with
his dying breath he exhorted young Henry to pursue, with inveterate hate, his brother, and the whole party to which he belonged,
promising him for every murdered Protestant, a bright reversion in
heaven.

Henry had no sooner paid the last duties to his departed parent,
than he hastened to meet his brother, from whom he had so long
been separated. Far from exulting in the superiority of fortune he
now possessed, his fondest wish was to divide it with a brother he
tenderly loved; their meeting was productive of the greatest joy
to both, and from that hour they were inseparable; both married
amiable and virtuous women, and the birth of sons, on either side,
crowned their mutual happiness.

The two young men were brought up together, their studies and
pursuits were all formed on the model of virtue; but Henry in his
choice of a tutor, was more fortunate than his brother, who, open
and generous himself, was ever liable to be deceived, and mistook
the superficial lustre of a pleasing exterior, for the more solid virtues of the mind. The Abbé La Haye was selected by him to form
the manners, and complete the education of the young Marquis
de Lusignan;* the latter was naturally of a reserved and suspicious
disposition, and sufficiently inclined to envy and dislike his cousin,
whose progress and advancement, superior to his own, excited sentiments of revenge and hatred. La Haye, attentive only to his own
interest, which he hoped to forward by widening the breach that
already seemed to exist between the the young pupils, incessantly
repeated to Frederick how much he was injured by his grandfather's
will, which bequeathed the family estate to the younger branch in
prejudice of the elder.

Frederick listened in silent disgust to these insinuations. His cousin, who bore the title of Comte de Clarival, differed wholly in disposition; candid, modest, generous, a stranger to artifice or disguise, his youthful mind expanded to the calls of affection; nevertheless, as Frederick, by his ill-humour, kept him in a state of constant irritation, quarrels became frequent, and as Frederick was always the aggressor, the chastisement was usually his. Jealousy soon ripened into inveterate hatred; and this common education, which was intended to cement their union, became, by an unforeseen fatality, the source of perpetual discord.

The Marquis of Lusignan, whenever he received what appeared to be a new injury, retired to pour his complaints into the bosom of his tutor, who, as he was but a few years older than his pupil, had great influence with him. One day when he was bitterly lamenting his inability to take ample vengeance on Clarival, La Haye, with a countenance that seemed to convey some pleasing intelligence, embraced his pupil, telling him he had made such a discovery as would enable him to satisfy his desires.

"I will put into your hands," said he, "the means by which you will effectually subdue the pride and arrogance of Clarival; all his possessions are your's by an entail which your grandfather had no power to annul; patiently wait your father's death, and you will have no difficulty in proving your incontestable right to the alienated property."

With tears of joy Frederick received this information;—a character of violence and impetuosity, was seldom so strongly marked as in this young man, even at the age of fifteen, and as time increased its developement, it became gloomy and severe. Prone to the wildest excesses, he already hated the world, and never seemed happy but when he could contribute to destroy the happiness of others; he would have desired to die, had not the hopes of being avenged on Clarival, attached him to life; he dwelt with unspeakable delight on the idea of seeing him reduced to poverty, nay beggary, imploring his pity, which he beforehand determined never to exert in his favour, though it might preserve his existence; all these ideas were deposited in the faithful bosom of La Haye, who omitted no opportunity or endeavours to cherish his resentment.

One day as Frederick, after a warm disagreement with Clarival, had retired to meditate on the banks of a river, which ran through the park, his foot accidentally slipped, and he sunk to the bottom. Clarival was at some distance, a spectator of the accident; he flew with a generosity natural to him, and, at the hazard of his life, preserved Lusignan's, who with great difficulty he rescued from certain death. Glowing with delight at the exploit he had achieved, he watched with anxious solicitude the effects of the remedies that were administered; and was no sooner convinced of their success, than embracing him with unfeigned affection, he congratulated him on returning life.—That life Frederick more than ever abhorred, since to his rival he owed it.

After this accident, which ought to have produced an entire reconciliation, their quarrels became so serious, that a separation was deemed unavoidable; for several years they never met, during which time both married.

Frederick had only one son, the Comte de Clarival one daughter;—by the demise of their fathers the former became the Duke de Meronville, and turned his thoughts, with the most serious attention, towards the recovery of his property. Many years were employed in procuring documents, and witnesses, previous to the commencement of a suit, which aimed at nothing short of stripping Clarival of all his possessions: in the meantime his son grew to years of maturity, and was sent on his travels. After the strictest researches, Meronville almost despaired of success, as the papers, on which his chief dependance rested, were no where to be found; impatient under this delay, he became almost frantic, when, to his inexpressible joy, a brother of Madame de Meronville, sent him certain information, that the deeds in question, were deposited in the archives of a Convent, of which he was Superior; they had been conveyed there during the civil wars, as a place of the utmost security. He at the same time requested this might be kept a profound secret, and that Meronville would either fetch them himself, or depute some person on whose fidelity he could rely.

The Duke at that time was in a very bad state of health, and incapable of undertaking the journey, as he resided at Paris, and the Convent was situated near Bayonne; in this perplexity he determined, notwithstanding his extreme desire to terminate the affair, to wait the young Marquis de Lusignan's return from his travels, as he had no person on whom he could depend, but the Abbé La Haye, who then accompanied his son; he therefore wrote to hasten their return, and they were no sooner arrived, than taking Lusignan into his closet—

"My son," said he, "the affair I am now confiding to your discretion, is of the highest importance; remember the advantage will be all your own; my life hangs on a thread,—your's is only now commencing; the immense estates, dependant on those documents will, when added to your paternal inheritance, render you the richest subject in his Majesty's dominions. Remember this, my son, but chiefly remember, you are assisting my revenge; that all my remaining hopes are centered in you; that should this affair fail of success I have nothing left to cheer my passage to the grave. Go, and shew yourself worthy the house of Meronville."

Lusignan promised to exert his utmost endeavours in promoting his father's wishes; he was a stranger to the merits of the cause he undertook, and the will of his parent had ever been a law, for the austerity of his temper admitted no relaxation, nor ever gave way to paternal feelings. Lusignan set out with only a confidential servant of his father's, and his own valet, who had been attached to him from his infancy; it was agreed that he should assume another name, for two reasons, the first, that no suspicion might be excited at the Convent where Madame de Clarival had many relations; the second, because it was customary at that time for heirs of great families to travel with large retinues, and Lusignan preferred a more private mode of travelling.

La Haye remained at Paris, to lend every assistance in his power towards bringing this work to perfection, which he claimed the sole merit of suggesting; he had, indeed, become necessary to Meronville, whose passions he soothed, and to whose desires, however extravagant, he implicitly conformed; besides, to his congenial breast, he alone dared to communicate his schemes of vengeance.

CHAP. II.

"Grace in each step, Heav'n in her eye,
"In every gesture, dignity and love."

Lusignan mounted his horse early on the following morning, and took the road to Gascony; his journey was not attended with any remarkable occurrence, and he arrived on the third day at the Carthusian Monastery,* where his uncle presided. He was received with much hospitality, and easily obtained permission to search the archives, where he found the rights of his father, as head of the house of Meronville, incontestably proved; he immediately communicated the joyful intelligence, requesting, at the same time, that he might be allowed to proceed to Montpelier,* where much company was assembled for the season.

Meronville's joy when he received these dispatches, is hardly to be described; the long expected hour was now arrived, and he might defy the perversity of fortune to disappoint him. For the first time in his life he felt inclined to contribute to the happiness of another; he granted Lusignan the first indulgence, and to testify his extreme satisfaction at the manner in which he had executed his commission, permitted him to pass the winter season at Montpelier.

Lusignan had just completed his twentieth year; his figure was tall and graceful, his countenance expressed the feelings of a benevolent, generous, and susceptible heart. The natural vivacity of his disposition had been considerably checked by the restraint his father's presence always imposed; hilarity in those around him he considered as a reproach to the sullen equanimity of manners, which became contagious to all around him; habit, therefore, had cast a shade of melancholy over the features of Lusignan; but a short absence easily removed it, and the slight remains rather resembled diffidence, and served to render his appearance truly interesting. His external advantages indicated those of his mind; he inherited all the virtues of his grandfather, but accompanied with a degree of impetuosity which sometimes prevented their full effect; generosity was his chief characteristic, and the few failings that obscured his merit, were forgotten in this, and he was universally admired and esteemed.

With a heart dilating with joy, and pleasure beaming in his countenance, he took leave of his uncle, the Abbot of Semur; it was the first time liberty attended his steps.—Accustomed to perpetual restraint he felt emancipated at once from every grief, all Nature smiled, the fertility of the country through which he passed, and the beautiful landscapes which every where met his eye, elevated his thoughts to rapture; he almost fancied that some magic power had formed the scene for his enjoyment, that magic power was liberty; and Lusignan now felt persuaded that life was an enamelled path, and sorrow a mere chimera, a phantom of his father's clouded imagination.

Arrived at Montpelier, he hastened to mix in a group of persons, whose cheerful countenances bespoke them, like himself, free from care; he had not yet learned, that under this disguise was frequently concealed a discontented spirit and an aching heart. They were hastening to the public rooms, where, as the company was usually select, ceremony was wholly banished, and the pleasing exterior of Lusignan soon gained him admittance to all parties; the name of the handsome stranger was anxiously enquired by all the surrounding females; his unaffected vivacity, which now appeared the faithful transcript of his heart, charmed all who approached him. As all females claimed his attention, he repeated with peculiar care and grace, those common place civilities which a man of gallantry bestows indiscriminately upon the sex, and ere three days had elapsed he was the theme, and no party of pleasure was formed in which he was not included.

A *fête champêtre** was announced at the Marquis de la Valette's; Lusignan promised himself every delight which the novelty of the scene could inspire. He arrived early at the appointed place, the ladies were already assembled, he joined them and was resuming his usual mode of entertaining them, when a lady in deep mourning entered the room; there was a dignity in her appearance, and the remains of so much beauty, as for a moment fixed the wandering attention of Lusignan. But it was soon riveted by an object which, at one glance, seemed to penetrate his inmost soul—her daughter, a young person of seventeen, whose exquisite charms were considerably heightened by her mourning garb, with which a gentle air of melancholy seemed to correspond. Her figure had every thing in it of elegance, that might have been chosen to portray the Medicean Venus;* her extreme modesty prevented her raising her eyes to the surrounding circle, whose all of attention was fixed on her.

From that moment Lusignan's gaiety forsook him; his very features sympathetically caught the impression of her's. Love, to punish his former indifference, developed all its power, and by one look enslaved his affections. For a moment he stood mute, and lost in excess of surprise and admiration; the ladies to whom he had before devoted his attention, rallied him on the sudden alteration of manners, and endeavoured in vain to restore his vivacity; his thoughts were all engrossed by one object, and he could not command his features, or appear unconcerned. He readily determined to address himself the first opportunity to the mother of the fair incognita, and to use every means of introducing himself to her society.

As they were almost as much strangers as himself, he had no difficulty in procuring a seat near them; and as a walk of some length was proposed, he requested permission to assist the ladies with his arm; his offer was accepted with thanks, and before they returned some accident separated himself and the young lady from the rest of the party; both were so much embarrassed that not a word escaped either till they rejoined the company. Lusignan was astonished at his own imbecility; he had been frequently in female society, where all were indifferent to him, yet he had always contrived to exert his politeness, and make a thousand speeches, he did not [feel???], now when his whole heart paid homage to this unknown divinity, he had not power to utter a simple expression of admiration.

"This angelic creature," said he, "must think me the most insensible of mortals; accustomed as she must be to the adoration of all who approach her, she can only attribute my silence to the coldest indifference."

He returned to his lodgings thoroughly dissatisfied with himself, and determined, when another opportunity should offer, to convince her, if possible, that he was not the child of insensibility. Never had he felt thus before, he was restless, perturbed, and impatient, night came but he vainly endeavoured to take repose; as soon as day appeared he quitted his apartment, and strolled out as though he expected to meet the object he sought at that early hour, when every eye, his excepted, was closed in sleep. The silence that prevailed every where excited his astonishment, till after wandering some hours, he involuntarily consulted his watch and found it was hardly yet nine o'clock; disappointed and blaming his own folly he returned home, resolved at least to enquire the abode of the fair stranger; but when he had an opportunity of so doing, he for the first time recollected that he had not the preceding evening been sufficiently master of his voice, to ask their names.

Great, therefore, as his impatience was, no remedy appeared but that of waiting till he met them at the rooms, which he hoped would be that evening. The hours appeared an unusual length, but the moment at last arrived, he entered the rooms before they were lighted, or prepared for the reception of strangers; he enquired why they were so unusually late, and could hardly conceal his impatience, when assured the company seldom assembled till two hours later.

A few persons at length arrived, and he endeavoured to beguile the tedious moments by conversing on general subjects.—Whilst he was addressing the Chevalier de St. Amand, the two ladies in black entered the room; the Chevalier, who was loquacious, and too much an admirer of himself to bestow much attention on others, condescended, however, to observe that those women were really handsome, and then, without remarking the effect their arrival had on Lusignan, was proceeding in an elaborate eulogium on his own conduct in a little *affaire d'honneur*,* in which he had been lately engaged; but Lusignan little disposed to listen, eagerly enquired their names.

"Their names!" said St. Amand; "why where, my dear friend, have you been entombed, not to be acquainted with that? Besides, I have seen you converse with them!"

"Doubtless you have," replied Lusignan; "but I will candidly confess that her charms so pre-occupied my ideas, that I never thought of asking their name or rank."

"As that is the case," continued the Chevalier, "I have no doubt you will consider those charms as doubly valuable, when I tell you their possessor is the rich heiress of Montalte, and only daughter of the late Comte de Clarival."

A thunderbolt would have affected Lusignan less than did this unexpected intelligence.

"Emily de Montalte!" repeated he to himself—"the object of my father's hatred!"

The Chevalier, eager to return to the subject of his own merits, turned to some person who might be more disposed to listen, and did not observe the impression his information left on the countenance of his auditor.

Lusignan dared not pause, or allow himself time to reflect; he instantly joined Madame de Clarival, between whom and her amiable daughter he divided all his attention; after accompanying them to their hotel, and obtaining permission to wait on them the following day, he retired to meditate on this extraordinary adventure. A train of opposing ideas rushed on his mind; the happiness of being near Emily, and of seeing her daily, produced such exquisite delight, that he most unwillingly relinquished the thought, to consider the circumstance in any other point of view. Here indeed the association of ideas was far less pleasurable; he saw only the opposition he must encounter from his father's enmity; he trembled at the violence of his passions, when inflamed by the least opposition; and above all, he shuddered at the idea that she had, perhaps, been taught to regard him as her inveterate enemy.

He now congratulated himself on the circumstance of his real name being unknown at Montpelier (for he had still retained that of Comte d'Everil, which he assumed at the Abbaye of Semur);* he flattered himself that under this disguise he might by his assiduities recommend himself to her; and that when she discovered his real rank, it would no longer be in her power to hate him, firmly resolved at that early period to sacrifice every consideration to love, should he ever be fortunate enough to engage her affections.

Emily de Montalte, indeed, justly claimed his admiration; her external charms borrowed new lustre from the virtues of her mind, the exact model of a mother, whose every wish was to bring her as near to perfection as possible—herself a pattern of female excellence—she wanted no accomplishment, which nature, improved with the nicest care, could bestow. Emily and Lusignan seemed formed for each other; but an almost invincible barrier was placed between them.

CHAP. III.

"Ah! cruel love, thou bane of every joy,
"Whose pains, or sweets, alike our peace destroy;
"Equal the woes, from thee mankind endure,
"Fatal thy wound,—and fatal is thy cure!"*

Lusignan having decided on the course he was to pursue, became more tranquil; he constantly attended Madame de Clarival, and each night returned more enamoured of his Emily.

One evening as they were walking with a large party in the public gardens, near the town, Emily, in pulling off her glove, let fall a bracelet, to which a miniature of herself was attached. The Chevalier de St. Amand picked it up, and after examining it attentively, put it in his pocket with an air of effrontery peculiarly natural to him. She at first gently requested he would return it, but as he seemed little inclined to comply, she assumed a more commanding tone; but St. Amand, who had been accustomed to think himself irresistible, felt but little disconcerted at her reproof.

"Since Fortune," said he, "Madam, has kindly bestowed this prize on me, you would not have the cruelty to counteract her friendly design.—I trust," continued he, in a half whisper, "that when my sentiments are known to you, you will, without difficulty, acquiesce in her decree, and confirm me in the possession of the original as well as the copy."

Then, without waiting the reproof such conduct would have called forth, he hastily withdrew, with a look of complacency and self-satisfaction not to be described.

Fortunately Lusignan was at some distance, or his indignation would certainly have betrayed itself in some rash act of jealousy; he seldom quitted her, and never but for a moment. Hearing her now speak in rather an elevated tone of voice, he approached; she was relating the adventure to her mother, with a great degree of emotion. Madame de Clarival felt not less resentment at such unwarrantable behaviour, and assured her she would on the following day insist on his restoring the portrait, to which he could have no claim.

Lusignan listened attentively, but took no notice of what passed, yet he was far from being unconcerned; had Emily only been dis-obliged, it was sufficient to excite his warmest resentment, but here was an attempt at rivalship, and St. Amand had, in his opinion, by presuming to withhold the portrait, infringed his right. With apparent unconcern, however, he continued to entertain her, and was even more gay than usual as he hoped Fortune had thrown in his way a method of obliging Emily.

Full of this idea, and a heart devoted to love, he retired to call on the Chevalier; he found him at home, and without losing a moment he entered on the subject of his visit.

"Chevalier," said he, "what passed this evening between yourself and Mademoiselle de Montalte, can certainly be meant only as a joke; you are too much of a gentleman, and a man of gallantry, to persist in retaining the portrait of a lady against her wish; and you must by this time be sensible, that you can have no claim to that of Emily de Montalte."

The Chevalier had been so little interested in the theft he had committed, that by this time the circumstance had fairly escaped his memory. This appeal, however, of Lusignan, awakened his recollection, and with it his vanity, which was sensibly affected by the latter part of his observation. He would willingly have made it appear, that he was a favoured admirer of the lady in question; not that, in fact, he was enamoured with any thing but his own sweet person. But as she was universally admired, his self-consequence was interested in general opinion; deeply, therefore, offended at the right Lusignan assumed in calling him to account, he answered with great warmth—

"I am a stranger, Sir, to your pretensions, and the powers with which Mademoiselle de Montalte may have invested you to become her champion and my monitor; but one thing I must inform you, I seldom submit to be advised, and that your counsels are therefore likely to prove ineffectual, except in confirming my design of keeping a bauble, in which you appear so interested. For," continued he, with a tone of irony, and a sarcastic smile, "as you are known to be a man of taste, I begin to conceive there may be more value in it than I first imagined."

Lusignan, beyond measure irritated, drew his sword.

"There is a method," said he, "I hope, of reducing those to reason who are above submitting to advice."

The Chevalier, not less enraged, drew his; they fought. Lusignan received the first wound; but, animated with love and resentment, he rushed on his antagonist, and at one thrust deprived him of the power to contend. Seeing him fall——

"St. Amand," said he, "I have no wish to deprive you of life; I am even sorry that our mutual impetuosity has given rise to an affair which, for a time, may be attended with unpleasant consequences to you.—Let it, however, not diminish our mutual esteem—accept my hand in token of reconciliation, and let the affair from this hour be forgotten."

The natural frivolity of St. Amand rendered his manners frequently disgusting; but he had a fund of generosity in his disposition, that would not permit itself to be outdone.

"Lusignan," said he, "take the miniature, I acknowledge it is your's by right of chivalry, no less than it is due to your generosity; from this moment we are friends, and I freely confess that I have no pretensions to the honour of becoming your rival."

Lusignan having seen that every attention was paid to the wound his friend had received, retired to have his own dressed, which, though slight, became painful. But not withstanding the peremptory commands of his surgeon, that he should go to bed, and remain quiet, he fully determined to pass the night in copying the portrait. He could paint a little, but was far from being an adept; Love, however, guided the pencil, and he succeeded so well, the copy could with difficulty be distinguished from the original. It instantly occurred to him, that he might substitute the one for the other, by retaining the one Emily had worn, and thus obliging her unknowingly, to grace his labours by attaching them to her arm. The idea was too pleasing to be abandoned; he dexterously adjusted the bracelet that the deception might not appear; and fully satisfied with his own ingenuity, he determined to attempt some repose, the want of which his fascinating employment had prevented his observing, though the rising sun now gilded the atmosphere.

The agitation of his mind yielded with difficulty to the wants of nature, and his slumbers were short and disturbed. The pleasure of receiving thanks from the lips of Emily was ecstacy, and he had no doubt she would thus reward his labours.

When the surgeon arrived, he found a considerable degree of fever accumulating, and was really alarmed for his patient. He insisted that Lusignan should not quit his bed that day; assuring him, that the least cold or agitation might be of fatal consequence. To the impatient mind of Lusignan, this appeared absolute coercion; but he recollected that any imprudence might, perhaps, confine him for weeks, and deprive him of the society of Emily.

This conclusion once formed had a more powerful effect than the wisest injunctions could have produced; he used every endeavour to compose himself, and a few hours consequent repose, almost restored his wonted vigour.

It now occurred to him that Madame de Clarival would, probably, take some measures to oblige the Chevalier to make restitution, and this might have superinduced an explanation, and a relation of facts he wished to conceal from her. The difficulty then was, how the portrait should be returned, without leaving room to suspect the means by which it had been acquired; this was hardly practicable, since his being absent a whole day, he flattered himself, could not pass unnoticed. In this perplexity he determined to send it, accompanied by a billet, in which he lamented that letters he received the preceding evening, obliged him to go into Languedoc; that his business, however, he hoped, would not detain him more than a few hours; and the following day he should have the unspeakable pleasure of paying his devoirs to the ladies.

Emily was no less rejoiced to find herself indebted to him for the recovery of her bracelet, than at the circumstance of recovering it. She watched the countenance of Madame de Clarival, to see what effect this acceptable piece of gallantry would have on her before she ventured to express her sense of it.

Madame de Clarival really felt much indebted for it, but the non-appearance of Lusignan alarmed her; she thought the reason he alledged did not wear the face of probability, and the real cause forcibly struck her imagination. She, however, did not mention her suspicions to her daughter, who suffered no intensive thoughts to disturb the satisfaction this affair gave her. The necessity of passing a long day without seeing him, however, was a real calamity. She was surprised at the degree of indolence she felt, and at her disinclination to dress, and go to the rooms. She persuaded herself it was only an effect of her impatience, to discharge a part of her obligation to Lusignan, by returning him her warmest thanks. The lassitude and *ennui* she felt in the midst of the gay circle, where she was the object of envy to her own sex, and admiration to the other, were attributed to the same cause.

Madame de Clarival observed it, however, not without uneasiness. Lusignan had acquired her esteem in the highest degree; but his rank and connections, as well as private character, were unknown to her.—Besides, though his admiration of her lovely daughter, was too evident to escape detection, he had as yet made no declaration that could justify the gift of a heart such as Emily's. She therefore determined to address her on the subject, certain that her ingenuous mind would conceal no emotion from the solicitude of maternal tenderness.

"My Emily," said Madame de Clarival, "you seem less entertained, less happy than usual, this evening."

Unconscious why, Emily blushed.

"I am very happy, my dear mother."

"I would not distress you, my love; but the absence of the Comte d'Everil seems to affect you. Tell me, is it not so?"

Emily blushed still deeper.

"Why my dear Madam," said she, "should I attempt to conceal, that I do feel a pleasure in his company, which no other can bestow. To your discerning eye he must already have appeared distinguished from the general class of men that frequent the rooms; the superiority of his mind and conversation, cannot have escaped you, and that alone induces me to give him a preference, which is confined, I believe, to the amusement of the moment."

Emily spoke these words with visible confusion. Madame de Clarival almost reproached herself for having caused it.—She tenderly embraced her daughter; then continued——

"My child, I place so firm a reliance on your virtue and good sense, that when I consider them, all my apprehensions vanish; but I would chiefly guard you against the errors of sensibility, and a too fervid imagination. Amiable as is the former, when duly controuled, and tending only to excite our sympathy, for the real sorrows of our fellow-creatures, it leads, by the least excess, to the most dangerous consequences.—So narrow is the boundary between virtue and vice, that a single inconsiderate step may bewilder your path.* Your unbiassed mind readily ascribes virtue to every thing which wears the semblance of it; but the world is full of deceit and dissimulation, few persons appear in their proper garb. Your rank, fortune, and connections, will procure you the apparent homage of those who consider them as the only valuable possessions, and will readily forget the more estimable advantages of the mind."

"D'Everil," exclaimed Emily, "is too generous, too disinterested!" She blushed, and paused——Madame de Clarival smiled.

"Here," continued she, "fervour of imagination may mislead you. Never expect, my Emily, to find perfection in a human shape; mediocrity is the real standard of our nature. I mean not to make you a misanthropist, nor entirely to make you despise that world in which you are placed, but only to guard you against its delusions. Preserve with the strictest care, that candour and ingenuousness—the noblest gift of Heaven! Let it not be perverted by the discovery, that all do not equally possess it. I will freely acknowledge that d'Everil has appeared to me every thing I could wish; but a judgment formed on such slight grounds, is ever to be distrusted. And above all things, avoid engaging your heart irretrievably, till you are not only certain of an exchange, but even an exchange worthy of it."

Here Madame de Clarival was interrupted, and soon after they retired to their apartments.

With silent concern Madame de Clarival had observed that the Chevalier St. Amand was absent from the rooms that night; a circumstance so extraordinary that it seemed to confirm her worst apprehensions. By Emily it passed unobserved.—Lusignan she knew was absent; all others were indifferent to her.

The next morning they had scarcely entered the breakfast parlour, when a visitor was announced, and Lusignan, almost equally to the joy of both, appeared.—Madame de Clarival expressed her thanks to him in the warmest terms; with Emily's were mixed a degree of embarrassment and confusion, in the midst of which Lusignan thought he discovered a secret satisfaction, that would have repaid him for a thousand wounds. Both hearts dilated with secret rapture, and neither would then have thought that any thing could disturb their mutual happiness. The hour, however, approached that was to bring a mournful reverse, and a storm at that moment impended, which would plunge them in the deepest affliction.

Notwithstanding the care that Lusignan and his antagonist had taken to conceal their *rencontre*, it soon became public. The Chevalier was confined for several days, and a servant he discharged in anger at that time, published the cause with exaggerated circumstances. The affair now became the general topic; many declared that St. Amand could not recover, and that his father was arrived to take his last farewel of this only son, on whom he fondly doted.

The pathetic and marvellous thus united, was repeated from one to the other, till it reached the ears of Mademoiselle de Montalte. The ladies who had never forgiven her for depriving them of Lusignan, omitted no circumstance that might increase her distress; and accused her of having intentionally engaged two gentlemen in a duel, by encouraging the addresses of both.

Emily, unconscious how much of envy was mingled in their reports, was sensibly affected by them, and had almost persuaded her mother to quit Montpelier;—when the Chevalier, to the astonishment of all, appeared in perfect health and spirits, leaning on the arm of Lusignan, the very day when all reports concurred in declar-

ing that he had expired, and that his remains had been privately
conveyed to a neighbouring Convent. Those who had been most
industrious in propagating the late rumours, now most sedulously
paid court to Emily, assuring her they had never given credit to
them, but waited to refute them, as they knew the Chevalier would
soon appear, to contradict them all.

Emily was but little interested in these professions, nor could
they remove the real injury herself and Lusignan received from the
publication of such reports.

It was observed, that when the latter left Paris, a confidential servant of his father's accompanied him; but not till he had previously
received instructions to attend scrupulously to his conduct, and
to inform La Haye, should any imprudence occur, that he might
represent to his disadvantage.* He had been faithful to his mission, and from time to time transmitted accounts of his union with
Madame de Clarival, and her daughter. La Haye secretly rejoiced;
but knowing the impetuosity of Lusignan's temper, waited till it
should appear in some effective step, before he communicated it to
Meronville, when the information would, from being unexpected,
strike more forcibly.

His agent did not fail to relate the event of the duel, with every
exaggeration it had accumulated in passing through so many hands;
adding, from the fertility of his own imagination, a circumstance
that could occur only to him, viz. That Madame de Clarival was
acquainted with his real rank, and had neglected no pains to attach
him to her daughter; representing them both as dangerous and
designing women.

La Haye now thought it time to open his battery. He bore no
enmity to Lusignan, but thought his own interest might be for-
warded, by occasioning a breach between the father and son, who
both had been in some degree his pupils. He had a powerful oppo-
nent in the Duchess de Meronville, who loved her son with more
than maternal affection.

The mildest virtues that adorn the sex were conspicuous in her;
united by one of those early marriages (in which interest is primar-
ily concerned), to a man whose pursuits and sentiments were all at
variance with her's, she had, in obedience to her parents, formed
vows at an age in which she knew not their value, and to which
in a more advanced period, her heart never assented. Conscious,

however, of the duties those vows imposed, she had devoted her life to sooth that ferocity of nature no efforts could subjugate. She sometimes succeeded, and began to hope her influence might be productive of reformation; but some secret power counteracted all her endeavours. This power was that of malignity, personified in the Abbé La Haye; he bore an inveterate hatred to Madame de Meronville, because she alone shared the confidence of his pupil with him. But profoundly skilled in the arts of dissimulation, he almost persuaded her their endeavours co-operated to the same end; and represented all his views as the offspring of benevolence.

He foresaw much opposition from the affection Madame de Meronville had for her son, in the project he had now formed for disinheriting him. He knew that from her all the obstacles would arise to the success of his wishes; and, therefore, determined to ensure success, before she could be aware that any such attempt was forming. He had here a fresh stimulus, that of revenge; for the Chevalier de St. Amand, though only acknowledged as his nephew, might, in truth, boast a nearer degree of consanguinity, and to this fruit of an illicit connection, he hoped to transfer the paternal patrimony of Lusignan.

CHAP. IV.

"Where'er my lonely course I bend,
"Thy image shall my steps attend;
"Each object I am doom'd to see,
"Shall bid remembrance picture thee."

In the meantime Lusignan every day increased in the good opinion of Madame de Clarival, and her lovely daughter; and after every interview returned more inebriated with the delicious poison of love. No extraneous idea was ever suffered to obtrude, lest it should disturb the visionary joy. He had never declared his sentiments; but they were not doubtful. The boasted eloquence of the eyes, was mutually expressive; and souls congenial like their's, could not long misunderstand each other.

Two months had now elapsed since his arrival in Montpelier; partial Time seemed to have extended his wide pinions, and to have flown with unusual swiftness.* Lusignan seemed to have forgotten that he must soon return to Paris, and that any ties existed, but those that detained him at Montpelier.

One evening as he was as usual sitting with Madame de Clarival and Emily, the servant delivered a letter into his hands, which he said arrived by an express from Paris, and required immediate attention. He involuntarily trembled, as with difficulty he divided the seal; but the vital current seemed for a moment suspended, as he hastily read these words:——

———————

"I am informed of all your guilt, and the disgrace that your imprudence has brought on the house of Meronville. As you value my malediction, return immediately to Paris; but not till you have informed those artful women, whose intrigues have enslaved you, that I am determined to proceed, without loss of time, in a suit which, Heaven be praised, will reduce them to penury. I only want the papers in your possession, and all my lawyers assure me the most undoubted success. Return then without delay, or dread the vengeance of your offended father,

"DE MERONVILLE."

———————

For an instant Lusignan stood petrified; his emotion did not escape the anxious eye of Emily. He paced the room with hasty steps, striking his forehead as in despair.

Madame de Clarival ventured to enquire if he had received any unpleasant intelligence. He seized Emily's trembling hand, who, terrified beyond description, could with difficulty support herself.

"You will hate me!" said he. "You will hate the wretch who has deceived you. And, alas! too cruelly deceived himself."

A long drawn sigh concluded this ejaculation. Emily responsively sighed. Addressing her mother, Lusignan then continued—

"Suffer me, Madam, to complete my guilt, by declaring that my whole soul is devoted to your angelic daughter; and I here solemnly swear, that no opposition, no persecution, shall have power to disunite us, if I can be fortunate enough to obtain your approbation, and the invaluable gift of Emily's heart."—He paused.

Madame de Clarival, scarcely less agitated, entreated him to explain himself.—His whole frame seemed convulsed, he struggled for utterance; then, with an effort that exhausted his remaining strength, he exclaimed—

"Know then, that I am the wretched heir of the house of Meronville!"

The effect of a thunderbolt would have been mild compared to these words.—Life fled from the cheeks of Emily, a livid hue succeeded, and she fell lifeless in the arms of her mother. Lusignan had thrown himself in an agony on a sofa, and seemed absorbed in forgetfulness. The danger of Emily roused him, he flew to her assistance, and this proof of her interest for him revived all his hopes; by degrees they all became more composed. Lusignan then endeavoured to convince them, that his father's enmity would yield to his entreaty; that his mother idolized him, and had great influence with her husband; that independent of that, if they could only be prevailed on to accede to his wishes, he should set at defiance that authority which, though parental, had never been enforced but to imbitter all his hopes.

Madame de Clarival shook her head.

"Marquis de Lusignan," said she, "let us no longer deceive ourselves, I am too well acquainted with your father's implacable animosity to have any remaining doubts; never will he consent to such a union, and it is in his power to oppose invincible barriers to your wishes."

"No power on earth shall oppose them!" ejaculated Lusignan.

"Listen," continued Madame de Clarival, "to maternal solicitude; believe that it is the voice of Reason that addresses you, and that I am not a cold or insensible observer of your sorrow. Unions formed on the basis of filial disobedience are ever baneful in their effects. Return to Paris, and let no recollection of Montpelier disturb you in the exercise of your duty. Remember that paternal commands are sacred; that Nature has made this one of her most inviolable laws, which no fortuitous tie can weaken. Should you succeed in obtaining his consent, mine will not be withheld; but as the chances are so unequal, let us part as we do after every casual connection, without regret, and endeavour to feel indifferent whether chance may favour any future meeting."

Emily's tears flowed copiously. The night was far advanced, and

Lusignan could not refuse to set out early in the morning; he had not power to bid her adieu, the words quivered on his lips; at length he faintly said—

"Farewel, my Emily! to happiness and you, a long, long farewel!" And then hastily quitted the room.

He gave orders to be awakened at six o'clock the following morning, and entrusted to St. Pierre, his favourite servant, the care of preparing every thing for his departure. He threw himself on the bed, but not to rest; his father's letter had chased every bright illusion, and shewn him the full extent of his misfortune.

He formed a thousand plans which quickly destroyed themselves; the law-suit now occurred to his imagination, its odious consequences were not forgotten, how to prevent them he could not devise. On a sudden the idea of destroying the papers he possessed occurred to him; this would finally terminate his disquietude; he was astonished this project had not sooner presented itself, as by so doing he should prevent his father from recovering the alienated property, except by consenting to their union; and should this be still denied, he was firmly resolved never to administer to his unjust resentment.

He then recollected the charge he had received when the care of recovering the entail was consigned to his discretion; he had been told that he was labouring for his own advancement; that he would become the richest subject in France. All this concerned only him, and he had a right to divest himself of that property, since it could not be purchased but at the expence of all his happiness; and if his father should think himself injured, he would, by way of compensation, transfer to him an estate he had inherited by his maternal uncle.

All obstacles vanished at the voice of love, and he no longer hesitated. He collected the papers, and committed them to the flames;* as each consumed, he exalted with joy.

"May every attempt to injure my Emily," said he, "thus perish! should we ever be united, she will know the sacrifice I have made; if not, the satisfaction of having essentially served her, will sooth every future hour of distress."

Elated with the idea, he felt relieved from a weight of anguish; and full of Emily, closed his eyes in sleep.

CHAP. V.

"These are thy glorious works, Parent of good,
"Almighty, thine this universal frame,
"Thus wondrous fair; thyself how wondrous then!"

The sun now dawned in the eastern horizon, gilding the proud summits of the distant Pyrenees; and extending its rays to the smooth ocean, scarcely a breeze agitated its translucent waves. Vessels scattered in every direction gently glided on the calm surface of the sea; all was still, save when borne on the breeze, the mariner's song reached the shore, hailing the return of morn; it was a scene no pencil could delineate. Lusignan silently contemplated and admired it, his perturbed mind was soothed by the prospect; he had risen earlier than he had given orders to be awakened, and sat down to await the appointed hour of departure.

St. Pierre at length entered the apartment; and with a heart almost bursting with anguish he set out. He must necessarily pass the abode of Emily, the lattices were all closed; "She sleeps," sighed he, "unconscious of my woes." Just as he passed the house, turning to take a last view, he observed a female figure half-concealed, at one of the windows; his heart told him it was Emily; in fact, it was her, who after passing a restless night, had hoped to see him once again, ere he quitted her for ever. She, however, shrank from his eye; but not till he had been convinced it was her, and fondly flattered himself that he was not forgotten in some degree; elated with the idea, he continued his route.

It was the month of May, nature, luxuriantly clothed, every where met the eye; but it was no longer for Lusignan the scene he had so lately viewed with admiration, other objects now engrossed his undivided attention. In vain the rural choristers filled the air with their gentle melody, that seemed in gratitude for the return of day—reproaching the ingratitude of man. The peasants with cheerful countenances, hastening to begin the labours of the day, greeted with rustic grace our sorrowing traveller.

How little, thought he, is that happiness which reigns in courts, and is so much valued in the haunts of luxury, compared with this; here nature limits our desires to our possessions; here no consideration of interest disturbs the rural lovers. Ah! why was not Lusignan placed here?

Being arrived at the village where he designed to pass the night, he allowed himself the unspeakable delight of addressing a line to Emily; he assured her nothing could withstand his entreaties, his despair. His father's heart, though formed of adamant, must yield; but above all, his mother would plead for him. He conjured her not to forget him, not to forget that his destiny depended on her; and that his heart was committed to her care. His whole soul seemed developed on the paper; he dispatched St. Pierre with it to Montpelier, with orders to rejoin him at Paris, as soon as possible, he purposed to arrive there himself the following night.

The reception he was likely to meet, could not be recollected without uneasiness; sometimes he flattered himself, that the hopes of uniting the divided honours of the family might induce his father to retract; since ambition, and more sordid avarice, were his governing principles. The thought, however, was evanescent, hatred and revenge would still preponderate; as he approached the metropolis his fears increased, his heart sunk. A criminal waiting his last sentence, never presented himself before the tribunal with more terror, than Lusignan entered the paternal residence; nor did ever the most austere judge, pronounce with less gentleness, less clemency, than the Duke de Meronville.

"Degenerate wretch!" said he, "you have descended to love my enemies, and have attached yourself to them without once recollecting the duty you owe me, the respect due to yourself; your audacity may even have formed more odious projects."

Lusignan threw himself at his feet.

"Yes, my father," said he, "I am guilty, but involuntarily guilty; at this moment when prostrate at your feet, and imploring your clemency, it is not in my power to purchase it at the price of repentance. I feel that nothing can tear from my heart, those sentiments that excite your anger; if nature yet pleads within your bosom, pity your child, withhold not your pardon, persist not in your unjust hatred; let this moment extinguish those resentments that have lasted too long. Heaven warns you by my voice to forget your animosity; it has inspired Mademoiselle de Montalte and myself with a mutual passion, to reunite us all, and destroy the sins of enmity. My father, I am your only child, relent, I conjure you; all my misfortunes will fall with double weight, since they are the work of your hand. A fatality of which I am not master, has made me offend you; have I ever before opposed you? No, my father, in every thing that I can command, your word is law; forgive me then, since Heaven, and not me, has implanted this sentiment in my breast."

Meronville regarded him with indignation, and made no attempt to raise him;—whilst he spoke he seemed struggling with anger, which at length found vent.

"I have listened to you," said he, "with an excess of patience, which really surprises me, for I did not think myself capable of so much forbearance. It is, however, the only indulgence you have to expect; retract all your promises to that artful and intriguing woman, who encourages you to contemn my authority; exert all your endeavours to forward my impending suit, or from this moment I disown you. But what do I say? it is not in your power to impede my success; return me instantly those papers you received at the Abbaye de Semur, you are unworthy the trust I reposed in you."

Had the Duke yielded to the voice of Nature, or suffered himself to be moved by the entreaties of Lusignan, this request would have embarrassed him, he would have felt some compunction for the injury he had done his father; but his inflexibility inspired him with courage.

"Those papers," said he, "are no longer in my power, they are consigned to the flames. Take all the property I lately acquired, to repay the loss you may sustain, I value it not. Give me Emily, restore me to your affection; but dispose of your possessions as you may think proper."

Meronville's eye-balls flashed with fire; he drew his sword, and would inevitably have embrued his hands in the blood of his only child, who made no effort to resist him, had not the Duchess at that moment entered the apartment. She threw herself between them——

"Desist," she exclaimed, "it is your child, your only child!"

Some secret power withheld the arm of Meronville; he paused, and in the short interval Lusignan was compelled by his mother to quit the room, and wait her return to her own apartment. A moment's recollection restored all Meronville's rage, he again drew his sword, unconscious that the object of his revenge was no longer near.

"Why did you prevent my taking instant revenge on that wretch, I once honoured with the name of son? Heaven, however, executes the malediction of a father; and I here solemnly swear by all the powers that protect me, by all my hopes of pardon in another world——."

"Stop! in mercy stop!" cried Madame de Meronville. "Vows formed in anger, are ever followed by repentance; leave to me the care of making Lusignan sensible of his duty."

He gnashed his teeth and raved with every symptom of distraction; with words of tenderness and affection, his Duchess tried to sooth and tranquillize him. While Lusignan, scarcely less distracted, paced his mother's apartment, and awaited her arrival. It was now no longer fury and reproach he had to encounter; it was now no longer an inflexible father he had to combat; it was the mild reproof, the gentle remonstrance, the tender solicitude of the best of mothers. Lusignan's manhood forsook him, he mingled tears with her's.

"My child," said she, "is it possible that a mistress, and one that you have known but a few weeks, can make you forgetful of a mother whose only consolation you have been. Did your happiness, alas! depend on me, it would be cheaply purchased at the expence of life; but you have a father who will be obeyed. He is meditating the most violent resolutions against you; I have only prevailed to have them suspended. My child, would you drive me to despair; stifle, I conjure you, a passion that can only render us all unhappy."

"Dearest, and best of parents," replied Lusignan, "no future tie can weaken my affection for you, I would willingly sacrifice my life to it; but were you to see my Emily, you would yourself confess, that having once hoped and obtained her affections, nothing could induce me to relinquish them. You would love her, she would adore you; she possesses all your candour, your fascinating sweetness, she would share your affections with me. Could my father, obdurate as he is, once see her angelic smile, he would consider himself vanquished. Can I betray her? can I recal the vows I made? can I banish from my heart those sentiments that, however opposed, will still form the only charm of life?"

He then repeated to his mother all that had passed between them, and her ignorance of his real condition till the last night when he received his summons to quit Montpelier. Madame de Meronville told him nothing would convince his father that Emily had not been prompted by her mother, to exact the sacrifice of the entail; she blamed him for having burned it, and prevailed on him, at least for the present, to feign compliance with father's orders; which were, that he should the next morning retire to a castle of his, situated on the coast of Normandy, as he positively refused to see him, or listen to any concessions short of absolute obedience.

"I acknowledge," continued she, "his anger has lasted too long, even had his hatred been just: no endeavour of mine shall be wanting to soften his resentment; but in return you must promise to exert all your strength to overcome this passion, and to renounce it entirely. Should it appear that Mademoiselle de Montalte is not equally attached to you, absence may on both have more effect than you suppose. Then go, my child, and may Heaven's blessing attend you!"

Lusignan promised all that his mother desired. He now regretted having sent St. Pierre to Montpelier, as he had no person on whom he could rely to attend him on this journey; he begged Madame de Meronville to send him as soon as he returned, and to correspond regularly with him. Madame de Clarival was soon to return to Paris, as the extreme heat of the weather prevented her remaining in the south. Lusignan ventured to request his mother would try to see Emily, and sometimes mention when she wrote, and having obtained that promise, he took an affectionate leave of her, and retired to his apartment. The night was far spent, and ere day-light appeared, the conductor Meronville had appointed informed him they must set out.

Whilst Lusignan was thus exposed to his father's anger, Emily, inconsolable for his loss, sought in vain those walks once her chief delight, when with him she admired the surrounding prospect, rich with every accumulated beauty of nature. The scenes which appeared to her truly elysian, when he pointed out those features formed to charm the eye and fix the traveller's attention, were now neglected; they seemed robbed of attraction, and to her preoccupied mind presented only the voidness of a desert.

Madame de Clarival observed with the deepest concern this alteration in her manners; she vainly employed every endeavour to soothe and dissipate the melancholy which pervaded every feature.

Emily gratefully acknowledged the design, but felt conscious of its inefficacy. To her usual vivacity, and even eagerness to participate in the amusements, which at Montpelier were diversified and adapted to the various tastes of its multifarious visitants, succeeded a listlessness, an unconquerable *ennui*, which made her dread the returning hours of relaxation. Pensive and sad she wandered, and frequently perused the letter of Lusignan, weeping over those lines his hand had traced. Madame de Clarival permitted her to answer it, confiding to her discretion the choice of terms. The hopes he had endeavoured to inspire were evanescent. She wrote as follows:

———

"I know not why my heart refuses its assent to the hopes you wish to communicate; accustomed to consider your father as inexorable, misfortune only presents itself to my view. Why, why, Lusignan, did you ever deceive me? why not appear in your real name? It would have taught me to shun you; it would have taught me early to suppress those sentiments which are now no longer in my power. Yes, Lusignan, my heart is your's, I will not conceal it; I feel pleasure in avowing that preference, for which you are not indebted to rank or fortune, but it is an homage I can only pay to superior merit; but remember it is my unalterable resolve to sacrifice inclination to duty, whenever called upon to do so. Imitate my example. Your father may claim submission while he bears that name, however cruel his orders may appear. Obedience is no longer a virtue when confined to those points in which inclination and duty may happily unite.* If this consideration wants weight, let love at least prevail. Emily can never be truly wretched, but in the consciousness that for her sake you have deviated from the path of rectitude. Submit then, dear Lusignan; be reconciled, at my request, to your offended father; let us depend on time to soften his resentment; and let your affection be as disinterested as is that of

"EMILY DE MONTALTE."

———

Emily had been nurtured in the bosom of virtue, which strengthened her mind, and rendered it capable of exertion, but could not subjugate a keen sensibility, too often fatal to female happiness. To Lusignan she would not betray her weakness; but when alone her affected composure all forsook her.

The summer season, which now approached, had filled Montpelier with an innumerable assemblage of valetudinarians; frequently she strayed towards the baths where those resorted in search of that health dissipation or a colder climate had impaired. Emily's sympathy, ever awakened at sight of human misery, was forcibly attached by the appearance of these victims of chronic disorders; she had often observed a young person of a very interesting figure, who seemed struggling with a gradual decline.—She had none of that delusive gaiety, the usual attendant on that flattering disorder; her countenance, which had more of interest than critical beauty, beamed resignation, blended with a consciousness of the decay of nature. Gentle melancholy tinged her features, and sorrow was mingled in the smile of benevolence, with which she greeted her fellow-sufferers. Her pallid cheek flushed with something like the bloom of departing health when she beheld Emily, who had frequently addressed her in the language of sympathy. Congeniality of soul early united them, and a permanent friendship was formed in less time than is usually requisite to sanction a common intimacy.

Youth is the season of candour, when the mind loves to expand in unrestrained communication. Anxious to conceal from maternal scrutiny her cares and uneasiness, she poured them uncontrouled into the bosom of friendship, which opened to receive the sorrows of love. Her cheerfulness in some degree returned; at least in the presence of Madame de Clarival she disguised those emotions, which flowed unrestrained in the breast of Caroline Montfort, whose health, however, rapidly decayed.

Emily, alarmed at her encreasing debility, pressed her to communicate that secret sorrow, which, grown more pungent from concealment, evidently preyed on her mind, and counteracted all the efforts of medical skill. Frequently urged, not by curiosity but friendship, she at length yielded, though apparently fearful of entering on a subject so painfully interesting.

CHAP. VI.

"Through life's mysterious vale, from day to day,
"Man, wretched pilgrim, journeys on his way,
"Here towering palaces attract his view,
"There the lone hovel shews its tatter'd crew;
"And if some casual flowers his senses greet,
"Still rending brambles cling about his feet."

"My misfortunes," said Caroline, "are of a nature so uncommon, and so incurable, that I unwillingly wound your sensibility with the recital; their period I feel fast approaching, life seems only for an hour suspended, and ready to take its flight from its enfeebled mansion. Merciful God! thou has appointed death to equalize us all;— grant that my sufferings may expiate my own sins, and the guilt of those from whom I drew breath, whose offences have indeed been visited on my devoted head." She deeply sighed, and continued, "My father was the younger son of a noble family of Italian extraction, but which had distinguished itself in the service of Henry of Navarre, and been naturalized in France. As the property, by right of primogeniture, all devolved on his brother, his sole patrimony was a commission in Henry IVth's body guards.* He was attached to a very amiable woman, whose personal charms had unfortunately captivated the heart of his brother, a man without principle or natural affection; he used every unlawful method to obtain her, and finding those ineffectual, so far overcame his aversion to the married state as to offer her his hand, more with a view to supplant his brother, the mediocrity of whose fortune he doubted not would yield to his superior advantages, than for any gratification of his own. His resentment, when he found himself rejected and a preference given to Henry, knew no bounds; he found means to prejudice his sovereign against him, and thus deprived him of his almost only means of subsistence. Notwithstanding this Adelaide refused to separate her destiny from his; they were united; he placed her in a Convent, where he knew she would be safe till his return, and then enlisted as a volunteer in the service of his country. For several years he followed the profession of arms, and had the good-fortune to save the life of Count d'Armenteau, whom he rescued from the enemy at the moment when they were ready to sacrifice him to their revenge. This procured him a multitude of promises, and some little preferment; but after long years of toils and perils, finding his fortune but little improved, he determined to quit the service, and seek some new mode of increasing it. He flew to his Adelaide, and in her arms forgot that after years of labour and absence he brought home no reward but empty fame. Unfortunately my father was strongly biassed by that popular prejudice which, in France, attaches the idea of degradation to every thing which is connected with commerce. He had several opportunities of engaging in it to great advantage, all of which he rejected while a ray of hope remained that he might rise in the rank to which he was born; but this feeble gleam, which irradiated his existence, lessened perceptibly, and soon dwindled into obscurity. He had no alternative, but unwillingly to enter into a species of traffic then offered him, and promising much emolument; but conceiving the employments of a *roturier** as derogatory to the dignity of a noble ancestry, he fulfilled them reluctantly and with negligence, in spite of the remonstrances of my mother, who, seeing their family yearly increase, began to apprehend that poverty which was approaching with hasty strides. They had already three children. She endeavoured to reason her Henry out of that ancestored pride, which was incorporated with his nature. He passionately loved her, and for some time appeared to have conquered his ruinous indolence; soon however he relapsed, and as debts rapidly multiplied, he saw himself, in spite of the tears and supplications of my mother, dragged to a common gaol. She flew distracted to the house of his brother; with difficulty she obtained access through a crowd of menials, who awaited his orders. Magnificence, and the highest wrought luxury, raised their proud heads, and seemed to reproach her poverty; she threw herself at his feet, imploring his compassion for his distressed relative. He would have spurned her from him, but that his selfish passion still preponderated, and recollecting that misfortune might have subdued her spirit, a smile of malicious triumph illumined his countenance, and he hesitated not to offer the liberty of her husband as the price of her honour! Indignant, horror struck, and humiliated, my mother quitted the house, determined to secure herself from his attempts by sharing the prison of her husband. With design to convey her family

thither, she retuned home; but what was her astonishment and
horror to find the deserted mansion occupied by bailiffs, who had
seized on their little remaining property to satisfy the demands of
a rapacious creditor. She embraced their knees, intreating them to
defer the execution of their orders but for a few days, as a distemper,
which had lately attacked her children, rendered a removal dangerous. The ferocity of their looks proclaimed how successless was
her suit; compassion never penetrated their relentless hearts, accustomed to convey misery wherever their steps were bent. My mother
was compelled to remove her wretched offspring in the small-pox;
the disorder increased; one early fell a victim, another soon followed, and eventually one grave enclosed them all. She was at that
time pregnant. A straw pallet, placed in a dungeon whose limited
dimensions could hardly contain it, supplied to her the place of all
those comforts she had lost. Here she lived with my father on the
prison allowance, contented to share his sorrows as she had shared
his pleasures. Mutually insensible of their own wants, and solicitous
only for those of each other, their miseries hourly augmented; their
health impaired by the pestilential vapours they inhaled, and condemned to associate with wretches whose crimes had made them
the outcasts of society, they were sinking under their accumulated
woes, when my mother was delivered of a female infant. Born in
misery and nurtured in affliction was that unfortunate being who
now addresses you."

At this period of her narrative Caroline was interrupted by convulsive sobs; her friend was no less affected. Exhausted by the effort
she had made in speaking so long, she felt almost unable to continue, and Emily insisted that she should defer it till the next day.
On the morrow she hastened to enquire after her, and finding her
more than usually languid, would have persuaded her to again postpone her recital; but Caroline looking on her with a smile of ineffable sweetness, assured her she felt relieved by the communication.

"The subject," said she, "has weighed heavy on my mind, because
deprived of friends or relations, who would have known how to
commiserate my affliction, I have fostered it solely in my own
bosom. To meet a sympathetic friend is a comfort not to be esti-
mated. My mother's recovery was slow, yet less so than might have
been expected considering the deep malady of her mind, which
increased as the prospect of my father's enlargement became more

apparently distant. Affection for me induced her to forego the consolation of retaining me with her, and she consigned me to the care of an old nurse, who had always attended her. One day, when she had been to see me, whom a trifling indisposition confined, she felt so weak that sitting down at a nobleman's door she fainted; just then a carriage drew up, and the Duchess of Meronville alighted; it was at her door my mother lay. This lady, whose benevolence and humanity adorn the rank she holds, immediately gave orders to have her taken care of, and visiting her when she was restored to life, felt warmly interested in her appearance and manners, which had something, probably, of dignity in them superior to the situation in which she appeared. My mother, no less charmed with her affability and sweetness, answered her interrogatories with the utmost candour, and even related all the circumstances of her misfortunes—The Duchess promised to exert her influence with her husband to obtain the sum for which my father was confined, deeply lamenting that so much was not in her own power; she, however, relieved her present embarrassments, and taking her address, dismissed her with every expression of kindness and compassion. She flew to cheer my father with the hopes of liberty, but it hardly forced a smile upon his countenance; the deep humiliation he had suffered preyed on his mind; he had witnessed so many instances of depravity in his fellow-creatures, that he became almost a gloomy misanthropist; and that pride, the only inheritance he derived from his ancestry, had been so deeply wounded, that death alone could relieve his inward and mortal anguish. He revived, however, at the prospect of seeing his adored Adelaide once more mistress of the few comforts his emancipation might enable him to procure for her, and their thoughts were now all employed in considering a mode of life that might be most eligible. Nevertheless a month elapsed, and brought no advices from Madame de Meronville. My mother gradually relapsed into her former languor and dejection, and began once more to consider death as the sole termination of her woes; but one day, as she was repining at my lot and her own, a carriage stopped at the prison gates, and our kind benefactress entered. The sight of so much misery astonished her gentle mind; she knew not that humanity was subject to such cruel vicissitudes; she was agitated, and could scarcely speak, but at length collected resolution to assure my mother they might quit this abode of horror immediately.

'The unavoidable delays,' said this angelic woman, 'in the proceeding requisite to the Chevalier's release have affected me no less than they have you; could they have kept pace with my wishes, you would have been emancipated from the hour I had the happiness of seeing you. I feel truly grateful to Heaven for the opportunity it has given me of being serviceable to you. None of us,' continued she with a sigh, 'are exempt from misfortune; but our worst ills are forgotten, when Providence kindly bestows the power of alleviating the sorrows of our fellow-creatures.' She then informed my mother there was a small house furnished, which she begged her to accept as a present from herself; adding, that she was much concerned to clog her husband's release with a condition, which might one day render it ineffectual; but she could only obtain the necessary sum from the Duke's *intendant*,* on a promise that in three years it should be repaid. She, however, promised that should any difficulty then arise with respect to the payment, her good offices should not be wanting to have this clause remitted. I need not assure you that my mother's gratitude was as unbounded as the generosity which inspired it. Madame de Meronville, overcome by its first effusions, quitted her abruptly, engaging to see her soon and frequently. My father now felt the necessity of exertion. Nature, as though to supply the parsimony of fortune, had endowed him with every noble faculty: these had for some time lain dormant under the chilling hand of penury; the benevolence of one human being made him forget the depravity of many, and he became again the same Henry my mother had first loved, candid, generous, sincere. He again entered into a mercantile connection, and succeeded beyond his hopes. After providing with great frugality for the current expences of his household, he reserved his superfluous gains as an accumulating fund, by which he hoped to discharge, at the appointed time, the debt he had incurred to the Duke de Meronville. The hour rapidly approached when it became due; the Duchess frequently visited my mother, and would as frequently have reiterated her benefactions; but my mother firmly refused to accept any further obligation, but that which her presence always conferred. The last interview they had, she assured her the sum would be deposited in a banker's hands the day it became due; and though the Duchess insisted that my father should not hurry himself, her generosity only stimulated his, and he became more anxious about it. Madame de Meronville was then going to spend some months at an estate in the Cevennes. She could not take leave of my mother without regret, to whom she had become fondly attached, and the latter felt more acutely the pangs of separation as she was her only female friend; the parting was, therefore, mournful to both, though they flattered themselves with the hopes of soon meeting again; but it was a happiness my mother was never more fated to enjoy.

"My father seemed now to have forgotten that pride which formerly impeded his success; it was a passion now never exerted but to prompt his virtuous endeavours for the support of two objects equally dear to him. After the labours of each day he returned to the affectionate embrace of his loved Adelaide, who was more dear to him than the first hour they had met; his comforts seemed even increased by the pains he took to procure them. I was then three years old; their mutual affection was only shared by me. Alas! the endearing caresses of parental tenderness were soon torn from me for ever! A week previous to the day of payment my father received a letter from the banker at Bourdeaux, in whose hands his money was deposited, informing him, the loss of a rich ship, in which a considerable portion of his property was concerned, had occasioned the failure of his house; that he regretted the inconvenience this might be to him, but hoped it would eventually be no loss, as his great connections gave him reasonable hopes of being able in a few years to refund his little property. This news threw my father into a state little short of distraction; he had a very strict sense of honour; and though he felt secured by the patronage of Madame de Meronville from any coercion, it made him only the more desirous of discharging the debt, lest he should appear to presume on her kindness. This failure proved the wreck of all his hopes, and reduced him to despair; for some days he refused to communicate to my mother the cause of his uneasiness; but his sombre dejection alarmed her so extremely that she insisted on sharing his grief, let the cause be what it might. When informed of it she sought to reassure him by all the arguments in her power, and only begged he would compose himself, and leave the rest to her, engaging to write to the Duchess, who, she was persuaded, when informed of the real circumstance, would do no less justice to their desire of acting honourably, than if the money had been actually repaid. The few days remaining of the unexpired term were wasted in fruitless deliberations on the course they should pursue, and as no other scheme could be devised, my father consented, though with extreme reluctance, to enquire the address of Madame de Meronville, and permit his wife to write to her. Before this could be accomplished, next day, as they were partaking of a very scanty meal, for they had curtailed their usual expences, two men entered the apartment. My mother had once witnessed the ferocity of sheriff's officers, and could not for a moment doubt that these were such; she sunk lifeless on the floor; my father started from his seat. Insensible as I was of the cause, the looks of those ruffians alarmed me, and I screamed convulsively. They produced their credentials, it was in the name of the Duke of Meronville—'You are our prisoner, Sir,' said they, 'and must immediately follow us.'—'Impossible,' cried my father, 'the Duke never could have acted thus, never could be thus inhuman!' 'Our business, Sir,' resumed the foremost, 'is not to examine the merits of your cause, but to execute our orders; I, therefore, trust you are prepared to follow us.' My father was chafing the temples of his wife, and endeavouring to restore her senses; she opened her eyes, they were fixed on the ruffians that stood before her; she shrieked, and instantly relapsed. I clung round her neck, in an agony for which I knew no cause; but certain it is the scene so deeply impressed my mind, that nothing has since been able to efface it. My father embraced us both with the most moving tenderness. The man who had spoken last attempted to use violence to detach him from our arms. 'Inhuman villain!' he exclaimed, 'is one moment long to thy insatiate cruelty? Canst thou look there and not feel the first emotion of pity that ever entered thy relentless breast?' The other man, who, in the exercise of an office which accustomed him to scenes of misery, had not grown callous to the sufferings of humanity, but retained some little of the milk of human kindness, then offered to fetch the lawyer who employed him, as it was possible he might so represent the affair to his Grace as would induce him to grant a short reprieve. My father entreated him to do so. He soon returned with a gentleman, who seemed shocked at the situation into which he had thrown us. After enquiring into the reasons of his non-payment, and the probabilities of his being more fortunate in future, he promised to exert his influence with his client to obtain his release; 'but,' continued he, 'I have not much hopes of procuring a long respite, as the debt is transferred by his Grace to the Abbé la Haye, a man little inclined to remit any of his rights, or to be moved by the voice of sup-

plication; relying, however, upon your honour, I, on my own responsibility, allow you three days to consult your friends, and to take, if
possible, more effectual means than reliance on the generosity of a
man, who never yet appeared to have any.' He then retired with the
sheriff's officers, leaving my parents distracted. 'My Adelaide,' said
my father, after a long pause, 'wherefore should we seek to prolong an
existence, which every hour renders more burthensome; the gift of
life was designed as a blessing; when it is no longer such, sure we may
return it to the bestower.' He spoke these words with an excess of
wildness in his countenance that terrified her; she endeavoured to
sooth him with those caresses which still had power to penetrate his
inmost soul. 'My beloved Henry, let us not despair, Heaven in mercy
chastens, and, perhaps, is now preparing some period to our sorrows;
inscrutable are its decrees; let us submit to them with humble resignation; but never let the worst calamity induce us to renounce that
reliance on its Providence, which never yet was known to fail to those
who faithfully depended on it; nor let us sully by any rash act that
rectitude and virtue, our best support in the midst of calamity.' With
such reasoning she prevailed on my father to represent his case to
some of those persons who lavishly bestowed the epithet of friendship on him, when he had no opportunity of putting it to the test. He
had, indeed, but little hopes, and his proud heart reluctantly submitted to the measure; but he had a beloved wife, an helpless infant, and
no longer hesitated. The two succeeding days were spent in fruitless
applications; all lamented their inability to serve him, and dismissed
him with every profession of regard; but none offered the least assistance. He returned home the second night, wearied and humiliated
with attendance on the levees of the great; he threw himself on a sofa,
and cried, 'It is all over, and now I have but *one refuge!*' On a sudden
he recollected that the Count d'Armenteau, whose life he had formerly preserved, was then at Paris, and as his promises had been
boundless, he hoped in a trifling instance they would be remembered. He flew to his house, and presented himself before him with a
voice and appearance which proclaimed extreme distress; he was
welcomed with the appellation of, dear friend, kind preserver, &c.
&c. and the Count enquired if he could serve him, assuring him that
he might command his person and fortune, which were justly
devoted to the preserver of his life. My father began to rejoice in his
success, and stated his embarrassments as concisely as the subject

would admit; but notwithstanding his studied brevity, d'Armenteau
was evidently constrained while it lasted; he paraded the apartment,
adjusted his cravat, and gave orders to his servants. My father perceived he was thought importunate, and concluded. The Count
affected much concern, and again repeated that his life was at his
command; but lamented that some late payments had taken all his
ready money, and bonds he had invariably disliked, and indeed never
gave any. Seeming, however, to recollect himself, he requested my
father would return the next morning, as it was possible he might
think of some method to relieve him. My father quitted him with the
utmost indignation, and would certainly never have again subjected
himself to such treatment, had he alone been concerned; but his wife
and child had still power to make him submit to another degradation. Previous to his departure in the morning he made some trifling
arrangements, embraced his wife, and left her not without hopes; for
he thought that the impulse of shame, which had induced
d'Armenteau to recant the preceding evening, might, probably, still
operate, though from his generosity or gratitude he had no expectations. His heart beat when he knocked at the door; he enquired for
the Count—he had left Paris early in the morning. Was he soon
expected to return? Not for some weeks. Had he left any message?
None. Montfort stood petrified for a few moments, then retired
from the inhospitable door, fully resolved to end at one stroke all his
misfortunes. In the meantime my mother anxiously awaited his
return; every noise startled her, every voice she hoped was his; the
tedious hours rolled on, he came not, hope and fear by turns agitated
her; he might be settling the business; for a time the thought cheered
her, but soon her heart sunk, for night approached. I sat on her knee;
she wept over me; the door opened, and my father appeared! She was
hastening towards him with a gentle reproach on her lips; his wildness terrified her, and suppressed the trembling accents ere they were
uttered. He sat down in silence, and in a moment drew two phials
from his pocket, then, with an averted glance of horror, presented her
one.—'This,' said he, 'is the cup of oblivion, and will end our woes!'
My mother comprehended his meaning; she kneeled, she supplicated, she placed me in his arms, and implored his pity for an helpless
orphan. Contending passions strove within him for the mastery. At
one moment he wept with her, at others seemed to recover resolution. The wildness of his features was succeeded by pensive melan-

choly. He informed her of the ill-success of his application, not doubting but d'Armenteau, apprehensive by a direct refusal of subjecting himself to farther importunity, had made use of the evasion of desiring him to return, with a view to dismiss him more easily. The Chevalier had next addressed himself to La Haye, but could obtain only this answer—'My money, Sir, or a gaol.' The injuries my father had suffered in a commerce with the world had deadened his noble feelings; reason had no longer power to control him; his resolution was fixed and immutable; he uncorked one of the phials; applied it to his mouth, and, whilst he presented the other to my mother, averted his eye, and drank it to the dregs. A statue placed before him would have possessed more power to prevent him than his wife, who sat perfectly motionless and petrified, till the violence of the deadly poison he had swallowed began to operate, and he sunk on the floor; her torpid faculties then revived; she threw herself in an agony upon him; he grinned horribly.—'It is done,' said he, 'merciless creditors, now wreak your vengeance on my senseless corpse!' then seeing the other phial untouched, 'My Adelaide,' said he, 'we have lived, one pang and then we part, since you refuse to die with me; oh! what in death can terrify? is it not the refuge of the wretched? One pang alone it costs to terminate our worst of ills! Would you render my last moments happy, drink, I conjure you, to the dregs, that sweet oblivious draught!' He had scarcely power to utter the last word, a convulsion seized him, and he ceased for ever to breathe in a world where he had known only misfortune; life was extinguished; he lay an inanimate corpse! My mother had not till now recollected that an antidote might preserve him. Old Annette, the sole domestic she had reserved, had taken me to rest; I slept unconscious that this fatal hour deprived me of both the most affectionate of parents. My mother rang violently, and requested she would hasten with all possible dispatch for advice. The poor faithful creature, whose terror rendered her more dead than living, obeyed; but it was past midnight, and she traversed half Paris without being able to procure the aid she required. In about an hour she returned; her mistress, to her infinite surprise, had quitted the corpse of her husband; she sought her in my apartment; she was not there; in vain she called on her name; no answer was returned; every thing in the parlour was precisely as she had left it; but my mother never again appeared! Left then to the protection of old Annette, who indeed loved me as her child, we removed next day to her humble roof. My father was as decently interred as her slender means would admit. She next made every inquiry for her beloved mistress, but in vain, not a single trace could be discovered; it is still a mystery which I long hoped time would develope. A few months after, Annette, rising early, found a packet attached to the lock of the door, and on examining its contents found a manuscript, and a letter addressed to her; she opened it; it was my mother's signature—'God be praised she lives!' sighed poor Annette, 'and you, my little Caroline, have still a mother.' Those words I have never forgotten. She read as follows:

'My departure must have occasioned the utmost astonishment to my faithful Annette, and I am not permitted to remove it; the only liberty allowed me is, to say I was carried off by violence a few moments after you left the house. Judge, Annette, of my cruel situation, the tortures of the mind assisting those of the body. Does my beloved husband still live? Tell him his wretched wife will be faithful while her heart beats with vital strength; but no, he is no more, I saw his parting agony; his voice no more shall chase anguish from the bosom of his once beloved Adelaide! But, my child, dear image of her departed father, she lives and is denied a mother's care; tell her, Annette, if heaven prolongs her existence, that she once had parents who adored her; tell her, the miserable being to whom she owes her's, will endeavour to preserve life with no other hope but that of being one day restored to her, that she may then feel the powerful effects of maternal tenderness. But I am ordered to conclude.—Adieu, dear Annette, remember your unhappy mistress, and in pity love her child!'

"Inclosed was another manuscript, and a letter addressed to the Duchess of Meronville, recommending me to her care, with the full account of her misfortunes; by this they were transmitted to me, and the Duchess herself has told me what it did not or could not contain. She no sooner received my mother's letter, than taking me home she engaged to provide for me, and gave Annette my father's house; we went into the country, and on our return, this faithful domestic, probably from necessity, had sold the house, and we could not learn her abode. It would be a real satisfaction to me to see her once before I die. Madame de Meronville placed me in a Convent, and has ever since almost supplied the place of my lost parent; but this angelic woman too has felt that in this world happiness is not always the reward of virtue, but she has taught me to expect it in the next. United to a man who shares not her generous emotions, that alone prevented her from adopting me, as she has only one son. She often told me that I had a rich uncle, whose heir, if he remained unmarried, I must be, but could never discover him, though certain he was a man of rank from what my mother said of him. The name of Montfort she suspects is not my real one. However this may be, I never regretted the want of fortune, till I attracted the attention of a man, whose attachment, purely disinterested, soon obtained the return of mine; but we had both experienced the fatal effects of uniting poverty; he left me with a determination never to return, but possessed of a fortune equal to his wishes, and embarked in a vessel trading to the coast of Africa. For near two years I have heard nothing from him, and as several ships have been lost returning from thence, there is but too much reason to suppose he has perished, particularly as his last letter conveyed the intelligence that he was on the eve of embarking for Europe. The dangers he has encountered for my sake, and their probable consequences, weigh on my mind, and frustrate the kind intentions of the Duchess, who with her wonted goodness, sent me here from the Convent of Clarivana, where I was a pensioner. But why should a being, destined from her birth the outcast of society, seek to renovate that existence which is a burthen? Such, my Emily, is the narrative you requested; I fear I have tired you; but I feel sensible relief in confiding my cares to the bosom of friendship."

Emily embraced her with the warmest affection, and endeavoured by every endearing attention to supply to her the place of those she had lost. Her narrative had been peculiarly interesting by the grateful mention she made of Madame de Meronville, whom Emily had already learned to love, both as the mother of Lusignan, and because she represented her as possessing every female excellence.

Caroline knew not her connection with the family of her bene-

factress, and her commendations were therefore unbiassed, as well
as the encomiums which in her letters she made on Emily; for
though the latter had frequently mentioned the Marquis of Lusignan, it was only as her lover, and not as son to the Duke de Meronville.—Secretly Mademoiselle de Montalte resolved, that should
Caroline's intended husband ever revisit his native land, fortune
should no longer be an impediment to their union; in the meantime
she devoted her time to her wholly, and derived a double advantage from this exercise of benevolence; she had the satisfaction of
seeing Caroline's health visibly improve, and her own spirits return.
Madame de Clarival, no less delighted to see Emily's melancholy
wear off, became much attached to Caroline. The two friends were
a source of mutual happiness to each other.

Emily had by nature an excellent disposition, which, improved by
the best education, had given her a turn of thinking, and a solidity
of judgment, seldom discovered at her age; a romantic spirit, which
in a small degree is, perhaps, inseparable from youth, made her at
first yield to affliction for the departure of Lusignan; but the relation of Caroline de Montfort's misfortunes corrected her views; she
compared her own situation with that of this amiable orphan, and
how favourable to her was the comparison, each day she felt less
inclined to murmur at the dispensations of Providence, whose gifts
she found more impartially distributed than at first appears.

Regular and undeviating as is the system of Nature, which denies
perfect happiness to any of her creatures, her best endowments are
clogged with some condition which diminishes their value, and
brings their possessor to a nearer level with those who are denied
them. So thought our heroine, and prepared to meet with fortitude
whatever changes time or chance might present.

CHAP. VII.

"Day spreads her beams, the lofty forest tree
"Shakes from its moisten'd head the pearly flower,
"All Nature feels the renovating hour,
"All but the sorrowing child of cold adversity."

The castle, which was chosen as a place of exile for Lusignan, was situated at the foot of a rock, on a remote part of the coast; it had more the appearance of a regular fortification than an habitable mansion, having been several times besieged during the civil wars. A perpendicular rock on one side rendered it impervious to the traveller's eye; the vast ocean served for its bulwark on the other; and its stately turrets and lofty towers gave it an air of gothic grandeur, which astonished rather than charmed the beholder.

Night had spread her sable mantle when Lusignan approached his dreary abode; the moonbeams, playing on its moss-grown battlements, discovered to him that his journey was at an end, and threw a sublimity on the scene, which inspired a degree of awe, distinct indeed from fear, but not untinctured with it. He alighted at the outward gate; his conductor pulled a bell, whose long reverberating sound seemed echoed on the opposite shores. They entered a drawbridge, which was instantly withdrawn. Lusignan felt himself coerced, and sighed for lost liberty.

The hall prepared for his reception, though the smallest in the castle, seemed only calculated for a guard-room; it was surrounded with javelins, casques, shields, and fragments of various coats of mail. Lusignan calmly surveyed them; it brought to his recollection former days, and "tales of other times;" many of these arms bore the insignia of the Crusades.*

"What various and innumerable weapons," thought he, "has the ingenuity of man invented for his own destruction!"

He passed some hours in desultory contemplations on these subjects; but as it was four nights since he had taken any repose, he early desired to be conducted to his chamber, determining the next day to satisfy his curiosity, by examining minutely every vestige of antiquity in this isolated spot.

Emily, however, did not for a moment leave his thoughts; he flattered himself she would not let St. Pierre return without some little answer to the letter he had written; and to that he looked as a compensation for solitude, exile, and parental rigor. At any rate he would, probably, have seen her; he could make a multitude of enquiries how she looked, what she said. Full of this expectation, when he arose, he resolved to employ his time as much as possible in the various contemplations his novel situation afforded, to divert his attention till the return of evening, which he hoped would bring with it the return of his faithful domestic. Several days, however, elapsed, he came not; hope rose with the morning sun, and disappointment succeeded with the night shades.

A parapet wall surrounded the castle, and from its extreme height commanded a vast and distant prospect; the Albion Coast was distinctly seen on one side, the vessels majestically sailing from its numerous ports. Lusignan envied the perils they must encounter ere they returned; he melted at the thought of the happiness they would enjoy when, after long roving on foreign shores and seas unknown, tossed by rude winds and faithless billows, their dear native isle should rise to greet their longing eyes. He sighed for England's chalky cliffs, and would willingly have resigned all his prospects of gilded slavery to share with Emily liberty and a cottage in that happy land.* He turned unwillingly to where Paris reared its stately towers, its gorgeous palaces.

Each morning he returned to this elevated station, when the sun from the east diffused its radiance to the western shores. The hour of the returning day, which revives all nature, at first occasioned youthful hilarity in him; but this soon wore off, and he yielded to despondency. How false is that policy which hopes by rigour and seclusion to conquer love. Had Lusignan been permitted to remain in Paris, variety of scenes and amusements would have diverted his attention, which in dreary solitude could fix on one sole object, which became more dear, as it was his only source of happiness.

At length one evening, when, as usual, he had spent the day in fruitless hopes of seeing St. Pierre, he discovered through the spreading gloom a horseman galloping towards the castle, his heart flew to meet him, but he was denied the pleasure of accompanying it. Soon, however, the bell sounded; the massy gates turned on their dissonant hinges, and St. Pierre alighted. He brought with him Emily's letter, and one from Madame de Meronville; the latter solicited him in the strongest terms to return to his duty and liberty. But with the energy of new-born love, he cried, "Never, liberty has no charms without Emily; with her a prison is a palace."

He now spent all his time in writing to her; for though he never sent his letters, they were reserved in hopes she might one day learn how his hours were passed in her absence. To his mother, however, he paid the just tribute of gratitude and filial affection. All her letters assured him of her unalterable tenderness, and the affliction his confinement gave her; but they contained no hopes of pardon. In the last of them she informed him that Madame de Clarival had furnished her with an opportunity, which she should certainly not neglect, of seeing her often, and without giving umbrage to his father.

Caroline de Montfort, still ignorant of the favour she conferred, always mentioned Emily in such flattering terms to her benefactress, as increased her desire of being personally acquainted with her; though it made her still more apprehensive that Lusignan would never be prevailed on to yield to his father's peremptory commands.

Madame de Clarival was hourly expected at Paris, and Caroline had requested leave to spend some time with her there. Without difficulty Madame de Meronville granted this petition, and the more willingly, as it would serve as a pretext for her to see Emily frequently, and judge for herself of those merits which were painted in such glowing colours. She almost wished to find her less perfect than she had been taught to expect; but the first time they met, Lusignan himself was not more struck than was the Duchess, and every future interview corroborated her opinion, that his choice was founded on principles too firm to be shaken, even by parental authority.

Six weeks had elapsed, and Lusignan heard nothing from his mother; in vain he mounted the parapet, and fatigued his eye in search of messengers; none appeared; his situation became more melancholy, and fancy portrayed new horrors, when one evening a carriage entered the great court. How interesting is the pause of suspence between hope and fear! Lusignan's heart beat. It was night, and he could not discern who alighted; but in a moment a thousand ideas succeeded each other; conjecture, however, ceased, and La Haye entered. He was welcomed with more apparent cordiality than the Marquis felt; his discernment had long discovered to him, that under the mask of candour and religion, this man concealed the deepest and most infernal hypocrisy. But he came from Paris, from his mother, perhaps from Emily. It was sufficient, and Lusignan forgot his aversion. La Haye accosted him with a smile of condescension, and more than ordinary self-consequence.

"I am charged," said he, "with a commission which will, perhaps, surprise you, as his Grace's lenity and affection are most conspicuously displayed in your favour. I may, indeed, congratulate you and myself on the victory my influence has obtained; his concessions are the happy effects of my influence. But I need not to boast, desiring no other reward than that of having served you in so distinguished a manner. Considering you both as my pupils, it gives me great concern that any difference should arise; but his Grace, desirous that I should perfect the work of reconciliation, as becomes a minister of Heaven, has entrusted me with such proposals as will immediately strike you with compunction for having offended such a father."

He paused to see the effect of his elaborate preface on the countenance of Lusignan; it had not undergone the least alteration. He was too well acquainted with the speaker to feel much elated; but requested he would explain himself.

"His Grace," continued he, "consents to restore you to his fortune and affections, and to banish every reminiscence of past errors; nay, to forget the entail you destroyed so rashly, and exacts in return one only compliance, if that can be called one which all France would regard as a distinguished honour. Mademoiselle de Foix, one of the first fortunes and connections in the kingdom, is offered you. In the humble walks of life her beauty and amiability would entitle her to your admiration; but here is every advantage united, and held out for your acceptance; it brings with it also your restoration to liberty, and a father's benediction, which alone would render it inestimable. Your silence convinces me this excess of good-fortune surprises you. Believe me, with profound humility I speak it, it required some address to make the Duke, your father, my honoured patron, concede thus; but, having once obtained his consent, I gave him no time to retract, but set out immediately."

"If these, Sir," said Lusignan firmly, "are the only proposals you have to make, I am truly concerned that your journey should be likely to prove so ineffectual. I render all due acknowledgments for your endeavours and my father's condescension, and beg you will add one favour to those you have enumerated; that of assuring him, I am ready to submit to every command of his, where my cousin, Mademoiselle de Montalte, is not concerned; that it is my fixed and unalterable resolution never to resign her, unless compelled by herself to do it; and that even then I have too much honour ever to possess myself of any lady's person and fortune, when my heart not only cannot be her's, but is irrevocably devoted to another. This, Sir, is my definitive answer, which you will oblige me by conveying to the Duke de Meronville."

La Haye secretly rejoiced at his contumacy, which, indeed, he had expected, yet affected the greatest amazement.

"Is it possible," he cried, "that paternal kindness and authority are rendered equally ineffectual by the machinations of two intriguing women, who have had power to exact such sacrifices as must for ever alienate the affection of the best of fathers?"

Lusignan's indignation arose.

"I do not submit my actions, Sir, to your scrutiny; nor do I desire your arbitration. Those ladies would not feel the least injured by the opprobrious language they would learn of me to despise."

La Haye forgot his accustomed coolness, his choler rose high.

"His Grace," said he, "is not deceived; he is perfectly informed that your mother, whose character is not improved by the discovery, has connected herself with these women, and holds intelligence with you, as an encouragement to contemn his orders."

Lusignan could contain himself no longer. This imputation on his mother awakened all his native impetuosity, and taking La Haye by the shoulders, he shoved him rudely out of the apartment, advising him never to return till he had learned the respect due to his superiors. The Abbé, terrified, mortified, and exasperated to the last pitch, retreated from the door, meditating plans of revenge, which he had it fully in his power to execute.

A little self-command would have been more serviceable to Lusignan; but he was attacked in the tenderest point; and his contempt for the speaker past all bounds of moderation. Irritated and agitated to excess, he sat meditating on the scene just concluded, when a gentle tap at the door interrupted his reverie; on opening it he found a servant of his mother's, who, putting his finger to his lip in token of silence, entered, and cautiously fastening the door after him, delivered a letter from the Duchess. Lusignan inquired why St. Pierre did not return? The man replied, that La Haye having discovered that he conveyed letters to Luneville Castle, had told his Grace, who ordered him to be confined.

"The poor fellow," added he, "is more concerned on your account than his own, and prevailed on me to secrete this letter, depending, Sir, on your discretion not to betray me; for Monsieur La Abbé's resentment would have no bounds should he find it out."

Lusignan assured him he need have no fears on that subject; and with promises of future remuneration dismissed him.

His mother's letter informed him that St. Pierre had been interrupted by some person unknown; that, in consequence, the Duke's displeasure had been great; but she had contrived, in some degree, to soften his resentment; that she was ignorant of La Haye's intentions, but understood he was on the eve of departing with proposals to Luneville; and she conjured him to make every concession, and return to Paris. She concluded by saying she had seen Emily frequently, and was indeed charmed with her; but she seemed wretched at the idea of estranging him from his family, and intreated him to return to it.

This letter conveyed the only real pleasure Lusignan had experienced since he took his melancholy farewell of Emily. His mother's approbation of her added lustre to her charms, and seemed to sanction his choice. Never had any female appeared to him so perfect as herself, till he saw Mademoiselle de Montalte. To be convinced, therefore, she admired and esteemed the woman he adored, afforded him the purest delight; and, he thought, justified his most obstinate perseverance.

He wrote to her, and painted his gratitude and affection such as it really was; assuring her that the letter he had just received amply compensated for the long days of sorrow he had experienced; and intreating her to mention him to Emily, whom he durst not address, lest he might offend her delicacy. He expressed much solicitude lest his mother, by her attention to him, should incur her husband's resentment; and consented freely to relinquish this his only pleasure, rather than implicate her in his misfortunes.

This letter he entrusted to the same messenger; and though still a prisoner, and surrounded with difficulty, hope enlivened his prospects, and he felt relieved from every care.

Early in the morning La Haye requested to see him before he returned to Paris; but Lusignan, little inclined for another interview, excused himself. The Abbé, whose character cannot be better described than by saying he was born with every quality that can constitute the finished villain, deeply resented this refusal, and yet more the contumely and disrespect with which he had been treated the preceding evening. Hitherto he had nourished the displeasure of the Duke, less with any view of his own than from the habit of perfect acquiescence in every foible of the person on whom he depended. But to the ignoble mind resentment once excited knows no bounds, nor stops at any thing short of utter destruction to the offending object. During the night he had revolved his wrongs, and formed a scheme of vengeance, by which he hoped to overwhelm his victims with despair.

Emily became no less obnoxious to his prospects, because he was assured that every calamity in which she was implicated would fall with double weight on Lusignan. Dissimulation was perfectly natural to him, and he concluded disguise was necessary to the success of his designs. He, therefore, wrote the following lines, which he committed to a servant as he jumped into the chaise:

———

"Your treatment of me last night may have induced you very reasonably to suppose that you have created an enemy in the person who, when he arrived yesterday, was your most devoted friend; but the sacred profession I have chosen, which prescribes universal philanthropy, and forgiveness of injuries, will not permit me to harbour resentment. The character of mediator and peacemaker best becomes the garb I wear; as such then rely on my good offices with the Duke, my noble patron. The influence our holy function bestows is best displayed in the glorious work of reconciliation. Notwithstanding your injustice, of which, according to the Gospel laws, I shall be avenged, by returning good for evil, I go to perfect this work; and you, through the blessing of God, will soon reap the benefit."

———

Lusignan threw his eyes over this composition with ineffable contempt, equally disregarding his promises and the threats which he had heard muttered between his teeth the preceding evening, when he turned him out of his apartment. He was, however, more in his power than he imagined.

Arrived at Paris, he was introduced to the closet of the Duke of Meronville, who eagerly enquired the success of his mission. La Haye, with a mixed expression of countenance, which he knew well how to assume——

"I grieve," said he, "to have no better intelligence to communicate. Ah! Sir, some power more successful than parental kindness, has planted obduracy in the bosom of your son. All my persuasions and entreaties have been fruitless. The Marquis of Lusignan opposes nothing but obstinacy to my more solid arguments. I conjured him as a father and a friend, for so the church enjoins its members to conciliate the disobedient; reproach and violence were my sole rewards—treated with contempt and indignity —I am insensible to that—the consciousness of doing right is an all-sufficient compensation; but your wrongs, Sir, strike at that heart devoted to your service. There can remain no doubt but your deluded son is secretly encouraged by your enemies.—Persuasion fails, and you have only to depend on coercive measures for restoring him to his duty."

The Duke was already sufficiently exasperated; hatred and revenge, the effect of early prejudices, corroded his heart. He conjured La Haye to suggest some means of compelling Lusignan to submit, assuring him there was no chastisement he should think too severe.

La Haye thought he hazarded nothing in affecting moderation at first. The conversation he had with the Marquis convinced him he would not yield to any thing that derogated from the passion that governed him; and lenity at present might recommend his future projects, when the Duke should be prepared to adopt all the violence of his measures.

It was therefore agreed between them, that the Duke de Foix should, with his daughter, be invited to accompany him to Luneville Castle, not doubting but that the sight of Eugenia would vanquish Lusignan's obduracy. The scheme was accordingly proposed and acceded to. A train suitable to the magnificence of both houses was sent down to prepare for their reception.—Nothing was omitted that could add splendour to the scene. The numerous vassals were all summoned to attend their lord; and every effort of feudal pomp and ostentation was exhausted to do honour to their noble guests. Those spacious halls, which for ages had served only as a refuge to some hostile crew, whose vaulted roofs had echoed only to the din of war, were now adorned with costly trappings, and prepared for scenes of social joy and festive mirth. The cheerful blaze, now kindled on the long neglected hearth, dislodged those solitary tenants, who by prescriptive right had built their nests in the lofty chimney's top.

Lusignan, informed by his mother of the cause for these mighty preparations, beheld them with unconcern. He doubted not of being able to convince Mademoiselle de Foix of his aversion for an union, which could have no charms for her; and he hoped she would herself raise obstacles that would relieve him from this dreaded persecution.

On the eve of that day when the Duke de Foix was expected to grace the Castle with his presence, a splendid retinue announced the arrival of the Duke de Meronville. Lusignan approached to welcome his father, but a frown of displeasure warned him to retire, till the numerous vassals dependant on his domain had paid homage to their imperious lord. Each bowed the knee as he approached, whilst he received their submission as a debt they justly owed to his exalted state. He flattered himself that Lusignan, struck with the dignity attached to superior rank and fortune, would be eager to connect himself with a family whose demesnes extended farther than those of any other subject. But far otherwise was the effect it had on him; slavery in every shape was abhorrent to his nature; he felt convinced, that although a subordinate class was necessary to preserve order in the system of nature, yet it was the duty of those to whom chance, rather than merit, had given power, to exert it only with a view to render all happy who were subject to them; and if he ever desired to possess that power, it was with design to lighten the yoke of servitude, which was a component part of the feudal system.

When those ceremonies were concluded, his Grace condescended to admit Lusignan to a cold embrace, accompanied by an observation, that he hoped to find him more submissive than when they parted last. Lusignan bowed assent. The evening was spent in cold formalities and distant attentions, with evident restraint on all sides. At midnight each retired to their respective apartments.

That of Madame de Meronville was separated from her son's by a long gallery hung with family portraits, between which, at intervals, were placed a kind of arched cavity, large enough to admit statues of those persons who had principally distinguished themselves in the service of their country. For a considerable time the footsteps of servants retiring to rest impeded her design of visiting Lusignan, whose altered looks and dejected spirits had greatly alarmed her, though she had restrained her maternal feelings in compliance with the strict injunction of his father. She had also with her a letter from Emily, which she might not have another opportunity to deliver; she therefore determined, when all should be still, to traverse the gallery, and seek his apartment. She cautiously opened her door and listened—all was still. She left her taper burning, and advanced towards the centre of the gallery. On a sudden one of the statues moved; she trembled, but persuading herself it was only fear, she advanced more hastily, yet fearfully looked behind her; the statue moved again, and a hollow voice said, "Beware!" She uttered a faint shriek, and equally dreaded to advance or retreat, for at that moment a voice from the extremity of the gallery exclaimed—"Beware!" All was utter darkness. The statues were of marble, and might, therefore, be distinguished in the surrounding gloom.

While Madame de Meronville stood in motionless terror, debating on the safest course to take, a dark figure crossed the end of the gallery nearest Lusignan's apartment, bearing a small lanthorn. Terror prevented her recollecting that this might be any other person but the one she sought—"Lusignan, my son!" she exclaimed, and was rushing towards him, but found herself forcibly detained by her robe. Unused as was Madame de Meronville to every species of alarm, her gentle frame could no longer sustain itself; she sunk lifeless on the floor. When she recovered, to her infinite surprise she found herself in her own apartment, without the least appearance of having quitted it. A confused recollection of the past scene reminded her that some extraordinary adventure had befallen her; yet she almost discredited her senses, and was inclined to attribute it all to one of those visions that often disturb our sleeping hours. Feeling, however, for the letter, which she was convinced she held in her hand, it had disappeared; her taper burnt dim; she explored the room, but in vain; no letter was there. No doubt could now remain of the identity of her recollections. She was so apprehensive that any person but Lusignan should find Emily's letter, that she summoned all her resolution to attempt again the ominous gallery, and seek it there; but thrice her hand pressed the lock, and thrice her courage forsook her. The voice issuing from the cavity still vibrated on her ear,* and, terrified beyond expression, she retreated to the other end of her chamber. The taper was now almost extinguished. She pressed her repeater; it was three o'clock.* She retired to rest, but had scarcely closed her eyes when the castle bell sounded a long hollow peal, which at that solemn hour seemed to shake the neighbouring battlements. The menials were in a moment roused. The portal grated on its hinges; and the tread of horsemen was distinguished in the court. Madame de Meronville concluded it was some of the retinue of the Duke de Foix, and again endeavoured to compose herself. When Gabriella attended in the morning, she enquired the cause of the night's alarm.

"Why, Madam," replied Gabriella, "there is a strange bustle in the castle, and nobody knows what it is about. An express arrived, they say, from his Grace of Foix, and my Lord Duke was awakened immediately. La France tells me he read a letter, and seemed so agitated that he grinned, and raved, and stamped, and frightened poor La France, who I am sure, though I say it, is a lad of great courage. But the best of all is, Monsieur La Abbé seems so very busy; he strides about the hall, orders one servant, countermands another, and, in short, looks more consequential than ever. Now, Madam, if you will excuse me for saying so, the servants heard at Paris that the castle is haunted, and they think his Grace may have heard the same, and so don't chuse to come. And I hope, my Lady, you will not mention it, but La France got up first, when the bell rung this morning, and as he descended that winding staircase that goes into the corridor at the end of the picture gallery, a ghost, dressed in black, and carrying a dark-lanthorn, ran before him; but he says these spirits are so light that it slipped away, and he could not overtake it, though he almost broke his neck down stairs. When it got to the gallery it stood quite still, and looked on him with such a look! He trembled when he told me. Then it took the flap of its black robe, put it over its head, and vanished, lanthorn and all."

Madame de Meronville could not help smiling at this account, though it seemed connected with the subject of terror she had herself experienced. She had no propensity to superstition, but thought it not improbable that some plot was carrying on that required the aid of supernatural appearances. She, however, reproved Gabriella for her credulity, and affected to disbelieve the whole; she was soon summoned to attend her lord in his own apartment. He told her in a solemn tone of voice, that they must instantly return to Paris; that some evil genius, who had borrowed the shape of his unnatural son, thwarted all his measures; that on the eve of her departure for Luneville Castle, Mademoiselle de Foix had been carried off from her father's hotel, and that the fugitives could not be discovered.

"I have no doubt," continued he, "that Madame de Clarival, her daughter, and the Marquis de Lusignan, are the contrivers of this diabolical scheme; but it will not forward their views. I shall order a dungeon to be prepared, and try the effect of that on his obstinate spirit. You may see him before you leave the castle, and assure him my malediction rests on him, and will never be withdrawn till I see him at the hymeneal altar with Eugenia de Foix."

Madame de Meronville in a moment saw the injustice of these suspicions, and neglected no pains to convince her husband of it. By caresses, tears, and intreaties, she at length prevailed on him to defer his return one day, and to see his son, who might have an opportunity of justifying himself.

She then went to his apartment, and found him addressing a letter to his intended bride, to prevail on her to raise those obstacles he had vainly opposed to his father's orders. She embraced him, and related the circumstance she had just learned from the Duke, and the suspicions that had consequently fallen on him. She then advised him to repair immediately to his father, and by gentleness and submission to avert his menaces.

Lusignan, though he could not but rejoice at this unexpected deliverance, fully acquiesced in his mother's opinion, and, throwing himself at his father's feet, assured him that he was innocent, and implored his mercy, as he never offended him but involuntarily, and suffered more from his displeasure than could possibly be described. The little remains of affection that the Duke retained for his son were awakened by his supplicating posture, and the alteration in his looks, where health no longer appeared. He raised him with something like kindness, and promised to suspend his judgment till some more certain discovery was made as to Mademoiselle de Foix's elopement, but still insisted he should remain at the Castle till he should engage to relinquish his views with respect to Emily. He retired to his apartment. The first thing which presented itself was a letter directed by her hand. The seal was broken. He read as follows:

———

"The fury of the Duke de Meronville has informed me of all I owe you; of the sacrifice your generosity has made, and your consequent confinement.

"For the last time, dear Lusignan, I let you see all my sensibility; but it is to teach you to sacrifice your own, since duty calls for it. Treading in the paths of Virtue, happiness will never forsake our steps.

"Mademoiselle de Foix possesses every qualification that entitles her to love and esteem; do not hesitate, Lusignan; transfer your affections to the object heaven has designed for you.

"We set out to-day for Montalte Abbey. I shall endeavour to forget the hour we met. I shall find difficulty in the attempt; but time brings fruition to every virtuous undertaking. All your prospects are bright, look forward to them without suffering any reminiscence of the past to interrupt your delights. Be happy, dear Lusignan, most generous of men, and forget that such a being exists as

"EMILY DE MONTALTE."

———

Lusignan read this letter a thousand times, and bathed it with tears.

"How insensible," thought he, "must that man be who could relinquish such a heart, when he had once flattered himself with obtaining it; and how inconsiderable are all the gifts of fortune compared with this."

He formed a thousand delightful projects, which only waited her consent. It was possible, he thought, to escape to the opposite shore, where liberty is the right of the meanest subject; there, in some obscure corner, he might with his beloved Emily forget the splendor he had left behind. He almost fancied himself there.

He wrote a dozen letters, and destroyed them all, for none expressed the feelings of his heart. On a sudden it occurred to him to enquire who had forestalled his happiness, by the first perusal of Emily's letter; for he now for the first time recollected the seal was broken. Fearful, however, of a discovery, he hastened to his mother, hoping she might explain the mystery.

She related to him the whole adventure of the preceding night, not forgetting her extreme terror. They were perfectly agreed that some human beings had been the actors of this scene, but could not possibly discover its design.

Lusignan had long considered La Haye as capable of every nefarious undertaking; but concealed his suspicions from his mother, who persuaded him from making any enquiries as to the person who had read his letter, since it might lead to the discovery of his having received one.

He acceded with difficulty to this necessary forbearance, and having at length written a few lines sufficiently passionate, he committed them to his faithful St. Pierre, who had attended Madame de Meronville to the Castle.

During the remainder of the day Lusignan endeavoured, by his attention and assiduities, to make his father forget he had ever offended him; and he was so well pleased, that he had once determined to permit his return to the capital.

But some secret monitor, who opposed all his best designs, persuaded him to defer this indulgence till he was more certain it was merited.

La Haye, who, fortunately for himself, held familiar converse with the spirits of darkness, could have best developed the mysterious warning in the gallery, for these aerial beings had on their swift pinions borne to him the letter addressed to Lusignan;* and as he had long been accustomed to consider the turpitude of an action as a mere chimera, except only as far as it might impede his designs, felt within his breast a very strong impellant to break the little bit of wax, which he had no doubt confined something he might wish to know. Finding, however, the contents perfectly innocent, another thought instantly struck him.

Lusignan and Emily were his devoted victims; he had sworn their destruction, and no means were to be neglected.

He had a surprising and dangerous talent of imitating written characters; he sat down and copied this so exactly, that the copy or original could hardly be discovered.

He durst not, however, trust it to the lover's eye; and, therefore, restored the original to Lusignan's chamber, depending on concealment, as he alone was apprised of the attempt.

He then wrote a letter, couched in ambiguous terms, which he might afterwards explain as the event made necessary, in Mademoiselle de Montalte's name; it contained hints of the expected elopement of Eugenia de Foix, and congratulations on Lusignan's happy devise to rid himself of this intended bride. The whole was so artfully compiled, that he could adapt the meaning exactly to any circumstances that might appear relative to her escape.

Having finished this work to his satisfaction, he reserved it to be employed as opportunity should direct. He behaved with unusual civility and even obsequiousness to Lusignan, who was at no pains to disguise or suppress his profound contempt.

Early in the morning his Grace with his retinue proceeded towards the metropolis, leaving our disconsolate exile to his melancholy rumination.

Madame de Meronville shed abundance of tears as she bid him farewell. Nor was his grief less poignant; he loved her with the tenderest affection, and her undeviating kindness claimed his warmest gratitude.

Impressed with these sentiments he saw her depart with extreme regret; and after observing the cavalcade from the parapet wall, which commanded a very distant view, he sighed profoundly, and retired to his apartment.

Eugenia de Foix had just completed her fifteenth year, and was still in the Monastery where she received her education, when informed that her father designed to unite her fortune to that of the Marquis de Lusignan.

She had never seen him, consequently could form no estimate of his merits, but she had read some romances, which taught her that love was the business of life.*

She hourly lamented not being born in those ages of chivalry, when some valiant Knight would have gloried in expiring at her feet, to avenge a rent in her robe, the work of a rival.

She wished as much as possible to restore in her own person

those halcyon days; and her fancy daily pourtrayed the delights of a second Amadis the Gaul* expiring at her feet.

To accept, therefore, at once, the lover her father had chosen, would have destroyed all the romantic visions of her soul; and would not have entitled her to become the heroine of one of those charming compositions.

Besides, the Chevalier d'Aubignac, with whose sister she was intimately connected, had, notwithstanding the vigilance of her monastic guardians, contrived to whisper soft entreaties, and had engaged to brave the most perilous adventures for her sake; he would fly to the remotest extremity of the habitable globe in search of dangers, and claim no reward but her gentle smile.

D'Aubignac at first appeared rather disagreeable to her, but these promises won her heart; and she determined to enlist him as her head champion.

Her first step, therefore, when apprized of her father's intention, was to acquaint him with her situation.

She collected fragments from all her favourite authors, to paint her distress, her inviolable constancy, and her determination to oppose the rigidity of paternal commands; declaring that no violence should tear his image from her heart.

The effect she expected from this delectable composition was, that he should propose to convey her to some remote castle, where love and liberty should guard the entrance, and his single arm defend her from a host of enemies.

But there were such things as Lettres de Cachet,* and the house of Foix was very powerful; these considerations, notwithstanding the valour of her adopted knight, had some little weight, and he persuaded her that on such occasions the most renowned heroines of antient romance had employed only tears and entreaties, which, unless his Grace's heart was truly adamantine, could not fail of the desired effect.

Eugenia agreed that such means ought not to be neglected; but was now determined to try something more effective.

By the means of Mademoiselle d'Aubignac, (and perhaps the connivance of her brother) she obtained male apparel, and in that disguise easily escaped; lamenting, indeed, the facility of it, as it gave her no opportunity of signalising her intrepidity in the cause of love.

D'Aubignac had engaged by verbal assurance to meet her at the appointed hour and place; but the Lettre de Cachet was still an object of terror, and he failed in his engagement.

To neglect a rendezvous was an unpardonable crime; but Eugenia had no doubt his detention had been occasioned by her pursuers, of whom he had very probably killed at least a score.

As her projects were, however, by this accident defeated, she purchased some female attire, and exchanging it for that with which she had left the Convent, presented herself to the Superior of St. Clair, determined to remain in that asylum till rescued by d'Aubignac.

She assumed a counterfeit name; and assuring the Abbess she was related to the first families in the kingdom, who would well reward the care she might bestow, was without difficulty admitted.

She had a little elegant figure, fine black eyes, and a natural vivacity that made her really pleasing, though not handsome. For a considerable time she heard nothing of her champion; nor could her friends, by all their researches, discover her retreat, as St. Clair was situated in a remote part of Champagne.

In this asylum we shall, for the present leave her, to return to Montalte Abbey.

CHAP. VIII.

"There placed aloft presides the Omniscient Cause,
"And orders all with just and equal laws;
"Above the confines of this earthly scene,
"By wrongs unsearchable to mortal men;
"There on eternity's unbounded throne,
"With triple light he blazes three in one!"*

Montalte Abbey was situated on the Norman Coast, nearly at the entrance of St. Michael's Bay;* it commanded a vast diversity of prospect, and nature seemed here to have combined those various beauties which are usually scattered with a frugal hand.

To the eastward a beautiful ridge of rocks, called the Casquets,* which, at low tide, formed a beautiful seat, whence the inhabitants had an extensive view of the Old Ocean; the small island of Alderney was completely traversed at one glance; and to the west the ports of Cherbourg and St. Maloes were distinctly seen.

The Abbey itself was a monument of antiquity, it being the first taken possession of by the celebrated Rollo;* but that part which the family inhabited had been somewhat modernized.

At the back of it some small eminences rose perpendicularly, to shelter the fertile dales from the detrimental north winds; and these, by the regularity of their position, formed a kind of natural amphitheatre, covered with brushwood of various tints.

A small rivulet ran at the bottom, whose gentle course was sometimes interrupted by enormous stones, which appeared at a short distance to form beautiful cascades and waterfalls.

From the Abbey windows the eye soared many leagues beyond this, and on a clear day the distant towers of Paris might be discerned.

Wild and terrific scenery sometimes interrupted this mild prospect. Ships were frequently wrecked, or in imminent danger, in that narrow channel which separates the island from the coast, and called the Race of Alderney.*

Emily's heart had often melted at the sight of that distress no human efforts could alleviate.

At this spot Madame de Clarival, her daughter, and Caroline de Montfort, arrived at sun-set; the declining rays of that resplendent orb played on the surface of a calm and transparent ocean. Emily and her friend felt a calmness of spirits in unison with the scene.

Caroline had learned, with inexplicable delight, the connection that subsisted between her benefactress, Madame de Meronville, and her friend, whose gentle and persuasive admonitions had restored serenity to her bosom.

Frequently, as she contemplated the vast expanse that rolled beneath, she would sigh at the recollection, that in its bottomless gulph her happiness had perhaps been buried; but Emily persuaded her to hope better things.

"My hopes," would she say, "are wrecked on land, yet, my Caroline, there is a power that alike protects the weary traveller straying through unfrequented wilds, and the mariner who braves the tempests, and seeks danger on the distant ocean's waves. Something whispers that your Edward will be restored; and that in your happiness we shall find the reward of patient resignation."

As she spoke the tear of sympathy fell from her eyes, which were raised to Heaven, and beamed the effulgence of youthful hope; their days glided away, if not happily, at least with that cheerful serenity which is ever the companion of the virtuous. It was disturbed, however, by accounts from Paris, which mentioned Lusignan as still a prisoner, and under the displeasure of a despotic parent.

His violence had informed Madame de Clarival, previous to her leaving Paris, of the suppression of those papers on which the rights of the Duke of Meronville were founded.

Curtailed as were his hopes of success, he had determined to attempt the suit; and spared no expence, nor omitted anything the ingenuity of a lawyer could invent, to ensure a decree in his favour; every due and undue advantage was taken, but to no purpose.

The entail, which alone could have established his claims, Lusignan had burnt; and the Duke could only display his inveterate hate and malignity, without reaping any fruits.

In open court he charged the Countess with having taught her daughter to require this sacrifice from his son, and declared, that to obtain her ends she had not scrupled to throw irreconcilable division into his family.

Madame de Clarival was now, for the first time, apprised of Lusignan's generosity.

His mother endeavoured as much as possible to counteract the effects of the Duke's violence, and to persuade her to co-operate with the endeavours of their numerous relations to accommodate all differences, and unite the several branches of the family.

The Countess's affection for her daughter, and admiration of Lusignan, powerfully supported these entreaties, and they were all requisite to induce her to admit a thought of alliance with a man who had so grossly insulted her.

Forgetting her injuries, however, she consented to second, with all her influence, the steps that should be taken to procure a reconciliation.

This affair, however, had induced her to retire to the Abbey, as it made much noise at Paris, and was the general topic in the higher circles. For the sake of Emily, she desired that their absence should give the tumult time to subside.

Madame de Meronville, who already felt a mother's fondness for Emily, had taken leave of her with extreme regret; she had mentioned her husband's design with respect to Mademoiselle de Foix; and engaged to convey Emily's letter to her unfortunate son; promising, that should any thing impede the intended union, she would persuade the Duke to forego such attempts in future.

"My dear Emily," said she, when last they parted, "how complete would my happiness be, could I ever call you by the endearing name of daughter; believe me, no blessing that fortune, from her inexhaustible stores, might bestow, could bear comparison with this. As to my son, if a mother's partiality does not blind me, he is worthy your affection; and, alas! deserves a better fate!"

"Your approbation, Madam," replied Emily, "leaves an impression so flattering on my mind, that time can never efface it. When first I knew the Marquis of Lusignan, his merit claimed my esteem; but his generosity and disinterested attachment has since bound my heart to his in ligaments too strong to be broken. Could I see him happy, though united to another, I should not feel worthy of commiseration; it is his suffering which occasions mine. Why, my dear Madam, was such a son given to such a father?"

"The ways of Heaven," said the Duchess, "are just, though impenetrable to our conceptions, and too profound for our superficial enquiries; our state here is merely probationary; fortitude and resignation, in the support of adverse fortune, entitle us to the future rewards promised by the Gospel. Were every blessing our portion here, still must the enjoyment be short, and even interrupted by the certainty that death must early terminate them all. I would not have you insensible to the events of this transitory world, nor too anxiously awake to their effects; insensibility too frequently degenerates into apathy, and the noblest qualities are destroyed in the stagnant mind. The contrary excess ruins our peace, and even by its consequences frequently becomes a formidable vice, though the best support of virtue, if exerted only to inspire universal philanthropy, and that charity and zeal for the interests of our fellow-creatures which may be called an emanation of the divine nature."

"These lessons," said Emily, "I have frequently received from my mother; yet cannot reconcile the idea of so many created beings, formed to prove the various degrees of misery to which we are subject."

"Justice and infinite mercy," continued Madame de Meronville, "are the great attributes of the divinity; both must be satisfied, and of both we are the objects; by the former our sufferings here are appointed to expiate the sinfulness of nature; by the latter we shall be raised beyond the boundaries of fortune. No casualties or fortuitous events can disturb that immortal bliss, which Heaven in its mercy prepares for those who have calmly submitted to the trials they have here sustained. A real christian, my Emily, never despairs: when all her prospects here are bounded by impenetrable gloom, she looks forward with undiminished hope to that resting place where every grief shall be forgotten!"

"My circumscribed experience," said Emily, "has already taught me that vice is often successful, and triumphs over oppressed virtue."

"Most assuredly it does," resumed the Duchess, "and erroneous are the tenets of that moralist who would teach us to expect an immediate reward for the exercise of virtue. On earth it is seldom found; but awaits us in another world. Let us never be discouraged by present evils; they are the preludes to future happiness. Reason is given as an antidote to the passions, and if listened to is all-sufficient.* It is the best support of hope, that hope which points to blessings certain and immutable!"

In such conversations was their last interview spent; Emily often recollected it, and found her virtue strengthened by such a bright example.

Nevertheless, as the issue of Mademoiselle de Foix's visit to Luneville was uncertain, she could not help feeling some uneasiness as to the result.

One evening as she with Caroline was walking on the coast, lost in admiration of the vast expanse, which no eye could compass, they strayed beyond their limited distance from home.

The sky, which had been clear and serene, was suddenly overspread with dark thick clouds, that seemed to portend a gathering storm; the sun declining in the west, shot from the pallid horizon streaks of firy red; the wind blew a hurricane.

Alarmed at these appearances the young friends quickened their pace, in hopes to reach the Abbey before the storm burst, but were soon overtaken by a violent shower, which obliged them to seek shelter in a deserted hut, erected by some absent fisherman.

From hence their view of the ocean was uninterrupted; they observed a ship tossed by the waves, whose pilot vainly endeavoured to steer beyond the narrow strait, whose rocks and shoals strike the intrepid mariner with fear.

Impelled by the fury of the swelling billows, he entered it, and then made every possible signal of distress, which were answered from the light-house on the shore; boats were sent off, but as often the waves, with irresistible violence, obliged them to return; the danger increased momentarily, and the vessel seemed ready to split on the rocks.

Emily and her friend trembled in silent agitation at this awful scene.

The rain had ceased, and the moon, majestically rising, struggled in vain with the condensed clouds which surrounded her.

The terror of the feathered tribe, shrilled in the omens of an approaching tempest, convinced Emily they had better seek the Abbey ere its violence increased; but as they attempted to leave the hut, the wind roared, the rain again fell in torrents; a wave almost enveloped the ship—another succeeded—the third dashed it against the dreaded Casquets—it instantly split.

Emily and Caroline now felt all their sympathy awakened for the unknown sufferers: some climbed the rocks, others attached themselves to rafts, and fragments of the shattered vessel; some endeavoured to swim, and by their exertions hoped to reach the distant shore; but destruction overtook them all; the merciless waves engulfed them for ever; in vain they extended their arms, and implored the aid of those who from the shore witnessed their distress; their supplicating looks, their uplifted hands were vain; it was beyond the power of human effort to relieve them.

Emily had followed with her eyes a man who made towards that part of the shore on which they stood spectators of the dreadful scene.

Borne on a raft, three times he almost reached the coast, but as often the impetuosity of the waves hurled him anew into the ocean; each effort he made grew fainter—her heart beat with anxiety—he sunk—she shrieked, and almost lost her senses.

Servants at that moment came up with lights, to conduct them home. When they had almost reached the Abbey, she turned to look at the spot where she had lost sight of the unfortunate man—a billow threw the raft on the shore—he still clung to it.

She immediately ordered the servants to return and bring him to Montalte, that no efforts might be wanting to restore that life he had endeavoured with such infinite labour to preserve.

Having satisfied the calls of humanity, she hastened to dissipate the fears of Madame de Clarival, who had been greatly alarmed at their absence, during so violent a convulsion of the elements, which had shaken the ancient structure to its very foundation, and even destroyed a part of the old building, which had hitherto survived the wreck of time.

The concussion was dreadful, and the Countess trembled for her children;—when they at length appeared she offered prayers to heaven, in gratitude for their preservation.

Emily related with great emotion the accident which had befallen the vessel; and before her narrative concluded, a servant entered to inform them the man was brought in, but without any signs of life; but her terror is not to be described, when told the hut, in which they so lately thought themselves secure, was carried into the fathomless ocean.

The Countess attended herself to the operations by which the family surgeon endeavoured to restore the unhappy stranger; after much exertion a faint flush overspread his countenance, he breathed gently, and every symptom appeared of returning life.

Emily leaped for joy.

He had a leathern bag suspended to his neck, which, with a shirt he had on, was all that escaped with him the universal wreck.

Having been conveyed to bed, in a few hours his reason returned, and he enquired whose hospitable mansion sheltered him from the storm. When informed, he expressed his gratitude to heaven and his kind preservers in terms which surprised Madame de Clarival.

There was something in his speech and manner so superior to the vulgar, that she wished to enquire his adventures; but thought it more discreet to wait his own communications.

"There is one thing, Madam," said the stranger, with great agitation, "which I value even more than the life your benevolence has restored, a small leathern bag, containing the only possession I have long cared to preserve: will you permit me to enquire if that has fortunately escaped?"

Madame de Clarival with pleasure assured him it had; and immediately gave orders to have it delivered to him.

He untied it with some difficulty, and drew from it a portrait and a letter, the characters of which were nearly effaced by the effects of the water, which the leather had not entirely repelled.

He kissed the miniature with fervour, declaring it the talisman which had preserved him in the midst of such dangers as no mortal had ever escaped; then taking the letter—

"These lines, Madam," said he, "were intended for an amiable and adored female, from whom, for five years, fortune has detained me; should she still breathe her native air, if her virtues still adorn that country, which for her sake I abandoned, this letter will recall her to my embrace. Alas! I quitted her to seek those riches which a single hour has deprived me of; a constant and affectionate heart is still all I can offer in compensation for that poverty which fate decrees to be my lot. Five years of labour and sorrow are past, and the produce buried in the unsearchable deep."

He sighed whilst he spoke. The Countess endeavoured to offer some comfort, and entreating him to take repose, which the surgeon had declared to be indispensably necessary, promised to send one of her own people with the letter to whatever part of the kingdom it might be addressed; she then left the room, giving orders that he should be left in tranquillity, and not disturbed but by order of the surgeon.

Emily and Caroline were in the vestibule, anxiously waiting the issue of this conference, and the opinion Monsieur le Saxe should entertain of his patient, for whom they felt peculiarly interested as their protégée.

The Countess gave a favourable account, and produced the letter, that they might decypher the superscription, and send it to its destined possessor.

She examined it carefully, and changed colour repeatedly as its blotted surface became more intelligible; she was confused, and hastily repeated the words he had spoken, adding, that the lady he mentioned would be truly enviable when apprized of his safe return.

She looked at Caroline, whose intelligent countenance betrayed the interest she felt in this detail; an enquiry seemed ready to issue from her lips; but mingled hope and apprehension deprived her of articulation.

"What say you, my love?" continued Madame de Clarival, "you seem much interested in this adventure. Should you not think the lady worthy of envy?"

"Most truly so, my dear Madam; but tell me what means your emotion, and that tremulous tone of voice?"

Her own was no less tremulous. The Countess affectionately embraced her.

"I need have no fears," said she; "the person who has so well supported adversity, will not be thrown off her guard by unexpected good-fortune. Heaven grant that all your misfortunes may thus terminate."

She put the letter into her hand; it was addressed to Caroline de Montfort, Convent of Clarivaux; she could read no farther, the paper dropped from her hand, excess of joy and surprise deprived her for a moment of reason; but it was soon restored.

She would instantly have flown to his apartment; but Madame de Clarival, with a smile, said she was sorry to delay the meeting of two such constant lovers. But as she really wished to preserve them both, prudence obliged her to request the interview might be deferred; for as extreme delight had such a powerful effect on her in full health, its consequences were to be greatly apprehended in Mr. Dorville's weakly state.

"Let us, my dear Caroline," continued she, "try the effect of Le Saxe's remedies first; the sight of you, as most efficacious, we will reserve for the crisis."

Caroline readily acquiesced in this decree; her impatience to see a man who had done so much for her, yielding to the fear of impeding his recovery.

"Happy, happy hour," said she, "my Emily, which conducted our steps to the beach; without this he might have perished, and I have witnessed his return only to mourn my irreparable loss. By such unforeseen expedients does heaven bring relief at the moment when it appears most distant."

Emily could not sufficiently express her joy.

"He is returned," said she, "my sweet friend. How complete is your happiness; and how truly blessed is your Emily, who may have it in her power to contribute to it."

Caroline answered only with a sigh.

She now recollected the obstacle that prevented their union before he left Europe; and that obstacle seemed revived with double force by the effect of the late shipwreck.

She took her station at the door of his apartment, and repeated her enquiries to every person issuing from it. A slight degree of fever appeared, which his Esculapius thought more occasioned by his anxiety respecting the letter, than the effect of the damps.* When assured it was sent, and that an answer would speedily arrive, he was more composed, and fell into a gentle slumber.

Caroline could now no longer be withheld from entering his chamber, to assure herself that it was indeed him. She approached the bed; but her consternation is not to be described, when she beheld a stranger! She crept out of the room, her heart sinking within her.

Emily waited at the door, shocked at her altered looks, which she could only attribute to his indisposition, which was, perhaps, worse than she had expected.

She eagerly began to console her, saying, that Monsieur le Saxe was a man of much professional merit, and would not have given them hopes had they not been well-founded.

Caroline fell on her neck in a state bordering on annihilation, she sobbed, and her tears fell in torrents.

"Speak, I conjure you," said Mademoiselle de Montalte. "What has so deeply affected you, who but a moment before was in an ecstacy of joy?"

"Oh! my friend, it is not he, it is not my Edward."

With difficulty she articulated these few words.

Emily retreated a few paces; she doubted the evidence of her senses.

"Was not that letter," said she, "from him?"

This mention of the letter revived Caroline's drooping senses; they descended together to the apartment of Madame de Clarival, who was truly shocked at this catastrophe.

She blamed herself for being the cause of such fallacious hopes, and dreaded the violence of such opposing and violent emotions, as those Caroline had experienced; and which on a frame so delicate as her's might be of fatal tendency; yet the letter seemed not doubtful.

It was inclosed in an envelope thus inscribed:

"The last token of my affectionate regard for an object who had engrossed my living thoughts, and to whom is devoted my dying breath. Compassionate stranger, whoever though art, that shall find this sad testimonial, I conjure you, as you value your eternal happiness, convey it where it is addressed, it will ensure a blessing on your head."

The letter contained these words:

———————

"Has not my beloved friend accused my long silence, and thought me the most worthless of beings? Necessity, dire necessity, has been alone the cause. Never for a moment has your image been absent from my heart; in the midst of perils and dangers, the hopes of returning to you has cheered my gloomy soul, which must otherwise have sunk under its various depressions.

"Thrice have I been on the eve of quitting the inhospitable shores of Africa; and thrice has my wayward fate consigned me a prey to savage nations.

"The storm now howls around me; the angry billows burst against the sides of our devoted vessel. I see that much loved shore where breathes my Caroline; but never must I reach it.

"Should fortune, satiated with my woes, relent when I am no more, and convey this memorial of affection to thy dear embrace, oh! pardon my unintentional neglect, and do not refuse a sigh to the memory of one, is addressed to Heaven in your behalf.

"The storm increases—the clouds condense——dreadful lightnings burst from Heaven!——The vessel is on the wreck.—Adieu! adieu! my Caroline."

———————

A perusal of these lines convinced Madame de Clarival, that the mystery which seemed to envelope this transaction arose from an alteration in Edward Dorville's appearance, the effect of fatigue and change of climate. She communicated her suspicions to Caroline, who shook her head, and refused to be again deceived. The eyes of a lover could indeed penetrate beyond the casual effect of absence. His features must have remained, and these were quite different to those of Dorville.

To elucidate this mystery the Countess repaired to his chamber, and as soon as he awoke took an opportunity of enquiring the name of the lady he was so solicitous to hear from.

"Julia d'Ermancy," was the answer.

Convinced now that some unaccountable mistake had arisen, she shewed him the letter addressed to Caroline de Montfort. He started from the pillow; some sudden recollection seemed darting across his mind; he sighed deeply.

"Oh! my friend," said he, "how must my heart be altered, since, till now, I had forgotten the dangers to which you were exposed. Unhappy Dorville, fate has not then ceased to persecute you!"

After some moments of recollection he addressed Madame de Clarival in these words:

"I had a friend, Madam, who left his native shore under the same circumstances as myself. Coincidence of fortune and sentiments united us so strictly that we never separated; our joys and griefs, our good and bad fortune were in common. We embarked for Europe in the same vessel, and congratulated each other on a view of the distant much-loved coast, when on a sudden the serenity of the atmosphere changed to the most convulsed, and the storm you witnessed, Madam, succeeded. The pilot and Captain both declared there was no hope or prospect of escape; and the whole crew commended their souls to God. Dorville and myself retired to our cabin, agreeing to write to our prospective brides, for such we considered them; and putting the letters into bags, we tied them to our necks, and tenderly embracing one another, we awaited the splitting of the vessel on those rocks it was impossible to avoid. By a strange fatality the bag containing Dorville's letter fell to my lot, and, doubtless, he preserved mine. Heaven knows where he is, though I fear too surely he has perished. I saw him clinging to a raft at the moment when I sunk myself, and lost all recollection. This, Madam, has occasioned the mistake, which I sincerely lament, as it appears to have given you so much concern. I feel my own strength so renovated by your kind attentions, that I shall probably embrace my Julia sooner than your messenger could arrive. Expression is so inadequate to explain my gratitude, and my power of return so limited, that I can only beg you to accept the blessings of two beings who will owe every future hour of enjoyment to you."

Madame de Clarival then related the effect this mistake had on the hapless Caroline, whose hopes, she now feared, were for ever ruined.

Marsillac (for such was the stranger's name) wept the misfortunes of his friend.

"Ah! Madam," said he, "had you known him! He was deserving Mademoiselle de Montfort, such as you describe her, the most generous, noble, disinterested soul that ever animated a mortal form."

Madame de Clarival knew not how to return to the saloon; she had no comfort to impart, no hopes to communicate; she was deeply afflicted at the disappointment reserved for her disconsolate guest.

All her woes were doubled by this sudden extinction of every hope; she sent for Emily, and after recounting all she had heard from Marsillac, left her to the care of consoling her unhappy friend.

Emily's affectionate heart shuddered at the grief she must communicate; yet there remained a possibility that he might have escaped, and on this she founded her only hope.

"My dear Caroline," said she, with a forced cheerfulness, "all is not lost; your Edward may still return; his most intimate friend is our guest, and he may, by the aid of Providence, have been no less miraculously saved. Nay, dry those tears; you distress me, my love; will you not listen to the voice of friendship?"

Caroline answered only by pressing her hand, and a suffusion of tears.

Emily then repeated what she had just learned, adding, that she would at least have the satisfaction of knowing all that had befallen him.

"And we shall to-day," continued she, "send messengers to different parts of the coast, to enquire whether any person has escaped the wreck." The result of these enquiries might prove satisfactory, and, indeed, she saw great reason to hope it would.

The remainder of the day was spent in calculating on the chances of the good or bad news the morrow should bring with it.

Caroline was evidently apprehensive, agitated, and alarmed; but tried to conceal her emotions from the anxious scrutiny of her friend, and always met her regards with a smile of ineffable sweetness.

They retired early to rest, or to indulge in solitude the various conjectures and ideas to which the events of the day had given birth.

Early in the morning Emily repaired to the apartment of her fair protegée. Certain of finding her wakeful, she stole to her bedside. The curtains were closed, the sun pressing through the casements, had not awakened her. A blush of innocence suffused her cheek, a tear stood trembling on her closed eyelids; yet a sort of smile seemed to give serenity to her modest countenance.

Emily gazed on her with delight; she sat down near her, and

imprinted a soft kiss on her vermilion lips. She awoke—her first smile was devoted to friendship.

"My Emily," said she, "I have had delicious dreams; sure the sylphs that guard our sleeping hours cannot have deceived me. Edward lives, and will return to chase the gloomy presages of my mind."

Emily embraced her, and concurred in her opinion; they descended to the Countess's boudoir, where breakfast waited for them. The first enquiries related to the stranger, who in a few moments entered the apartment, and made his warmest acknowledgments to all the ladies for their care, and the attention he had received.

Caroline scarcely ventured to lift her eyes on him, when she recollected the disappointment his first view had occasioned her; yet he was the friend of Dorville, and she could not be uninterested.

He had been warned not to mention Edward, unless requested to do so; and as all were fearful of introducing so interesting a subject, the breakfast hour was spent in desultory enquiries respecting his adventures. As soon as it concluded, he mounted a horse, and set out for Besançon,* where Julia d'Ermancy formerly resided, promising to see her only a moment, and then return, to unite with them in using every possible method to discover their lost and mutual friend.

END OF VOL. I.

LUSIGNAN.

CHAP. I.

"Thou art return'd; but the felicity
"Thou brought'st me last, is not return'd with thee.
"Thou art return'd,—but nought returns with thee,
"Save my last joys——regretful memory!"

Though Emily's concern for her beloved Caroline had lately occupied her undivided attention, and driven from her recollection every extraneous subject, Lusignan, in solitude and seclusion, thought on her alone; days, weeks, and months rolled away, and were marked only by a monotonous recurrence of the same uninteresting pursuits: his hours of repose, those sweet intervals of oblivion, when nature is respited from all its woes, were shortened by the perturbation of his restless mind. No sooner did daylight appear, than he repaired to the most elevated battlement, and, from its extremest height, surveyed the winding road which led to Paris; and, when night again returned, he murmured at the chaotic power which interrupted his views. No friend appeared to cheer his heavy hours, or listen to his tales of sorrow; he was separated from the whole universe; an isolated, melancholy, and neglected prisoner. Such had been his state since the splendid retinue left Luneville, which had been attracted there by the supposed arrival of the Duke de Foix. His mother had promised to write; St. Pierre had attended her to Paris, in order to convey any intelligence to the Castle, but no tidings of either interrupted the settled gloom of his ideas: memory, by recalling past joys, only rendered his present situation, by contrast, more dreary. Frequently pondering on it, he thought of endeavouring to escape, but the Castle was so well guarded, that this appeared impracticable; and, even if he should succeed, how little would his situation be improved! Emily had convinced him she never would consent to a clandestine union, and that was the only thing which could make him happy.

During these ruminations, a letter at length arrived. Madame de Meronville gave him hopes; his father seemed to relent; the friends of all parties had united in endeavouring to procure an accommodation, and Lusignan was permitted to leave the Castle during the day, for the purpose of exercise and recreation, on giving his word to return before dark.

Depressed as were his spirits by anxiety and long confinement, his heart was still open to the impressions of youthful hope; his elastic mind bounded at its touch. He interrogated St. Pierre as to the state of things at his father's. This faithful domestic wept at the languor and dejection which pervaded his once animated features; he informed him that, soon after they left the Castle, the Duke held a long conference with Monsieur La Haye, in consequence of which he appeared more than ever exasperated, and even treated the Duchess with disrespect and harshness; that, by degrees, this had worn off, and though moments of violence sometimes recurred, he yet seemed, on the whole, softened, and less inexorable. Mademoiselle de Foix had hitherto eluded all her pursuers, nor could the strictest search discover any trace of her situation. Lusignan then dismissed him, with an injunction to observe all that passed, and return in eight days at farthest.

Wholly occupied with the new hopes he was now permitted to cherish, his former vivacity returned; his long-neglected books again appeared a source of amusement; exercise and air, while they invigorated his body, fortified also his mind. He strayed beyond the Castle walls, conversing with the neighbouring peasantry, and partaking their rural enjoyments. Nature smiled again: his heart, lightened of sorrow, almost promised him that his exile would expire with the eight days to which he had limited the return of St. Pierre; and he rather rejoiced in his past sufferings, since they gave him an additional claim to the heart of Emily, for whose sake they had been endured.

La Haye seemed to have forgotten his resentment, since the Marquis's persecutions were remitted; but far otherwise, he only took a circuit where the road straight before him, though shorter, was less infallible. He had now two schemes in view, and one seemed likely to obstruct the other; it required, indeed, the skill of an artful politician to unite all parts of a machine which was constructed like his; but much may be done where nothing is allowed to interfere but the dread of detection. The Chevalier d'Aubignac was very nearly related to him, and he was very anxious to maintain his claims to Eugenia de Foix, yet he had intended to make her the source of division between the Duke and his son, but her own elopement had prevented the objections Lusignan would doubtless have made to a union with her. No sooner, however, was he informed that d'Aubignac was the person for whose sake she had deserted the paternal roof, than he saw the course he must pursue; he took every precaution to assure her concealment till the Chevalier could with safety marry her, and then considered how he might best turn to account his knowledge of her retreat.

On his arrival at Paris he readily perceived his patron on the eve of relenting. Nature raised a few scruples in his heart, and he had felt a pang of remorse at the sufferings of his only child. Madame de Meronville had during the journey assiduously cherished this spark of remaining affection, and really hoped much from it, particularly as Fortune, rather than Lusignan, had rendered his designs abortive. La Haye easily discovered that this was not the season to press vigorous measures, but he opened his batteries by degrees; his projects were not formed on system, but always adapted to existing circumstances; and the versatility of his attempts rendered them less suspicious, but more to be dreaded. He now hesitated whether to abandon Lusignan to shame and his father's resentment, or to persevere in his revenge; the insult he had received still preyed on his mind, but all doubts were removed by the arrival of the Chevalier St. Amand, who, with his usual vanity, boasted that he possessed much influence with Mademoiselle de Montalte. La Haye thought every thing was possible to him, and he concluded that by depriving her of all hopes of Lusignan, he should induce her to become the wife of St. Amand; he knew the effect of disappointment on the female mind, and that he resolved to try by first giving her well-founded hopes that the Duke would forget his resentment; by this he should also gratify his revenge against the Marquis. With his plan, therefore, concerted, he entered the closet of Meronville. "I was going to send for you," said his Grace: "I am growing old, La Haye, and more so from infirmity than years. I have sometimes thought my son might be a comfort to my declining age. On your friendship I can rely; tell me, are all my proceedings, with respect to him, guided by equity? As my spiritual father, tell me, is my conscience clear?"

La Haye, though rather alarmed at this preamble, yet thought it a good opportunity to begin his design; assuming, therefore, an air of sanctity, he said, "The vengeance of Heaven, Sir, lights on the children of disobedience, and it is fit a father should chastise his rebellious son; your inclination to mercy does you honour; pursue it, it is the attribute of divinity, but let not justice be forgotten: have you duly weighed the guilt of the Marquis, and are you satisfied with the punishment it has incurred?"

"He has suffered much," said Meronville; "and my displeasure seems not to be the least of his misfortunes."

"Is he then, Sir, disposed to obey you," said La Haye; "for what other proof can he give of contrition? His crime is that of the first man, and for which the great Creator has punished all his descendants. Heaven has delegated its power to parents, and their authority is a type of the supreme power, from which it is derived."

"Mademoiselle de Foix," resumed his Grace, "eludes all our pursuits; it is she who throws obstacles in the way of my wishes; Lusignan seemed disposed to comply." (La Haye shook his head.) "She may," continued the Duke, "be, ere this, united to the man who prompted her to forsake the parental asylum."

"Would you then, Sir," said La Haye, "consent to the union of your son with Mademoiselle de Montalte?"

"I have had," replied the Duke, "applications from several quarters to that effect. It is thought eligible to unite the numerous estates and honours of the two families."

"Meronville was a rigid Catholic, though his ancestors had been Huguenots," La Haye observed; "the Comte de Clarival was a heretic."

"My uncle was," replied Meronville; "but my late cousin and his daughter were admitted into the pale of the Church. My ancestors, like their's, were in error."

"Which makes it the more necessary," replied La Haye, "to guard against the propagation of such apostacy. Madame de Clarival herself was, and I believe is, a Protestant; the blood of heresy is mingled in the veins of her daughter with that of true believers. Be careful, Sir, not to contaminate your spotless race. Heaven is my witness! to conciliate differences, to restore peace, and promote universal charity, is my governing principle; but I dread to sanction, by my authority, an union that might pollute our holy religion!"

Meronville was staggered. "Would to Heaven," said he, "Mademoiselle de Foix would return!"

La Haye again shook his head, with insidious meaning,—"I fear she is too powerfully detained; it is an iniquitous plot!"

"Plot!" exclaimed the Duke; "whose plot, whose infamous contrivance?"

The Abbé, seeming to recollect himself, affected concern at the knowledge he had betrayed; he hesitated,—"I was to blame," said he; "proofs are wanting; we are, perhaps, too credulous. Pardon me, my Lord, I was too unguarded."

"You torture me," said his Grace; "speak, is my son——"

"Far be it from me," rejoined the hypocrite, "to sow divisions, or add corrosives to a father's sufferings: no, my Lord; permit me to be silent; there is only the evidence of a letter, perhaps I am deceived——."

"This is past endurance!" cried Meronville. "Speak, as you value my favour."

La Haye knew the effect of suspense; he tried it, till his patron was wrought to the highest pitch of impatience and curiosity. He then produced the letter himself had forged, whereby it appeared that Emily and Lusignan held intelligence respecting the concealment of Eugenia. The Duke paused not to weigh probabilities,—he could no longer contain himself,—"By my God," said he, in a paroxysm of rage, "and all my future hopes of mercy, I solemnly swear never to forgive him! Oh degenerate son! Oh wretched father! but it is enough; I disinherit him; nor shall any future concession be deemed an atonement."

With profound hypocrisy La Haye lifted his eyes to Heaven, and, falling on his knees, with a deep sigh pronounced these words:— "Recording spirits, that note the words of man, blot from thine eternal register this sacred oath! and all ye sainted spirits, that intercede for sinful mortals, pour repentance into the deluded heart of Lusignan!"

Meronville, by this time grown calm, requested again to see the letter, and asked how it came into his possession?

The Abbé said he was not permitted to develope this secret; but, tearing off the address, permitted him to ask the Duchess if that was the handwriting of Emily?

So accurate was the forgery, that she indiscreetly acknowledged

it. Here, then, was no room for doubt. Meronville told him he
was resolved to conceal his son in the western turret of the Castle;
that his confinement should be unknown to any person except one
on whom they might depend; and that, to prevent importunity,
he would himself affect ignorance of his abode, and join in the
researches that would be made to discover him.

La Haye approved of this plan in part, but said his assertion
would hardly be credited, as it was known Lusignan had, by his
order, been confined. A *lettre de cachet* would be more eligible;* but,
as that would take time to procure, he desired three days to form
a plan that should answer every purpose, by implicating also the
female who had seduced his son from the path of duty, and, therefore, like our mother Eve, the original sinner, his Grace acquiesced;
and during this interval it was that the Duchess felt his displeasure; but he no sooner acceded to the scheme proposed by La Haye,
the success of which depended entirely on dissimulation, than he
assumed a lenient air, and gave her hopes his resentment was no
more. Under this impression she had written to Lusignan, and her
unsuspecting heart, no less than his, dilated to the hope of reconciliation.

After the eventful days just passed, the young friends of Montalte, little inclined to repose, rose with the sun, and left the Abbey,
in hopes of meeting some returning messenger who might bring
intelligence of Edward Dorville. The grey horizon, not yet emancipated from the shades of departing night, seemed pregnant with
rain; but, as they advanced along the coast, the sun gently emerged
from beneath the clouds, shedding on all surrounding objects that
soft but animating tint so beautiful and picturesque, and the cool
breezes issuing from the ocean tempered the sultry heat of an
autumnal morn.

This part of the coast, remarkable for its extreme fertility, formed
a delightful contrast with the more northern shores, which partake
the sterility and barrenness usually produced by the neighbourhood of the sea.* The heart of Caroline beat with something like
hope; she knew not why, but an unusual gaiety had succeeded to
the long melancholy which had so long been the companion of her
thoughts: yet soft apprehension was mingled with it, and the novelty of the sensation surprised her.—Emily was delighted with her
cheerfulness, which, with the credulity of youth, she attributed to

the presentiment of some impending good fortune; and, invited by the bleating of flocks in a neighbouring pasture, and the lowing of the more distant herds, they entered an extensive plain, whose smooth and luxuriant verdure was alike grateful to the eye and feet; the fatigue which extreme uniformity gives the eye was relieved by clumps of various shrubs, scattered in every direction, under whose shade the modest lamb reclined. The melodious notes of the shepherd's pipe filled the air, and completed the harmony of the scene: the plain was bounded by a wood of considerable extent, whose variegated foliage, rich with innumerable shades of green, attracted the admiration of our fair wanderers, and they directed their steps to its entrance, where a group of children were at play; they soon discovered several cottages, from whence these issued. A shepherd, tending his milk-white flock, saluted them with a degree of urbanity peculiar to that polished people. Emily returned his civility, and made some enquiries respecting his family and condition.

"I have three children, Madam," said he, "whom you see near yonder sheepcot. Heaven has given them the blessing of health, and me strength to work and support them. My wife spins, and takes care of our cottage; she would be charmed if such ladies would accept some trifling refreshment. Antonia," said he, calling to his wife, "these ladies will honour our little cot with their presence."

Antonia instantly appeared; her ruddy cheeks and dark eyes proclaimed her one of the beauties of the sylvan scene: her only ornament was a knot of pink ribbons, which decorated a neat straw hat; a long jacket, and clean white apron completed her attire, and made her a pattern of rural elegance. She welcomed her guests with a modest curtsey, and a blush that gave a deeper tint to the glow on her cheek. Emily was charmed with her appearance, and yet more with the neatness that distinguished the interior of the cot: the floor was of brick; the table and chairs of dark brown wood, polished with such nice care, as gave them the brightness of a mirror; cleanliness in every shape was visible; a large bowl of cream, some rye cakes, and nuts gathered in the neighbouring woods, formed the rural feast which Antonia gracefully spread before her fair guests. The children came running to gaze on the strangers, for so unfrequented was this delightful abode, that it was almost a wonder to see any but the rustic tenants of the wood. Emily, after thanking Antonia for her kind hospitality, enquired if their little dwelling was not sometimes endangered by the violent storms so frequent there?

"The trees, Madam," said she, "protect us; but we often shelter the benighted traveller, and our humble roof but now received a stranger wrecked in the storm this week."

Her husband, who was entering as she spoke these words, gently reproved her, saying,—

"Antonia, let us never boast such deeds as these: if Heaven permits us to succour our fellow-creatures, let us be grateful for the opportunity, and attribute the good to Him, and not to ourselves."

Caroline and Emily, who were more interested in this subject than the good people were aware of, pressed them to explain the circumstance to which Antonia alluded; after much importunity, Bazil consented.

"'Twas a sorry night," said he; "the tempest, so violent, shook yon Abbey, and destroyed some of the old building. I had strayed from home, and taken refuge, with my flock, in a cavern in yon rock (pointing towards the coast). My comrade Pedro was at no great distance. I had heard signals of distress fired from some vessel, but the rocks prevented my seeing it split. However, I had no doubt some terrible accident would happen; when, all of a sudden, I heard a great noise like something falling. I looked towards the place, and saw a board with a man clinging to it; and just then a wave carried it floating into the sea. I called to my comrade. 'Pedro,' says I, 'hast a mind, friend, to help a poor sufferer?' 'God be praised!' said he, 'Pedro was never known to flinch: what's the business, honest Bazil?' So I shewed him the raft, and said, if we could pull it to shore whilst there was a moment's calm, we might save the man; so to work we went: I must own I was terrified, the sea looked so tremendous; but Pedro, God bless him! never thought of danger when he could serve a fellow-creature; so he fairly leaped into the water, and got hold of a piece of rope tied to the board, and then we both pulled till it came on shore; a moment longer, and it had been too late, for the sea got so boisterous, that we must have been lost ourselves. We soon brought the man to the cavern, but he seemed dead; and it was so dark, I could hardly see, so we stayed till the storm abated, and then, putting him on our shoulders, brought him here. 'Wife,' says I, 'we have brought you a prize; here's a man, child, but whether dead or living we must find out;' so Antonia lighted a fire of brush wood, and wrapped him in a blanket, and he soon came to life; and when he had been put to bed, why next day he was quite brisk, and as comely a youth for a sea-farer as you shall see."

Caroline listened attentively.

"Is he still here?" enquired she.

"He's but now gone," replied Bazil: "he seemed somewhat impatient to see his friends, and said he should find a bride as fair as my Antonia when he got home; and he talked so about gratitude, and being obliged to me, and all that, and God knows, I only did my duty; and he promised to return, and, in spite of all I could say, would talk of paying; and, to be sure, he had only a shirt on, and a round piece of gold about his neck, and he would give me this piece of gold. 'Take it, honest friend,' says he, 'and when I come back, you shall give it me again.'—I would fain have persuaded him to keep it, as he might want money before he reached his friends; but he said no; God had been his best friend, and would be still; so he gave it to little Margery, and told her to keep it for his sake, till he brought her something better."

Emily, more than ever interested, and seeing her friend much agitated, requested to see what he had left.

"Go, Margery," said Antonia, "shew the lady your present."

Margery ran, and soon returned with great delight, bringing a little red case.

Emily opened it, and found within a circle of gold, which had been the setting of a miniature, but the painting was taken out; on the back it had the initials C. M. and lower down E. D.

Caroline uttered an exclamation of delight when she recognised what had contained her portrait when Dorville left France.

She had been prepared for this adventure: something like prognostic* conducted her to the cottage, and her surprise at this developement, was, therefore, less evident than her extreme joy, to which, however, she seemed fearful of yielding, as she had been once disappointed.

Antonia seemed surprised at her emotions; but, when informed of the cause, almost wept for joy. She could give no account of the road he had taken; but there was no doubt of his safety; Caroline, certain he would apply to Madame de Meronville, who was informed of her abode, doubted not of seeing him in a few days. The tear trembled in the eye of Emily. She proposed returning to the Abbey; and, after amply rewarding the good cottagers, who had been the harbingers of such pleasing intelligence, they took leave, promising soon to return.

They were not long in reaching Montalte. Madame de Clarival had just entered the breakfast-room, and was waiting their arrival. As they passed the windows, the pleasure beaming from their countenances proclaimed some fortunate event. Emily eagerly related the adventure of the cottage, and the consequent discovery they had made;—the Countess heard the detail with real and heartfelt satisfaction; she loved Caroline with maternal tenderness, and wished nothing more ardently than to see her happy. During their morning repast, nothing could be talked of but this interesting adventure; when it ended, Caroline, taking her long-neglected lyre, strung it to the softest notes of rapture; Emily accompanied it with her voice. Directing her eye towards a woody enclosure to the east of the Abbey, she observed a man listening, in mute attention, to the gentle melody that issued from the window. Finding himself observed, he continued to advance, and she lost sight of him as he entered a winding path which led to the offices. In a few moments, the door of the saloon opened, and a servant informed the Countess a stranger, escaped from the wreck a few preceding evenings, requested to see her, as he was unable to pursue his journey to the south, where his friends resided, not having succeeded in saving any part of his property, though his life was miraculously preserved; he added, that his design was only to procure the loan of a trifle, which should be repaid as soon as he reached Paris.—Madame de Clarival ordered him to be immediately admitted. The young friends were so attentive to their own occupation, that they did not hear the message, nor perceive that any person entered the saloon. A most uncouth figure soon appeared,—a remarkably tall man, with a large blue *surtout*,* a flapped hat, and shoes infinitely the worse for wear;—his address, however, was the direct contrast to his appearance; he bowed respectfully to the Countess, and declared the occasion of his intrusion in a few words, but in an elevated tone of voice, which withdrew the attention of the female musicians from their own employment, to fix it on the speaker. Caroline turned her head;—she caught his eye,—a moment's suspense succeeded,—the next he was at her feet; it was Edward Dorville. His surprise at finding her there is not to be described; a mixture of doubts, fears, and hopes crowded on his mind, and deprived him of power to express them. A moment of eloquent silence decided it; the unfeigned rapture her artless countenance displayed soon chased apprehension from his heaving breast; he pressed her to his heart,—

"And is it, indeed, my beloved Caroline? and is she still faithful to her long lost lover? Does relenting fate at length restore you to my arms?"

"Yes, Edward," said the blushing Caroline, "it is, indeed, herself; and Oh, what has she suffered by your long, long absence!"

Dorville now addressed himself in the language of apology to the Countess, saying, his extreme amazement at meeting Caroline so unexpectedly, when he thought her at some hundred leagues' distance, had made him, for the moment, forget the respect due to her.

The Countess answered with a smile,—

"Though you are unacquainted with us, allow me to assure you you are not a stranger here; on the contrary, you may consider all present as your friends: Caroline shares my affection with an only child, and we have all long participated in her anxiety for your return."

Dorville bowed his thanks.

The Countess gave orders that an apartment should be prepared for him, and apparel more suitable to his condition.

"I make no apology," said he, "for my uncourtly garb, for which I am indebted to some good cottagers; I am sufficiently happy in being restored to you with life. One thing only I have preserved," continued he, drawing from his bosom the portrait he had detached from its enclosure when he left the cottage; "this has never forsaken me; it has been my faithful friend and companion in every danger since I left my native land."

Caroline could only look her gratitude as he retired to exchange his rustic habit for that provided by order of the Countess. Emily embraced her friend with the sincerest congratulations, and, when Dorville returned, could not sufficiently admire his manly features, and graceful deportment. He had resided five years in Africa, and he was now eight-and-twenty years of age: the effect of a hot climate had given a dark hue to his complexion, almost resembling that of the dusky natives, but it accorded so well with his black eyes and arched brows, that it was rather an advantage to him. The delicate features of Caroline had greatly improved since he saw her; though ill health had somewhat impaired the lustre of her azure eyes, it gave an interest to her countenance which fully compensated for that loss. Dorville gazed on her with silent rapture, nor was his admiration withheld from her fair friend, whose beauty far exceeded any thing he had seen since he left Europe. They informed him of the safety of Marsillac, about whom he expressed much concern, and of the intelligence they had received at the cottage where he had been sheltered, which made his arrival an expected event. He spoke in terms of infinite gratitude of the hospitality he had met with from its worthy inhabitants, and hoped he should not be denied the happiness of rewarding their unbidden kindness: "though," added he, "in the course of my desultory rambles I have not met in low or elevated stations a family whose every want seems so truly adapted to their possessions. An increase of wealth might, perhaps, bring with it a diminution of happiness by promoting factitious wants; but they have children, whom, I hope, it may one day be in my power to provide for; and the best and truest remuneration they can receive is, I doubt not, already their's,—that of the heart, which, by its suffrage, never fails to reward every good action."

Madame de Clarival assured him they should not be forgotten, and, in the meantime, hoped he would give them some account of his adventures, and the accidents which had detained him so long on a foreign shore. Caroline seconded this request, and he did not hesitate to comply. His narrative will be the subject of the following chapter.

CHAP. II.

"To sailors then, who, wand'ring o'er the main,
"Have long explor'd some distant coast in vain,
"In seas unknown, and foreign regions lost,
"By stormy winds and faithless billows tost:
"If chance, at length, th' expected land appear,
"With joyful shouts they hail it from afar;
"They point with rapture to the wished-for shore,
"And dream of fortune, toils, and fears no more."

"My adventures, though distressful," said Dorville, "are but little connected with the marvellous and extraordinary circumstances that are usually appendant to the traveller's narrative; and, as I am addressing myself to friends who, I hope, will feel equal interest in the most simple events, as in the most surprising, I shall confine myself to unadorned fact, reserving all embellishments for a period when I may endeavour to attract the interest of a credulous public.

"The success of the first years of my absence you are already acquainted with; my fortune was considerably increased, and I hoped to return to Europe with such a competence as should ensure our future comforts. Marsillac and I had laboured conjointly; we were strictly united by congeniality of sentiments and pursuits; and as many persons, engaged in the same trade as ourselves, were such as had quitted their country for deeds of, at least, a doubtful cast, we did not care to form any connection with persons whose reputation was suspicious.

"Two nights previous to our intended embarkation, having, during the day, undergone much fatigue in hastening the preparations, the sultry heat of the climate had completely overcome our strength, and we stretched our weary limbs on the beach, and soon fell into a sound slumber. The night was far advanced; the sun had sunk in the west, and, long ere we awoke, every surrounding object was lost in impenetrable darkness. Roused by an uncommon sort of motion that I could not account for, I began to rub my eyes, and look around; but my astonishment was not small, when I discovered myself in a sort of canoe, so light that it cut the waves with incredible rapidity. Conceiving it to be the effect of a dream, I called aloud to Marsillac, who still slept profoundly, but was awakened by my voice; he started, and began also to enquire by what strange accident we were exposed on the wide ocean? Convinced by this of the identity of my recollection, I became greatly alarmed, supposing we had fallen into the hands of pirates. The moon was hid behind a cloud, but from the light reflected from the transparent sea, we could distinguish five or six persons, and were afraid to communicate our mutual suspicions, lest any person on board should understand us. Soon, however, the moon, emerging from concealment, threw its silver beams on our vessel, and we distinctly saw six men arrayed in habits resembling those of the Asiatics, that is, in tunics, and something like turbans round their heads, with plumes of various colours;—they remained invariably silent, and scarcely betrayed life by a single gesture.

"We soon discerned, at no great distance, a vessel approaching, of far greater magnitude than our own; and Marsillac and myself, who now, for the first time, ventured to express our fears, determined to hail her, not doubting but she was the property of some European, who would rescue us from these lawless depredators. The profound silence they observed made us conclude they apprehended what we so earnestly desired, and this confirmed us in our design of imploring their assistance.—We were ignorant of the vast extent of sea we traversed in a few hours; indeed, the extreme rapidity with which this little vessel scudded, prevented our forming probable conjectures by comparison with any former voyage. To our great astonishment, twilight already glimmered in the east, and we began to fear we had passed the limits of European traders; the vessel, however, advanced, and, on a sudden, our companions cast forth such shouts as seemed to rend the air, while they struck consternation to our hearts, and deprived us of all remaining hope. We were rowed alongside the large ship, and a man, who seemed the commander, addressing us in the Arabic dialect, which we perfectly understood, ordered us to ascend a ladder they had let down for that purpose. We looked at one another in silent dismay, but the vast expanse that surrounded us, which seemed immeasurable, as we could not, on any side, descry land, offered no prospect of escape; obedience was, therefore, the effect of necessity. We soon discovered that we were captured by an Algerine corsair,* with whom it was usual to make descents by night, and carry off any booty they could catch. From their signals, we concluded they were perfectly satisfied with the prize this attempt had procured. Having taken on board all our boat companions, who, we observed, were armed with scimeters and cross-bows, doubtless to defend themselves in case of any resistance, they secured us in the hold, and then continued their voyage. So surprising was the whole of this adventure, that we were still half persuaded it was the mere illusion of fancy; but the fetters applied to our arms and legs convinced us more of the reality of the circumstance than we could have wished.

"After we were left alone, we continued a few moments silent. At length, Marsillac, as though awakened from a dream, cried, 'By Heavens, Dorville, we have made but a sorry business of it!'—'In good truth,' said I, 'we shall remember sleeping on the beach.'—'Could I,' resumed Marsillac, 'form any conjecture as to the part of the country to which they are conveying us, I should have no doubt of escaping when once we reach land; but dangers surround us every where, for all this part of the globe is inhabited by savage nations, more terrible even than the Algerines.'—We then agreed that it would be more politic to affect compliance at first, that they might place more dependance on us, and, perhaps, furnish us with some opportunity of escaping.

"The time seemed long ere we landed. At length, however, we drew near the shore, and were ordered to disembark. Our conductors were men of an unusual height, swarthy complexions, and long dark whiskers, which gave them a most ferocious appearance; their habits were splendid, and we had no doubt they held the first rank amongst their countrymen, for those who crowded to gaze on us were hardly covered, and no habitations appeared but huts scattered in all directions over a plain of boundless extent. We travelled on foot towards the interior of the country. Our guards were mounted on camels; for several days we were not suffered to take more than the repose of an hour, and even pursued our route with great celerity by night, which prevented our marking the road;—at last we stopped in the suburb of a great city, and were exposed, with three other white men, to sale: fortunately we both fell to the lot of the same purchaser, who immediately conveyed us to his abode, highly satisfied with his bargain. The employment allotted to us was that of cultivating a large garden adjoining the house; we were yoked, and in that condition lashed with whips by a Mahometan slave, to quicken our proceedings, which were much impeded by being fastened together:—at night we were secured in a kind of subterraneous vault, which received air only from an aperture in the roof.

"My friend and I now began seriously to despond, our thoughts ever running to Europe, and those scenes of social happiness to which we were hastening when this cruel adventure had ruined our hopes; and the improbability of ever escaping reduced us to despair. The pains of perpetual servitude were considerably increased by the impossibility of sending any communication to Europe, or informing our friends of our cruel destiny. I could not but hope my Caroline would regret her absent lover; and yet to inflict on her gentle bosom the pangs of suspense tortured my inmost soul.

"Two months had now elapsed, and no ray of hope illumined the dark prospect before us, or offered its aid to sooth the rigours of absolute slavery. One day we observed, by the increasing rays of the sun which streamed through the aperture in our cell, that Benazer (so was our jailer called), had let pass the usual hour of bringing our food, which he generally did at daybreak, and then conducted us to the garden where we worked. We could not devise any reason for this neglect; as there was no probability of our being left to perish in this dungeon, for the interest of our purchaser was too much concerned in preserving our existence.

Whilst we were ruminating on this extraordinary circumstance, we heard a great bustle over our heads, and concluded some uncommon event had taken place. Divided between hope and fear, we thought it not impossible that some revolution had happened, which is not unfrequently the case amongst the savage nations, and which might procure our emancipation. Our conjectures on this subject were interrupted by the unbolting of the door, and Benazer's grim black visage appeared. He brought our usual allowance of raw corn and water; and whilst, to satisfy the cravings of nature, we eagerly devoured what we should have blushed to set before hogs in Europe, he informed us his master, the Assaff Assuddin Melachnasser, was that day celebrating his nuptials with the daughter of a neighbouring Assaff, and that, in consequence, all the black slaves were exempted from their daily toils. Whilst he spoke, he lashed his whip over our heads, ordering us to end our meal as soon as possible, that he might conduct us to our labour, and then enjoy one day of freedom. When we had finished, he drove us out, and, with uncommon energy, applied the whip, doubtless to denote his joy, and singing the whole way. Cruelty and the abuse of power are inherent in the breast of man. This vile slave, subordinate himself to some rigid taskmaster, who exercised every species of inhumanity on him, avenged his sufferings on us, and seemed happy in his wretched state of servitude, since it enabled him to gratify his propensity to cruelty on two helpless human beings. He informed us, when he retired, that he should not return till night, and fortunately forgot, in his great joy, that we were not, as usual, tied together;—we easily perceived the advantage of this omission, and began to hope we might escape, as the whole people were engaged in the nuptial festivities. The height, however, of the walls which surrounded us, seemed to oppose an invincible barrier to our wishes; but what difficulties will not despair, the love of liberty, and sense of oppression surmount! I climbed a large tree, very common in this country, and called a guava, and then jumped on the wall, which was above two feet in thickness. Just as Marsillac was preparing to follow me, I observed a cavalcade approaching, our master, the Assaff Assuddin in the midst, and the dreaded Benazer in the crowd following. I called to my friend to desist, and, terrified beyond expression, as I knew the consequences of detection would be fatal, I stretched myself on the wall, and, from its extreme height, escaped notice. I had not, however, much time to congratulate myself, for at that moment a key was applied to the door, and the Assaff entered! Surprised to see Marsillac alone, who affected to be busily employed, he enquired for me. My friend answered, that Benazer had allotted me another employment that day; and, to lull suspicion, he pretended to complain of our separation, as an additional hardship;— the Assaff, to my astonishment, seemed satisfied with this reply, and left the garden.—No time was now to be lost; he would, there was no doubt, soon discover the deception, and to deliberate was ruin. All was profoundly quiet beneath; Marsillac climbed the guava, bringing with him the rope with which Benazer usually confined us, and which might facilitate our descent. When I looked at the perpendicular height of the wall, my heart sunk, for to escape seemed impracticable; yet to descend to the garden was now no less difficult: I therefore paused no longer, but giving one end of the rope to my friend, he held it while I reached the ground; he then fastened it to the wall, and followed me. Here then we were, but our prospects were far from enviable;—entirely ignorant of the country, and the most likely method to elude pursuit, we struck into a forest that lay before us, and, when we had reached the thickest part, sat down to deliberate on the next step to be taken. To reach the coast appeared impossible, as we must have passed through innumerable hordes of savages, who would all impede our progress, besides that we were wholly at a loss to conjecture what part of the country we were now in;—we had no means of procuring sustenance, and as wild beasts of every kind tenanted the woods, destruction, in all shapes, presented itself to our view. As all these circumstances crowded on our imagination, we began to regret having quitted our former confinement, the horrors of which seemed light compared with our present situation. As some step must, however, be taken, we continued advancing in the woods, where no human track appeared; the branches of trees were so entwined and interwoven, that with difficulty we could sufficiently disentangle them to procure a passage through the enclosure. This circumstance, however, promised us safety while we continued there, though every leaf that moved in the breeze made us start, and fancy the hated form of Benazer;—on a sudden we saw a human figure, apparently flying at our approach; it flitted before us with uncommon swiftness. No less terrified ourselves, we made no effort to arrest its flight, but lay still to avoid suspicion, concluding it to belong to some of the savage tribes. Continuing through innumerable windings of this woody labyrinth, we perceived an aperture at no great distance, which seemed the mouth of a cave. We now hesitated whether to explore its recesses, or avoid it, as the probable haunt of an enemy. Necessity prompted us to court danger;—we descended some steps, evidently the work of man; all was darkness, and still no human vestige appeared. At length, light penetrating through some inlet we could not perceive, discovered to us an abode, which had nothing barbarous in its construction; a prayer-book, a crucifix, and a cruse* of water were placed on a table apparently hewn in the rock; we looked round, and saw, in a more remote recess, a lamp burning, a kind of couch, some fire-arms, and every appearance of a human abode. While, lost in astonishment, we were contemplating this phenomenon, footsteps descended the stairs by which we had entered, and echoed through the windings of this vaulted recess. Concealment was now impossible, and we prepared to meet danger in any shape. The solitary tenant from the wood soon approached, and, uttering an exclamation in our native language, shrieked horribly, and fled. Convinced we had nothing to fear, our efforts were bent to recal the poor wanderer, whom we had driven from his melancholy retreat; the sound of our voices, and the language we spoke, dissipated his alarms, and he returned.

'Strangers,' said he, 'what dark design has led you to this isolated retreat? Are you come to take the sad remains of life, or, like me, the children of adversity, do you seek concealment here?'

'Pardon me, father,' said I, 'we meant not to intrude; chance directed our steps hither, as we fled from savage masters; we are, indeed, the sport of cruel Fortune, and wish only to reach the coast, where, probably, we may find an opportunity of regaining Europe.'

'Hope it not!' replied the recluse; 'the far distant ocean is intercepted by whole nations of hostile negroes, whose hate to white men will not permit your return. Unhappy strangers, if you have left wives, mothers, sisters, or children to deplore your loss——never must you see them more! Never shall the social blaze be kindled at your approach; never shall the smile of love greet your wished return; fatherless are your babes; your widowed brides shall weep in vain! Alas, poor strangers!'——

"The venerable old man dropped a tear as he spoke; there was a benignity in his aged countenance that might impress the callous heart, and move the savage breast to pity; his silver locks and wrinkled brow proclaimed the ravages of care,—its furrows marked his woe-worn cheek.

'Tell us, good old man,' said I, 'what strange event has placed you in this impenetrable solitude; your speech and manner bespeak not a native of the woods; you are not by birth a stranger to the haunts of man.'

"He raised his humid eyes to heaven.—'For twelve long years,' said he, 'I have inhabited this lone recess, nor has it in that time ever been visited by a human being; deprived, by the relentless stroke of death, of the only tie that united me to a world of misery, I live here, sequestered alike from the joys and griefs of man. Strangers, you seem not uncourteous; pardon these unbidden tears—they flow from recollections of scenes long, long past; the sight of you has rekindled those feelings I thought dead; stagnant indeed they were; at sight of you they flow with native warmth.'

"I was so moved at the impressive tone with which he spoke these words, and so affected with their import, that my tears fell with his; he seized my hand.—'What, have I made you weep?' exclaimed he. 'Alas! this aching heart has long forgot the tear of sympathy!'— Then seeming to recollect himself, he continued, 'I have lived so much alone, I am become an egotist. Pardon my neglect; the few refreshments my solitude can offer are your own; you seem fatigued; when you have eaten and drank, my couch invites you to repose; security, at least, you will here find.'

"We thanked the good old man for his hospitality, and partook his frugal meal; it consisted of fruit, goat's milk, and wild corn.

'Do not spare it,' said he, 'the wood supplies me abundantly with provisions. Sometimes,' added he, pointing to his gun, 'I do with that obtain a change of meal, but, for many years, I have not used it; I love not to make war on helpless animals, who are my only companions; they here enjoy that liberty the neighbourhood of man curtails; their early notes chase sleep from my pillow, and I listen in rapture to their gentle melody.'

"Whilst we were devouring the delicious fruit he set before us, he was busied in preparing beds, though with many apologies for their mediocrity.

'Father,' said I, 'it is long since we knew the comfort of repose; cold stones have been our beds, and here is luxury indeed.'

"He smiled.—'Then sleep, gentle strangers,' he said; 'and when the morning sun shall gild the atmosphere, Theodore Velasquez must haste to his daily labour. You will then witness his mode of life; he offers you to share his humble cell, but should you resolve to brave the dangers that await your farther progress, he has nothing to bestow but his blessing, and the prayers of a recluse.'

"So saying, he retired to the inmost cave. Marsillac and I sought repose, which, though somewhat disturbed by the desultory events of the day, was more delightful than any we had experienced for months.

"In the morning we arose enlivened and invigorated. The advice Theodore had given us, to remain in the cavern, was, we were aware, most prudent, and least exposed to Fortune's vicissitudes; but to live in solitude and supine security was not consonant to our wishes, for the most sequestered spot cannot exclude past reminiscences—recollection will obtrude in deserts. To one who, like Velasquez, had lost his only remaining tie, the world could offer no allurement; but we were more fortunate;—the reward our labours were to meet in Europe was an incentive to the wildest temerity; dreadful must those dangers be, the remembrance of which a smile from Caroline could not obliterate."

Caroline smiled.

Madame de Clarival said "she was sorry to interrupt a narrative which awakened so entirely the interest of his auditors, but they had been summoned to dinner some time, and must, therefore, defer the pleasure of hearing the remainder."

During the repast, Dorville charmed the Countess by his animated and pleasing deportment.

Caroline, adorned with the blush of innocence and happiness, looked all that fancy can paint. Emily alone was pensive. Her fears with respect to her friend being now subsided, she returned to the contemplation of her own less fortunate situation. No pleasing retrospect or joyful future presented itself to her imagination. Lusignan was still a prisoner, and it was she who deprived him of liberty: the Duchess, his mother, had given her hopes, but her long subsequent silence made these appear futile. When alone, she frequently pondered on this circumstance, but of late she had been so employed in exertions to keep up the drooping spirits of Caroline, that self had been wholly forgotten. The happiness now displayed by her and Dorville made Lusignan's melancholy contrast more visible;—in vain she endeavoured to seem cheerful like them; in vain she sought to conceal her emotion;—her countenance, the true index of her mind, betrayed every idea; the tears which stole down her cheeks were carefully suppressed, yet frequently returned; and, finding herself unequal to the task of concealing them, she, early in the evening, complained of a headach, and withdrew to her apartment. A flood of tears there came to her relief.—"Lusignan, Lusignan," thought she, "can you pardon, and even love the destroyer of your peace and happiness? Could I, by devoting every future hour of my life to your comfort, testify my gratitude, how gladly would I do it! but relentless fate has doomed us both to misery, which shall end but with our days!" She threw herself on the bed, and lay in agony inexpressible; she thought her present feelings foreboded some approaching evil; by degrees she reasoned herself into composure. Sleep, which flies only from the pillow of guilt, soon brought relief,—she sunk in sweet oblivion of care.

CHAP. III

"Court not the luxury of tender thought,
"Nor deem it impious to forget those pains
"Which hurt the living, nought avail the dead!
"Go, soft enthusiast, quit the cypress grove,
"Nor to the riv'let's lonely moanings tune
"Your sad complaint! Go seek the cheerful haunts
"Of men, and mingle with the busy crowd."

The sun no sooner illumined the heavenly concave, and shed its genial influence on the world below, than Emily was awakened by a gentle tap at her chamber door; it was Caroline, who proposed to her a ramble to the cottage, which she hoped might assist in dispelling the gloom that, in spite of her efforts, had not escaped the affectionate eye of her friend. Emily hastily arose to accompany her.

There is something reviving in the breath of early morn,—something in animated nature that imperceptibly glides to our heart, and raises our drooping spirits. Emily acknowledged their effects; she felt her despondency wear off as she gazed with delight on scenes which, though familiar to her view, never wearied, but each day seemed yet new; the lark and linnet, with their gentle notes, seemed thanking the Creator for the comforts they enjoyed.

"These, Almighty God!" she secretly said, "are the works of thy hand! All these blessings thou hast made for man; and shall he, ungrateful, murmur if, amid so many sweets,—if amid the many roses that adorn his path, a thorn is sometimes planted?"

They soon reached the cottage, where they found a crowd of villagers assembled, who were decorating the rural cot for an approaching festival: Antonia's sister was, in a few days, to bless the arms of a neighbouring shepherd, and the day was to be spent in Bazil's modest dwelling. Emily determined to contribute to their delight by furnishing the children with bridal habits; she did not, however, mention her design, but fearful, by her presence, of imposing restraint on the happy group, she soon left them. Dorville was enraptured with this picture of genuine happiness; to them he owed his, and their's was not a little increased by the recollection. Nature had implanted in their untutored minds such sentiments of true benevolence and humanity, as would do honour to the most elevated station.*

Scarcely had our young friends reached the Abbey, when Emily, looking from a balcony on the enamelled lawn beneath, discovered an equestrian advancing towards the house. Her heart beat; she looked, doubted, hoped, feared, and recognised the well-known figure of Lusignan. She flew to meet him. As she crossed the lawn, her white robes waved in the breeze, her auburn tresses flowed in luxuriant ringlets over her fine-formed shoulders; she looked a sylph descended from the world above. Lusignan could not mistake her; never was joy more complete than their's at this happy moment;—it was long since they parted, and feared never to meet more; the various events which had progressively intervened confirmed this apprehension, but one hour of virtuous ecstasy repaid an age of sorrow. A thousand questions each uttered; but, occupied only with each other, waited no reply. As they entered the saloon, an exclamation of joy escaped from the Countess, and she introduced the stranger to the wondering Caroline, who had never seen him. A susceptible heart will be at no loss to conceive the happiness of all parties at this unexpected meeting. A mind which expands to the impressions of love, will feel their raptures;—on the child of insensibility description were spent in vain.

Lusignan had received letters from his mother, which gave birth to the most sanguine hopes. He discovered, while conversing with his tenantry, that Montalte was distant only eight leagues from the Castle, and, as he had leave to quit it during the day, he set out early for the Abbey. A happier circle could not be found than that now assembled in the saloon;—nothing but perpetuity was wanting to complete it; but the rapid hours revolved unconscious, and, though he protracted his departure till the latest moment, the approach of evening compelled him to return before he could conceive the sun had run its midway course. He promised, however, to visit the Abbey on the day appointed for the village wedding, fearful to renew his happiness more frequently, lest it should be suspected, and counteract his father's lately acquired moderation. Emily saw him depart with extreme regret; but the hopes he left with her supplied his absence, and she looked forward with renovated confidence to the future. Dorville was now requested to resume his narrative, which had been delayed by such pleasing interruptions; and, happy in the entertainment it afforded, he thus continued:—

"Though Marsillac and myself determined not to remain long in the cavern, we judged it prudent to seclude ourselves there for a few days, while the search after us would probably continue, and we might hope, by this means, to escape the vigilance of Benazer, and his master, the Assaff Assuddin Melachnasser.

"Velasquez, who had been abroad some time, soon returned with a supply of fruit and corn; he milked a goat caught in the woods, which he had tamed, and now loved with the tenderest affection; the beast seemed sensible of his regard, and actuated by more than an instinctive principle of attachment to her protector. I related to Velasquez the accident which had conducted us to his retreat; he appeared concerned at our sufferings.

'My children,' said he, 'the lot of man is wretched; various are the ills he is doomed to suffer. In the wide world danger attends his steps. In this seclusion neither the villany of man, nor the shafts of adverse fate, can penetrate. Live with me; renounce your intention of revisiting Europe: pleasure, it is true, comes not here, but evil greatly preponderates in the scale of life, and you will gain more than can be lost.'

'Father,' replied Marsillac, 'misfortune has made you a misanthropist; the world has many joys. Have social comforts no power to lure you from this sad abode?'

'Social comforts!' said the recluse, with energy; 'ah, name them not! Once they were mine; once this heart expanded to love; once——but hush! recollection is maddening! be still, thou busy flutterer! Oh Maria!'—After remaining some moments absorbed in grief, Velasquez continued;—'Never shall the sad relation of that fatal event, which placed me here, pass these lips; they are no more who might have recalled me to a world I hate; then name it not; nor seek to change a resolution irrevocable as the stroke that made it! These woods, that have preserved my miserable existence, shall receive my bones.'

'Venerable old man,' said I, 'I would not torment you, but methinks the solitude in which you live nourishes your grief; society, by diverting your thoughts from the melancholy subject of your afflictions, would lessen their poignancy.'

"He forced a smile on his countenance; it was rather the smile of despair than conviction.—'That melancholy I love,' said he; 'yes, I cherish it at my heart; 'tis the first great good,—it is a vital principle; it alone animates me, and my heart shall cease to beat, ere it shall cease to grieve. Should I revisit the cheerful haunts of man, how should I be there received? No sympathetic friend to share my woes, no gentle smile to sooth affliction's sting! contempt would mingle in the pity granted by the aged; the young would consider me as an object of ridicule! The wide universe contains not a friend to Theodore Velasquez!'

"Finding argument fruitless, I quitted a subject that seemed so afflictive to the venerable recluse. He tried, in his turn, to prevail on us to remain with him, by representing the real danger that awaited our egress from the forest. Of this we were truly sensible; but no consideration could induce us to resign the hope of returning to Europe. Finding our resolution invincible, the old man offered us his gun, and the small remains of powder and shot he possessed; for, as the Africans were entirely unacquainted with the use of fire-arms, he had experienced that nothing to them was so great an object of terror; and he concluded, that if any thing could protect us against their attacks, it was this. We accepted the offer with grateful acknowledgements; but, recollecting that we were, perhaps, depriv-ing him of his only means of defence, in case his retreat should be discovered, we retracted our assent, and begged him to preserve it for his own use.

'On my own account,' said he, 'I have no fears. When first I became an inhabitant of this cave, I found it necessary to terrify the savages by firing upon them, and they soon were persuaded that some supernatural power tenanted the wood; to this conceit I attri-bute the security I have enjoyed. I have lived so long unmolested, that I have no doubt the few remaining days allotted me by Provi-dence will pass without interruption; and death has no terrors for me, who long have loathed existence.'

"We continued three days in the cave. Velasquez had an hour-glass, which marked the lapse of time, and, at the close of each day, he cut a niche in the rock, by which he kept an accurate account of the revolving years. It was not without regret we bade him adieu, and consigned him a prey to his own reflections. A heart glowing with benevolence deserved a better fate; at the sad hour of depart-ing life, no friend shall be near to hear his parting sigh,—no sym-pathetic tear shall grace his cold remains. We were probably the last human beings whose breasts would heave with sorrow at his melancholy fate."

Caroline, at this period of the narrative, could no longer restrain the effusions of sorrow occasioned by the grief of the poor recluse; she enquired anxiously if they had really abandoned him to distrac-tion?

"We had no alternative," replied Dorville, "since no arguments could prevail on him to accompany us; and, indeed, we could only ask him to share dangers whose issue was very uncertain, and he had no motive for encountering them; we, therefore, reluctantly bade him farewel; he conducted us to the skirts of the forest, and, bestowing a parting blessing, instantly darted into the woods, and we lost sight of him for ever.

"The world was now before us, but where to direct our steps as most likely to lead to some wished-for port, we were profoundly ignorant. Keeping the road straight before us, we wandered for some time without meeting any person; but, shortly, we discovered an assemblage of huts, which proclaimed the abode of a savage tribe. We endeavoured to avoid observation, but in vain; for one of the swarthy natives discerning us, raised a howl, that soon brought a multitude of his countrymen about us; they issued from the huts like swarms of bees, and, as we perceived they were preparing their bows and arrows, we discharged the gun amongst them. At the sound of this they dispersed, even more suddenly than they had collected, struck with a dreadful panic: partly by signs, and partly by the Arabic language, which they understood, we enquired of them the road towards the coast, assuring them we should do them no hurt. The heart, uncontaminated with the depravity of polished society, and untaught by any laws but those of nature, yields without difficulty to the voice of kindness;—these poor people not only directed us to the ocean, but even offered us provisions and a night's lodging. We accepted the former, as it was not likely we should always encounter such *civilized Barbarians*,* but did not think it prudent to halt so near the habitation of Assuddin Melachnasser; we, therefore, pursued our journey.

"Night advancing, we dreaded the approach of wild beasts, with which we understood the country to abound, and from whose ferocity we had every thing to apprehend. Trusting this to the care of Providence, we took precautions only against human beings, one of us watching whilst the other slept. The night passed in perfect tranquillity; and, in the morning, we advanced pretty rapidly, surprised at the little interruption we experienced in a country tenanted by absolute savages;—we encountered, indeed, vast hordes, and they at first appeared hostile, but the gun, our never-failing resource, always reduced them to compliance. We had reason to remember Theodore Velasquez with infinite gratitude, for without him we must have perished,—in one instance particularly. Grown careless by security, we both slept profoundly, when some blacks, who had watched us, came up in swarms, and completely secured us. Our hands being tied, we could not employ the magic gun; but after they had all examined this object of terror, one ventured to take it up, when, being doubly loaded, it went off, and killed the offender on the spot;—this completed their dismay; they immediately released

us, and ran away with the most dismal cries. With concern, however, we found our powder and balls nearly all expended; for a considerable distance the report of the formidable weapon we carried
spread amongst these untutored people, and the sight of it procured
us respect, and provisions in abundance.—But, at length, we drew
near the shore; Europeans were known here, and white men held
in abhorrence; they had taught these harmless savages the barbarous policy of destroying their fellow-creatures; some of our most
polished nations have exercised such cruelties as the most ferocious
barbarians would blush to commit. The sea was covered with a multitude of canoes, and we determined, by night, to seize one of them,
and, under the guidance of supreme Power, to consign ourselves to
the wide ocean, hoping to meet some vessel which might convey us
to an European settlement:—but Fate had decreed otherwise; for,
whilst we were deliberating on a place of concealment, till darkness
should enable us to execute our design, a party of Moors fell upon
us, and, deprived of our only resource, the gun, all our toils began
afresh! I pass over slightly our adventures here. We were not carried
far from the coast; our employment consisted in searching with the
natives for gold dust, which, though it may appear a gentle task,
was by no means enviable, exposed as we were to the meridian rays
of an almost vertical sun; we were always guarded at night by two
men armed with bows and arrows, so that to escape was impossible.

"A female savage, who had often looked on us with an eye of
compassion bordering on Christian charity, one day took an opportunity of addressing us; and though we could but little comprehend
her words, by signs and gestures she conveyed her meaning, which
was, that she commiserated our sufferings, and wished to relieve
them.

"There is an herb, common in this part of Africa, whose effect
is so soporific, that, applying it to the nostrils of any person, will
throw them into a slumber so profound, that for some hours nothing can awaken them from the stupor it occasions.—Yaratilda, for
so we called this benevolent woman, made us, at length, comprehend that we should apply this to lull our guards. A considerable
time elapsed before we developed her design; but, at last, we learned
to converse in the Moorish tongue. Yaratilda, rejoiced at the progress we made, now offered us her brother to conduct a canoe, which
we might seize by night when the soporific herb should operate on

the senses of our guards. When our scheme was quite concerted, we fixed the day for its execution, and endeavoured to persuade Yaratilda to accompany us herself; she consented. The morning came. We observed a great stir amongst the natives; many appeared whom we had before seen. A considerable heap of wood was prepared in the midst of the plain; we thought ourselves betrayed, and, knowing that it was the custom here, concluded that we were to be destroyed by fire. In solemn consternation we awaited our sentence. Yaratilda and her brother were amongst the spectators who formed a large circle around the pile, which was set fire to; and then some negroes advanced, adorned with beads and plumes, their bodies and faces painted, and, singing aloud, they bore the victim in the midst. The crowd, for a time, obstructed our view; but our horror was indescribable when we beheld a native of Europe, bathed in blood, roasted at the fire they had kindled. The sight overcame my strength and fortitude; I sunk on the ground. This cruel scene was acted just before the hut in which we were confined. I even now shudder at the remembrance. We had happily escaped hitherto, but had no doubt, if the attempt we were about to make should be discovered, the same fate awaited us, and, sooner or later, we should be sacrificed to the carnivorous appetites of our sanguinary masters. Having satiated their hunger, the savages danced round the pile with every demonstration of joy, and the festivity ended but with the day. I trembled as the moment approached which must set us free, or devote us to destruction. Yaratilda had supplied us with the opiate; our guards usually slept towards morning, but the fatigues of this jovial day made them sink earlier to repose. We pretended ourselves to be lost in sleep, and, when we observed them snoring, dexterously applied the magic herb. Yaratilda soon appeared with her brother; they released us from confinement, and, in profound silence, led towards the shore. The sleeping Moors reposed in perfect security. A canoe was ready; Yaratilda attempted to enter it, but she had never been exposed on the vast Atlantic; her courage failed, and no persuasion could induce her to brave the dangers to which we were hastening; we had no time to lose; the sea was calm; we embarked;—poor Yaratilda beheld us from the shore as we rapidly glided away, never more to return. Her terror displayed itself in natural but expressive gestures. She threw her eyes to Heaven, imploring our safety of the planets she adored, unconscious that

an all-protecting, though invisible, Power reigned there.* We reluctantly left her, and kept our eyes fixed on the spot where she stood
long after the gloom of night concealed her from our view. Never
were the elements more profoundly calm; the pellucid waves that
sustained our little vessel resembled the smooth surface of a mirror;
the firmament above, resplendently decked with myriads of stars,
whose individual lustre almost eclipsed the mild effulgence of the
moon. We advanced with extreme celerity, our skilful guide dreading to be overtaken by his enraged countrymen. The day appeared,
and no pursuers had checked our rapid flight; but, just as Yaramanza
had assured us we had nothing to fear, a speck in the distant ocean,
magnifying by degrees, shewed us three canoes in full chase. In
vain we endeavoured to escape them. They had discovered us, and
plied their oars with such uncommon swiftness, that we resigned
ourselves for lost,—when, at this crisis of extreme danger and fate
inevitable, we descried an European vessel drawing near. Yaramanza
exerted himself to reach it. The Africans, no less alarmed than we
were delighted at this unhoped-for relief, tacked about, and left us
in security. The master of the vessel received us with all possible
humanity, and conveyed us to the next settlement. Yaramanza, to
whom we were indebted for our escape, remained with us. I found
my own countrymen had not treated me with much ceremony;
for the Captain, who had received my merchandise on board his
ship previous to my being captured by the Algerine, imagining I
should never return, had quietly possessed himself of my property,
and could not be prevailed on to give any account of its amount. I
would not, however, suffer this to detain me on such an inauspi-
cious shore, hoping that an appeal to the laws of my country would
be more efficacious than any arguments I could use. This attempt
I am determined to make; but should it prove equally ineffectual, a
sum I have realised, and confided to a Banker at Paris, will procure
us all the comforts of life; for its luxuries we must depend on love.
If mediocrity of fortune cannot alarm my Caroline, I have nothing
to fear. One thing gives me inexpressible concern: poor Yaramanza
perished by my side, vainly imploring that succour which was not
mine to bestow. I saw him sink in that dreadful storm from which
we so hardly escaped. The pleasure of shewing my gratitude would
have been to me one of the first joys of life; and of all the treasures
buried in that fathomless gulph, him only I regret."

Dorville's interesting narrative here concluded. His fair auditors almost lamented its ending so soon, though Caroline could
not refuse a sigh to many dangers he had encountered; but it was a
sigh not unmixed with pleasure, when she recollected that he had
happily escaped them all, and was now secure from future wrecks,
reposing in the bosom of love and friendship. The unexpected and
unhoped-for arrival of Lusignan had chased sorrow from the heart
of Emily. Madame de Clarival, as an affectionate mother, had felt
her affliction, and now participated her happiness. To all reflection
was a source of enjoyment, such as memory must ever prove to those
who can only look back on virtuous struggles. Then memory from
her exhaustless mines brings forth unnumbered treasures to cheer
the passing hour; time or place cannot interrupt her joys,—those
joys so truly our own, which can arrest the flight of that incompre-
hensible principle, thought, when, trembling, it darts into doubtful
futurity, and recalls it to past pleasures which nothing can destroy.

CHAP. IV.

"I envy none their pageantry and show,
"I envy none the gilding of their woe."*

The day approached when the village nuptials were to be celebrated
in Antonia's cot. Emily had ordered habits to be prepared for the
three children of Bazil; they were of dark brown, ornamented with
pink; she added to them knots of rose-coloured ribbons, to decorate
their favourite lambs, and a bridal robe for young Lauretta of spotless white; she carried these little presents herself, desirous to witness the joy such trifles confer on the youthful mind. As she drew
near the cottage, they flew to meet her, charmed with the caresses
she had before bestowed upon them; but when she displayed the
little treasure she had brought, they leaped with delight, their little
hearts swelling at the hope of outvying all their rural guests.

Whilst Emily was enjoying the rapture she had caused in their
innocent minds, a gentle tap at the door sued for admittance. Margery opened it, and, with smiles on her face, was beginning to relate
the joyful event that occasioned them, when, seeing a stranger, she
blushed and drooped her head. Not so our heroine. She rose to greet

the unexpected but welcome intruder by the name of Lusignan.

"My sweet Emily," said he, "will you pardon my impatience. The appointed day was far too distant for my wishes. I could not refuse myself that happiness it was in my power to obtain."

Emily's intelligent countenance expressed the pleasure his arrival communicated. One of the children sat on her knee; another reclined on it with a look of half envy at his sister's situation; the third, climbing on the back of the chair, played with her auburn tresses. Antonia just then entered. She thanked her, with a modest courtesy, for her kindness. Emily looked more interesting than Lusignan had ever seen her. He gazed with excess of rapture, repeating to himself,— "Oh, my father! could you witness such a scene, how would you rejoice to give your grateful son such a bride!"—They now left the cottage; the wedding was fixed for that day se'nnight; it was the birth-day of Caroline; Emily promised to join with her the rural dance, and then directed her steps towards the Abbey.

She leaned on the arm of the enraptured Lusignan. The fragrance of the morn, and the fresh breezes from the ocean, increased the bloom of youth on her lovely cheek, and gave an indescribable animation to her countenance. Innocence and pleasure were blended in the smile of love with which she looked on Lusignan. He shewed her a letter from the Duchess de Meronville; it contained but a few words.

"At length, my beloved child, fortune smiles on your wishes; and your happy mother is enabled to communicate intelligence that gives her no less pleasure than yourself; the Duke for some time has mentioned you in terms of affection he never used before; he has even praised your Emily; I have but a moment to write; but of this be assured,—that if no unforeseen reverse takes place, in less than a month I hope to bring Emily, who shall herself release you from confinement, certain as I am that liberty received from her will be of double value. Farewell; be prudent, and hope the best."

"I know not why," said Emily, when she had perused these lines, "I hardly dare to hope these appearances are real. Your father's extreme inveteracy, which so lately seemed inflexible, subsides without any new motive. You know my heart is your's, and I need not, therefore, blush to add, my happiness is no less implicated in his decision than your own; and this makes me fear to yield too readily to hopes whose fallacy would be doubly afflictive if too fondly cherished."

"Angelic Emily," replied the Marquis, "suppress, I conjure you, all doubts, nor seek to lessen my happiness by the intrusion of unfounded fears. Nothing but certainty would have induced my mother to write thus. She knows the energy of my feelings, and would not for worlds inflict a disappointment on them. My sanguine heart tells me all our sorrows are past. Henceforward shall the path of life be strewed with flowers; secure in your affections, each hour will glide in happiness almost celestial; devoted to your service, how enviable will be my lot! how enviable are my future prospects! Oh, my Emily, did you but feel as I do, no doubts could distress your anxious mind!"

Emily smiled.

"Doubt," said she, "Lusignan, is the companion of love; the more our hopes are fixed on one event, the more we dread its failure. Is your mother informed of your visits to the Abbey?"

"She is," rejoined Lusignan. "I could conceal nothing from so affectionate a parent."

"I had myself designed to have informed her," continued Emily; "yet I fear she will think me imprudent to admit them. Should they reach the Duke's ears, his displeasure may rekindle."

"No one knows," said Lusignan, "how my days are spent. Since I had leave to quit the Castle walls, I have usually left it early, and returned only with the evening shades."

As he spoke these words they reached Montalte. Caroline rallied her friend on the solitary ramble she had made.

"Had you," said she, "gone out with the person in whose company you are returned, I could have pardoned the treachery of memory which made you forget me; but as you really were alone, I should have been delighted to accompany you."

"I left the Abbey," replied Emily, "at so early an hour, that I was unwilling to disturb your slumbers, which have, indeed, been too frequently invaded of late; and the Marquis," continued she with a smile, "will acquit me of having made a rendezvous at the cottage."

The day was spent like the former one; and when Lusignan departed, Emily exacted a promise that he should not return till the wedding day. A tedious week intervened, but, as she insisted on the propriety of her request, he at last reluctantly consented.

The following morning the carriage was ordered at an early hour; the Countess and Emily took the road to Paris. She had not mentioned her intention to Caroline, nor invited her to join the party, but only said they should return in the evening, and, embracing her as she jumped into the carriage, hoped the day would not seem long in her absence. Caroline followed the vehicle with her eyes, but its rapid motion soon concealed it from her view; she was wholly at a loss to conjecture the meaning of this mysterious proceeding; Emily had hitherto communicated every thought soon as it had birth; her natural candour and ingenuousness rendered concealment impossible; now, for the first time, she had a secret from her friend. Caroline felt almost chagrined, but, having exhausted conjecture in vain, she concluded that night would bring a solution to her doubts, and, resuming her wonted gaiety, returned to Dorville. He took the opportunity of soliciting her consent to an immediate union.

"Fate," he said, "had opposed so many obstacles, that he feared, by delay, to give birth to new ones."

Caroline, though fully sensible of propriety, disdained the affectation of prudery. Her regard for Edward had never been concealed; she, therefore, assured him she should not seek to procrastinate their union, except till she had the concurrence of the Duchess, who had been to her more than a mother; and gratitude to Madame de Clarival made it also requisite that her consent should be asked; these, however, she doubted not to obtain immediately.

Hilarity was painted on the countenance of Emily when she returned; but she made no communication to her friend, who, surprised, and even hurt, yet knew too well the line that duty prescribed to let her curiosity appear, or betray her into an enquiry after what seemed intentionally withheld.

The visit to Paris was for several days repeated, and still its motive was enveloped in mystery. That it gave real satisfaction to Mademoiselle de Montalte was evident, and her affectionate attention to Caroline received daily some increase. Why then this concealment, was a question that Caroline frequently asked herself, but asked in vain.

At length the tedious week expired; the day arrived which gave birth to Caroline, and was to crown the felicity of the village lovers. Emily descended early to the garden, to select the choicest flowers, as a bouquet for her friend; myrtles, roses, jessamine, and a variety of evergreens, composed it; she entered her apartment ere the bright beams of the sun had chased sleep from her yet closed eyelids.

"My beloved Caroline," said Emily, "accept this offering of tender regard, and with it my best wishes for your every happiness. May each revolving year bring some increase of virtuous pleasure."

She put the bouquet into her hand, and with it a sealed paper. Caroline opened it; it contained a gift of a small estate in Switzerland, situated in the Valais. Caroline was so affected at this unexpected kindness, that she for a few moments gazed on her friend in silence, the big tear trembling on her eyelid.

Emily embraced her with the tenderest affection.

"Oh, my Emily," said Caroline, "you are too kind indeed! Take back this gift; your invaluable friendship supplies my best wishes; do not overwhelm me with benefactions I can never, never repay."

"Would you," replied Emily, "deprive me of so much pleasure? This day I consider as one of the happiest of my life. Wherefore, my Caroline, was wealth bestowed on us? And how can it in any other way contribute to our happiness, but as it enables us to increase the comforts of those we love?"

"This spot," said Caroline, "I have heard you mention with rapture, as the scene of your earliest enjoyment."

"Hear me," continued Mademoiselle de Montalte. "My possessions in France are so large, and so infinitely exceed my wants or wishes, that I would willingly relinquish them all, and retire with you to Ivy Cottage; but there are duties which superior rank imposes, and we should be criminal to neglect them. These duties compel us to reside on our estates, that we may know the real situation of our vassals and tenantry, and apply our superfluous wealth to the relief of their indigence. I have seen too much of the selfish policy of intendants and stewards ever to submit the welfare of so many human beings as are dependant on my estates to their rapacity; careful only to enrich themselves, and obliged to supply the inordinate extravagance of their masters, who lavish with criminal profusion in the great metropolis that affluence hard earned by the sweat of many a sufferer's brow, they deprive these poor peasants of the common comforts heaven designed for all, and, by their practice, imply the belief that a subordinate class of beings was created only to administer to the artificial cravings of intemperate luxury. In my latest hour such conduct would rise up in judgment against me. No, my friend, never could I bear the reproach of conscience for misusing the means Providence has so liberally bestowed on me to confer happiness on hundreds of my fellow creatures. Should I ever marry," added she, with a sigh, "I trust I shall find in the companion of my choice an assistant willing to second my views, and, by his activity and knowledge, better able to forward an undertaking arduous only in prospects."

"The rectitude of your benevolent heart, my Emily," rejoined Caroline, "is so well known to me, that I need no additional proof; but, while you are providing for the happiness of others, let not your own be neglected. There are times when you might rejoice to quit the splendour of your paternal domains, to enjoy in retirement the fruit of your labour, the reward of your generous exertions; such a retreat the Valais offers you."

"It is impossible, my dear friend," replied Emily, "to confer happiness, and not at the same time receive it. My motives are less disinterested than you suppose. Ivy Cottage I give you in trust. Some future time, when weary of the bustle of the great world, I shall for a time forsake it, I hope to retire to the bosom of friendship. The charms of the Valais will not be diminished by its amiable possessor. It is the spot where your Emily drew breath; the scene of my infant joys, my earliest and best delights; not a tree or shrub but is endeared by some sweet remembrance.* How grateful to our hearts is the recollection of those happy days, when the mind, undepraved by luxury, uncontaminated by the cares of a corrupt world, derived enjoyment from every source! Oh, my Caroline, it was here I first knew the tender caresses of paternal affection; and it was here I lost them for ever! My venerable and ever-to-be lamented parent here breathed his last!"

It was the first time Emily ventured to mention her departed father. Her tears flowed copiously. Caroline kissed them as they fell, and mingled her own with the pious sorrows of filial reminiscences. Emily smiled through her tears as she thus continued:—

"Let us avert all painful retrospects; this day, to love and friendship sacred, shall be devoted only to pleasure; Lusignan will soon be here; the village festival began with the dawn; we must, my Caroline, partake their rural felicity, far more real and exquisite than that found in courts."

"Ere we descend," said Mademoiselle de Montfort, "let me, my beloved Emily, make a confession that weighs on my conscience. Your journies to Paris, of which my happiness was the object, really gave me uneasiness; pardon me, I almost accused you of unkindness."

"I should have thought your affection less lively," replied Emily, "had you been unconcerned at my apparent neglect."

Lusignan was just then crossing the lawn; they descended to meet him.

"My sweet Emily," said he, "this long week is elapsed, and your happy Lusignan once more at your feet; one quarter of the time to which the Duchess limited my confinement is also past. You do not, Emily, look half so rejoiced when we meet as I do. Tell me whence this pensive look? Are you not well, my love?"

Emily's features had not yet recovered the impression the mention of her departed parent had left on them; her eyes were still humid; she tendered her hand to Lusignan with a smile of inexpressible sweetness, assuring him she was both well and happy.

Soon as breakfast was over, the whole party moved, on foot, to the cottage in the wood; the morning was delicious; the resplendent rays of the meridian sun, tempered by refreshing breezes from the sea, seemed grateful even to inanimate nature; and the gentle notes of the rural choristers filled the air with ineffable melody. Soon, however, they were overpowered by the sound, no less harmonious, of the shepherd's pipe. The rural festival had already began, and the friends from the Abbey, ere they entered the plain leading to the cot, saw the happy group dancing, with rustic grace, the merry Lavolta.* They no sooner observed Madame de Clarival, than, forming themselves into a line, they advanced in couples to meet her, bearing garlands of innumerable flowers that grow spontaneously on this fertile coast. The bride and bridegroom advancing first, presented Emily a wreath of myrtle and jessamine entwined with the nicest art. The Countess begged the dance might be renewed, but could only prevail on condition that Lusignan and Emily, with Dorville and Caroline, should join them. They consented, without hesitation, to this request. The natural and unfeigned delight that beamed in the countenance of these untutored peasants communicated itself to their visitors; they joined the dance with light hearts, and would, at that moment, have resigned willingly their splendid servitude for the liberty and happiness of a cottage. Emily, however, was glad to retire at a small distance from the sportive throng, that she might observe their unmingled delight. The young Lauretta had a beautiful face, and a form that would have attracted the admiration of courtiers; the cares of the world had not yet made an impression on her artless countenance; happiness seemed personified in each individual of the village group; they performed with equal ease and agility the various motions of the graceful Lavolta.

"How little do we gain," said Emily to Lusignan as he approached, "by the tutelage of those mercenary teachers, fertile in their inventions to distort Nature, and rob her of that inimitable grace attached to all her followers!"

"Your reflections, dearest Emily," said Lusignan, "have been in unison with mine. I have been lamenting the rank in which fortune placed me, which has so long withheld me from the knowledge of scenes fraught with such pure delight. How enviable are these obscure villagers, from whose abodes luxury and care are banished!"

Antonia now entreated Emily would partake of the little refreshment prepared for the bridal guests; but just as she was preparing to comply, a servant from the Abbey advanced across the plain, directing his steps to Madame de Clarival. At sight of him, an undefinable emotion communicated itself to the hearts of the lovers. Emily felt as though the rural festival was likely to be interrupted: her contemplations of the enjoyments of innocence were, indeed, interrupted,—she was summoned to far other scenes.

"My dear Emily," said the Countess, "we are obliged to return to Montalte, by the arrival of unexpected visitors: Philip knows not who they are, but says their train is magnificent, and their retinue very numerous."

Emily and Lusignan felt chagrined at this unseasonable intrusion, but rose to follow the Countess. Dorville and Caroline soon joined them. As they walked towards the Abbey, they endeavoured vainly to conjecture who could be the unexpected guests; but were not long in doubt, for at some distance they discovered a servant wearing the Meronville livery. Emily turned pale; her quivering limbs hardly supported her fragile form; she leaned on Lusignan's arm; her agitation could not be concealed from him, but communicated, like a contagion to his heart.

"Be not alarmed, sweetest Emily," said he, "it is probably my

mother, come to surprise you: she can bring none but pleasing intelligence."

His looks, whilst he spoke, evidently contradicted his assertion.
Emily trembled.

"Shall I," continued he, "retire, ere we approach the Abbey?"

"Concealment," replied Emily, "implies criminality, and disguise
may be misconstrued:—the sensations of my heart are unaccountable even to myself: some unforeseen event has surely brought the
Duke to our abode."

"It cannot be," resumed Lusignan. "My mother has not written
to you; she means to surprise you by her unexpected arrival."

"No, no," said the foreboding heart of Emily; "she never travels
with a retinue so splendid; but, be it as it may, we will encounter
whatever Fate may design for us: we are free from guilt; let us not,
by forsaking candour, wear the semblance of it."

"Be composed then, my beloved Emily," said Lusignan, as they
entered the woody enclosure that opened on the lawn;—the pavilion overlooked it; the casements were all unclosed.

Lusignan soon discovered his father, and was not long unobserved by him. A scowl of indignation more deeply shaded his austere brow: he was on the point of betraying his rage, when a sudden
recollection restrained him, and ere the party reached the pavilion,
his features had resumed their wonted composure.—Madame de
Meronville started when she saw Lusignan, and, fixing her anxious
regard on her husband, beheld not without terror the impression
it made on his disturbed countenance: she felt so agitated, that,
when they entered, she could with difficulty address the Countess; Caroline, however, relieved her, by falling into the arms of her
benefactress. Lusignan received the cold embrace of his father with
a truly filial warmth. The latter, without expressing any surprise at
the unexpected meeting, bowed in the most respectful manner to
the Countess, saying,—

"I hope, Madam, the business that has brought me to your mansion will offer an apology for this apparent intrusion, and that our
future union will obliterate all recollection of past animosity."

"I am ever sensible," said Madame de Clarival, "of the honour
of entertaining the Duke de Meronville, which renders all apology
superfluous. It has long been my sincerest wish to conciliate all differences, and I trust the connection, thus renewed, will be produc-

tive of happiness to all concerned in it. Permit me," continued the Countess, "to present to your Grace my only daughter, who will be proud in the honour of embracing her uncle."

Emily approached as she spoke these words: she had sunk on a sofa as she entered the apartment, but relieved by the interval of a few moments, and still more by the words uttered by the Duke, which she had indistinctly heard, she drew near with a modest but graceful address; her pallid cheeks animated by a blush that heightened her native beauty. The Duke could not refuse a smile of approbation, and could almost, at that instant, have declared himself vanquished. Lusignan watched the effect her appearance had on him, and augured much from his relaxed features. Emily then embraced the Duchess, whose cordial and sincere affection could not be concealed. All felt happy, save only the Duke, whose corroded heart had long excluded every social regard, and with it every genuine delight: he endeavoured, however, to appear animated, and in some degree succeeded. He requested a private interview with Madame de Clarival, in which he informed her it was his wish to promote the happiness of Lusignan and Mademoiselle de Montalte, and that his consent should be freely given; concluding,—

"For the sake of our children, Madam, I hope you will forget the injuries you have received, which have been the effect, not of personal but hereditary prejudice: I shall bury them all in oblivion, and trust you will not be unwilling to second my designs."

Madame de Clarival assured him there was nothing she so ardently desired; but thought it necessary to account for Lusignan's appearance at the Abbey, which would, in all probability, draw forth some animadversion. He appeared perfectly satisfied with the account she gave him, yet, under his affected moderation there was an evident restraint, a want of cordiality, that left the Countess but half satisfied; but she attributed it to some slight remains of his yet unextinguished animosity, which she doubted not would, by degrees, entirely subside. She endeavoured to prevail on him to remain at Montalte, and make it his residence till the intended union should take place; but this he constantly refused, saying, some affairs required his presence at Paris, and that he wished the nuptials to be celebrated on his own estate, for which purpose he selected Luneville Castle, as his numerous tenantry and vassals there would add splendour to the bridal scene, such as the dignity of the two families required. The Countess, though she could have wished it otherwise, yet did not withhold her concurrence, and it was concluded that, in a week, the family from Montalte should remove to Luneville.

When the Duke left the room, Madame de Meronville gave vent to the affectionate feelings of her heart, which were now engrossed by three equally deserving objects.

"I recommend prudence to you, Lusignan," said she; "yet, when I see the object that makes you forget its dictates, I feel more than half disposed to pardon your offence; but, indeed, my love, I trembled when I saw you here, fearing that it should revive your father's dormant resentment, as his lenity has appeared to spring only from the idea of your sufferings by long confinement and total seclusion: you must, however, return with us to-night, and apologize to him for your appearance here, lest it should have dangerous consequences."

"I will assure him, my dear Madam," said the Marquis, "that I only availed myself of his permission to leave the Castle during the day, and have always returned ere it was dark;—he has seen my Emily, and will not wonder that, being at only the distance of eight leagues from her, I could not resist the happiness of seeing her, which the proximity of our abodes seemed to offer. I saw him, my Emily, no less struck with you than his enraptured son; his features relaxed into a smile of approbation, which they but seldom assume. Suffer me, my dear mother," continued he, "to express, if possible, the grateful feelings that animate my soul for all your exertions in my favour: the success they have had, though far from expected, adds nothing to the obligation I should, in any case, have felt;—I almost now distrust the excess of happiness I seem already to possess, and, like the miser, find the abundance of wealth a source of inquietude, from the fear of its decreasing: such a bride and such a mother were surely never designed to bless one man!"

The Duchess embraced him with tender affection, and was going to add some observation; but, recollecting her time was short, she turned to her amiable protégée;—

"I must not forget my sweet Caroline," said she. "Where is Edward Dorville? You do not introduce him to his mother."

Caroline, kissing the hand of her benefactress held out to her, replied,—

"The many interesting subjects, my dearest Madam, which your arrival here has given birth to, made me unwilling to intrude my affairs; but the happiness which Edward's return has occasioned me is still incomplete, as it wants the sanction of your approbation. Will you permit me to summon him?"

"Most willingly, my dear child," replied her Grace. "I am no less anxious than yourself to be acquainted with the man to whom I must entrust the future welfare and guardianship of my beloved Caroline, though I am almost jealous of his influence, which may rob me of mine; yet remember, the place you occupy in my heart will never be transferred to any other object."

Caroline's tears fell fast; she threw herself at the Duchess's feet.—

"Never, never," said she, "will the remembrance of your kindness be effaced from this grateful heart: could any future tie weaken its impression, I would, from this hour, renounce them all. Your inestimable friendship has so long formed the only charm of life, that should fate even restore my long lost parent, she would still divide with you the affections of her child."

As she spoke these words, Dorville entered the pavilion. She arose to present him to the Duchess, who was much pleased with his address.

"I have long wished," said he, "for the honour of seeing the Duchess de Meronville, and of soliciting her consent to obtain the hand of her lovely ward. The splendour of rank and fortune is unhappily not mine to offer. Caroline has generously condescended to accept, as a substitute for affluence, a faithful and constant heart, whose only wish is to guard her from every future misfortune. Inferior as are my claims to her merits, if you, Madam, will deign to second my request, I have hopes of seeing my most sanguine wishes crowned with fruition."

Taking the cold hand of the blushing Caroline, Madame de Meronville put it within his.

"My only motive," said she, "is the happiness of this darling child; and I have so much confidence in her choice, that I unreluctantly give my fullest consent. Be assured the gift of her affections is an inestimable treasure: I resign them to your care; but, in so doing, cannot relinquish my own claims. In any future hour, should maternal counsel or regard become necessary, I reserve to myself the exclusive privilege of being addressed in the character of the most affectionate mother:—and you, my beloved Caroline, never forget that you have a claim to every service it may be in my power to bestow; and that a sincere and unalterable friend will be never wanting to you, while heaven prolongs my existence."

With these words she tenderly embraced her. Caroline's heart was too full for utterance. She left the apartment as the Duke and Madame de Clarival entered it. After partaking an elegant collation, the illustrious visitors quitted the Abbey. Lusignan asked leave to accompany his father to Paris, which was granted without difficulty, and they all set out together.

When Emily retired to her apartment, her thoughts were all occupied in revolving the various occurrences of this eventful day. The magnificence and splendid retinue of the Duke de Meronville, which, in his route, had brought out crowds of admiring villagers, left no impressions on her mind, but that care and anxiety was the exclusive privilege of wealth and worldly grandeur. She saw in his clouded and austere brow none of that pure and natural delight which characterised the features of the humble peasants she had left when summoned to the Abbey. In vain she sought, in the pomp and ostentation of his polished manners, any of that mild benevolence which charms the impartial observer, and receives its own gratifications, whilst it confers happiness on others; in vain she sought, in the trappings of luxury, that simple delight, those unbidden smiles, that had charmed her in the rural festival. She found nothing to fix her attention. Riches and honours still left a vacuum in the generous mind. Virtue, thought she, elevates its possessor, however humble may be his lot, to the highest dignities of man. Vice, though gilded by splendour and independence, reduces us below the level of the poorest subjects. She could have said,—

> "Sublimer happiness can titles yield?
> "Can wealth or grandeur greater meed bestow?
> "Unbias'd nature scorns the blazon'd field,
> "And every finer feeling answers——No!"*

CHAP. V.

"At each response the sacred rite requires,
  "From her full bosom bursts th' unbidden sigh:
"A strange mysterious awe the scene inspires,
  "And on her lips the trembling accents die."

Madame de Clarival's chief care was now to prepare for the celebration of Caroline's nuptials, as they were, in a week, to remove to Luneville. She wished not to take leave of her till she had secured for her a protector who would ensure her future safety. She summoned her to her closet, and communicated her intentions.

Caroline at first started at the apparent precipitation of her marriage, but was soon convinced that, as she could not accompany Emily to Luneville, there was but one step, consistent with propriety, she could adopt: she, therefore, submitted entirely to the decision Madame de Clarival should make, and retired to pour her doubts and fears in the bosom of Emily.

The ceremony was fixed for the third day, and they were immediately to set out, and take possession of their little cottage in the Valais.

Caroline could not, without the deepest concern, see the hour approach when she must bid a long adieu to her friend, and enter on a state of life so different to that which habit had endeared her. She was fondly attached to Edward Dorville, but at the awful moment when she sacrificed every thing to him, and formed, in the presence of Heaven, vows that must influence and controul every future action of her life, she could not entirely subjugate her fears, nor conceal from her beating heart that the issue of her union was doubtful. Emily participated the anxiety that disturbed her friend; the night previous to the intended solemnity she remained late in her apartment, and shed torrents of tears at their approaching separation.*

"Will not absence, my dearest Emily," said Caroline, "and the splendour to which you are called, efface from your heart the friendship we have mutually vowed? Shall I still live in your remembrance? Tell me, will your affection survive the lapse of time,—Memory?"

"How little do you yet know me, my Caroline," replied Emily, "if you can suppose that an attachment formed in my bosom is subject to time or place! Congenial souls, though separated by mountains, seas, and worlds, will still beat in unison. Whatever be my fate, to combat the rude shocks of adversity, or resist the allurements of more formidable prosperity, still shall I look forward, with undiminished delight, to the happy hour of again meeting my beloved Caroline. Then dry those tears. To-morrow's dawn unites you for ever to the man of your choice. You have nothing but happiness in perspective."

"Alas, my friend!" replied Caroline, "such were the prospects with which my unhappy parents were united! How soon was the bright sunshine of their early days lost in impenetrable gloom! So uncertain are all our hopes,—so subject are we all to the casualties of fortune, I tremble when I think on my ever-to-be lamented mother, and recollect how little virtue secured her happiness!"

"Most true it is," said Emily, "that we are all liable to vicissitudes and fortuitous events which no human foresight can avert: but, my Caroline, if virtue and religion do not exempt us from trials, which are the portion of humanity, they, at least, teach us to bear them, and keep always in reversion a hope, which no sorrow, no persecution can destroy,—that of a blessed immortality:—this only remains with us in that hour when we feel, past all doubt, that our soul is taking its flight to another world,—that hour which wealth and magnificence can no longer gild, nor acclamation exhilarate."

As Emily spoke, her eyes were raised to Heaven, with an expression of such sweet resignation to its will, as almost assimilated her to a celestial being. Caroline was so oppressed with the various sensations of her mind, on the eve of a day which was to decide her fate for ever, that she felt the necessity of endeavouring to take repose, which could alone invigorate both body and mind, and render them equal to the exertion they must suffer: Emily therefore retired, entreating her to be composed, and sought herself that repose which is never long absent from the pillow of innocence.

Caroline was early awakened by her woman bringing a letter, that had arrived by express from Paris; and she was not a little rejoiced when she recognised the handwriting of the Duchess de Meronville: she bestowed a kiss on the insensible paper, and, sighing as she broke the seal, read these words:—

"I hope these few lines, dictated by affection, and flowing from maternal tenderness, will reach my beloved Caroline in time to prepare her for a solemnity which will call for all the native energies of her cultivated mind. Too frequently is marriage considered only as a ceremony, which unites the fortunes and honours of those who embrace it, rather than their hearts and social interests. With such ideas annexed to it, it inspires none of that awe, that tremulous solemnity of feeling, with which every person, who forms an adequate conception of the engagement into which they are entering, is impressed in the bridal hour:—to say no more, you are making vows in the presence of Almighty God, and calling on him to consecrate them: enrolled in his eternal register are those vows, which every hour offers to many a temptation to violate. I have too much confidence in your virtue and integrity of heart to have any apprehensions on that score: but our fragile nature is ever prone to error; and the counsels of age may strengthen and support the instability of youthful resolutions. Consider well, ere you tie the indissoluble knot, the many duties it imposes. Remember, Dorville is the arbiter of your future destiny: all your wishes must centre in his affection, all your actions be regulated by his will: in prosperity, you must rejoice with him; in adversity, sooth his anguish; supply by your tenderness the deficiencies of fortune, and obliterate by your caresses the frowns of adverse fate. Such, my child, are the indispensible duties of a wife;— those of a mother may soon be added. On you principally devolves the education of your children: they are, indeed, wholly consigned to your care. In that age when the foundation must be laid of every future principle, it is you must form the pliant mind to virtue, ere the perversions of the world have given it a contrary bent;—you must prepare by precept what you will inculcate by example. The texture of the youthful mind is delicate, and ready to receive every impression. Be careful to let none be made you would not wish to be indelible. A thousand obstacles will impede your progress. Should Heaven bless you with a numerous family, diversity of disposition and temper will require diversity of treatment; and your best hopes will frequently, without any personal neglect, issue in disappointment;—this will be a source of grief and care to your anxious heart. I turn with pleasure to the bright reverse. The exercise of your duty as a wife will ensure to you the confidence and affection of your husband, who will acknowledge, with grateful sensibility, that to you he owes his happiness. Your children, in the common course of nature, will look up to you as their guide and protectress; and, by their endearing caresses, will gild the social hour, and make your home the centre of enjoyment. You may reasonably expect these fruits of your care; but, should they fail, by any fatality of which you are not the mistress, the consolation will still remain of having done your duty, of which no perversity of fortune can deprive you. I could much more largely expatiate on this important subject; but I am not writing to a person in whom virtuous principles must be formed, but only confirmed. If, after examining your heart, my child, you declare it capable, which I have no doubt it is, of fulfilling obligations I have pointed out, you may approach the altar with confidence and security; you may look forward to that happiness your virtues claim: yet be prepared to meet adversity and disappointment; they are always mingled with our enjoyments here, to wean our hearts from this temporary state, and fix our hopes on another and a better world. Adieu, my dear and much-loved Caroline! Your welfare is now deposited in other hands:—yet surely you will not leave France without affording me one sigh, one last embrace. If your husband is in no haste to arrive in Switzerland, come with Emily, and spend at least a month at Luneville. Tell him it is a favour I claim, as due to your mother. Till we meet then, farewell!"

The perusal of this letter renewed the agitation of Caroline's mind, which a night of sweet repose had calmed.

She read it a thousand times; but her heart told her the exercise of her duty would be a source of perpetual happiness.

Convinced of this, she reasoned herself into that pensive composure which usually succeeds violent struggles, and felt prepared to meet Dorville at that altar which was to unite them for ever.

Emily came to assist her resolution, and prepare her for the approaching solemnity. The Abbey chapel was decorated for the occasion with garlands of flowers.

The tenants all attended to do honour to the bride. As they walked through a long avenue of elms and poplars that led to the chapel, the village maidens strewed the path with flowers, and offered prayers for their happiness.

Lusignan, to the surprise and delight of all, arrived ere the ceremony was concluded.

Caroline was several times nearly overcome, whilst the service was performed, with awful solemnity, by the pious chaplain, yet supported the scene with dignity, and more composure than Emily had hoped.

Her mind was much relieved by Madame de Meronville's letter, and the certainty of remaining some time longer with her friends; for Dorville felt no less happy than herself in the prospect of improving his acquaintance with her patroness.

Lusignan had leave to remain at the Abbey till Madame de Clarival removed to Luneville, which was but three days distant.

The Duke and Duchess de Meronville were already there, to prepare for their reception. The former was fully resolved to display all the pomp and ostentation imaginable on this occasion, and to supply, by this studied magnificence, the want of that cordiality which he vainly endeavoured to assume. The seeds of rancour and unconquerable resentment still lurked in his bosom; and to conceal them entirely was an effort beyond his strength.

CHAP. VI.

"———Thou cry'dst, 'Indeed!'
"And didst contract and purse thy brow together,
"As if thou then hadst shut up in thy brain
"Some horrible conceit.—If thou dost love me,
"Shew me thy thought."

La Haye accompanied the Duke to Luneville; and, as they ascended a steep hill, which calmed the velocity of their rapid motion, he enquired the issue of his visit to the Abbey.

"You will hardly credit me, La Haye," said his Grace, "but my resolution almost failed. There was a sweetness in the features of Mademoiselle de Montalte, equalled by nothing but that which beamed in the countenance of the Duchess de Meronville, when first I led her, trembling, to the altar."

"I have understood," said La Haye, "that she was uncommonly beautiful; and, indeed, we may attribute to her some extraordinary charms, since they have power to make the Marquis de Lusignan forsake his duty, and contemn parental authority."

"Syren!" exclaimed the Duke, "and hence my vengeance shall pursue thee:—yet," continued he in a softened tone of voice, "she may be guiltless. Is it possible that so much sweetness can conceal a heart so black?"

"Else," resumed La Haye, "her influence were not formidable. Did depravity appear in its own disgusting form, we should be armed against it; but, when it assumes the semblance of virtue, it is then we must dread its affects. In looking on Mademoiselle de Montalte, you perhaps, Sir, forgot Mademoiselle de Foix?"

"Ah!" said the Duke, "there, again! Destruction light on thy head, thou pleasing sorceress! Yes; that letter proves her guilt. By torture Lusignan shall be forced to confess the arts that have concealed Eugenia."

"Not so, my noble patron," said the Abbé. "Try gentle methods first. Time will reveal this hidden mystery. I have reason to hope I have discovered her retreat; but should you precipitate your enquiries, she may be again removed, ere I can certify my doubts. Promise me, my Lord, not to mention the subject till I assure you it may be done without danger."

"I do promise," said Meronville;—"but tell me, in return, what are the discoveries you have made."

La Haye was not prepared to answer this question. He assumed a look of concern and importance; and a jolt of the carriage at that moment gave him time to recollect himself.

"Suffer me, my Lord," replied he, "to remain in silence. I would not wound your bosom, already lacerated by filial disobedience. I could——but it is enough, my Lord."

"Speak!" exclaimed the Duke. "This silence tortures me. Is my son more guilty? Speak, that instant vengeance may overtake the deed!"

"Caution, Sir, is indispensable," said La Haye. "Precipitation may ruin our designs. When certainty has taken place of those doubts which at present involve my discoveries, it shall be communicated to you; till then it is better to be silent."

"The Duke de Foix is my particular friend," resumed his Grace. "I would remove the fears that agitate his bosom for an only daughter, seduced by some villanous pretence. You are entitled, by any discovery, to a vast reward his Grace has offered for her detection."

"Such rewards, my Lord," said the hypocrite, "cannot stimulate my exertions. To restore a child to her disconsolate parents,—to heal the wounds of parental solicitude,—to rescue virtue from the snares of villany: these are my motives, Sir—far more potent than the love of wealth: leave all, then, to my care, Sir.

"Within a month I will engage to restore, if she yet lives, Mademoiselle de Foix to her injured parents. I only request of you, Sir, firmness in the resolution you have made, and a strict adherence to the plan we have concerted."

"That firmness," said the Duke, "it will be difficult to preserve. Resolute as is my nature, the caresses of a wife, a son, and a lovely woman, may shake my resolves; and, as I have now no other means of recovering the family estates, policy may almost dictate compliance."

"I grieve," rejoined La Haye with a sigh of profound dissimulation, "at the necessity which wars against my nature, and compels me to urge revenge.

"My duty points out the conduct I must pursue.

"As your spiritual father, I must warn you to be aware of polluting Christian blood by a mixture with that of heresy. The evil this might entail on future generations would recoil on my guilty head, if I omitted any exertion to avert the deed.

"As a minister of Heaven, I must carefully guard the interests of the Catholic faith. Why was I placed in a situation which obliges me to do violence to the benevolence Nature has implanted in me?

"But these are trials to which humanity is subject. It is fit we should sacrifice our own gratification to the welfare of others.

"My inclination, Sir, no less than your's, points to lenity, but duty opposes it, and I willingly make the sacrifice.

"Remember, my Lord, by yielding to the wishes of your son, you may ensure his happiness here, but you destroy it hereafter. Heaven avenges the heterogeneous union of true believers with infamous apostates; and the sins of disobedience, if not punished on earth, will be recorded in Heaven and eternal perdition waits on successful villany!

"But I will urge no further:—you are not insensible to the voice of reason. Reflect on what I have said. Conscience is a monitor that cannot listen to it; and, above all, remember that the Comte de Clarival was an heretic."

"Then be it so," said the Duke; and as he uttered these words, the chaise entered the great portal of Luneville.

Mademoiselle de Foix was still immured within the walls of St. Clair. She had often written to D'Aubignac, and began to accuse his tardiness; but some artful evasion always was at command to extricate him from the unpardonable guilt of negligence.

Eugenia, in her last letter, told him the monastic life was little suited to her inclinations, and that she would even prefer returning to her father, though she had no doubt her chastisement would be grievous.

Perhaps for a time she might be confined within four walls, where she could have no consolation but in the remembrance of his love; and, whatever might be her sufferings, she would never permit his name to pass her lips: in the meantime, if he really loved her, he would not hesitate to rescue her from the tyranny of her offended father, and that she was prepared to follow his steps wheresoever they might lead.

D'Aubignac was now in the utmost perplexity. He had exhausted every subterfuge the fertility of imagination could furnish, and he knew her too well to doubt that, in search of romantic fame, she would follow any person who would become her devoted knight-errant.

Her large fortune and vast connections gave her an indisput-able claim to his attention, but the more powerful her family was, the more he dreaded the exertion of that power, which might con-fine him to the Bastile; and though she might attend him there, as became the heroine of romance, and by her sighs and tears move the obdurate jailer's heart, he felt his love not sufficiently disinterested to receive the single gift of her heart as an equivalent for the splen-dour and magnificence with which he wished it gilded.

In this exigency he applied to a secret monitor, who had before assisted him, and the result of the enquiry was partially transmitted to Eugenia in a letter, wherein he conjured her, by her past affection and future hopes, to remain yet a little while at St. Clair, assuring her that the procrastination, of which she complained, arose from a circumstance which he flattered himself would enhance his merit in her opinion; that he could not now explain the whole to her, but that he was preparing a castle to receive her, which must undergo repairs, but was now in a state of great forwardness, and that, when arrived there, she might defy the tyranny of parents and guardians.

He entreated her, at the same time, to mention him as her brother, for he was all impatience to throw himself at her feet, but dared not appear, apprehensive of subjecting her to the enquiries of the Superior; but if she would prepare them by the name of a brother, he should then, without fear, sue for admission within the walls, and this might facilitate her escape, whenever it should become expedient.

Soothed by this letter, Eugenia yielded without difficulty to his reasoning, and even wept at the suggestions of her heart, which told her that, perhaps, he suffered much for her sake, though his disinterested affection concealed those sufferings from her, fearful to wound her too susceptible nature. She therefore conceived it was her duty to repay him, in some degree, by permitting him to sigh at her feet, and forget, in her smiles, that Fortune ever frowned.

With this view she informed the Abbess that her brother would soon be in the neighbourhood, but would not, without requesting her permission, present himself at the convent gates.

This compliment the Abbess received very favourably, and consented, in this one instance, to overcome her aversion to the sex, and permit D'Aubignac to visit her. He lost no time in availing himself of it. He threw himself in breathless agitation at her feet.

She acted the part of a heroine with great effect; nor was his character as a dying lover ill supported.

The scene, on the whole, pleased Eugenia extremely, and she cared not how long nor how often it was repeated; but prudence, she acknowledged, made it necessary he should retire, and she now endeavoured, by her fortitude, to support his drooping spirits, as with difficulty he tore himself away, promising to return the earliest opportunity.

Before he retired, it appeared to him advisable to solicit an interview with the Lady Abbess, which was readily granted.

She was a short fat woman, about fifty; her countenance expressed more of cunning and acrimony than is strictly consistent with the Christian spirit, that prompts a seclusion from the world, and a renunciation of its concerns; her little black eyes, which, but for their extreme brilliancy, would not have been distinguished, enveloped as they were in fat, gave a keenness to her appearance, which conveyed much meaning; and a turn-up nose added to the asperity of her countenance.

It so seldom happened that any male was admitted within the convent, save the confessor, whose sable cassock and neglected beard had no charms for the discerning Dorothea, that she felt a sensation of pleasure at the idea of beholding a young handsome officer, which, I have no doubt, is very unusual to the vestal train.

With her veil half turned back, a smile on her countenance, and dimples in her cheeks, she entered the parlour where D'Aubignac waited for audience, and graciously enquired what had procured her the honour of a visit?

D'Aubignac surveyed her as she spoke, and could hardly refrain from laughter at her ludicrous appearance.

Checking, however, his risible propensity, he bowed with great respect, and said his sister was the subject on whose account he troubled her.

He then lamented the necessity which obliged him to desire a strict watch might be kept over her actions; but said that, as she had left her family at the instigation of some unprincipled lover, he yet feared she might be prevailed on to quit with him the asylum she had chosen, to obviate which he wished no man to be admitted to her but himself, and her walks to be circumscribed to the bounds allowed the pensioners in the convent.

He then enquired if any person had visited her since her arrival; and, on receiving a negative answer, concluded thus:—

"Your established reputation, Madam, and the prudent discipline for which your community is distinguished, leave me no fears, now that you are apprised of my sister's real situation; and I cannot but rejoice at the fortunate chance which directed her to seek protection under your roof, as the example you hold out to this little republic will fortify all her virtuous inclinations, and destroy every other.

"I may add, though certain your conduct will be little influenced by any worldly consideration, that she is related to the first families in the kingdom, who will not fail handsomely to reward the care you may bestow."

D'Aubignac's elegant person had not escaped the observation of Dorothea, nor was her heart rendered sufficiently callous by long confinement, and vows of hatred to the world, to make her wholly insensible of such a compliment, delivered by so graceful a speaker.

She knew not which most to admire, his politeness or discernment: both she thought very conspicuous, and silently acknowledged that the sex she had renounced were really so captivating, that it made her lament their being so deceitful.

This idea, however, she thought not proper to communicate, but, thanking him for his good opinion, said—

"I believe I may indeed boast that no community is better regulated than that which I have the honour to conduct. Heaven be praised, there are none but virtuous members of it! and you may rely, Sir, on my care of your sister, which shall be exerted to make her virtuous and happy.

"Her conduct has been strictly proper since her arrival, and it really merits an encomium. I shall, however, attend to your injunctions, and trust you will have no reason to repent the confidence reposed in me."

D'Aubignac soon after put an end to this conference, which the Lady Abbess was far from unwilling to prolong; and having obtained leave to repeat his visits as often as convenient, took a respectful leave, not at all dissatisfied with the success of his attempt.

CHAP. VII.

—————————————"But tell
"Why thy canonized bones, hearsed in earth,
"Have burst their cearments?"

Dorville began to be much alarmed at the non-appearance of his friend Marsillac, who had promised to return immediately, but from whom he heard no tidings, and the family were now on the eve of quitting Montalte, where alone he could hope to receive any intelligence of his fate.

He communicated his doubts to Madame de Clarival, who gave orders that any enquiries for him should be directed to Luneville, whither the whole party now removed.

A contrariety of emotions filled the heart of Emily, when Lusignan pointed out to her the cloud-capt towers of this ancient edifice.

The day was dreary. The autumn, far advanced, submitted to the gloomy reign of November fogs.

The building, as it seemed majestically rising from concealment, presented an object in exact correspondence with the day.

Its lofty turrets, its ponderous gates, and massy bulwarks, made Emily shudder as she surveyed them.

She imputed the sensation to the recollection that it had been the prison of Lusignan, and she endeavoured to feel happy in the idea that it would now be the scene of enjoyment; yet when she reflected that the Duke de Meronville presided, she again relapsed into terror and doubt, which the pleasure of meeting the Duchess could not entirely remove.

Lusignan observed her pensiveness, and endeavoured, by gentle reproaches, to restore her natural cheerfulness; yet, as the carriage wheels rolled through the huge portcullis at the entrance of the court, he almost sympathetically shuddered, and an unusual faint-ness almost overcame Emily.

A numerous train of menials were placed in two rows down the long passages through which they passed in arriving at the spacious apartment where the Duke waited to receive them.

The gloomy visages of these dependants, suited to the taste of their master, their antique liveries, and the correspondent horrors of the long-neglected castle, served not to dissipate the oppression of spirits to which Emily involuntarily yielded.

Madame de Meronville's affectionate embrace had a more pow-erful effect; but the austerity of the Duke's brow, which a forced smile but ill concealed, chilled her heart. She would have given worlds to be again restored to the dear abode she had lately left. She turned round, as though to see if an escape were practicable. She encountered the anxious eye of Lusignan, who, taking her hand, entreated her not on this day, which should be the first of his hap-piness, to appear so agitated, so oppressed.

Roused by this appeal, Emily smiled at her undissembled terrors, and felt the necessity of exerting herself to conquer them. In this attempt she partially succeeded, and the day passed less unpleas-antly than she expected.

The eastern turret was appointed for the accommodation of Madame de Clarival and her family.

It was a vast pile of buildings, which was the original Castle of Luneville; the remainder had been added by several successive Dukes. It had all the appearance of the greatest antiquity; and the suite of apartments appropriated to Emily had been for ages closed; and although the cheerful blaze was kindled in them all, it served only to condense the damp vapours which had accumulated by the long exclusion of light and air.

So spacious were the rooms, that she could not at one extremity discern the other.

They were hung with tapestry. Where once the workman's art had been displayed in the judicious choice of innumerable shades, to make living figures rise on the inanimate canvas, the hand of Time had long banished all distinction, and united the living colours with the sable ground-work.

Emily, nervous from oppression of spirits rather than natural timidity, requested, when she retired at night, that Gabriella, her favourite woman, might sleep in the contiguous apartment, and then reposed undisturbed during a tempestuous night.

Emily's first thought when she arose was to hasten to her windows, and see if the prospect without was less gloomy than that within her chamber;—but here no pleasing object met the eye, excluded as were all the views of Nature by immense walls, which seemed bidding defiance to the ravages of time.—"Many a poor prisoner," thought Emily, "has here been confined, here wasted his hapless days in sorrow, and viewed, in silent dismay, those invincible barriers to his escape!"

She sighed at the recollection, and turned to examine the interior of her apartments.

She opened a small door, and found it communicated with a staircase, which she descended, and then perceived another door: trying the rusty lock, it yielded to her pressure.

She entered a chapel, the floor of which was black marble: the arched Gothic windows, overspread with cobwebs and dust, scarcely admitted light enough to distinguish objects; but Emily felt impressed with awe at the solemn horror of the place. She advanced towards the altar, and kneeling, breathed a fervent prayer to Heaven.

The chapel was hung with black; achievements were every where dispersed; a large coffin, covered with a magnificent pall, was at the foot of the altar, whose only decorations were two skulls, and other insignia of the dead.

Emily was not superstitious, but she had never seen any thing that reminded her so forcibly of departed spirits. It was broad daylight, but the sun-beams never penetrated here.

She trembled, for the black hangings moved. She hastened to the door, then took one terrified glance at the gloomy objects before her, and hastily closed the entrance, determined to repeat her visit whenever she could collect courage to explore this long-deserted region.

While she sat musing at her window, her eye vacantly fixed on the dull wall before her, a gentle tap at the door dispersed her reverie, and introduced Caroline to her apartment.

After embracing Emily, she enquired how she had spent the night, and invited her, as it was yet early, to take a ramble on the ramparts, where the beauty of the prospect compensated for the want of any in her apartment.

She was happy to comply, and found herself so refreshed by the morning air, that at breakfast she was unusually cheerful.

The Duke did not descend till dinner time, so that the party was unconstrained by his presence.

Lusignan was overjoyed at Emily's improved spirits, and proposed a walk within his own domain. He conducted her to the most enchanting spots, and pointed out the beauty and diversity of the surrounding landscape.

He described to her the happiness he hoped to enjoy, when with her he should visit his numerous tenantry, and apply his superfluous wealth to the increase of their comforts.

He detailed a thousand plans of future enjoyment, and Emily, with a sigh of doubt, assented to them all.

At dinner the Duke appeared, attended by La Haye, whom he introduced to the ladies.

He regarded Emily with the deepest scrutiny, who had no opportunity of satisfying her own curiosity, which had been much raised by the description Lusignan had given of him.

He behaved to her with the utmost obsequiousness, and not less to the Marquis. He had seen much of the world, and on most topics was in some degree conversant.

His humour contributed to enliven the company, who seemed infected with the gloom of Meronville's countenance. They all retired early, and notwithstanding the assiduities of Lusignan, and the faculty to entertain discovered by La Haye, Emily began to wonder how it would be possible to spend a month in such a way.

The contrast, indeed, with the method of life at the Abbey was both striking and revolting—there all was liberty and virtuous unrestrained enjoyment; here the presence of a single person imposed a restraint quite incompatible with social harmony.

The sight of Emily had confirmed in the mind of La Haye a resolution he had for some time meditated, that of procuring her for his supposed nephew, the Chevalier St. Amand.

In a heart where ambition and every malignant passion preponderated, it is not to be supposed that the turpitude of any attempt would be allowed to interfere with its execution.

Lusignan's undissembled contempt wounded him to the soul, and to revenge the insult, no crime could he think enormous.

On the other hand, Emily's vast rental offered a mark to his ambition, to attain which he determined to sacrifice every thing. If half his projects succeeded, he would raise his family to the first rank in the kingdom.

The obstacles he acknowledged were powerful, but by perseverance he doubted not to overcome them.

All his acquaintance with the retreat of Mademoiselle de Foix had nothing marvellous in it, for the Chevalier d'Aubignac was also one of his protégées, and might boast the same degree of affinity with him as St. Amand, and, as he inherited all the malignity and baseness of La Haye, he never acted but by his advice.

This deep politician saw but one invincible barrier to his hopes, which was the consent of Meronville to the union of the two cousins, and this he bent all his address to prevent.

He seldom left him alone, conscious that in the most depraved heart reflection will sometimes sow the seeds of repentance;—and he saw clearly the charms and enchanting sweetness of Emily wanted not effect on the mind of Meronville.

The influence, however, he possessed, and which he knew sufficiently how to exert, was the foundation on which he built his hopes. He recollected with infinite pleasure the success of his former scheme, which had extorted an oath from the lips of Meronville, that he determined to employ against him if he ever appeared inclined to mercy.——

"By my God, and all the saints that intercede for sinful man, I solemnly swear never to forgive him, from this hour to disinherit him, nor ever deem any future concession an atonement for his guilt!"

These were the words he had uttered in a transport of rage, and these were deeply engraven on the memory of La Haye. His innocent and unconscious victims slept profoundly, whilst he devoted the hour of repose to the formation and execution of his schemes.

A few days after the party assembled at the Castle, the Duke's *Avocat* and *Homme d'Affaires** arrived, to prepare the necessary settlements when two such vast properties were about to be united.

Meronville and La Haye took the whole management on themselves, and sedulously added, by their endeavours, to the dilatoriness of lawyers.

Time, which constantly though regularly presses forward, soon elapsed, in spite of the tediousness of restraint, and the hour approached when Dorville and Caroline were to depart for Switzerland.

That hour was equally dreaded by Emily and her friend; but it imperceptibly arrived.

On the evening preceding their journey, which was to commence early in the morning, the supper hour was spent almost in silence; each was occupied in their own reflections; the unbidden tear started in the eyes of the young friends when their sorrowful glances met.

Caroline repaired to her apartment, to pour, for the last time, her tears in the bosom of Emily. So conscious were they both of the uncertainty of all human events, that they almost felt separating for ever.

With difficulty, after a thousand embraces and tender farewells, Caroline forced herself away, and left Emily absorbed in grief. She sat for some time meditating on her loss, and then, elevating her thoughts above the world and its concerns, she took her taper, and descended the stairs leading to the chapel.

The great clock struck twelve: its long reverberating sound echoed through the vaulted chapel's roof. Emily paused,——but ashamed of her fears, she unbarred the door, and entered the recess of the long-forgotten dead.

She kneeled before the altar, unconscious where she knelt, so entirely were her thoughts addressed to Heaven;—but as she raised her head, her taper burnt dim.

The place was dark and dismal. She was preparing to quit it, when a gentle noise made her look back. She stood transfixed! A figure in a winding-sheet rose from behind the altar. The ghastly paleness of death overspread its features! It held a crucifix, and fixed a mild but haggard look on Emily. It uttered a faint groan, and, as it vanished, said, in a hollow voice, "Unhappy Emily!" and instantly disappeared.

Emily sunk motionless on the marble, and for a time was unable to move.

At length recovering a little, she directed her tottering steps to her own apartment. Every breath of wind, every murmur of the night bird, startled her. She saw in every corner the horrible spectre rise, till, wearied with watching, she wrapped herself in the bed-clothes, and in welcome oblivion sunk to rest.

The gentle voice of Gabriella in the morning startled her, ere she had recovered from the profound stupor into which terror and long watching had thrown her.

With a faint recollection of the night scene, she awoke, saying,—

"Is it you, Gabriella?"

"Yes, my Lady, it is I," said Gabriella; "and glad I am to find us all safe, after the fright I had last night. I am sure not for worlds would I sleep alone again in that antichamber. Holy Maria! How terrified I was! And how much, my Lady, I thought of you. Did you see nothing, my Lady?"

Whilst Gabriella spoke, Emily had time to collect her senses not yet emancipated from the torpid influence of sleep. The hollow voice and compassionate look of the spectre were present to her imagination, and the recollection almost made the live blood stagnant.

Certain, however, that Gabriella could not have seen what she saw, and unwilling to sanction the errors of superstition, which are usually very predominant in the illiterate mind, she answered, that she had slept extremely well and undisturbed; and enquired what idle fancy had possessed her imagination?

"Idle fancy!" exclaimed Gabriella. "Holy Virgin! Had you seen it, my Lady, you would have said it was real enough. I have often heard talk of ghosts and hobgoblins, but never met with one before. I wonder I did not die, and become a ghost myself, though I am sure I will never leave my coffin only to come and frighten folks. Oh, St. Jerome,* how horrible it was!"

Emily, thinking her terrified abigail's alarm might be connected with her own, desired her to explain what she had seen.

"Why, my Lady," said she, "you must know that soon after I

left you, that is, about an hour after; it was when the clock struck
twelve, and they say ghosts always appear at that hour, I heard a
door open that leads out of the oak room, and thinking that you was
gone to bed, and knowing that nobody slept in these apartments
but our two poor selves, I thought I would just look out, and see if
you wanted any thing, never thinking of ghosts; so I looked out, but
nothing could I see, though two doors certainly opened——"

"Is this all?" said Emily, impatient at her long unmeaning discourse.

"Protecting Saints!" replied Gabriella, "I wish it had been all: but
where did I leave off? Oh, I was saying I could see nobody, so I
laid down, and tried to sleep; but about half an hour after, the door
opened again.

"Oh, my patience! why could not I lay still, and let the spirits
walk about as they liked? But it is all fate, my Lady. So I peeped out,
and there I saw, just coming through the door, up the little staircase,
such a ghost! it was dressed all in white;—I suppose it had just come
out of the coffin in its winding-sheet. It was very tall, and its face
not unlike you, my Lady, (if you will excuse me comparing you to
a spirit,) but so pale, and its eyes so black, and it held a taper that
burnt quite blue!

"Well, I did not stay to see where it went, but slapped my door
to, and locked it, though they say spirits get through the key-hole;
but I made the sign of the cross three times, and sprinkled my bed
with holy water, and so it never came;—but I am sure I do not sleep
there again; and I hope, my Lady, you will leave this nasty haunted
eastern turret, as they call it: they say it has not been inhabited these
hundred years, and so I suppose the ghosts walk about, and do as
they please.

"Lord have mercy, my Lady, why if you an't a laughing!"

Emily, indeed, could not help smiling at the terror she herself
had caused in the credulous mind of Gabriella.

The hour and appearance so exactly corresponded with her
return from the chapel, that she doubted not it was herself Gabriella
had seen, though she was too much terrified to know that any one
observed her, and she had no doubt her face was ghastly pale, from
the effect of the shock she had undergone; she felt it, therefore,
incumbent on her to destroy this prepossession ere it spread, which
she knew it would quickly do, if repeated by her woman to the

crowd of wonder-loving menials below, and might be of unpleasant consequence to the Duke de Meronville.

But she was at a loss how to do it, without discovering her secret visit to the chapel; she therefore paused a moment, and then, smiling, said,—

"Why, Gabriella, you tell a ghost story as well as any old woman; but I am not so credulous as yourself, and am rather inclined to think your fright was occasioned by something living than dead."

"Oh no, indeed, my Lady," resumed Gabriella, "I am sure it looked dead; and besides all the servants say they never go into this part of the Castle; so who could it be, you know, my Lady?"

"You were to blame, Gabriella," replied Emily, "to detail such nonsense amongst the household.

"The Duke will certainly be displeased when he hears of it; and I must insist upon it that you never again repeat such stories, and take every method of contradicting this.

"I am fully persuaded it was no ghost you saw, and in proof that I have no fears, you shall this night leave the antiroom, and I will sleep alone; but remember, if you fear my displeasure, never let me hear such a subject mentioned again, or such idle fancies disseminated by you amongst the servants."

Gabriella had lived with Emily from her infancy; she was strongly attached to her, and the dread of displeasing her could be exceeded by nothing but that produced by the sight of a ghost. Her mistress had never spoken to her so seriously before: she sobbed outright,—

"I would rather die than disobey you; but indeed, indeed, my Lady, it was a spirit, and this is not the first that has been seen.

"Monsieur La France, my Lord Duke's gentleman, met one, but that was in the north bastion, in the picture gallery; and Jacques, and Madelena, and all the servants, have heard noises, and seen lights; and——"

"All these stories, Gabriella," interrupted Emily, "your's has given rise to; and it therefore behoves you to put an end to them. I know what it was alarmed you last night, and know that it was a living being; so let me hear no more of it, but go and contradict your fallacious assertions, if it is not too late. The Duke will be greatly displeased, should it come to his ears."

Gabriella obeyed, but shook her head in doubt as she left the room, and found it was much easier to raise fears in the credulous mind than to subdue the influence of superstition.

Emily, left to herself, revolved in her mind the events of the night, and held a debate with her fears, whether to communicate the apparition she had seen, or conceal the knowledge of it in her own breast. On the latter she determined, for she yet doubted the evidence of her senses, and thought the gloom of the place and hour might have conjured in her imagination this ideal form; yet the voice, the look, the words, were indelibly written on the tablet of memory, and so pre-occupied her mind, that she for some time endeavoured vainly to shake off the impression they caused.

Resolved, however, to prove the truth or fallacy of her conjectures, she thought of again exploring the mysterious chapel when the family should have retired. Having made this determination, she descended to the saloon, where she found Lusignan alone.

"My dear Emily," said he, "I have just bid adieu to your much esteemed friends. Caroline seemed quite oppressed. I made a promise that, as soon as we were at liberty, we would visit them at the Cottage. I hope, in so doing, I have fulfilled your intentions."

"It will indeed ever give me the greatest pleasure," replied Emily, the tear trembling in her eye, "to meet my beloved Caroline. She was my friend, my companion, when from you, Lusignan, I thought myself separated for ever."

"Thank Heaven, my Emily," said the Marquis, "those days of sorrow are past! The constraint my father's moroseness imposes I feel no less irksome than it evidently is to you; but I consider it as a prelude to my future felicity.

"United to my Emily, what shall ever have power to afflict me? At Ivy Cottage, or in any more remote region, with you alone I shall enjoy all of happiness that the world can bestow. Splendour, wealth, and fame, how secondary to this!"

The entrance of La Haye put an end to this conversation, which variously affected our heroine, and she was not sorry for the interruption.

The ladies soon after joined the party, and the day was spent in desultory amusements, as the weather would not admit of pedestrian excursions.

A week elapsed in the same style. Every night, when Emily retired to her apartment, she endeavoured to execute the design she had formed of revisiting the chapel, but her courage failed, and she each morning smiled at her own folly, and resolved to conquer it.

The comforts of the fire-side meanwhile increased. The Duke himself seemed emerging from his wonted severity: his aspect was more humanized.

Emily seemed to have subdued his rigid spirit. He almost felt inclined to love her; and his heart relented at the idea of destroying entirely the reciprocal happiness of Lusignan and Emily. He dreaded being alone with La Haye, who never failed to oppose all his inclinations to mercy and pardon.

He was too bigotted not to think himself bound by the counsels of his spiritual father, and could almost have wished that Emily would agree to a clandestine marriage with his son, to render his consent unnecessary.*

The artless cheerfulness of Emily, and the raptures of Lusignan while he gazed on her, or listened to the melodious notes of her lyre, softened him almost to affection, and removed severity from his brow; but a look from the Abbé soon destroyed this momentary smile, and his features relapsed into rigid gloom.

After a day thus spent, Emily retired to her apartment with a light heart, and a mind uninfluenced by fear or superstition.

Now was the moment, she thought, for visiting the altar. She took a book, and amused herself with it till the distant sound of closing doors had ceased. All was profoundly still, and midnight was passed. Then taking her taper, she gently descended the little staircase, and opened the door which disclosed the sable interior of the chapel.

Her heart beat; she looked fearfully around.

To assure herself no person was concealed she removed some of the black hangings. Something issued from behind them! She started! It was only a harmless bat, dislodged by the light of her taper.

She continued her researches. No subject for alarm appeared. She sat on the coffin, and counted the beadroll.*

Her eye glanced towards the place whence the phantom issued on the former night.

Slow rising from behind the altar, it lifted its wasted form! She trembled, and sat motionless, her eyes fixed on the haggard features of the dread apparition!

They resembled those of her departed father! She shrieked!

It motioned silence!——"Destruction awaits thee!" said a hollow voice. "Fly from it. Thou art the destined victim of love and hereditary hate! I shall meet thee once again, but it will not be till the hour that brings ruin to thy hopes!"——

It ceased and vanished.

Less animated than the cold marble which supported her stood the object of this warning.

Her eye rivetted to the spot, her senses absorbed in terror, her breath suspended, the taper fell from her hand;—she was left in total darkness.

She now groped towards the door. The marble columns that surrounded the chapel appeared to her repetitions of the horrid vision.

She stumbled at every step; but at length reached her deserted chamber. The dying embers on the hearth still emitted light enough to conduct her to the bed.

She threw herself on it in wild affright, and daylight dawned in the east, ere she closed her eyelids.

Gabriella entered her apartment at the accustomed hour. She slept so profoundly, that, unwilling to disturb her, she gently crept out of the room.

The sun had run its midway course, ere she awoke. Her bell summoned Gabriella. She was astonished to find she had slept so long. She fancied some horrid dream had disturbed her:—but fortunately all recollection of the real event was denied her. She was unconscious that she had visited the chapel.

Lusignan's voice in the antichamber enquired if she was not well. She assured him she was perfectly so, and expressed her surprise at having slept so long. He imprinted a kiss on the hand she held out to him, and told her he had good news to communicate, at least such as gave him indescribable delight.

The Duke's *Avocat* was that moment arrived, and assured him that in a week the settlements would be completed, and nothing but her consent wanting to his happiness. She returned no answer, but an eloquent look told Lusignan the intelligence was not displeasing to her.

Breakfast was no sooner over than Madame de Meronville requested she would accompany her to her closet.

"My dearest Emily," said she, "Lusignan has partly prevented my design, by informing you himself of the arrival of the Duke's Homme d'Affaires, but to me he has consigned the care of intreating you will fix an early day for the celebration of your nuptials.

"There is nothing I wish for more ardently than the happiness of calling you my daughter; and so many impediments to my wishes have occurred, that I fear a further protraction, and claim the privilege of fixing the day myself. Will you promise to accede to it, my love?"

Emily blushed deep while she spoke; and, throwing herself into the Duchess's arms, concealed her face, and wept.

Madame de Meronville was no less affected. Both were a few moments dumb. At length Emily broke silence.

"To you and my mother, my dear Madam," said she, "I submit the decision. I could wish a short delay, but do with me what shall appear to you most eligible."

Smiling, the Duchess replied,—

"My sweet girl, I take your wishes into consideration, and will, therefore, not appoint an earlier day than Monday se'nnight."

"Monday se'nnight!" exclaimed Emily. "Surely not so soon!"

"I have consulted Madame de Clarival," replied the Duchess. "She concurs with me, and your consent only is wanting. I know you, my dear child, too well, to think any motives of prudery or affectation can influence you; and therefore, though I can easily account for your reluctance to decide, I am persuaded you will yield to my entreaties, when assured they are dictated by prudence."

"Once more, my dearest Madam, then," said Emily, "dispose of me as you think proper."

Madame de Meronville embracing her, thanked her for this compliance, and left her to recover composure, saying, she had no doubt Lusignan was in the antiroom, waiting her reply. There indeed he was, and received with enraptured heart from his mother the confirmation of his wishes.

CHAP. VIII.

"'Tis strange! 'Tis passing strange!"

With downcast eyes Emily met Lusignan at the hour of dinner. The party was that day increased by some gentlemen who had arrived from Paris, which rendered the conversation more general. The Chevalier Dorimond sat next to Emily, and addressed her on various subjects of history, erudition, and the more common topic of fashions. He found in her a fund of good sense and information very rare in the sex, and which soon induced him to abandon the trifling observations he had been used to detail to every woman he met, and turn the conversation to subjects less general, but infinitely more interesting to a cultivated mind.

Emily herself felt pleased and relieved by his animated manners.

Lusignan kept his eye invariably fixed on her with an expression of delight, that spread a crimson glow on her cheek whenever her averted glance involuntarily met his.

Dorimond knew not which most to admire, her lovely countenance, her enchanting modesty, her elegant manners, or cultivated understanding; all equally delighted him;—he never had seen such an union of charms.

After dinner, he addressed himself to the Abbé, expressing the admiration Emily had excited, and trying, by indirect enquiries, to assure himself whether she was disengaged.

La Haye was not easily deceived: he understood the drift of these interrogatories, and was resolved not to leave Dorimond in doubt, as it was his intention to remove, if possible, every rival. Affecting, therefore, to acquiesce in his opinion, he said,—

"She is, indeed, very amiable; and I am almost tempted to envy the Marquis de Lusignan, who entirely engrosses her affections; and they are, by mutual consent of all parties, soon to be united."

"He is indeed enviable," faltered Dorimond, "and seems worthy of her approbation, for I never knew a young man more universally well spoken of."

La Haye bowed, and entered into conversation with the Duke,

who had approached too near for his purpose, and who might have heard an eulogium of his son, which the Abbé rather wished to conceal.

Dorimond pondered on what he had learned, and sighing, owned there were no hopes for him. Indeed, as a younger brother, and without fortune, he could never have expected to obtain her in an age when even reciprocal attachment was ever sacrificed, and made subservient to aggrandizement and the sordid considerations of wealth.

This, however, had not occurred to him; but, regarding her now as the property of another, he determined not to risk his peace of mind, which he found but too much endangered by this first interview, and therefore ordering his horse, he immediately returned to Paris.

The appointed week rapidly elapsed, though Time, in the ideas of Lusignan, had borrowed leaden pinions.

Emily thought otherwise. An involuntary dread possessed her mind when she thought on the wedding-day; the more unaccountable to herself, as she felt every day more attached to Lusignan, whose virtues and amiable qualities each hour developed.

The tenants looked forward to his residence at the Castle as the commencement of their happiness; and only one opinion prevailed amongst those who knew him, and that was decidedly favourable.

Soon as night returned, with it returned a confused recollection of some horrible dream to Emily, which, however, she could not analyze; yet it preyed on her spirits.

The eve, however, of this dreaded and equally wished-for day arrived. The Duke assembled all his vassals and tenantry, and the great hall, overspread with dainties, was thrown open, and reminded them of former days, and the hospitality of his ancestors.

The lofty roofs resounded with songs of joy and acclamations.

The guests all drank happiness to his Grace, and the young couple, in whose honour the entertainment was given. It ended but late at night.

Lusignan seemed so happy, that Emily could not but participate his joy.

The Duke fixed on them a look of compassion, and suddenly retired from the company. Forced, however, to return by the remonstrances of La Haye, his perturbation could not be concealed,—

it betrayed itself in his countenance; when, as they retired to rest, Emily and Lusignan threw themselves at his feet, and implored his blessing.

Never before had Madame de Meronville seen the tear drawn from his eye, where obduracy and insensibility seemed to have fixed their abode.

His trepidation was visible. The agitation of guilt overcame him. The stagnant feelings of paternal affection seemed to flow anew.

"May Heaven bless you, my children!" said he, in a tone of voice rendered inarticulate by his emotion.

"Oh, my father!" said Lusignan, "how shall I ever make you any return for the happiness I receive at your hands? Ask any sacrifice, any compliance; my heart, overflowing with gratitude, can withhold none."

Emily wept aloud.

"It is too much!" exclaimed the Duke, as he fixed his regard on the irritated and impatient La Haye, and darted out of the room.

The party separated.

The Abbé remained alone, biting his lips, and cursing the perversity of his patron's disposition.

"Another moment," said he, "had ruined my hopes! Another moment, and he had confessed his designs! It must not be. Now, Fortune, smile on me!"

The Duke had twice summoned him to his closet, ere he thought proper to obey. He dreaded a recantation, and wished to ensure the success of his own scheme before there was time to render it abortive.

The family had all been retired an hour. The clock struck one. La Haye entered the apartment of the Duke. He was pacing it in evident perturbation. Never had he been thus agitated.

"Approach, La Haye," said he, in a solemn tone of voice, "I have need of all your counsels; and, as you value my eternal salvation and your own, deliver your sentiments. I feel that I am about to destroy for ever the happiness and peace of mind of two young creatures, who have a right to look up to me for its ensurement. My conscience upbraids me! Their only crime has been that of loving too well. Does Heaven empower me to take vengeance for such an offence? Speak;—it depends on you to regulate their future destiny. Should I be guilty of a crime, on you may the malediction of Heaven light:

for by your counsels I am resolved to be guided. Remember, your own soul and mine are at stake. One word may ensure their salvation, or involve them in eternal perdition!"

La Haye was for a moment silent. He seemed struggling with internal conflicts. Depraved as was his heart, this sacred appeal made him tremble. Repentance was but momentary. He soon recollected himself.

"Would to Heaven, Sir," said he, "you had chosen some other monitor! I know not how to advise you. There is but one circumstance that divides my opinion; but for that, I should yield to my inclinations, and recommend lenity. But there is one impediment, one invincible obstacle——"

"Name it," said his Grace with energy. "If it relates to the apostacy of her ancestors, that cannot influence my decision. The most learned divines are of opinion that their re-admission to the pale of the church is an atonement."

"I have duly weighed this matter," said La Haye, "and far be it from me to differ in opinion with the supports of the Roman Catholic faith: but there is another objection, which I fear cannot so easily be obviated, and which my duty and sacred character oblige me to mention.

"In all ages the inviolability of oaths has been acknowledged. Pagans and Heretics confess their immutability. They are sometimes rashly made, and a strict adherence to them is prescribed as the punishment for such temerity. I lament the necessity of addressing you in language perhaps severe, but no alternative is left me,—I have no power to absolve you from the obligation an oath imposes. Reflect, Sir, on your words—'By my God, and all——'"

"Stop, in mercy!" cried the Duke. "Give me time to breathe! Yes, I have bound myself cruelly! Yet tell me, is there no method, no refuge? Oh my treacherous heart! Never, La Haye, did I feel thus wretched!"——

He paused and groaned.

"Yet a dispensation might be procured. Why did you not sooner tell me of it? All might have been well.—But to-morrow, ——yes—to-morrow,——"

He looked at his watch.

"Heavens! It is two o'clock! To-morrow is already here! My senses madden! Fly, La Haye, as you value my friendship,—my peace of mind! Fly, if it is not now too late! Oh, La Haye, save my child!"

He fell in agony on the couch.

His astonished auditor had not been prepared for a scene like this. He hesitated—but he had studied the human mind, and perfectly understood its various emotions: with that of Meronville's he was particularly acquainted—violent, imperious, irritable.

He doubted not but in a few hours his present agitation, caused by the explosion of a few latent sparks of affection, would subside, and he should have no difficulty in reconciling him to an event which he could persuade him was directed by Heaven, and prompted by chastening mercy. The slave of bigotry, he knew that, with such an assistant, he had nothing to fear.

The business now was to prolong this conference, as he feared to appear designedly inimical to his desires, and yet was resolved not to obey his orders.

"I go, Sir," said he; "but am I justified in yielding to your wishes, at a moment when, blinded by passion, and conquered by affection, you give orders, which in a calmer hour you may repent?"

"Never!" ejaculated Meronville. "At any rate let me have another day to give the cause a fair hearing. I can find some means of protracting the nuptials till the morrow; and then it will still be time——"

He fell into a profound reverie. La Haye stood aloof, and did not interrupt it. At length starting, he exclaimed,—

"Yes, I am resolved! Yes, I was right! La Haye, was you in time to save him? Are my orders obeyed?"

La Haye stammered—

"My Lord! Your orders, my Lord! I wait to hear them, my Lord!"

"How?" said Meronville. "Have you not heard me? Is my son safe?"

"I fly to rescue him, my Lord!" said the terrified Abbé. "I had not heard your decision."

The clock struck three.

"Oh God!" exclaimed Meronville rising, "it is, perhaps, now too late. Fly! Fly! La Haye! Delay not a single moment!"

La Haye now willingly obeyed, for he had no doubt the hour was long past. He left the room with affected alacrity, leaving his patron in a state little short of distraction.

While this passed in the Duke's closet, different scenes were acted in the apartments of Lusignan and Emily. The former, as he retired to rest, was addressed by St. Pierre in terms that, in spite of himself, affected him much. St. Pierre was tenderly attached to his master. He fastened the door cautiously, and then seemed struggling with some restrained communication.

Lusignan enquired what disturbed him?

He threw himself at his feet.

"My dear master," said he, "I fear your displeasure, yet cannot conceal my apprehensions that some dark design is formed against you."

"Against me!" exclaimed Lusignan. "You surely cannot mean what you say?"

"If you will permit me, Sir, to tell you the subject of my alarms," replied St. Pierre, "I trust you will, at least, pardon them, and may Heaven grant that I am deceived!"

"Speak," said Lusignan.

"You know, Sir," continued St. Pierre, "that the feast given by my Lord Duke brought a great concourse of people to the Castle: but amongst these two men came, whom nobody knew. There was something in their appearance I did not like, so I told my Lord's Maitre d'Hotel,* but he said it was all right, and Monsieur l'Abbé knew them.

"However, I watched all their motions, because I had some suspicions. So presently they went into the Castle, and met Monsieur La Haye, and he took them into the oak chamber, and fastened the door.

"Soon after, Gabriella, the Lady Emily's woman, came to me quite terrified, and said that she was in the closet, which is only divided by a thin partition from the oak parlour; she heard your name pronounced several times; so she was fain to listen; but they spoke so low she could hardly hear: only Monsieur l'Abbé several times said, 'the north bastion,' and seemed to be describing your apartment.

"One of the men said twice 'the Marquis de Lusignan.' The conference lasted some time. At last La Haye got off his chair, and Gabriella heard him say 'Two o'clock! Remember, two o'clock! The family will be at rest long before that hour!' He then left the room, and the men in it, and gave orders that no person should go into the oak chamber to-night. This, Sir, is what I wished to communicate. If my conclusions are false, I hope you will excuse them; but I entreat you not to neglect this warning. Indeed, Sir, I am terribly frightened!"

Lusignan was astonished beyond measure. There was a mystery in this affair that seemed to involve some great design. Yet he tried in vain to analyze his vague conjectures: they produced nothing like certainty. Unwilling, however, to publish his alarm, he told St. Pierre he had no fears, and Gabriella must have been deceived.

"She might, Sir," replied St. Pierre; "but I hope you will, at least, permit me to sleep in your antichamber, that I may be near to assist you, in case any thing should happen."

"By no means," rejoined Lusignan. "Who can make any attempt on me during the night?"

"Ah, my dear master!" said his faithful domestic, "you little know what stories are told of Monsieur l'Abbé. All the servants think him very wicked; and it can do no hurt to let me watch in the antiroom."

Lusignan thought as he did with respect to La Haye, but was still so unwilling to betray his suspicions, that he insisted St. Pierre should return to his own apartment.

The poor fellow in vain entreated. He was compelled to submit; but resolved, nevertheless, not to absent himself long or far. As soon, therefore, as he heard his master lock his door, he wrapped himself in his surtout, and took his station in a great chair in the antichamber.

Lusignan, though he had endeavoured to conceal the fears this intelligence gave him from St. Pierre, could not, when alone, deny them to himself. Of what nature La Haye's design might be he could not devise; but he had long considered him as a man not likely to be deterred by any considerations opposed to those of interest. He therefore resolved to watch the remainder of the night, that he might not be surprised whilst sleeping, and unable to make any resistance.

He threw himself on the bed, and the thoughts of that happiness the morrow would bring him chased not only sleep from his pillow, but every idea that might interrupt the visionary scene of bliss in which imagination placed him.

Such ideas he fondly cherished; and sure, since our best enjoyments are but ideal, we may be thankful whenever Hope's elastic spring animates our future prospects.

Lusignan thought so. He revolved in his mind a thousand plans of future happiness—Love and Emily the basis of every delightful chimera, he sunk into oblivion of all but her. But from this pleasing reverie a noise near his bed roused him. He started, and seized his sword. St. Pierre's words occurred to him, and in a moment every horrid suggestion rushed on his mind.

The noise continued. The lamp burnt in the hearth. He cast a wild look towards the place whence the disturbance issued. The tapestry near his bed slowly heaved, and two men armed with pistols appeared.

"At your peril stop!" cried the Marquis. "What midnight ruffians are you? And what is your dark purpose?"

The foremost advanced.

"In the name of the king, surrender," said he in a determined tone, and with a look of horrid ferocity.

Lusignan at these words felt his heart sink. The dreadful reality burst at once on his agonized soul. He examined the lettre de cachet, which he dared not resist.

"At least," said he, "let me see my father. He has credit to obtain my release."

"The Duke de Meronville, Sir," replied they, "is apprised of his Majesty's intentions. You must follow us without delay. You appear," added one with a malicious smile, "to be prepared, for you are dressed."

In fact he had not put off his clothes.

"My friends," said he, holding out his purse, "you shall be well rewarded, if you will only permit me to see my family one instant."

"Were you to offer us the world," replied they, "we could not grant your request. The King's commands are absolute, and must be instantly obeyed. We have already tarried too long. Come, Benedoit, lead the way."

"Impossible!" cried Lusignan. "Sure you are only trying my fortitude."

"We shall soon prove to you that the joke is rather serious," said one. "Come, Sir, march."

Lusignan, almost annihilated, obeyed. They led him down staircases, passages, and gloomy recesses, of which he had not the least knowledge, to a postern gate.* Here a carriage was waiting. They hurried him into it. Benedoit seated by his side, and his companion on the box, it drove off with the rapidity of lightning.

Lusignan was bewildered,—lost in a maze of conjectural doubts. The clock struck three as he entered the chaise. In six hours he was to have been for ever united to Emily. Distraction followed the recollection. The velocity of the motion almost precluded reflection. He thought it was a dream. Relays of horses they found at every stage. They stopped not. Every turn of the wheel removed him from Emily. He sighed, and resigned himself to despair!

END OF VOL. II.

LUSIGNAN.

CHAP. I.

"What beck'ning ghost, along the moonlight shade,
"Invites my steps?"

Emily, when she left the saloon, retired to the apartment of Madame de Clarival, to pour her anxious fears in the bosom of maternal tenderness:—the Duchess attended her to the door, and affectionately embracing her, entreated Heaven's blessing on the vows she was on the morrow to form.

Emily shed a torrent of tears.—

"I know not why, my dear mother," said she, "I feel such poignant anguish on the eve of that day we have all so ardently desired,—a day that is to cement the union of a long-divided family, and ensure to us the blessing of social harmony. Idea portrays happiness in the brightest form, but my heart refuses its assent to the fairy vision,— it seems prophetic of woes to come; tell me, my dearest Madam, whence this happens?"

"My beloved child," replied Madame de Clarival, "I am not surprised at your agitation at the approaching hour, which must fix your destiny for life; the happiest marriages are not exempt from evils, and thus, my child, I felt, when I resigned my hand and heart to the best of men, your ever to be regretted father: the moment was awful, but it was the last pang I ever experienced, till that fatal hour which deprived me of every comfort but my Emily, that alone is left to cheer my passage to the grave. Methinks I now see him, stretched on the bed of death, commending you to the protecting care of Providence.—But let us, my Emily, forget all painful retrospects; in your conjugal felicity I shall find the renewal of my own. Retire to rest,—you require it to compose your agitated spirits; collect your fortitude to support the solemn scene that awaits you, and ever remember, that in all stations, situations, and events, virtue is the peculiar care of Heaven; it vouchsafes its guidance to all who pursue the path of rectitude, and will, I have no doubt, my Emily, still watch over your interests."

"With such a mother, with such an example," said Emily, as she quitted the room, "I shall have no excuse for deviating, even transiently, from the path of virtue."

Arrived in her own apartment, she resolved, by one effort, to stifle the emotions that oppressed her, and seek that repose which she felt indeed the necessity of finding: but vainly she endeavoured to still the trepidation of her mind; it momentarily increased, for now the recollection of the chapel scene recurred forcibly. She could not conceive how it had so long been forgotten; she was much inclined to return to her mother, but there were several long galleries to pass, and she could not command resolution to attempt them at that silent hour;—those terrible words the phantom uttered, "We shall meet again!" vibrated on her ear, and rendered her quite a coward. She looked round her spacious apartment:—it was profoundly dark; her taper was extinguished,—no dying embers in the hearth interrupted the impenetrable gloom. She arose and unclosed her lattices; the moon shone feebly; she cast a fearful look around, persuaded she should again see the horrid spectre;—something white caught her eye; she shrieked,—it was only her own robe carelessly thrown on the chair, which acquired in her disordered imagination a thousand dreadful forms. She recollected that the figure bore the features of her dead father; she knelt, and prayed,—

"Shade of my departed parent," said she, "thou that twice hast deigned to quit the blest abodes of eternity, to visit your wretched child, if ethereal spirits are permitted to guard the tenants of this nether world, support me, I conjure you, in this hour of trial! And Oh! if you again condescend to warn me of approaching evils, direct me how I may best support them; infuse into my mind that fortitude, the best gift of Heaven,* and grant me strength still to pursue the path of virtue, though it should be strewed with thorns!"

She ceased,—and, seating herself near the window, awaited with more composure any event that might befal her.

The clock struck two;—its hollow sound startled her; she looked to the extremity of her apartment, which was bounded by an arched recess;—the dreaded phantom stalked towards her; its garments only she could discern; they were of spotless white. She would have endeavoured to fly, but had not power; motionless she sat, awaiting her sentence from the prophetic ghost.

"Emily," said the phantom, "I am the ghost of thy departed father, suffered to revisit these mortal abodes, to warn my child of the evils she is destined to undergo. This moment is fatal to you,— this moment witnesses the triumph of successful villany; yet fear not; be virtuous, and never despair; your trials will be hard, but the end of them is glorious!"

"Oh my father!" exclaimed Emily, "tell me in pity, must Lusignan also suffer?"

While she spoke, the moonbeams fell on his haggard countenance, and gave it a more livid hue. She trembled,—the cock crew!

"My hour is come," said the ghost: "morning dawns; the east already glows with orient red,—I must return to my eternal habitation; for the last time I am permitted to quit it, but not to reveal the secrets of futurity: Lusignan's fate must remain concealed, till time developes it. Adieu! Remember thy father!"*

It vanished.

"Remember thee!" said Emily: "yes, till this heart shall cease to beat and grieve, thy image shall be present to remembrance. Oh Lusignan! thou to whom my virgin love is given, why was I born to make thee wretched, to darken all thy prospects, to plunge thee in irretrievable misery?"

Long after the spectre had vanished, she sat with her eyes fixed on the spot where it stood, as if expecting to see it rise again; but all was still as the grave. She had recourse to her pillow in vain; rest was flown from her agonized heart; she equally longed for and dreaded the return of day. The mysterious words, "This moment is fatal to you!" what could they mean? In the solemn hour of night perhaps the blow of an assassin deprived Lusignan of life. The dark forebodings of her soul could not be analyzed; a labyrinth of conjectures bewildered her imagination; she fell into a short perturbed slumber, but started in a fright, fancying a phantom more hideous than the former appeared to her; it wore the form of La Haye. Vice was engraved in shining characters on his forehead;* she screamed, and awoke.

She now resolved to seek the apartment of her mother, and relate to her the terrors of this eventful night. She fleeted through the long deserted galleries, trembling at every step. It was just six o'clock; in three hours the nuptial ceremony was to be performed. Emily was not prepared to sustain the scene. She knocked gently at the Countess's door. Rather alarmed at the unusual intrusion, Madame de Clarival opened it, but started at the tremulous voice which told her it was Emily. Darkness prevented her seeing the livid countenance that accompanied it.

"For Heaven's sake, my dear Emily!" said she, "what has disturbed you thus early?"

"Oh Madam!" replied Emily, "did you but know what I have suffered since I left you!"

"My child," returned the Countess, "I thought you had more fortitude;—is the bridal hour then so fraught with terrors?"

Emily, in broken accents, related to her the vision she had seen, and the thrice repeated warnings.

Madame de Clarival now shared her terrors, but endeavoured to moderate their excess by persuading her that the whole was the fiction of a perturbed mind. Emily's reason told her it was otherwise.

"I will try to adopt your opinion, my dear mother," said she, "if all is well when the family assembles; but too surely I believe the hour past. Oh Lusignan! dear Lusignan!"

She continued absorbed in grief, from which no efforts could rouse her, till a tap at the door announced the probable arrival of some intelligence. Gabriella entered with a terrified air, but seemed somewhat relieved when she saw Emily.

"Oh my dear mistress! Heaven be praised you are safe!" said she: "I thought you too had been spirited away. Oh Madam! have you heard what has happened?"

Too much shocked at this confirmation of her fears to enquire the meaning of Gabriella's speech, Emily sat, her eyes fixed with vacant attention on the speaker, while Madame de Clarival ordered her to explain herself.

"Why, my Lady," said she, "you must know that the Marquis de Lusignan has been spirited away during the night, and nobody can guess what is become of him. He could not come out of his room by the door, because it was locked this morning, and besides St. Pierre was in the antiroom; and all the servants say the north bastion is haunted, and so a ghost must have carried him through the keyhole; and yet do you know, my Lady, St. Pierre will not allow that it was a ghost. I never was angry with him before, because it is so obstinate,

you know, my Lady.——Holy Virgin! how pale my Lady Emily
looks! Shall I fetch you any thing, my Lady?"

Emily sat perfectly mute during this relation; her countenance
exhibited no marks of animation, nor did she utter a single groan.
Madame de Clarival, when sufficiently recovered herself to observe
the insensible figure before her, was more terrified than she would
have been by the most violent expressions of grief.

"Look not thus piteously, my Emily," said she, "there is some
unaccountable mistake in this affair; but I doubt not it will soon be
all explained. Then take comfort, my love, and do not drive me to
despair by that sad look."

She embraced her; her tears bedewed the pale cheeks of Emily in
vain, whose quick agitated respiration alone convinced the spectators
she still lived. Her fixed eye, her wan cheek, her lifeless pulse shewed
the agony of her soul, which she sought not to express by a sigh or a
single tear; a heart of adamant would have melted to see that countenance, so lately animated with the smile of love, now insensible as
marble.* Madame de Clarival knew not what to do; she wrung her
hands in despair. Another sufferer soon appeared to share her grief
and terrors—the unfortunate Duchess de Meronville. After trying
in vain to sooth by the kindest caresses and expressions the speechless Emily, she informed the Countess that St. Pierre had slept in the
antichamber; that about three in the morning, he thought he heard
a noise in the Marquis's room, and several persons talking; that he
endeavoured to enter, but the door was locked, and in a moment all
was hushed; so that supposing he had been in a dream, he again fell
asleep. At eight he knocked, as was his custom, at his master's door;
but receiving no answer, after repeating the summons several times,
he forced it open, when, to his utter astonishment, the bed and room
were vacant, and not the least traces of any person having been there
but the Marquis.

"What fatal event has happened," continued the Duchess, in tears,
"I am wholly at a loss to conceive. I sent to request I might see the
Duke, but received for answer that he was too much shocked to see
any body but La Haye, who brought me this message. We must omit
no endeavours speedily to elucidate this mystery, but our first care
must be this dear suffering angel. I will order Le Saxe to prescribe for
her, if alas! the disease of the mind does not baffle the physician's art."

Le Saxe thought it advisable that Emily should lose blood; this restored her in a small degree to her senses, but the faculty of speech was gone, and even her feelings remained nearly in the same torpid state of annihilation.

While this passed in the apartment of the Countess, Meronville raved and deplored the execution of the order he had given. La Haye affected great concern at having arrived too late to prevent it, though it was his fixed purpose to do so. He had now an arduous task to perform, but he had two powerful auxiliaries, Bigotry and Shame:—by the former he hoped to persuade his patron, that the coercion exercised on his son was the work of Heaven; by the other he doubted not of prevailing to keep him silent as to the share he had in the disappearance of the unfortunate Marquis. His first step was to keep him wholly secluded from the intercourse of every person but himself, till the acute sensations of remorse should subside, to effect which he employed every argument most likely to prevail; and in the course of one day he already found his scheme began to operate. Madame de Meronville in vain requested to see him; she was always answered that he was not yet sufficiently composed to meet her. La Haye rightly judged that a very short time would restore all his influence, and destroy that of natural affection, which was in general a dormant principle in the mind of his patron, though of late inflamed by the raptures of Lusignan, and the mild effulgence of female excellence.

For a week poor Emily continued in the state of insensibility to which Gabriella's information had reduced her. At length nature yielded to the violence of sorrow; she fell into a kind of hysteric fit, and a flood of tears restored her recollection of the deplorable evils she had suffered. She enquired for Lusignan; the dejected countenances around told her there was no pleasing intelligence to communicate;—a dangerous fever succeeded.

It had lasted some time, and been attended with the most alarming symptoms, when Meronville, who had not yet quitted his apartment, consented to admit the Duchess. He told her, after the fatal event that had happened, he could no longer bear to remain at Luneville, where every thing reminded him of it; that he was therefore resolved to return immediately to Paris, where he was more likely to make some discovery, and that she was at liberty to remain with her friends, for whom he expressed the greatest concern and esteem.

The unsuspicious heart of his Duchess gave full credit to these professions of sorrow; and indeed they were not wholly false; every latent principle of equity or virtue reproached him with the horror he had committed through the unjustifiable thirst of revenge which he indulged without controul, and he could not even endure the regards of his timid Duchess.

La Haye promised himself much advantage from this removal; absence in all cases operates powerfully, and where nothing occurs to revive the recollection, it soon loses its poignancy. The severe illness of Mademoiselle de Montalte was less favourable to his views; but he judged of her by comparison with those depraved females who had been his associates, and doubted not but she would readily accept another lover, when the one she had chosen appeared for ever lost to her. He accompanied Meronville to Paris, and there had daily the satisfaction to witness the progress of time and absence; for ere long the Duke appeared to have forgotten that any thing had disturbed the equanimity of his austere soul.

The Duchess de Meronville accepted with delight the offer of remaining at the Castle, to aid the Countess, and administer, if possible, comfort to the disconsolate Emily. Her long fits of delirium hardly admitted a hope of recovery, as the lucid intervals were but transient, and in them she always expressed her resignation, and hopes of soon being released. Madame de Clarival attended her night and day, and the effect of anxiety and perpetual watchings soon appeared on her delicate frame.

One day when Emily, contrary to her usual custom, had fallen into a profound and tranquil slumber, the Countess retired for a few moments, to leave her undisturbed. On her return she was surprised to find the door unclosed. She approached the bed, and gently drew the curtains aside,—Emily was gone!—She called for assistance; Gabriella and the faithful St. Pierre attended;—they sought her through the innumerable apartments of the Castle. Madame de Clarival pursued the path pointed out by the expanded doors, which she had probably unclosed;—this led her to the ominous chapel, where she had never been before. The fragile form of Emily there presented itself, leaning against a marble column, whose snow-white surface was rivalled by the wan cheek of Emily; the violence of a delirious fever had given her strength to reach the chapel.

"For mercy's sake, my sweet Emily," said her mother, "return with me!"

"No!" said Emily, in a solemn tone, and a look of terrifying wildness, "I am come here to be buried; here my father appeared to me,—here, Lusignan, we may be united. You would not be so cruel, Madam, to take me away! Where is my mother? Send her to me,—I hate strangers.* Oh my poor heart! Well, it is just breaking! Tell my mother not to weep for me; I shall go to Heaven, and pray for her, and pray for my dear Lusignan: he loved me much, but not more than I loved him. Oh, no! no! no!"

By this time the servants, drawn by the cries of Madame de Clarival, arrived, and conveyed her away, though she resisted with a force almost supernatural, and which entirely exhausted her remaining strength.

The physicians now declared her disorder was coming to a crisis, and that on the morrow she must either die or amend. Of the latter but little hopes appeared. The Countess watched a lucid interval to call in a priest, who should administer the last sacrament. Towards night she grew more composed; they sent to a neighbouring convent for a confessor, who soon arrived. He waited but a few moments, for her senses now returned. When she saw the venerable man, she welcomed him with such sweetness and angelic resignation, as drew tears from all present.

"Holy Father," said she, "I have but a few hours to live; my soul is ready to quit its mortal confinement; it is fit my remaining moments should be spent in prayer; assist me to support this awful scene, to elevate my thoughts to Heaven. Oh God! thou that knowest my inward soul, bear witness that I die in peace and charity with all men. I have secret enemies;—I know them not, but my pardon rests with them. Pardon them, merciful Lord! and pardon my sins, particularly that of having loved too well, and placed that affection on a created being, due only to thy Divinity."

Whilst she spoke, a faint flush overspread her wan cheek; her dim eyes were animated with celestial hope; she looked an angel.*

"Daughter!" said the venerable Friar, "be comforted; Heaven accepts your prayers, and absolves you, by my mouth, from your offences. Enviable is your lot in being thus early torn from the temptations of a sinful world, while yet your heart is uncontaminated by it. Daughter, be thankful to Heaven for this blessing, and join with me in prayer."

He put a crucifix and bead-roll into her hand; she kissed it with fervour, and remained for some time in devout prayer: but the Friar, observing her increasing paleness, now summoned the family to receive her last breath.

As soon as she saw Madame de Clarival and the Duchess enter, she entreated them to approach. Drowned in tears, they knelt in silent agony over her, while she spoke thus:—

"My beloved mother, and you, my dearest Madam, who have vouchsafed to me a parent's fondness, let me not see you thus oppressed! Can any happiness be compared to that of feeling, past doubt, that your soul is about to be translated to its eternal habitation;—that, relieved for ever from the woes inseparable from humanity, you henceforward partake the divine nature? To leave you, best of mothers, costs me indeed a severe pang, but believe me, we shall soon meet again. A reunion with those we love is the most exalted of pleasures, and that will surely not be denied to us in the realms of bliss.* My career has been short; in the flower of my youth Heaven deigns to take me to itself. Could I be sure of leaving you happy, how gladly would I resign this intellectual being! It yet grieves me not to see once again my much-loved Caroline; tell her that with my latest breath I implored the blessings of Providence on her! Oh! if I yet dare name that being to whom my early love was given, tell him it is my dying wish that with some virtuous object he should forget that ever he loved his Emily; tell him that, if after death we are permitted to communicate with terrestrial beings, I will still watch over him, and, as a guardian angel, protect him!* Above all, charge him, as my last request, to conform to the wishes of his father. I fear it is the curse of disobedience which has rendered our lives a scene of woe. May Heaven, avenged by my death, accept the expiation, and may he henceforward be restored to happiness!"

She embraced her mother and the Duchess, and then continued:—

"Farewel, dearest mother and best of women! dry those tears, I conjure you; we part but for a season. My soul, elevated to its God, feels no pang in separating from mortality, but that of leaving you comfortless. I go to intercede——"

She could proceed no further;—exhausted by the effort of speaking thus long, she fainted. Sobs and convulsive groans echoed from all parts of the apartment; soon, however, she again revived, and endeavoured to speak. The physician felt her expiring pulse, then looked at the Confessor, who understood his meaning, and, presenting the crucifix, said—

"Daughter, commend your soul to Heaven."

Madame de Clarival was now conveyed from the chamber in a state of insensibility; the Dutchess remained, expecting to receive her last breath. Emily kissed the crucifix, then returned it to the Friar, and, closing her eyes, remained silent. The physician ordered every person to leave the room. Madame de Clarival, herself almost a corpse, obeyed, and waited every moment the information that she had expired. Contrary, however, to all hopes, she still breathed in the morning, which the Doctor had mentioned as the crisis; her pulse was now animated; he began almost to hope, but would not communicate it, fearful to aggravate the disappointment, should it prove such; and it was still so doubtful, that every moment might be her last. She remained without motion, but she breathed gently, and soon fell into a sweeter slumber than any she had yet experienced. Want of rest had proved so destructive to her body as well as mind, that Le Saxe hoped a return of it would restore both. He ordered every thing to be kept perfectly tranquil, and positively prohibited Madame de Clarival or the Duchess from entering the apartment. They received this injunction with rapture at the moment when they expected to hear that Emily had expired. She still lived, but so feeble, so wasted, that the prospect of her ever regaining strength every day lessened.

Whilst his victim thus lingered on the verge of eternity, La Haye enjoyed the success of his schemes. So entirely was the Duke reconciled to the want he had so lately deplored, that he seemed to have forgotten his son, or only remembered to execrate his disobedience, and wish him united to some great family, whose rank and connections would extend the authority, and add splendour to his family.

He now began to wish the return of his Duchess, who had remained too long at Luneville, and mentioned his design of summoning her to the Abbé. The latter wished to postpone this yet a little while, till Emily's death or recovery could be ascertained, and he had regular advices every day of the progress of her disorder. He hoped then to make the recal of her Grace conducive to his views, by making it appear that she had abandoned Emily, or at any rate to remove from her a person whose amiabilities he could not but acknowledge would attach Emily every hour more strongly to Lusignan.

The latter had arrived, without interruption, at Belleisle Priory, an ancient structure, situated in the Cevenni mountains,* and which was the destined seat of his confinement. He was inclosed in a tower, where the breath of heaven could scarcely penetrate; it was only six feet square, and he was never permitted to leave it, even for the purpose of exercise. The furniture consisted only of a stock bed, a chair, and table. Books, pen and ink, and every thing that might have lessened his misery, or beguiled the tedious hours, were denied him. One of the men, who had assisted in forcing him from Luneville, each day brought him his limited nourishment, which was of the meanest kind. But he was wholly insensible to the rigours of his situation, excepting as they were connected with his removal from Emily. The recollection of the event which had separated them appeared so astonishing, that he could hardly convince himself it was real. Sometimes he felt persuaded it was a mere vision, a delusive dream, from which he should soon awaken. Petrified he stood!—then in a fit of phrenzy would attempt to burst the strong barricadoes by which his prison was secured, but his efforts were impotent and fruitless. He wished to ascertain by what right he was there confined, but his jailer was inviolably silent. The lettre de cachet, he thought, must have been procured by his father's desire; yet he had appeared to relent; and wherefore should he, by affected lenity, have raised his hopes only to plunge him in a gulph of disappointment? He now ruminated on the words of St. Pierre, so coincident with his own opinion of La Haye, and lamented that he had not permitted him to watch as he requested, since he could then at least have informed Emily of the coertion practised against him. Now a thousand doubts must perplex her soul; perhaps she might think him false—that, he hoped, was impossible; perhaps she might suppose him murdered—at least he trusted she would shed a tear to his memory; perhaps she might be induced to give her hand to another—distraction accompanied the suggestion. He paced his cell, he stamped, he groaned, he felt emasculated. Another idea soon presented itself; he thought of her sweetness, her gentle affection, her delicate frame; he feared the shock might be fatal to her—he

saw her expiring, calling on his name in vain—he heard her not. Far
from feeling relieved by the consciousness that their sufferings were
mutual, his were increased by the apprehension of occasioning her's.
"Oh my Emily!" would he exclaim, "forget for ever the wretched
being that adores you, more wretched in the certainty that but for
him you would have been happy in the exalted state to which your
rank and virtues entitled you!"—In these melancholy ruminations
Lusignan wasted the live-long day. He could not by any means
ascertain the flight of time, as his watch had been purloined by the
ruffians who escorted him from the Castle; and the partial rays of
the sun, admitted through the grated aperture in the roof of his cell,
enabled him not to mark its diurnal revolutions.

CHAP. II.

"The suffrage of the wise,
"The praise that's worth ambition, is attained
"By sense alone and dignity of mind."

Emily's recovery, though slow, now appeared certain. Every day
accelerated it; her reason was perfectly restored; and though it
served only to bring to her remembrance the horrors of her situation, it had no other effect than that of reducing her to a settled
state of melancholy. She enquired for her mother and the Duchess.
Le Saxe permitted them to see her, hoping to divert her mind, and
animate her absorbed faculties. The first meeting was distressful to
all parties. Emily felt as though she was actually restored to life,
and Madame de Clarival and the Duchess could hardly persuade
themselves it was her, whom they had lately considered as lost to
them for ever.* The altered looks of the Countess, now scarcely
less an invalid than her lovely daughter, were not unobserved by
Emily. She silently accused herself of being the cause. She longed to
enquire about Lusignan, but dared not trust herself with his name;
and Le Saxe, fearful of fatiguing her, desired the interview might
not be prolonged.

St. Pierre, whose suspicions of La Haye were too just to be easily
extinguished, resolved to examine the apartment of the Marquis,
hoping to discover some trace of the fraud by which his vigilance

had been eluded. After diligent search, he discovered the hidden door through which the miscreants had penetrated. Rejoiced at his success, he took a lamp, and descended the stair-case, supposing his master might be concealed in some of the subterraneous caverns. He sought in vain, and was returning somewhat disappointed, when a paper on the floor attracted his attention; he stooped and picked it up, and, returning to the light, examined its contents. It was only a fragment, but contained a clue which gave St. Pierre the greatest hopes of at last discovering the abode of Lusignan, though it might not be in his power to release him. The words were as follows:—

"Secure him; remember your reward is unbounded, but your secrecy must be inviolable. The lettre de cachet will be sent to you in a few days, and will exculpate you from all blame. I take the responsibility on myself; be assured his Grace lends me his authority. Belleisle Priory is situated——"

The remainder was torn off; but St. Pierre had read enough to convince him this fragment had fallen from the pocket of some person employed by La Haye to secrete his ill-fated master, for he doubted not the writing was his, and that the blackest designs were executing against the Marquis. He lamented that the words extended no further, as he was now in doubt how far Belleisle Priory was connected with the disappearance of Lusignan. He now debated with himself whether he should communicate his discovery to Madame de Meronville immediately, or wait till further investigation should elucidate his doubts. The latter plan he could have wished to pursue, but his ignorance of the situation of the Priory made him resolve to consult the Duchess, who could inform him whether any of the family estates were so called. He therefore took an early opportunity of requesting a private interview with her, in which he delivered the intelligent scrap to the astonished Duchess. That such depravity existed she had no previous conception, and she began to doubt the reality of what her domestic said; but when he repeated to her what Gabriella had heard, she could no longer dispute or deceive herself: the enormity of La Haye's conduct was lost in that of the man to whom she had at the altar and in the presence of Heaven vowed obedience; how could she ever meet him again? how conceal her horror at sight of him? She commended the fidelity of St. Pierre, and dismissed him with strict charge not to let his knowledge of this business escape him, and promising to consult on the best mode of proceeding, and communicate to him her determination.

Left alone, she wept in bitter agony her fate, and the misfortunes of Lusignan; but though she had no hopes of procuring his release, she yet trusted, by the means of St. Pierre, to convey a letter, which might alleviate his sufferings. She resolved to repeat to the Countess alone what she had learnt, and to conceal, if possible, even from her, the share the Duke had in the affair; but while she was thus meditating, a letter from Paris was delivered to her. It contained a summons for her to quit the Castle, and a request that Madame de Clarival and her daughter would remain there till there was no longer any danger attending a removal, and some studied lamentations as to the impossibility of discovering the Marquis de Lusignan.

Madame de Meronville read this letter with mingled emotions, all of them painful to a sensitive mind. To quit Emily, she felt was quitting all she now loved, and at a moment too when her presence might be necessary to sooth her affliction and divert her melancholy. The Countess had all the appearance of a rapid decay; she was reduced almost to a skeleton, and her sallow complexion and sunk eye were very alarming symptoms. On the other hand, by remaining at Luneville, she was more likely to be of effectual service to Lusignan, than she could be immersed within the walls of Paris; and, above all, the duplicity and moral turpitude of her husband's conduct, so revolting to her nature, made her shudder at the idea of meeting him again; besides, being certain of having to support the presence of the detested La Haye.

All these considerations weighed heavy on the mind of the Duchess. She stood in the attitude of affliction when Madame de Clarival entered. She put Meronville's letter into her hand, and when she had perused it, said,—

"I am obliged to quit you, my dear Madam, but my heart, believe me, remains here. My orders, you see, are peremptory, and I dare not even ask a short reprieve. How I grieve to leave my beloved daughter, (for as such I shall ever consider her) before she is fully restored to health; but alas, I am bound, and have no power to contest the authority which summons me to scenes of gaiety, where I shall carry an aching heart."

"My Emily," said the Countess, mournfully, "will break her's at this unexpected separation; and Heaven knows I am but little able to support her sorrows and my own!"

"One subject, my dear friend," resumed the Duchess, "however painful, I must not neglect; this is perhaps the last opportunity I may have of addressing you undisturbed, and without witnesses,—I have discovered the fraudulent attempts that have been made to conceal my son."

"Your son!" exclaimed the Countess.

"Yes," replied the Duchess, with a deep sigh; "the basest and most detestable plot has been executed against him, and my heart bleeds while I am obliged to confess, that his father has, in some degree, been accessary to it, though I am convinced that want of resolution is the culpability of his conduct: the contriver and executor I believe to be La Haye, who, under the mask of religion does not blush to form the most odious and criminal designs against innocence and virtue."

The Duchess then shewed Madame de Clarival the fragment found by St. Pierre, and related to her the circumstances which gave rise to his suspicions.—She then continued:—

"I have no doubt a lettre de cachet has been procured, not by the desire, but connivance of the Duke, and that Lusignan is in virtue of it now confined at Belleisle Priory, which is situated in a remote part of the Cevenni mountains, where but for this accident we were not likely ever to have heard of him. Of what nature his confinement may be cannot now be ascertained, but I shall endeavour, by the means of St. Pierre, whose fidelity may be relied on, to convey a letter to his prison-house, which will be a source of consolation to him. Would you think it advisable, my dear Madam, to mention our discoveries to Emily, and give her an opportunity of writing to him herself?"

"At present," replied the Countess, "I think her mind is not in a state to receive with composure any intelligence which so nearly concerns the Marquis. Her delicate susceptibility would be deeply wounded by the consciousness that for her sake he is deprived of liberty, and I fear the least irritation of spirits might be fatal to her. Till she is, therefore, in some degree recovered, and reconciled to her fate, silence will be more prudent; but indeed I fear your departure will sensibly affect her."

"It is to me," rejoined Madame de Meronville, "a melancholy necessity; but it is not my fortune ever to be continued in the enjoyment of what I love."

"I go then," cried the Countess, "to prepare her for what is inevitable. How much I lament the absence of Caroline. It is my fixed purpose to go to Switzerland as soon as Emily's health will permit; the air may be of service when she is convalescent, and no less so to me;—my strength has been much impaired by the violent shocks it has undergone."

Madame de Meronville answered only by a look of assent that spoke her concern, and then hastened to give orders for her departure on the morrow.

While the Countess went to prepare Emily for the new trial, to which her fortitude was destined, she found her reclining on a sopha, her eye, humid with the unchecked tear, fixed on a full-length portrait of Lusignan which hung over the chimney. There was a look of plaintive sadness in her countenance that expressed the feelings of her widowed heart. She smiled as her mother approached, and endeavoured to conceal her emotions, but they were too visible to escape a parent's eye.

"My Emily," said she, "I have a scheme in view which I hope will give you some pleasure. It is my intention to visit Ivy Cottage as soon as your health will permit. Caroline, I am sure, will rejoice to see us, and it will, I hope, equally conduce to your happiness."

"Happiness!" said Emily, the tear starting in her eye: "Ah, my dear Madam, it was never meant for me."

Seeing her mother affected, she added,—

"Pardon me, dearest of mothers: I would not afflict you; it was an involuntary exclamation. Wounded as is my heart, I trust I am not insensible or dead to the feelings of a friendship generous as is my Caroline's. Nothing can give me such real delight as a journey to the Valais, and your health requires it, I fear, more than mine; but while Madame de Meronville remains at the Castle, I would willingly remain also. Perhaps it may be the last opportunity we shall have of enjoying her society, and I would very reluctantly curtail moments so precious."

"I fear," replied Madame de Clarival, "the Duke will not permit her to remain long with us, and to quit Luneville is what I anxiously desire. She has had a letter this morning pressing her return to Paris."

"Surely she will not leave us," said Emily.

"She has no alternative," resumed the Countess: "if his Grace demand it, obedience has long been her only choice."

"And how soon," rejoined Emily, with a faultering voice.

"My beloved child," said her mother, "this one more sacrifice is required of you. Bear up, my love; I have no doubt we shall one day assemble again. A long life is before you, and, I trust, fortune has exhausted her malice in your youth, to leave uninterrupted the joys of futurity: The Duchess must leave us in a few days."

"Oh my dear mother," replied Emily, while her tears flowed rapidly, "I cannot lose her! Pardon me; with such a parent I ought not to repine; but she is so dear to me, for her own sake, for that of——"

She could proceed no further, but fell into the arms of the Countess. Their sighs and tears were mingled, when Madame de Meronville entered the room. No less affected herself, she knew not how to address Emily; but by an effort, of which she alone was capable, she soon turned the conversation to other subjects, and the evening approached without any further mention being made of her departure.

Emily, during her illness, always retired early. She was yet ignorant that the Duchess intended to set out the following morning, and the Countess wished to conceal it from her, thinking she would be sooner reconciled to an event which had actually taken place, and for which there was therefore no remedy, than to one in reversion; besides, the exertion of taking leave might exhaust her yet feeble frame. When the hour, however, of separation arrived, the Duchess, whose fortitude had sustained her through the day, could no longer command her emotions. She wept, she embraced Emily, she quitted the apartment thrice, and as often returned to it, still lingering near the object she almost idolized. Emily could not help noticing her more than usual tenderness; and recollecting the conversation she had in the morning with her mother, began to suspect the truth.

"You are going to leave me," she exclaimed; "I am sure you are going to leave me. No! do not be so cruel."

"Soon I must, my love, and oh! with what regret!"

She stole from the room, and nothing could prevail on her to return, so truly was she concerned at her own imprudence, which had discovered what she wished so much to conceal. Emily passed a restless night, convinced that the Duchess meant to depart in the morning, ere the sun should gild the distant horizon; and, in fact, the moon had not yet resigned her dominion, when the noise of horses in the court below left her no room to doubt her conjectures were accurate. Soon after she heard the noise of the portcullis, and could not refrain from unclosing her lattices to take a farewell view of the amiable Duchess. The imperfect rays of light which dimly issued from the grey east, hardly permitted her to distinguish the vehicle which conveyed her much loved friend; but as the wheels, with rapid motion, rolled over the draw-bridge, Madame de Meronville looked back. Emily doubted not it was her. The stillness of the hour, the massy walls before her, the gloomy presages of her mind, all concurred in the parting sigh with which she returned to her deserted pillow. Lost in misery, and overwhelmed with grief, she lay; but her native virtue and firmness soon asserted their empire: she accused herself of impiety to Heaven, which had permitted an accumulation of woes, perhaps only to try her fortitude. She resolved to repine no more, but closing her wearied eyelids, forgot in ideal bliss, real and effective misery.

CHAP. III.

"Hark! the death-bell sounds!"*

One day as Lusignan, in his solitary prison, was mourning his wayward fate, and weeping his lost Emily, he was surprised by the entrance of a new jailer, whose countenance bore not so evidently the traces of native ferocity as did that of his companion. There was an impression of sorrow in his eye as he fixed it on the emaciated form before him. The sympathetic tear seemed ready to fall; his hand trembled as he delivered the scanty pittance allotted to the unfortunate heir of Meronville. He seemed desirous, yet fearful, of speaking. Lusignan, struck with his features and appearance, as the rays of the lamp developed them, determined to make an effort to procure the means of addressing Emily, which he felt would compensate for his worst of misery.

"Friend," said he, "you seem not ungentle; tell me, can pity warm your breast for a wretch cruelly oppressed, deceived, persecuted past endurance?"

The young man sighed and shook his head, and in a half whisper, said,—

"I dare not speak."

Lusignan looked towards the door, and saw the shadow of a man, who doubtless stood there to observe the motions of his companion, and detect any attempt at indulgence; he therefore forbore to add any thing further; but as the rusty bolts were again secured, he perceived a slight glimmering in the corner of his cell. He approached and examined it; it was a dark lanthorn, which, turned to the wall, gave only light sufficient to be distinguished in the extreme darkness that surrounded it, but, when trimmed, illuminated the whole cell. His heart bounded: there was also a book under it. Here was a luxury from which he had so long been debarred, that he felt inexpressible delight.—"Now," thought he, "kind benefactor, only allow me pen, ink, and paper, and you restore me to life. Oh my Emily! I may then inform you of my cruel state, and my inviolable constancy."

Occupied with this idea, time seemed divested of its leaden pinions, and his dungeon was again unclosed long before he could have hoped the sun had accomplished its diurnal course. Apprehensive of a discovery in case his former jailer should return, he again concealed the lamp as he had found it; but the youth who brought it once more attended. He whispered his gratitude, and ventured to request implements for writing, but he was answered only by a shake of the head. Looking round when he retired, Lusignan discovered a scrap of paper he had dropped. Not doubting but that it contained some information to him, he eagerly unfolded it, and read thus:—

"I am deeply concerned at your fate, and would give worlds to relieve you. At present it is not in my power; but if you are prudent and silent I do not despair. Depend on my best endeavours. Your former jailer is in a weak state of health, which is the reason that his employment is deputed to me; but never would I have accepted it, but in the hopes of rendering you some service. I do not know you, but misfortune in any shape is entitled to commiseration. Examine the roof of your dungeon; there is a trap-door, which is perhaps not fastened, and you may, by forcing it, enjoy at intervals the light of heaven, but be careful to have it always closed at the hours of meals."

The words here ended, and seemed broken off abruptly. Lusignan fell on his knees, and breathed thanksgivings to Heaven for this ray of hope, calling forth blessings on the compassionate stranger. He then proceeded to search for the trap-door, and soon found it, but his efforts to force the bolts were ineffectual: in vain he applied strength and dexterity; he was retreating in despair, but determined to make one last effort. He exerted his whole force; aided by hope and desperation, the bolt yielded, the door unclosed, his heart dilated with joy, but night prevented his deriving any present fruits from his labours: he closed it cautiously, and longed for the return of day.

The smile with which he greeted his youthful jailer, when he entered early in the morning, convinced the latter that his endeavours had been crowned with success; and he was no less rejoiced than the enraptured prisoner, who was no sooner left alone, than he repaired to the trap-door, opened it, and felt the breath of Heaven descend to refreshen his feverish brain. He now thought it not impossible to ascend, and putting his hands on one side of the aperture, he sprung with extreme agility, and soon found himself emancipated, and at liberty to range over a vast parapet, commanding an extensive prospect, but so elevated that objects beneath appeared all in miniature. The morning was delightful; the birds, guarding their nests built in the lofty pines, filled the air with delicious melody; the nightingale warbled her farewell notes, as she retired from the approach of day. Lusignan thought himself under the influence of some magic enchantment. Wherever he looked some beautiful landscape met his wondering eyes, so long a stranger to the display of Nature's plenteous stores. He had arrived at the Priory in that dull season when the snow-girt mountains and fading verdure proclaimed the gloomy reign of winter; now every thing shone, and seemed gladdened with vernal bloom. On one side the distant Appenines raised their majestic summits, towering to the skies, and appeared ready to fall on the enamelled plains beneath. Here the fertile valleys of Switzerland, covered with a fleecy brood, white as the driven snow, charmed the eye; here the beholder almost trembled at the splendour of Alpine grandeur. On the other hand the broad Rhone extended itself in innumerable windings; its fertile banks covered with living verdure, and shaded by luxuriant woods. Lusignan turned towards Paris, where he supposed his treasure lay, but it was too distant for the eye to trace.—The peasants, hastening to their daily labours, almost excited the envy of the Marquis, who listened to their rustic songs as they ascended on the air, whilst with frugal hand they stored the rich land, and hoped from Providence an abundant increase. In a neighbouring pasture the shepherd's boy tuned his pipe to notes of love; Lusignan's heart beat responsively; he listened, he gazed, and reluctantly retired to his solitary cell only when the gloom of evening reminded him of the rapid flight of ruthless time.

He judged by the surrounding prospects that he was at Belleisle Priory; for as he had travelled there by night, or with the blinds closed, he could not before form any accurate conjecture as to the scene of his seclusion. He now found that he had traversed the kingdom from west to east, and so wide was the distance which separated him from all he loved; he sighed as past occurrences crowded to his imagination, but was not insensible of the little alleviation Heaven had that day granted to his misery; and, fearful of discovery, and consequent deprivation, he hastily closed the trap-door, and resumed his situation in the dungeon.

Several days passed thus, and Lusignan, who had perhaps only been delighted by the scenery around him with a view to more happiness in reversion, began to despond as before. The kind stranger still attended him, but, always observed by the ferocious jailer, durst attempt no further amelioration of his fate. He regularly brought him fresh oil when that of a former day was expended, so that he was now no longer subject to darkness, even during the night; but by long confinement and inertion his faculties grew torpid, and his native strength of mind relaxed: a gradual but deep melancholy took possession of his soul; he fancied himself not only resigned, but indifferent to every future want; he sometimes wondered at the oblivion in which he was buried, sometimes accused his mother, his Emily, of unkindness; sometimes thought his father the author of his woes; at others he blamed only La Haye, and resolved to be avenged should ever liberty be restored to him. In these ruminations he stood reclined against the tower, when looking at the road beneath, he discovered a man apparently examining, with critical accuracy, the situation of the vast edifice he inhabited. The distance was so immense from the summit of this tower to the base of the structure that he could hardly discern the features of the person, but thought he was not unacquainted with the figure, which was tall and well proportioned. The man looked towards the spot where he stood, and retired a few paces back to take a more concise view. Lusignan hesitated, hoped, feared, and recognised St. Pierre. The poor fellow was not long in doubt, but neither durst speak, though by signs and gestures they expressed mutual satisfaction at the rencontre. The Marquis could almost have leaped from the eminence to enquire for Emily, but certain destruction awaited the attempt, and before either had resolved on any method of communication, the night drew on, and impenetrable clouds separated them.

Certain that St. Pierre would not leave the Priory while any hopes of addressing him remained, Lusignan spent the night in forming plans, which destroyed themselves, as he could not admit St. Pierre to the knowledge of them.

Early in the day, before he had ventured to open the trap-door, because his morning sustenance had not been brought, he heard a knocking, proceeding to appearance from the roof of his cell. He looked towards the grated aperture, and saw his faithful domestic, who let fall a letter. Exulting with new-born hope, he unclosed the door, and in a few words desired him to remain there till he returned, which should be as soon as the accustomed visit of the jailor should set him free till evening. Almost before the bolt was fastened, he heard the massy key applied to the lock, and Vicenza entered. His visit was as usual short; he set down the cruse of water and allowance of bread, and without uttering a syllable retired. Lusignan flew to the door, and admitted St. Pierre, who, overcome with his emotions at the melancholy state in which he saw his beloved master, threw himself at his feet, and remained speechless. The Marquis raised him affectionately, and enquired how he had discovered his abode, and by what fortunate chance he had reached the summit of the eastern turret.

"Oh my dear master," replied he, "you remember the warning I gave you on the night you were so basely betrayed, and though you would not permit me to watch near you, I remained in the antiroom; and, alarmed by the voices in your apartment, attempted to enter, but the door was fast, and all being soon silent, I thought myself mistaken, certain that no one had passed through the anti-chamber. The next morning, however, finding by your disappearance all my prognostics verified, I could not doubt but there was some direct outlet to your chamber, by which the emissaries of La Haye entered to execute their murderous purpose. By long search I discovered it, and descending the spiral staircase, found part of a letter, which discovered the place of your confinement, and convinced me that in fact the Abbé was the author of it. I communicated what I learnt to my Lady Duchess, who gave me the letter which you now hold."

Lusignan, though delighted to hear from his mother, looked half disappointed to find it was not from Emily.

"And, Emily!" he exclaimed: "has she not written to me?"

St. Pierre shook his head.

"Alas, my dear master," said he, "the lady Emily has suffered much. We all thought she would have died; she received the last sacrament, and bade us all adieu, but Monsieur le Saxe says, youth and an excellent constitution restored her, when he thought it impossible she could recover."

"Death and destruction!" said Lusignan: "and all these sufferings for my sake! Is she informed of my situation?"

"My Lady Duchess," replied St. Pierre, "durst not tell her till she was more recovered, but I believe she suspects the truth, though she seems fearful of mentioning your name."

The Marquis, after perusing his mother's letter, the characters of which were almost effaced by the tears with which she had bedewed it, made every enquiry about Emily which love could dictate. St. Pierre related to him all that had passed since his departure. Madame de Meronville herself informed him that the Countess and Emily were on the eve of a journey to the Valais, and entreated him to write a submissive letter to his father. "I know," said she, "my dearest child, that I require of you a sacrifice almost greater than life itself, but there is a necessity for it: consent, then, to relinquish Emily! Her excellent heart and superior understanding will assist her to conquer an attachment which can only make you both wretched; and I am convinced, that if she was assured that you were at liberty, and enjoyed tranquillity at least, if not happiness, she would feel infinitely relieved from the anguish which destroys her.—Make an effort, my child, worthy your noble nature; endeavour to appease your father's resentment; consent to live single, in compassion to a mother who adores you, and avert the dire calamities that await perseverance in an ill-fated attachment."

Lusignan acknowledged the force of this reasoning, which did not proceed from a heart callous to the sufferings it deplored, or accustomed to philosophize with stoic apathy on the misfortunes of others. It was dictated by maternal affection; but he was not equal to the sacrifice it required: possessed of the affections of Emily, he could never resolve to resign them. He thought on his sufferings with pleasure, since for her sake they were endured, and determined by fortitude and perseverance at least to merit her esteem, and prove to her that in such a course he was invulnerable. In the presence of his keeper he had several times written to his father, but had received no answer,* so that he resolved to attempt no more this means of conciliating his obdurate spirit.

The day seemed short which he spent in listening to the minutest detail of every word and action of his Emily; but the night approached, and St. Pierre must depart. Favoured by darkness, he descended unobserved the craggy sides of the Castle, promising in the morning to bring with him implements for writing, that he might reply to his mother, and on the third day it was concluded he should return to Paris.

Preparations, in the meanwhile, were making, with the utmost diligence, for the departure of Madame de Clarival and Emily from Luneville, which both were equally anxious to quit, since the gloomy scenes within and without were no longer forgotten in the enlivening presence of the amiable Duchess. Here every thing reminded Emily of her once happy days, and her absent lover. She felt indeed a mournful pleasure in the contemplation, which she would not have exchanged for the boasted ease of the philosopher. But her strict sense of rectitude told her it was a crime to yield so unresistingly to impressions which destroyed her health and peace of mind; besides, her mother suffered no less in seeing her thus devoted to despair. Determined, therefore, to exert herself, she hoped that the scenes of her early joys, and the soothing cares of friendship, would expunge from her heart that deep sense of misery, which preyed on her vitals. In this idea she grew more composed, and Madame de Clarival took an opportunity of relating to her, one evening, all she knew respecting Lusignan. Emily was more affected than surprised. She had guessed the cause, in a great degree, and attributed her present sufferings, like the former ones, to Meronville's unconquered resentment. She then resolved, that as soon as she arrived in Switzerland, she would write to the Duke, and consent to bind herself never to see Lusignan again, as the price of his liberty and restoration to paternal affection.

The Countess felt her health rapidly declining, and wished only to preserve it for the sake of her unprotected child.

"I know not wherefore, my Emily," said she, the night previous to their departure from Luneville, "but I feel very anxious to arrive in Switzerland. My life seems so precarious, that I should be more easy if you were in a safe asylum;—I should die in peace, could I see you with Caroline."

"Talk not so," said Emily, "my beloved mother; you drive me to distraction;—deprived of you, my only guardian and protectress, how could I support life? No! your Emily must die with you!"

"However burdensome may be our existence, my child," replied the Countess; "it is our duty to cherish and preserve it: fixed is the term of our lives, and Nature tells me 'tis I must first leave this terrestrial scene; the dearest friends must separate, when the fatal stroke is given, which disunites for ever our mortal and immortal parts. But surely there is nothing to regret: we exchange an intellectual state of woe for an inheritance of eternal joy. We shall soon meet again, my Emily, in those blessed regions where grief shall cease, where joy shall be uninterrupted—where, by the presence of an Almighty Father, peace shall abound, and every tear be wiped from every eye!"

"Oh my beloved mother!" exclaimed Emily; "with such a prospect in view, can you leave your child amidst the cares and delusions of the world?"

"The joys of our future state, my love, are proportionate to our sufferings here, and are only insured by our endurance of the woes incidental to humanity. Our post on earth is a post of danger and trial: if we desert it, our infidelity will be punished; but if, on the contrary, we sustain with fortitude the charge consigned to us, our reward is boundless: a few short years of misery are repaid by an eternity of bliss!—Let us quit this subject; it is late; we must rise early."

Emily threw herself into the Countess's arms, and implored her blessing.

"Heaven bless you, my child," said she, "and may its choicest blessings repay you for your dutiful regard!"

They now retired to rest, giving orders to be called early. Emily's heart beat with an unusual kind of apprehension, which she endeavoured to lull by the thoughts of soon embracing her much-loved Caroline; but in spite of all her endeavours she could not obtain a composed and refreshing slumber: a thousand ideal phantoms haunted her imagination;* she frequently started, breathless with terror, and trembled at the airy visions of night.

Not yet recovered from these impressions, she looked wildly at Gabriella, when she drew her curtains early in the morning; she eagerly enquired what had happened, and the expression of Gabriella's countenance did not help to subdue her imaginary terrors.

"Ah, Madam!" said she, "the Countess is——"

"What?" asked Emily, rising.

"The Countess, Madam, is very ill this morning," replied Gabriella; "and desires to see you! She cannot set out to-day, Madam."

"Heaven protect her!" exclaimed Emily, as with her robe-de-chambre she hastily left her apartment; but ere she reached that of her mother, her heart sickened; she slackened her pace; she faltered, hesitated, and reclined against the wall. Father du Secque met her, the same who had been summoned to attend her dying moments.

"Approach, daughter," said he; "animated by celestial hope, the Countess would see you. Be prepared for the worst, but hope the best: heaven is all powerful; my prayers shall be united with your's."

Emily, more dead than alive, drew near the bed, where lay her expiring parent.

"My child!" she said.

Her faltering accents failed; she had half raised herself, but fell lifeless on the pillow. Emily's senses instantly fled: Le Saxe applied all his skill to recover both; with Emily he succeeded, but the Countess was gone for ever.

Emily found herself surrounded with domestics, the venerable Friar, with uplifted hands and eyes, imploring heaven in her behalf.

"Where am I?" she said: "Where is my mother?"

"In heaven!" replied the Friar. "Her sainted spirit is fled to kindred angels. Weep not, my daughter; you have still a parent left, one who protects the fatherless, and defends children of innocence—one who looks from his exalted throne on the miseries of his creatures—one who chastens in mercy, and permits transitory grief to ensure eternal happiness! Elevate your thoughts, my daughter; thank that Providence which has taken your departed mother to the realms of endless joy!—Let us join in hallelujahs to his sacred name."

He presented the crucifix to her pallid lips; she kissed it fervently, and going to her mother's apartment, entreated to be left alone. The Friar respected her grief.

"The spectacle of death," said he, "is salutary; it reminds us that we are here but for a season, that we have hopes beyond the grave! The death of a true Christian is fraught with holy instruction. Look on that corpse, daughter, and learn to die! but let not your grief be excessive: think of your desolate state with reference to futurity, and bow in solemn resignation to the Author of Good."

After this exordium, the pious man left her to enjoy the luxury of sorrow.

She looked at first with a sort of passive composure on the sacred reliques before her, but soon her grief broke out in streams of bitter lamentations. She threw herself on the clay-cold corpse, and clasped it to her heaving breast. For hours she remained uninterrupted, till Du Secque thought it necessary to detach her from this scene of woe, lest the impression should be too deep. He prevailed on her to retire to her own apartment.*

Here she collected her scattered senses, and endeavoured to compose her mind; but, alas, it was impracticable. Wherever she turned her eyes, terrific objects met them. How desolate was her situation! Alone in a Castle, the property of her inveterate enemy; no friend to guide or assist her; thrown on the wide world, without comfort, without hope, the sovereign balm of life, where could she go? where conceal her head? where fly from the tyrant misery that pursued her steps? Thought darted with unspeakable velocity through the chaos of futurity, but it brought no solace to her woes; the more she endeavoured to penetrate, the deeper she was involved in a labyrinth of cares. She knew not to whom to apply. The Duchess de Meronville was the only person whose friendship she might rely on, but she feared exposing her to the resentment of her husband, by requesting any assistance for herself. Resolved, therefore, not to implicate her in the miseries of her lot, she gave up that source of consolation. Caroline was too distant to be of service to her: she must then depend on her own exertions, and alas, she was not mistress of any. Enfeebled by her late illness, and oppressed by a weight of woe, her mind sunk, and would no longer assert its native energies. In this perplexity she knew but one certain refuge—she sought it in the bosom of religion.

"Almighty Father!" she said; "thou that deignest to look with a pitying eye on the sorrows of thy wretched creatures, strengthen and support my fainting spirit! Grant me that firm reliance on thy Providence, which can alone rescue me from despair! Implant in my heart that true and invaluable piety which ever ensures the comfort of hope! And Oh! when it shall please thee to take me to thyself, grant that I may be reunited with the sainted spirits of my departed parents, and that, like them, I may quit this transitory state with a well-founded hope of rising to a blessed immortality!"

Heaven never denies its aid to those who seek it with sincerity and devotion. Emily felt the efficacy of christian faith. Her prayer, uttered from an unfeigned heart, was heard; she felt almost instantly relieved, and sending for Father du Secque, entreated him not to leave the Castle till the funeral obsequies of her mother were performed, and she was enabled to retire to some other abode. He lamented that, consistent with the rules of his order, he could not pass the night out of the monastery, but promised to return as soon as it was light, and to take upon himself all the care of the ceremony that should consign the remains of the Countess to their mother earth. They were to be conveyed to Montalte Abbey, and deposited there in the family vault. Emily resolutely refused to leave the Castle while her mother remained there, but consented, at the earnest solicitation of the Friar, not to accompany the funeral to Montalte. He advised her to spend the season of mourning in some cloister, where, occupied in the sacred offices of religion, she would sooner forget her causes of grief. This counsel was congenial to her feelings, and she readily subscribed to it. He recommended the monastery of St. Clair, where he had a sister professed, whose piety, he hoped, would sooth her sorrows. To this she likewise consented, and it was agreed that the corpse of the deceased Countess should in a week be conveyed to Montalte, and the same day she should set out for St. Clair.

Having made this arrangement, she was at leisure once more to reflect on her forlorn state, and to recollect the prophetic vision she had seen on the evening previous to her intended nuptials. In her accumulation of sorrows, she saw the accomplishment of her father's predictions, and rested in hope on his last words, "Your end shall be glorious."

La Haye was not long uninformed of the transactions at the Castle. The demise of Madame de Clarival seemed to offer a favourable opportunity to his ambition. By bribes and various arts he still detained Mademoiselle de Foix at the Convent where she had taken refuge, and had found certain means of securing silence on the part of the Abbess, who watched all her motions, and prevented all access to her, except when D'Aubignac presented himself. His design was to detain her there till she attained the age prescribed by the law, when he might without fear espouse her in the face of the universe. Here then La Haye thought himself secure; but he was unsatisfied whilst Emily resisted his attempts. By obtaining her for the Chevalier St. Amand, he united his family to the two first connections in France, and this by means of an illegitimate issue, which he dared only acknowledge to the world as his collateral descendants. The partner of his guilt had long been deserted, and lived, with no other patrimony but her shame, in a wretched hut on the confines of Bretanny.* She had long repented, and mourned her fault, in quitting the bosom of a family in affluent circumstances, to share the fortunes of a man who treated her with contempt when to his arts she had sacrificed her virtue and happiness. Certain that Emily was now unprotected, and hoping to find her an easy victim, he applied to this woman to secrete her during a few days, till she could be united to St. Amand, whilst he, without scruple, determined to perform the ceremony himself. Touched with remorse and horror at such a proposal, she determined to accede to it with a view of rescuing Emily from his designs. Having, therefore, learnt the name and abode of the person he meant to ensnare, she repaired with all speed to Luneville, and requested an audience with Mademoiselle de Montalte. Absorbed in her own sorrows, Emily at first refused to admit her, but being much importuned, at length consented. The woman then, without betraying the names of St. Amand or La Haye, informed her there was a design of carrying her off, and advised her not to walk out, or sleep alone, while she remained at Luneville; and, after saying this much, she positively refused to explain herself further, and immediately retired. Emily determined not to neglect this warning. Gabriella always slept in her room, and a male servant in the antichamber. The event proved the wisdom of these precautions. Four nights after the Countess's death, a noise at the windows, about midnight, alarmed her; she called to her domestics; they flew to her assistance, and discovered three men descending a ladder fixed to the chamber window. A firelock* discharged amongst them seemed to have reached the hindmost, for they heard a groan; but the darkness of the night prevented their discerning objects, though only at a small distance. Next morning traces of blood were visible in the court, and there could be no doubt one of the ruffians had suffered for his temerity. Emily's gentle nature recoiled at the thought of having been perhaps the means of endangering the life of a fellow-creature, and she became more than ever desirous of quitting an abode where persecutions and dangers hourly multiplied.

Without further interruption the eve of that day arrived which was appointed to solemnize the obsequies of the deceased Countess. In the still and solemn hour of night Emily repaired to the chamber of death, to take a last farewell of her dear and much-regretted parent. At sight of the sacred trappings, and the awful insignia of mortality, her fortitude fled; she knelt in inexpressible agony over the coffin.

"Dear, sainted mother!" she said; "behold your desolate and forlorn child, left unprotected and friendless. Ah! Why is my loathsome existence prolonged? Why must I outlive all that is dear to me? Why may I not be inhumed with thy sacred ashes? If the purest, the tenderest affections, still animate the soul when the body is confined within the narrow precincts of the tomb, Oh look with an eye of pity on my sorrows! Intercede with the Heavenly Disposer of events, that I may follow thee; but if Fate still destines me to support this scene of woe, infuse into my enervated mind strength to sustain the trials allotted me!"

She ceased; and, after embracing thrice the cold remains of her mother, quitted them for ever.

Father du Secque had prevailed on her to set out early in the morning, as the journey was rather long. Accompanied only by Gabriella and two servants on horseback, she took the route towards St. Clair. The venerable Friar had written to prepare the community for her reception, and had described her in such terms as made them all anxious to see and welcome their new pensioner. Emily could not help often turning to look at the deserted Castle, where she had experienced such various and contrary emotions, where she had witnessed events fatal to all her hopes. She recollected the impressions with which she first gazed on the mighty structure, and could not help discovering in them something ominous, and prophetic of woes to come. The whole journey passed in silence, her dejected and mournful countenance checking the loquacity of her domestic, who, however, could not sometimes refrain from exclaiming at the beauty of the prospect; but the beauties of nature could no longer delight or inspire Emily with that rapture she once felt. She gazed with a fixed and vacant eye, and arrived at the Monastery without suffering a single observation to interrupt the settled gloom of her ideas.

The convent was at this time full, and to accommodate Emily some apartments were opened adjacent to the quarter occupied by the nuns, and which had long been closed. The Abbess received her with the utmost courtesy, and endeavoured to prevail on her to accept some refreshment; but she desired only to be conducted to her apartment, as repose was particularly requisite after the fatigues she had undergone. With the utmost obsequiousness and officious care the Superior waited on her, and, with a thousand curtsies, left her for the night.

Emily's first care in the morning was to dismiss her attendants, retaining only her faithful Gabriella, who had been the companion of all her adventures. The novelty of her present life for a time wholly occupied her thoughts. In the seclusion of a cloister her mind, undisturbed, had leisure to ruminate. Lusignan, whose image seemed banished by the melancholy scene of death, which had pre-engaged her ideas, now recurred, and she resolved to put the design she had long meditated in execution, that of endeavouring to ransom his liberty. She wrote a pathetic letter to the Duke de Meronville, in which, after slightly adverting to her own misfortunes, she lamented that she had been the innocent cause of estranging the Marquis from his family, and concluded by informing him she was now an inhabitant of St. Clair; that it was not her intention to take the veil, but she was ready solemnly to bind herself never to acquaint Lusignan of the asylum she had chosen, and to do every thing in her power to prevent his discovering it, on condition that he should be restored to the situation he might justly claim. She sent this letter by a confidential servant, with strict orders to deliver it only to the Duke or Duchess. To the latter she wrote, by the same conveyance, an account of her late sufferings and present abode, and requesting her counsel as to her future conduct.

Having executed this design, she felt much relieved, and attempted to mix in the little enjoyments of the pensioners. Her story was well known in the community, and excited much interest, which was not diminished by her beautiful countenance, where melancholy sat triumphant. Eugenia de Foix thought her adventures so romantic that she was particularly anxious to form a close connexion with her. She introduced herself under a borrowed name, so that Emily had no idea who she was; her vivacity and good humour pleased her, though she sometimes sighed at her levity and inconsistency.

Eugenia, though informed of Emily's misfortunes, knew not that she was her rival with the Marquis de Lusignan, and often designed to communicate to her the reason of her remaining in a situation so little suited to her taste. She prevailed, after much importunity, on her to accompany her twice to the parlour, where she went to meet D'Aubignac. He who, till now, had never done homage to any charms but those of gold, was struck with the disconsolate orphan, whose last wish was that of attracting admiration. He made it his business to enquire who she was; and her real fortune and rank, magnified by those who repeated them, made him resolve to abandon the deluded Eugenia, and transfer his affections to her new friend. To recommend himself, however, was a difficult task, as he had never seen her but twice, and then only in the character of suitor to Mademoiselle de Foix. In this emergency he wrote to La Haye, and the result will soon appear.

Meantime Eugenia related her history to Emily, heightened with every circumstance her romantic fancy could suggest to make the recital marvellous. She painted her father's cruelty, her lover's attachment, and her hate to Lusignan, whom, however, she had never seen. Emily, though really concerned at her folly in committing herself to the guidance of such a man as she judged D'Aubignac by his conduct to be, yet could not help smiling at the detestation she expressed for the Marquis. She had extorted a promise of secrecy, which alone could prevent Emily from immediately informing the Duke de Foix of the situation of his daughter. Jealousy was a stranger to her bosom, yet she sometimes had fears, that should Lusignan be restored to liberty, her apparent neglect might induce him to espouse the woman chosen by his father. This idea, however, was evanescent. What right had she to impede his union with another, since she could never be his, and her utmost wish was to see him happy. She determined, therefore, to omit no argument to prevail on Eugenia to return to her family, and if that should prove ineffectual, to break her promise, which she thought it would be criminal to adhere to, since by violating it she might rescue innocence from the snares of villany.

CHAP. IV.

"The beauteous maid that bids the world adieu,
"Oft of that world will snatch a fond review;
"Still at the shrine neglect her beads, to trace
"Some social scene, some dear familiar face,
"Forgot, when first a parent's stern controul
"Chased the gay visions of her opening soul!"

Emily had exceeded the usual hour of retirement. One evening, when she was, in a letter to her beloved Caroline, pouring the sorrows of her lacerated bosom, to repose them in the heart of friendship—her apartment, distant from those of the other pensioners, was spacious and hung with tapestry—in an adjoining room she thought she heard the voice of complaint. She listened, and frequently the sound recurred. Ever alive to the distresses of humanity, she sighed at the idea that the voice probably issued from the cell of some victim devoted to seclusion by the tyranny of parents, and compelled, perhaps by the dictates of ambition, to form vows to which her heart could not assent. The proximity of her chamber to the cells of the nuns rendered this conjecture probable, and while she was lamenting that such distress was beyond her power to relieve, something fell against the wall of the apartment with a sound so distinct, that she thought the partition could be only slight; and knowing that in ancient buildings doors were frequently concealed beneath the tapestry, she determined to seek, hoping that by her sympathy at least she might alleviate the sufferings which admitted not of remedy.

Her research was not fruitless; she perceived a spring, which, on touching, instantly gave way. She took her lamp, as in the dark she could only discover an aperture, whence no sound issued, and she began to fear she had not penetrated to the right spot. Holding her lamp, however, she started with horror to behold a human figure, apparently lifeless, extended on the floor! She hastily lifted the hangings, and sat down to recover from the shock this sight had occasioned. She hesitated whether to return, but humanity prevailed over her fears; and, recollecting the groans she had heard, she hoped the poor nun might be restored to life. Shuddering as she entered, she applied to her nostrils sal-volatile, and chafed her temples with water. To her utmost satisfaction signs of life appeared. Soon as she hoped recollection was restored, she spoke in terms the most soothing. The stranger, long unaccustomed to words of kindness, looked on her with surprise, and eagerly enquired what angel was come to her relief? Emily informed her that their apartments were only separated by a slender partition, through which the lamentations had penetrated, and enquired if it was possible for her to be of any service? With some apprehension the nun asked the hour; and having learnt that it was an hour past midnight, she said,—

"There are three hours yet ere the community assemble at matins. As you, gentle stranger, have, at the call of humanity, sacrificed the season of repose to its relief, shall I trespass yet farther, and intreat you to listen to the melancholy sketch of a life now near its close? The benignity of your countenance tells me I am in no danger of being betrayed. Alas! the heart, long a stranger to the balm of sympathy, eagerly expands at the first appearance of it: but my state cannot be worse; I suffer the just punishment of violated vows! May Heaven accept the expiation, and blot from its eternal record the sins of my perjured soul!"

Emily assured her she might, without fear, unbosom herself to one who had also felt the heavy pressure of misfortune, and depend on her best endeavours to ameliorate her situation.

"Your mourning garb," replied the nun, "and the melancholy impressed on your lovely features, are but too sure indications of the hand of adverse fortune; but if, as your appearance proclaims, your sorrows are only fortuitous, and such as humanity is ever subject to;

if you are only an innocent victim to the machinations of villany; if you are a stranger to the reproaches of offended conscience, you know not what it is to suffer! Immolated, as I was, at the shrine of ambition, I fancied misfortune at its height; but the accumulated woes of years were light, compared to one pang of self-condemnation!"

Exhausted by her emotions, the poor stranger again sunk on the floor. Emily comforted her with a sweetness peculiar to her nature, and entreated her to defer the relation of her calamity till another opportunity, when she might be better able to sustain the effort.

"My fears," said the nun, "are, that such an opportunity may be for ever denied me. The consolation of meeting a compassionate being is so novel, that I relinquish with pain the happiness of communicating my sorrows; but it must be so; I am now too feeble for the task; the hours rapidly glide that bring intermission to my grief; and should the Abbess, when she goes to matins, discover that I have spoken to you, some other dungeon will be provided. For five tedious years have I been immured in this cell, nor has the light of Heaven ever visited these eyes. I have been subject of late to violent fainting fits, which daily curtail my strength, and make me hope the end of my miseries is near. I ask but the comfort of relating my melancholy tale to some sympathetic hearer, who may one day justify me in part to the man I first loved, of whose virtues I am unworthy. I shall then die in peace, and resign my soul to my Saviour and my God."

Emily, after again lamenting that it was not now in her power to render her any assistance, promised to return the ensuing night, when the bell should have summoned the community to rest; and then, fearful of discovery, closed the sliding-door, and retired.

The volatility of Eugenia, who spent the day with our heroine, could not drive from her recollection the isolated being she had met with on the preceding evening. She longed for the return of night, still hoping it would be in her power to alleviate her sufferings. Every thing claimed an interest with her that bore the semblance of misfortune; but there was something peculiarly attractive in the stranger, who now solicited her compassion. The hand of time had left her features unimpaired, and youth, though deprived of its bloom, still graced her woe-worn countenance, where traces of native beauty were still visible. She wore the habit of a nun. The cell

where she was confined was not high enough to permit her stand-
ing upright; and so contracted were its dimensions, that it hardly
admitted a second person. A heap of straw was the only furniture,
and daylight was for ever excluded.

Emily chid the lingering hours that detained her from the participation of her grief, and retired to her apartment long ere the
appointed hour, to await the sound of the night-bell. She listened,
and heard the neighbouring cells close one by one. At length the
bell tolled; hasty steps in the gallery told her the nuns, obedient to
its sound, were hastening to repose. All was in a moment hushed.
No longer mistress of her impatience, she entered the dungeon,
where the forlorn victim anxiously expected her. She embraced her
with the warmth of friendship, and tried to persuade her to sit in
her apartment during her narrative; but her limbs, contracted by a
continuance of the same posture, refused their assistance, and she
was compelled to remain, whilst she spoke thus,—

"My father was a man of considerable rank and property, proud
of his noble ancestry, and desirous, by his care, to perpetuate the
honours of his family. He had two only children, a son, in whom all
his hopes were centered, and myself. Very early in life he designed
me for a cloister, that his undivided property might revert to my
brother.* At the age of sixteen, having been always a stranger to
the world, I felt no reluctance to the state of life allotted me, and,
accustomed to obey, I considered my father's will as a sovereign
law, till chance introduced me to a man, formed in every respect
to attract my affection, and give me a distaste to a life of seclusion. Unfortunately, perhaps, for us both, our souls were too congenial not to inspire a mutual attachment. I informed him, however,
immediately, of my parent's design, and intreated him to avoid me.
Far from acceding to my request, he flattered himself with being
able to controvert a scheme formed from my cradle, and addressed
himself to my father. He had nothing, alas! but love to support
his pretensions; his fortune was very limited, and his offers were
peremptorily refused. Almost in despair, he applied to my brother,
who really loved me, and detested that common prejudice which
devotes younger children to misery for the aggrandizement of the
elder; he readily promised, therefore, to use his influence in procuring some concession in our favour, and succeeded in some measure. My father engaged to suspend the execution of his project till

Marsillac should have made a voyage to Africa, and if he returned with an affluent independency, he would then give his consent to our union. Marsillac asked no more,—time, absence, dangers, and perils, all vanished at the voice of love. He set out, animated with hope, after recommending, in the most solemn manner, his interests to my care, and exhorting me to act under the conviction that his heart and happiness were in my keeping. I promised, with a full persuasion of fulfilling my engagement; but, alas! I too cruelly deceived him.

"Soon after his departure, my dear brother set out on a tour, and left me alone with my father, who, regardless of his word, my tears, and supplications, conveyed me by a stratagem to these walls, and compelled me to take the habit of a novice.

"He tried, in vain, to set aside the usual year of trial prescribed by the ecclesiastical laws, and to obtain an order for me instantly to assume the veil:—that could not be procured; but apprehensive that should I make my situation known to Frederic or Marsillac, they would endeavour to counteract his design, he ordered me to be strictly watched, and was but too surely obeyed: he several times compelled me, in his presence, to write letters to Marsillac, containing professions of unalterable attachment, and dated from my home, to prevent all suspicions of the coercion I suffered. To contradict these, I made several attempts at sending accounts of my sufferings, but was as often betrayed.

"At length the year elapsed, during which the Lady Abbess had omitted no kindness, no concession, to make me a voluntary victim, but in vain. The day came when I was to be professed. Surrounded by a crowd of vestals, I was led to the altar, trembling, weeping, and in despair.

"The organ swelled a solemn peal;* the nuns united their voices in displaying the joys of a life devoted to the service of God; but my heart, dedicated to love, refused its assent. Methought the lamps burnt pale, Nature seemed to make a solemn pause, to view the sacrifice I made.*

"The priest read in an audible voice the vows I was about to make. At each response my voice faltered, and grew more faint; my cries and groans were lost in the sounds of harmony that issued from the choir; but when the crucifix was tendered to me, and I was called upon to complete the sacrifice, life deserted its station in my breast; I sunk senseless on the marble. I was conveyed from the chapel, and soon restored to that existence I could have wished for ever fled.

"The Abbess, in a tone of kindness, which she then for the last time used with respect to me, conjured me to summon fortitude: she feared that should the Bishop of the diocese, whose humanity is exemplary, be informed of the violence exercised against me, he would forbid the ceremony, and therefore wished to make me appear a willing sacrifice.

"I returned to the altar, but at the awful moment of completion, again lost my senses. The third time I succeeded, and pronounced the fatal vows that bound me for ever to a life of seclusion and misery.

"I turned and looked on the spectators, in whose countenances pity shone, all but in that of my father, who had witnessed the whole of this cruel scene without emotion.

"At that moment Frederic entered the chapel; I extended my arms in vain towards him. A quarter of an hour sooner, and he had saved me; now he could only display his extreme anguish in unavailing complaints. I have since learned that he had made enquiries for me at all the convents in France, and more than once at St. Clair; but so strictly was my father obeyed, that no one durst reveal the secret of my fate.

"Chance directed his steps to the chapel at the moment the sacred rites were concluded. With what dismay did this affectionate brother of my heart witness the horrid sacrifice! Fearful that I might implicate him in the guilt of his father, he wrote me a letter, the exact transcript of his affectionate nature.

"Oh! how my heart bleeds when I now recollect the emotions the perusal of it occasioned! His kindly compassionate look when I turned from the hallowed shrine, a pale, lifeless, and devoted victim, so impressed itself on my grateful soul, that it is still present to my imagination, unobliterated by the lapse of time, uneffaced by the desultory, but never-ending scenes of woe, that have succeeded.

"Pardon my prolixity, Madam; it is the first opportunity I have had of declaring my sorrows; your's is the first sympathetic tear that has fallen to sooth the woes of the wretched Julia.

"I could dwell for ever on the remembrance of my truly and deservedly beloved brother. Yet what pangs have I not inflicted on this dear object, who still engrosses more of my retrospective ideas than does the man who sacrificed his friends, his country, for my sake! If he yet lives, Heaven grant that some worthier object may fix his affection!

"Such has been the perversity of my fate, that I have rendered all I most loved wretched, and, like a contagion, have disseminated misery amongst all who are even remotely connected with me!—Excuse this digression. How is it that memory fondly dwells on scenes of such exquisite grief?*

"After the ceremony, which condemned me to a living tomb, was concluded, I remained in a state of absolute torpor for months; I performed the duties of my situation with a sort of mechanical accuracy, for which I cannot account.

"Sister Cordula always attended me, and strove by all means in her power to alleviate my grief, and avert the resentment of the Lady Abbess, who termed the deep dejection of my soul unpardonable contumacy.

"Roused at length from this state of insensibility, which I could have wished eternal, I tried by the aid of religion to feel reconciled to my fate; but at the age of eighteen, attached by so many ties to the world I had abandoned, my thoughts too frequently wandered to the dear social hours for ever past.

"At the sacred shrine, when my tears bedewed the marble, far from interceding for pardon of my offences, I supplicated rather for a miracle that might restore me to a world of temptations.

"To the sanctuary of religion I carried a heart fondly attached to a mortal, who more than shared my affection with the offended Deity, who heard indeed my prayers, and granted my petition, to be avenged, and plunge me in inextricable misery.

"Sister Cordula's office was that of attending the sick in the infirmary of the convent, where a certain number are admitted, and others, whose indigence prevents their purchasing medicines, have leave to apply daily, and are furnished out of the infirmary here with what they request.

"A violent storm had one night shattered the chimnies, and done much damage to the roof of the convent.

"While the workmen were employed in repairing it, the Abbess used to attend and overlook them, usually accompanied by one of the sisters:—this, in turn, fell to my lot; and whilst I was, from the elevated summit, casting a mournful look on the moving scene below, I observed a young officer gazing on me with surprise, and, I thought, admiration. I blush to own, that so little was my heart detached from worldly pursuits, I felt flattered by the idea of being yet admired, though certainly disfigured by the vestal habit. I contrived to attend the Superior the two following days, and still the same object met my eyes.

"Vanity was then my only crime; but it is a dangerous failing, which, if unrestrained, leads to the most fatal excesses in search of gratifications. Heaven knows, I should at that period have shuddered at the bare idea of violating, in the smallest degree, the vows I had been compelled to form. Yet it was infringing my duty to look on any man with a desire of being admired; and if we once pass the confines of Virtue's contracted dominion, there wants but a step to plunge us into absolute vice. This is an aphorism, which, by fatal experience, I can attest.

"A few days after Sister Cordula was taken ill, and the care of the sick devolved on me, I stood at the grate to hear the petitions of the out-patients: a cripple, covered with rags, presented himself, and requested relief.

"Instead of stating his case, he put a paper in my hands, which, he said, contained an account of his sufferings, which it was in my power only to relieve. He then hastily retired, promising to return for an answer the following morning, and conjuring me not to refuse compassion to his case.

"Unfortunately for me I was alone, and concealing the paper I received, took the earliest opportunity of retiring to my cell to peruse it.

"Never was any composition more calculated to conquer religion and virtue. It set forth that the writer had been a witness of my sufferings at the altar, which were light compared to his since. He had that day yielded for ever his affections to an object apparently torn from him irretrievably; that he had frequently lingered near the spot, but ineffectually, till the happy hour when I appeared with the Abbess on the parapet.

"He then urged every argument that villany could suggest, to prove that compulsatory vows are not registered or accepted in heaven; that we were formed for other purposes than those of secluding ourselves; that it was our duty to contribute to the happiness of our fellow-creatures, and that by resisting the tyranny employed in my confinement, I should much better answer the ends of creation.

"He then made protestations of the tenderest affection, and said, if I would consent to share his fortunes, he would retire to some isolated spot, where the tyranny of the world could not disturb our mutual happiness; and that if I rejected his suit, he solemnly swore never to survive it.

"A contrariety of emotions strove for the mastery, as I read these lines, and every latent spark of virtue kindled in my defence. I firmly resolved indignantly to reject his offers, and adhere to the line of duty; but I had not resolution to act as such a determination required.

"Instead of discovering the scheme to the Abbess, and requesting some other person might attend the infirmary, I persuaded myself it would be right to give the answer by my own mouth, which would prevent such attempts in future more effectually, than if I left him in doubt whether my refusal was the effect of compulsion or choice.

"I burnt the letter, and next day repaired to the grate, where he appeared. I spoke with energy and firmness, assuring him, that although my vocation was at first involuntary, I was now perfectly reconciled to it, and that nothing should induce me to violate the sanctity of my calling; adding, that should his attempts be renewed, I would impart them to the Superior, and there were means of severely punishing those who endeavour to seduce a vestal.

"He sighed, he entreated, he tried to alarm me by the desperation in his looks, and, I fear, discovered in mine less firmness than I could have wished.

"Not to tire you with a recital of the arts he employed, I will only tell you that his perseverance and my weakness prevailed—I promised to elope with him!

"Reason must certainly have been then suspended, or I could never have conquered all the obstacles that opposed such a step: the perdition of my own soul, the grief of Frederic, my sworn and unalterable love to Marsillac, all were forgotten in this hour of delusion.

"I persuaded myself that the protest I made when forced to the altar, absolved me from my vows; that my brother would rejoice at my emancipation; that though I could never love any one but Marsillac, gratitude, and the certainty that I could never be his, would induce me to grant esteem and confidence to the man who restored me to liberty. In short, my fragile heart persuaded me the crime I was about to perpetrate was meritorious, and all objections vanished.

"It was agreed that my seducer should have a vehicle ready to convey me to the coast, at the north wall of the great court; that he should let down a ladder to facilitate my ascent, and that I should hasten to him an hour after the community had retired.

"On the day previous to the elopement he brought me some apparel, the better to disguise my situation if I should be seen on the road, and every thing seemed to promise success to our scheme. Nothing but absolute infatuation could have supported me through such an undertaking.

"The night came, the nuns retired, I softly issued from my cell, and proceeded uninterrupted, till I reached a gallery, at the end of which was a large crucifix. Here I beheld—Heavens! how I tremble at the recollection! a nun counting her beads, and kneeling at the base of our Saviour's image. I stood for a moment petrified, doubting whether it was an apparition, but was soon convinced it was a sister, who had probably imposed a penance on herself.

"Her back was turned, and the fervour of devotion prevented my footsteps from disturbing her. I recollected myself, and took another road to the court, which I reached without further interruption.

"The night was so dark, that I could hardly distinguish the north wall; but on a sudden the moon, emerging from the clouds, shone forth with native lustre. I climbed the ladder, and turned from the summit to take a last view of the cloister. The moonbeams fell on the long grated windows, and I distinctly saw the sister who had been at prayers at a window, her eyes fixed on me.

"'We are discovered,' I exclaimed, and fainted in the arms of D'Aubignac."

"D'Aubignac!" repeated Emily.

"What have I done?" said Julia: "I had sworn never to betray him, and in an unguarded moment his name has passed these lips. Oh Madam! promise me not to make known his crime, or the death of a fellow-creature will be added to my already overcharged conscience!"

"Assure yourself," replied Emily, "I will never without your concurrence betray the trust reposed in me. Believe me, I am too much interested in your sufferings."

At this moment the bell rang for matins. Emily hastened from the cell, much disappointed at being deprived for the present of the conclusion of a narrative in which she felt the keenest interest.

The names of D'Aubignac and Marsillac had awakened her utmost attention. She trembled for the fate of Eugenia, whose virtue and honour were in the hands of a man capable of such baseness, for she doubted not he was the seducer of Julia, and resolved more than ever to inform the Duke de Foix of the danger she was in.

CHAP. V.

"What is this world? Thy school, Oh Misery!
"Our only lesson is, to learn to suffer;
"And he who knows not that,
"Has lived in vain!"*

Emily's letter had reached Paris, and penetrated more easily to the Duke, as La Haye, who would have endeavoured to retard it, was unaccountably absent.

He had disappeared very unexpectedly, promising to return in a day, but had written several letters, stating that business detained him. There appeared something very surprising in this affair, as it certainly endangered the success of his schemes, and he had never before willingly absented himself for so long a time.

In this interval, Emily's letter happily arrived, and Madame de Meronville did not neglect the opportunity it offered of exerting her dormant influence. She threw herself at his feet, and conjured him, by the voice of humanity, to pardon the involuntary errors of his unfortunate child.

The Duke at first felt confused at finding the share he had in Lusignan's confinement so well known; but the Duchess removed it by assuring him, they were all persuaded La Haye was the instigator, as well as perpetrator, of the deed they lamented.

She found his Grace not inexorable to the entreaties of Emily, strengthened as they were by her promise of concealment, and resolved to forward the business as much as possible during La Haye's absence, who had the happy talent of counteracting every good inclination in his patron.

The Duke de Meronville was now but fifty—his quondam tutor ten years older; but the latter, from his extreme activity, had greatly the advantage; nevertheless, at the age of threescore, he might be said to be verging rapidly towards his end, and made no preparations for the awful day of retribution, but by adding multiplied offences to his enormous weight of sins, rendered doubly obnoxious by the sacred character he had assumed.

The Duke, emancipated for a short time from the despotism of his councils, consented to give an order for reversing the lettre-de-cachet, and Madame de Meronville, overjoyed, immediately took every necessary means to accelerate the proceedings.

Some time must absolutely be expended in procuring Lusignan's release; but before the return of the dreaded Abbé, things were in such a train as ensured success.

His patron concealed from him the concession he had made, for so completely was he enslaved by the arts of this spiritual father, that he dreaded his reproaches, and trembled at his frowns.

Emily was soon blessed with a most affectionate letter from the Duchess, who assured her of her eternal regard, and lamented, with bitter anguish, that she was denied the happiness of endeavouring to supply the place of her esteemed and ever-regretted mother.

She then informed her of the success of her suit with the Duke, and hoped soon to acquaint her that Lusignan was restored to liberty.

This letter afforded a temporary consolation, and conveyed a ray of hope to her desponding heart. She hoped he might at least be happy, though peace had for ever deserted her bosom, and her benevolent mind expanded to something like pleasure, in the hope she had conceived of rescuing the poor nun from the tyranny of her oppressors.

She had contrived, during the day, to convey to her nourishment more salutary than that allowed by the Superior, which consisted only of bread and water, and even that bestowed with a parsimonious hand.

At night she was happy to find her rather less feeble, and able to proceed with the narrative, which she did in these words:—

"When I recovered from the temporary death, in which the fear of detection had plunged me, I found myself in the arms of my seducer, travelling with unspeakable velocity.

"He endeavoured to sooth me by every expression of regard and affection, and by assuring me, that the vows I should make at the Hymeneal altar would entirely efface those which persecution had extorted from me; but I no sooner found myself released from the hated bonds of confinement, than my sense of rectitude returned, and I shuddered at the crime I had committed. Repentance, however, came too late—it was no longer in my power to recede, and I endeavoured, by sharing the raptures of D'Aubignac, to forget the misery of my state.

"We embarked for England, and soon arrived there, proceeding without loss of time to the metropolis. During the journey his behaviour was perfectly respectful and submissive, but it grew every day less so. I frequently mentioned marriage; but though he still professed it his intention, he evaded it by a thousand vague excuses. At length, tired of dissimulating, he threw off the mask: 'Marriage, my Julia,' said he, 'is the link of slaves, the tie of vulgar souls, an unmeaning ceremony to bind discordant minds: love, far more free, unites us in his gentle fetters; hearts truly congenial, like ours, need no foreign aid to cement their union; love and liberty are inseparable. Human ties can form only an honourable servitude, a legal prostitution!* Why should we, who have overcome the prejudices of custom, again involve ourselves in the labyrinth of vulgar error? What is the world to us, or honour, that glittering bauble, invented for the use of fools?* No, my Julia; secure in our affections, let us not seek, by extraneous bonds, to weaken the more lasting charms of love.'

"I was at first so amazed by this developement of his intentions, that the power of expressing my indignation was denied me. He soon made me sensible how impotent and futile were my remonstrances. I was completely in his power, in a foreign country, a stranger even to the language.

"To all my supplications, he only answered, that men were too wise to depend upon the fidelity of a woman, who had not hesitated to renounce and violate her duty, even for their sakes; that oaths once broken through could no longer bind; and that my affected coyness was too flimsy to deceive him.

"What shall I tell you? Despair reduced me to a state of apathy; I yielded to all his requests, not with a view to any gratification, but merely to silence that importunity I had not resolution to repel.

Tired at length of his victim, he went out one morning, and left a
paper on the table for me: it contained a very small supply of money,
and a last farewell! Ruined, wretched, and almost frantic; my means
of subsistence daily lessened, and with it the civility of my hostess.

"She soon informed me I must quit her house, and, in spite of my
remonstrances, turned me out of doors.

"Vice abounds in a great metropolis. I was soon enrolled in the
list of those wretched victims, who, dead to shame and virtue, obtain
subsistence by their nocturnal debauches. Oh, Madam! nobody who
has not, like me, experienced it, can form an adequate idea of the
sufferings of these miserable beings.* Did inconsiderate youth but
know the horrors of vice, how would they fly from its first approach!
Frequently did the price of my accumulated guilt scarcely procure
me sufficient to sustain life.

"Four months elapsed in this manner, when one day I was discovered by my brother, who had crossed the seas in pursuit of me.
Oh, my beloved Frederic! how were your fraternal feelings lacerated
at the sight of your deluded sister! How did I shrink from your
regards! I tremble at the recollection.

"This affectionate brother tried at first, in vain, to rescue me from
this dreadful gulph of misery and perdition. I persisted in the resolution to die there. I was far advanced in my pregnancy. He carried me
by force to a place of security, where I was delivered of a daughter.

"A violent illness succeeded, which carried me to the verge of
eternity, and discovered at once to my frantic soul the enormity of
my conduct.

"All this while Frederic attended me with affectionate care, and
no sooner saw me awakened to a sense of my condition, than he
called in all the aids of religion to strengthen my repentance. Conviction burst on my senses, and gave birth to despair.

"The first sacrifice I made was that of desiring my child might be
taken away, and engaging never to enquire for it.

"As soon as I was sufficiently recovered to be moved, Frederic
offered to pay my pension in any convent, where my story should
be a profound secret, and where I might expiate, at the shrine of
religion, the errors I had committed in the world.

"But here I was inexorable: it was my firm resolution to return to
St. Clair, that the spot which had witnessed my crime might also
witness its expiation.

"My kind brother, prophetic of the persecutions I should suffer, omitted no arguments to change my resolution, but in vain; I persisted, and he conducted me here, recommending me, in the strongest terms, to the pity and prayers of the whole community, who were strangers to all but my first fault, and whom he endeavoured to interest in my favour by the repentance which induced me to return.

"The Abbess affected much concern and lenity, but in a few months declared that I was dead, and confined me to this dungeon. Frederic, I am sure, has mourned my loss. I never dared enquire for Marsillac, whom I had so mournfully, so cruelly offended. His generous soul has perhaps vouchsafed a tear to my memory.

"May his prayers and my sufferings be deemed an atonement at the tribunal of a just, but merciful God!"

The poor mourner here raised her eyes, humid with the tear of repentance, towards that Heaven whose azure concave was for ever hid from her sad dwelling.

Emily was for some time so affected, that the feelings of her heart were denied utterance. Somewhat recovered, she pressed the deluded sinner to her throbbing heart.

"Heaven is already avenged," she said. "Be comforted; remember that one penitent sinner has power to increase the joy of the seraphic spirits that surround the throne of mercy!"

"My chastisement, alas!" said Julia, "I confess to be infinitely light, compared with my offences. The rigour employed by the Lady Abbess I regard as the will of my God, and bow in humble resignation to the divine hand; but the tortures inflicted on the body are indeed insignificant, compared with the pangs of remorse preying on the immortal soul. The severest struggle I have endured, thank Heaven, was a penance I had the resolution to prescribe, that of stifling a mother's love, and resigning my wretched offspring to foreign hands. Oh! what did I endure when I suffered it to be torn from me, and refused myself the consolation of one embrace, one last maternal farewell. Mournful is the sentence that dooms it to suffer for the crimes of its parent. Yet I do hope, that, deprived of the fostering hand of affection, it has in this been restored to the bosom of a merciful creator."

Emily, after employing every consolatory argument, ventured to enquire if her name was D'Ermancy.

"That name I once bore," she said, "but have too cruelly dishonoured it. Oh, Frederic! how must your heart bleed, if you have indeed survived my sullied fame!"

Emily now no longer doubted that she was the person in search of whom Marsillac left the Abbey, but she dared not disclose her suspicions, fearful of renewing the grief of the disconsolate mourner. She then enquired if her confinement was authorized by the laws of the order, or by ecclesiastical appointment, and, on receiving a negative answer, promised, with heart-felt joy, to procure her release by an order from the Suffragan Bishop.*

"Allow me," said Julia, "with a heart overflowing with gratitude, to refuse your generous offers: I have been so long sequestered from the converse of my fellow-creatures, so long a stranger to the light of Heaven, that I should suffer by a renewed intercourse with that society, whose laws I have so palpably infringed. I should be exposed to the contempt of some, to the injuries of others; and those few compassionate souls, who, like you, can pity the unfortunate, and cherish the repentant sinner, would be withheld, by the fear of censure, from yielding to their benevolent inclinations. The few short years that are yet allotted me in the page of life will be best spent here; and when I am no more, my sufferings may furnish a useful lesson to the inconsiderate multitude. Events such as those which have marked my transient passage through the vale of tears are of moral utility: they teach the mind, untutored in the school of vice, to shun its approach as a contagion, that never stops till it has reached maturity.* I call Heaven to attest the sincerity of my heart, when I assure you, that from the moment I forsook the path of virtue, all traces, not only of happiness, but tranquillity, deserted my steps; nor can the most zested enjoyments of vice, through a period of years, be compared to the mild, but celestial rapture, of one self-applauding moment."

She had scarcely concluded these words, when the footsteps of the nuns repairing to matins warned Emily to return. With a silent embrace, she bid her adieu, and retired to meditate on the woes, infinitely various, to which humanity is exposed.

She had long been inclined to doubt if seclusion was indeed the will of Heaven; if there was not more merit in resisting the temptations of the world, and enduring with fortitude our appointed lot, than in forsaking the haunts of man, and cowardly flying from danger, rather than resisting it; in wasting, in criminal supineness, the hours destined to the active discharge of our duty in the sphere of life to which we are destined.

She weighed, with moral accuracy, the various motives that prompt the choice of a monastic life.

In some she found it the effect of indolence, operating on minds too weak to resist the allurements of vice. The same lethargy of nature made others seek seclusion to avoid the exertion necessary for their subsistence in the world. In a cloister they found, without labour, every thing provided for their daily sustenance: here was a powerful incentive. Others, denied that consequence in society which they found possessed by rivals, retired to foster, in the bosom of solitude, all those evil passions that made them hateful to the world. In others, the love of sway preponderated, and induced them to seek the means of tyrannic oppression over a few, which their circumscribed merits deprived them of in the great commonwealth; and lastly, others, wearied with disappointment, flew to retirement as the last refuge. Few, indeed, she found, who withdrew from motives of pure religion, and an unfeigned desire of consecrating their lives to that God from whom they were received. She found that in the contracted sphere of monastic society, amongst the professors of conciliating Christianity, every evil passion existed; rancour, malice, envy, and detraction, deserted the world, and were admitted here.

In the rigour exercised against the victim she had just left, she saw none of that mild philanthropy which should characterize the professors of religion.

"True piety," thought she, "impels us to compassionate the errors of weak mortals, to alleviate the sufferings of nature, to cherish repentance, and pardon others, that we may claim remission of our own offences. The power of avenging God never delegates, nor are we excuseable in arrogating it."

In such reflections Emily spent the night, and applied the first hours of the ensuing day in addressing a petition to the Bishop of the Diocese in favour of Julia. He was a man of singular probity, truly worthy of the ministry he had chosen, for the sole purpose of watching, with paternal care, over his flock. He returned an immediate answer to Emily's letter, informing her, that the day of his annual visit approached, which he usually remitted, but would make it his care to examine the convent of St. Clair, and redress the grievance she mentioned, for which she felt much indebted.

Satisfied with her success, Emily felt unusually exhilarated, but was not fated to see the accomplishment of her benevolent purpose.

The Abbess, who kept a watchful eye on Mademoiselle de Foix, frequently permitted her to ramble with Emily, whose prudence and discretion no one could distrust. Eugenia, whose disposition was really excellent, was charmed with her sweetness, and listened to her counsels as to the voice of wisdom;—these all tended to persuade her to return to the bosom of her family.

One evening, as she was thus exerting her influence in the cause of virtue, they had strayed to an unusual distance, and night's sombre shades involved the universe, ere they reached the convent gates. Suddenly two men appeared in an avenue through which they had to pass, who appeared to court concealment. The young friends, greatly terrified, hesitated how to proceed; but a romantic frenzy taking possession of the mind of Eugenia, she exclaimed, that somebody wanted to carry her off, and hastily ran towards the monastery with all imaginable speed, leaving the trembling Emily, who had not power to overtake her. One of the men advanced, crying,—

"Now is the moment!"

And seizing her, in spite of her cries, forcibly impelled her to attend them to a vehicle, which was in waiting at a short distance. Emily assured them they had mistaken her for some other person, and conjured them to release her.

"No," said they, "we know you well; you are the heiress of Montalte."

They proceeded for some time with great rapidity, till, suddenly stopping, a person entered the chaise, whose features the darkness prevented her discovering, but he spoke in the most rapturous terms of his love, and happiness in having acquired the possession of so inestimable a jewel.

During this rhapsody, Emily wept, and conjured him in vain to restore her to the monastery. His professions kept pace with her tears: he assured her that love alone had prompted him to the deed he had committed; that such heavenly charms as her's were never intended to be obscured in the gloom of a cloister; that in the sphere of life to which he was leading her, they would appear in native lustre; that at the Court of Versailles she would be the envy of one sex, and the admiration of the other; and that he doubted not of reconciling her easily to a change, by which she would be so great a gainer, particularly as the Marquis de Lusignan, he was assured, was contracted to another, and had obtained his liberty by that step alone.

Emily's astonishment could be equalled only by her despair. That she was in the power of some person acquainted with her affairs, appeared evident, by his mention of her love. She thought she was not a stranger to the voice, yet could not analyse her conjectures. But would Lusignan have indeed resigned her, and plighted his faith to a rival? The thought was distraction; the information came from doubtful authority; he had probably been released by her offers, and the entreaties of his mother; he could not, she was sure, so soon have forgotten her; yet if he had, ought she not to rejoice, since his attachment to her had been the production of so much misery, and his desertion might insure future happiness. This was the line of duty: but love was yet too powerful in her bosom to admit such generous conclusions, where a rival was concerned.

While she was revolving these things in her mind, d'Aubignac, for he was the ruffian who sat by her, remained silent, hoping, by the artifice of his insinuation, to have wrought jealousy in her mind, and induce her, perhaps, by resentment, to throw herself into his arms.

The silence thus preserved on both sides was suddenly interrupted by a violent concussion of the vehicle, followed by a complete overthrow. A huge stone in the road had overturned the carriage.*

Emily uttered a shriek; d'Aubignac bestowed a malediction on the driver.

Whilst he was employed in releasing her the tread of horsemen at that moment alarmed him, and caused a movement of joy in the heart of Emily, who was determined to implore the assistance of any passenger. As they approached, she redoubled her cries. D'Aubignac tried, by the most affectionate and respectful intreaties, to make her desist; and when the equestrians reached the spot, informed them of the accident, signifying that to it the lady's cries were owing.

"Oh, no, no!" exclaimed Emily; "I have been carried off by force, and this accident is my only chance of escaping."

"Heavens!" ejaculated a voice; "what sounds are those that burst on my wondering senses! Sure that plaintive voice is not unknown to me!—Lady," continued the speaker, "if I can be of any service, you need only command me; I am at your devotion, and shall rejoice in the opportunity of rescuing innocence from the betrayer."

"At your peril, desist," replied d'Aubignac, drawing his sword, "or thus shall your temerity be punished."

"Villain!" rejoined the stranger; "I contemn your threats, and despise your vengeance!—Draw!"

"Oh, Heavens!" exclaimed Emily, " 'tis Lusignan!"

The elevated tone in which the two competitors spoke had betrayed them both, for Emily now recognised d'Aubignac. Lusignan, animated by the well known accents, made a thrust at his antagonist that laid him at his feet. He then flew to Emily—

"Tell me, my love, what has placed you in the power of this villain, and how can I release you?"

"Oh, Heaven!" cried Emily, "convey me in mercy to the convent of St. Clair."

"It is too far distant," rejoined Lusignan, "but there is a hamlet in the vicinity, in which you may pass the night: protected by me, you can have no fears. Will you suffer me to conduct you?"

"Any where," said Emily, "that I may escape from these horrors."

He placed her on his horse, and, ordering his servants to follow, left d'Aubignac, with his attendants, on the road.

Guilt renders a man a very coward: the wretch, who did not blush to betray innocence in every form, whose courage was undaunted when helpless females fell into his power, yielded almost without resistance when attacked by a single adversary; and, though he was attended by six equestrians, not one offered to defend him, or contest with Lusignan the prize he had regained.

When they arrived at the hamlet, he ordered the best accommodation the meanness of the place could furnish. Emily, who during the short journey had recollected the insinuations of d'Aubignac, which seemed confirmed by Lusignan's actual release, regarded him with an eye of doubt, when he threw himself at her feet, ready to expire with joy at this unexpected meeting, and the opportunity it had furnished him of rendering her an essential service. She related the circumstance which had placed her in the situation from which he happily rescued her, and spoke in terms of gratitude of the obligation he had conferred.

"Talk not of gratitude, my Emily," said he: "Ah! how far above

price is the happiness I now enjoy. But tell me, are you still inexorable; will the turpitude of my father's conduct induce you to relent?
will it justify your consent to unite your fate with mine in defiance
of opposition?"

Emily was ashamed of having for a moment yielded to suspicions
so injurious to the constancy of Lusignan, and was rejoiced that she
had not betrayed them.

"Never," replied she, "shall I think any event capable of justifying
a breach of duty! No; I acknowledge to you that my happiness is for
ever destroyed, but I will still preserve that rectitude of mind, which
can alone support me through such varied scenes of woe. Alas! your
liberty has been obtained by my promise of concealment; and your
father, informed of this meeting, which he will scarcely believe accidental, may perhaps repent his lenity, and resume his rigour."

"What is liberty to me, my love," said the Marquis, "if purchased
at such a price! Let him add fetters to my bonds, let him add tortures to imprisonment, I regard them not! Deprived of you, fortune
has done her worst; her utmost malice cannot now affect me. She
seems not entirely to have deserted me, since she has permitted me,
before I die, to have the consolation of serving you."

He then informed her, that his release arrived the preceding
day, and that he was travelling towards Paris when arrested by her
cries; that he was now resolved to see her to a place of safety ere he
quitted her: but Emily positively refused this; she insisted that he
should pursue his route, and leave St. Pierre only to conduct her to
St. Clair; she should reach it before night, and during the day she
had no fears.

"Do you then envy me this short remains of happiness?" said
Lusignan. "Will you deprive me of the last pleasure I may ever
enjoy, and even curtail the parsimonious favours of fortune?"

"By virtue alone, Lusignan," replied she, "ought we to seek an
amelioration of our fate. Let us mutually promise never to be
betrayed by misfortune into any steps which may make either blush;
my attachment may make me wretched, but shall never have power
to make me criminal!—Are you incapable of that fortitude my
weaker nature displays?"

"I am capable," said he, "of dying, but never of relinquishing you.
But since you command it, farewell! Heaven protect you! Yet once
more assure me I am not indifferent to you."

"That would be needless," replied Emily; "you are sufficiently assured of that."

She held out her hand as she spoke; he clasped it in his: it was the last moment of joy he ever experienced. The sun was already risen, and streamed through the casements.

" 'Tis time I should be gone," said Emily. "Farewell, Lusignan!"

Her tears fell in torrents; she tore herself away; the chaise was ready; St. Pierre attended her; Lusignan watched the lessening vehicle as it disappeared, and, deeply sighing, took the route to Paris.

CHAP. VI.

"Ah, happy hills! Ah, pleasing shade!
  "Ah, fields! beloved in vain!
"Where once my careless childhood stray'd,
  "A stranger yet to pain!"*

For miles Emily forgot her own situation, and thought only of Lusignan. His father's unjust and unnatural severity presented itself in the most alarming shape, and she feared he would be exposed to its extremest rigour by the accidental meeting, of which she doubted not the Duke would be informed. She saw him either condemned to his former exile, or persecuted eternally to induce him to marry some woman, whose only recommendation was her rank or superior connections.

She had observed, with extreme regret, his altered appearance, nor had the excessive paleness of her once blooming countenance escaped the scrutiny of a lover's eye.

She had hurried away from the hamlet, where they spent the hours of darkness, with a speed that precluded observation; and when she left it, a thousand things crowded on her mind, which she would have given worlds to enquire; but the same prudent discretion that induced her to curtail their first interview, prevented her seeking another. So fully was she persuaded that they were for ever separated, that she considered every meeting as a dangerous indulgence, calculated only to increase their miseries.

Having wasted reflection on this subject till her heart sickened, she endeavoured to forget it, and turned her thoughts towards the monastery.

D'Aubignac first met her fancy: the multiplicity of his nefarious attempts struck her with horror, and she thanked her Almighty Protector, who had so miraculously rescued her from his villany. The unfortunate Julia appeared more than ever to her an object of compassion. Eugenia, another of his victims, she still hoped to rescue, and bent all her thoughts towards the means.

She was not, however, wholly without apprehensions with respect to D'Aubignac, though Lusignan had assured her he was but slightly hurt, though much frightened.

An unaccountable reluctance made her dread returning to the monastery; she hardly knew what reception she might meet with there from the Superior, and indeed the whole community, whose ideas, confined like their persons, prevented their acknowledging candour, even when it appeared most striking; and though she had nothing to fear from their resentment, she wished not to encounter their suspicions. The romantic spirit of Eugenia, who saw design in the most casual occurrence, made it not improbable that she would innocently lend her authority to strengthen the surmises of her cloistered companions.

Doubtful and perplexed, she turned her thoughts towards Switzerland, to which she had often looked forward as a temporary asylum.

To retire there appeared now the only eligible plan, and on that she resolved. Sending, therefore, for St. Pierre, when they stopped to change horses, she enquired how great the distance was from the Valais, and being assured it was a short day's journey from St. Clair, she determined to proceed without loss of time, as she thought herself free from danger at present, since D'Aubignac, from whom alone she had any apprehensions, must, by his wounds, be prevented from making any new attempt; and, once arrived at the Cottage, she considered herself as released from all cares, but those which were fostered in her own bosom.

Thus resolved, she communicated her design to St. Pierre, who highly approved it, and was ready to attend her to the remotest extremity of the globe, as he knew he could not render a more essential service to his master, to whom he was tenderly attached.

He advised her to repose that night at Monte-Sancto,* and to cross the mountains the next morning.

With this advice Emily complied. They arrived early at Monte-Sancto, where they spent the night. It was only at a league's distance from St. Clair, and she hesitated whether to make known her situation to the Abbess; but the dread of publicity determined her to remain quiet, till by her arrival in Switzerland she should be sheltered from all attempts.

Early in the morning, therefore, she resumed her route, and arrived on the confines of the Valais just at that hour when the declining orb of day reflected his parting rays on the delighted universe.

Emily was intimately acquainted with every spot in this Elysian country. Nothing she had seen, since she quitted it, could bear comparison with the diversified beauties Nature had been industrious to accumulate here.

The harmony that filled the air proclaimed the melodious inhabitants of Italy. Innumerable flocks grazed on the mountains that surrounded this peaceful abode of liberty. The distant hamlets, scattered over a vast tract of country, formed a coup d'œil truly enchanting. The groupes of peasants that filled the luxuriant valleys, shewed by their countenances that despotism was banished from their abodes.* The females had an air of elegance, which but for Switzerland would be thought incompatible with rusticity: even the children, taught hospitality by the example of their ancestors, attended the chaise that conveyed Emily, welcoming her with songs and cries of joy. She pleased herself with throwing from the windows pieces of money,* and with observing their innocent frolics multiplied in gratitude for her favours.

She could have wished to arrest the rapid hand of time, which momentarily spread a deeper shade over the fading scenery, and threatened to involve them in obscurity, and she began to fear being benighted, when the carriage stopped, and in an instant she found herself in the arms of her astonished but delighted Caroline.

After the first expressions of joy were over, Caroline expressed her uneasiness at the ill health visible in the countenance of her friend.

Emily related, in a few words, the occasion of her sudden arrival in the Valais. The young couple could not sufficiently testify their joy at a circumstance so much wished, so unexpected.

Emily cast a pensive look round the apartment: it was a library, opening through a greenhouse on to a lawn, enamelled with flowers, and had been the favourite retreat of her father. On one side hung a full-length portrait of the deceased Countess, and over the chimney a miniature of the Count. Her eyes were in an instant suffused with tears, which she vainly endeavoured to suppress.

"Excuse me, dear and valued friends," she said, "if my fortitude is not proof against the tender, but melancholy, recollections these scenes bring to my mind. I am come with my sorrows to interrupt your felicity."

"That felicity," said Dorville, while the sympathetic tear trembled in the eye of Caroline, "we owe to you: it admitted of no increase but that which your presence confers; and believe me, there is no emotion of your heart that is not participated by your Caroline, and, allow me to add, by the man who has the happiness of calling her his own!"

Caroline persuaded her early to retire to recruit her spirits, and seek in repose relief from those feelings which had been so painfully called forth by the sight of that spot, the scene of her infant joys, and the delight of her lost parents.

She awoke revived and refreshed, and yielded her heart entirely to the calls of friendship. In tracing each spot where she once strayed, a stranger to sorrow, she felt a pensive but pleasing sensation take possession of her heart.

The enjoyment of the present hour is too frequently destroyed by a doubtful futurity, but the delights of memory nothing can interrupt: in the most advanced periods of declining life, recollection fondly turns to scenes of infant pleasure; and, in dwelling on the retrospect, the hours seem renewed, and past joys can yet exhilarate the present moment.

Emily experienced the truth of this observation; her contemplations were no longer painful; each day found her less wretched, and her health and spirits improved beyond the hopes of her friends.

She had suffered a week to elapse before she had courage to address the Duke de Foix on the subject of his daughter, which she was, however, determined not to neglect. One whole day she devoted to it, addressing, at the same time, Eugenia herself, to whom she related her adventure subsequent to their parting, and entreated her to pardon a breach of confidence which nothing could authorize but the exigency of the present moment, when nothing but the exertion of paternal influence could save her from destruction.

She wished much to have informed Julia of her reasons for not revisiting her cell, as she could not doubt it would give her much uneasiness, but she dared not trust the romantic Eugenia with her secret, and she had no friend in the convent on whom she could rely.

She felt that in a situation such as Julia's the mind is more than usually sensitive, and awake to the least apparent neglect; but she had no means of removing her doubts at present, and therefore contented herself with inclosing a letter for her to the Bishop, with a request that he would deliver it when the period of his annual visit furnished him with an opportunity. All these were sent by a person deputed to conduct Gabriella and some other attendants to their mistress, as it was her design to fix her abode here entirely during her minority.

Caroline was far advanced in a state of pregnancy, and had been ordered to reside for a few months at Lausanne. She was concerned at being obliged to leave the Cottage at the moment when it became doubly dear to her by the presence of her friend, and she feared it would likewise be a disappointment to her; but Emily, without hesitation, offered to accompany her to Lausanne, assuring her all situations were alike, and local attachments were now but feeble in her mind.

"Endeared by the presence of those we love, all scenes are delightful," said she; "to follow you, my now only remaining friend, is the greatest pleasure I can hope on earth."

Caroline felt doubly grateful for this new instance of affection, and they only waited the arrival of Emily's attendants to fix their residence at Lausanne.

Before this took place, she had the happiness of receiving a letter from Julia herself, teeming with gratitude and joy. The good Pontiff, who had promised to extend to her his protection, had visited St. Clair, and given orders that she should be restored to her rank in the community; and, to prevent such oppressions in future, he declared, that any one who should be wanting in respect to her, or should reproach her for errors she so deeply repented, should be subjected to a severe punishment, which he, by virtue of his episcopal authority, would inflict. This, she said, secured her future peace, and, in gratitude for her deliverance, she hoped to consecrate the residue of her days to her Maker.

The result of Emily's exertion with respect to Eugenia was no less satisfactory. She was informed of it by a letter from the Duke de Foix, who rendered her warm acknowledgments for the favour he had received. He had hastened to the convent, and soon convinced the Abbess of the identity of his claims; but Eugenia had just left the asylum with her supposed brother, the Chevalier D'Aubignac.

This miscreant, in despair of the ill success of his attempt on Mademoiselle de Montalte, had hurried, as soon as his wound would permit, to St. Clair; and, assuring Eugenia he had received it in defending her cause, prevailed on her to consent to an immediate union.

He had secured a priest, and, under his protection, she was readily permitted to quit the monastery.

Not apprehensive, however, of any sudden discovery, he omitted the usual precautions, and the Duke arriving in the interim, easily traced him to the altar, where Eugenia was preparing to consecrate her vows. The wretch endeavoured vainly to escape. Notwithstanding the tears and supplications of his bride elect, he was dragged to prison, and she reconducted to the paternal mansion. Here, for some days, she was deaf to all entreaties, conceiving it her duty, as a disconsolate heroine, to personate despair; but the perusal of Emily's letter to herself, which was just then delivered, opened her eyes, and convinced her of the error she had committed in pursuit of romantic celebrity. She threw herself at her father's feet, and, having obtained his pardon, consented to receive the addresses of a nobleman, in every respect worthy her attachment.

Such was the issue of the adventures at St. Clair, and Emily could not sufficiently congratulate herself for having chosen an asylum that had furnished such a field for the exercise of benevolence.

The family now removed to Lausanne, and the novelty of the scene, for some time, occupied her attention, and detached her thoughts, in some degree, from past and future sorrows.

Caroline persuaded her, as often as she found an opportunity, to mingle in the enjoyments or amusements of those who resorted there, more for the purpose of recreation than health.

The society was fluctuating, and almost every new week brought with it a change of inhabitants. The contemplative mind might here indulge its propensities in analysing the different features, manners, pursuits, and interests of its multifarious visitants.

To such contemplations the understanding of Emily was peculiarly adapted. The study of human nature pleased and instructed her. She often attended the rooms, but less frequently than she might have wished, owing to the observation she ever excited, and which she anxiously wished to avoid.

Her train of admirers, in spite of her efforts, daily increased, and it soon became necessary to seclude herself almost entirely, to escape the importunities of her various suitors, whose pretensions were all equally irksome to her.

She was relieved, in some degree, by the confinement of Caroline, which was a sufficient plea for her own. She had given birth to a female infant, who claimed the affections of Emily as entirely as those of its parents. In listening to the maternal raptures of her friend, and almost partaking them, she found an undefinable increase of happiness.

She had informed Dorville of the fate of Julia D'Ermancy, and enquired if he had heard of Marsillac. He had seen him, but the victim of love and despair. He had learnt the history of her misfortunes from her brother Frederic, accompanied with the assurance that death had terminated them all; and Marsillac, unable to endure a world where all his hopes were wrecked, had retired to a monastery.

Amongst the pretenders to Emily's hand was the Chevalier St. Amand, who, having understood that her union with Lusignan was not to take place, thought this a favourable moment to urge his own pretensions.

A few years had improved his natural good sense, and destroyed that vein of self-love which once pervaded all his actions, and to which his noble propensities gave way. During his residence at Lausanne, he had formed an intimate connection with Dorville, which introduced him to the society of Emily at all hours, and his admiration of her matured into the most solid esteem and affection.

Dorimond, whom she had formerly seen at Luneville, was also an inhabitant of the gay scenes of Switzerland: modest, diffident, and unaspiring, he viewed her with an excess of admiration that almost deified her; but, while he secretly languished, an invariable silence concealed from her his wishes: yet to an impartial observer his feelings were evident; his looks, his actions—a thousand nameless attentions, bespoke him her devoted lover; his whole happiness seemed centred in attending her, and endeavouring to gratify every wish ere it was uttered; yet he never dared raise his hopes to a return of affection.

Accidentally, however, he learned that some misunderstanding between the families had disunited her from the Marquis; he had even heard that she was neglected by him, so partially had rumour, on its swift pinions, borne the story of her misfortunes.

Various conflicts arose in his mind on the receipt of this information; generosity forbade him to address her on the subject of a new connection, at a moment when the melancholy impressed on her features proclaimed her yet enslaved by a former one. On the other hand, now was the crisis when he might best hope success. He knew that renunciation of an attachment, which has long engrossed our faculties, leaves a vacuum that can be best supplied by some new passion. Could he ever hope to give birth to that, how enviable would be his lot! Even if he could only obtain her esteem, and with that her consent to an union, he doubted not his undeviating affection, his fond assiduities, when he became the arbiter of her destiny, would, in a mind like her's, soon give birth to more tender sentiments.

After much consideration, he resolved to address her on this darling subject, and should he unhappily be repulsed, to banish himself for ever from those syren delights that ruined his peace.

He had written many letters, and made many attempts to enter on the subject, but doubt and apprehension still sealed his lips, when one evening, as he sat with her and Caroline, at a late hour, an unexpected visitor was announced, and, to the astonishment of all, Lusignan entered.

Fatigue was visible in his appearance. His eyes, though brightened at the sight of all he loved, bore traces of deep dejection. Emily started from her seat, and, by an involuntary emotion, threw herself into his arms. The sight of him, in defiance of reason and conviction, made her hope some favourable conjuncture had directed his steps to Lausanne.

"My betrothed, my darling Emily," he said, "do I see you once again! do I indeed clasp you in these arms! would you but yield to the voice of love, never more should fortune separate us!"

These words recalled her wandering senses; their import convinced her there was nothing to hope. Without uttering a syllable, she threw herself on a chair, shocked at the indiscretion she had been guilty of.

Dorimond, astonished, dismayed, and bereft of hope, darted out of the house, finally resolved never to enter it more.

Emily at length recovered the power of speech, which surprise and horror had destroyed.

"In the name of Heaven, Lusignan," she said, "what has brought you here?"

"Love, distraction, and despair!" he cried. "There is but one way, Emily: if you do not consent to burst those barriers, imposed by a severe—a despotic world; if you do not consent, in spite of my father, to an immediate union, you urge me to the most fatal excesses. Never will I survive it. Shall the fetters of abject custom, the bonds of an ill-judging multitude, be compared to the sacred ligaments of the soul, which bind our destinies! No, my Emily; rise superior to such prejudices, consent to be mine, now—this very hour! doubt is distraction! Give me but a right to defend and protect you—make me, by the most sacred tie that unites the sexes, the arbiter of your fate, and no powers on earth shall separate us!—It is not alone the voice of love, it is that of reason which speaks, and urges you to resolve. Know, that I am once more a prisoner. On my arrival at Paris, my father, already informed of our meeting, which, however casual, wore in his corroded mind the semblance of design, refused to see me, to listen to my justification, and ordered me to return to the Priory. It was in my power to escape, to quit France, and seek liberty in a happier clime; but I still respected paternal authority, however abused. Ah! rather, my Emily, I still loved that country which contained my treasure. To breathe the same air with you, I consented to remain in a kingdom which had no other charm, and where I was for ever bereft of liberty; I returned to the Priory with less regret, as the court, the palace, were alike a desert to me. The illness of my keeper has furnished me with this opportunity of seeing you. If you are yet inexorable, it is for the last time!—You weep, my love; you are then not insensible to my misfortunes! You change them into bliss. By a single word, you render me the most fortunate of beings."

"Ah! say not so," replied Emily; "say rather I deprive you of the last consolation; the only one that can remain to you in the last hour, that of having done your duty. No, Lusignan; you would, in a calmer hour, blame that compliance you now solicit. Love is too frequently a source of error: let it in us become a principle of virtue. Never, O never will I add to the pang of misfortune the consciousness of having deserved it!"

"Such reasoning," cried Lusignan, "is the effect of indifference—cold, cruel indifference! Ah, Emily! how little do you participate the warm feelings of my heart! Reason, love, equity, all plead for me. You contemplate, with unconcern, my tortures—my agony! Then, farewell; I return to the bondage my father has imposed, less cruel far than you! There is a way, which to all is ready—one means of ending our worst afflictions: it is now my only hope—my last sad refuge!"

"Ah, Lusignan!" rejoined Emily, while tears of bitter sorrow bedewed her cheeks; "how unjust are your words! Recall them; do justice to my sufferings; summon to your aid, religion, virtue, fortitude; the day will come when you will bow in thankfulness to the author of mercy, who has alone prevented your taking steps, which, by destroying your virtue, would annihilate your claims to happiness here and hereafter! Return to the Priory; I will consult with the Duchess de Meronville; if she seconds your request, I fear it will no longer be in my power to reject it; but promise me not to make any rash attempt—promise me to preserve your existence for my sake, for that of your maker."

"What voice is it," said the Marquis, "that has power thus to calm the mighty tempest of my soul? Yes, I do promise, and may Heaven register the vow—still to live, since you command it; to drag through a weight of existence, till the appointed hour of retribution. But talk not to me of hopes; once returned to the Priory, they are all extinguished. My ferocious keeper will resume his station. I have no future chance of escaping. Will you then let me depart? Never, my Emily, shall we meet more; my boding heart tells me we part for ever!"

"Yes, Lusignan," said she, while sobs interrupted her speech, "it must be so: I am forced to pronounce that sentence which deprives me of life, or at least all that can render it estimable. Adieu! It is time this interview should end; it enfeebles us both; you require repose after the fatigues you have sustained. Retire! but seek not to meet me again; my strength is unequal to such conflicts."

She endeavoured to quit the room; he caught her robe.

"Hear me yet a moment, my love, my adored Emily!"

Scarcely able to stand, she tore herself from him, and just reached her chamber, ere life receded from her breast.

Lusignan, convinced he had nothing to hope, departed with the first rays of the sun. Emily rose dejected, pale, uncheered by hope—by all but the consciousness of having done her duty.

CHAP. VII.

"Her trembling tongue, the motive would explain
"That fix'd her thus, alas! to live in vain!
"Some dread remembrance of departed joy
"Beguil'd her reason, powerful to destroy;
"Left her like yonder leafless shrub to fade,
"Hid from the light, and withering in the shade!"

D'Aubignac had suffered the just punishment of his crimes. The Pontiff, whose zeal and equity had restored the lost Julia, exacted as an indispensable condition the revealment of the miscreant, whose arts had seduced her. Painful as was the effort, his arguments convinced her, and she named the Chevalier D'Aubignac.

Death is the penalty imposed by the ecclesiastical laws for a crime so heinous as that of seducing a vestal consecrated to God.

The Duke de Foix, finding in him the betrayer of his daughter, exerted his influence to prevent a mitigation of the sentence, as he conceived a person capable of such nefarious practices to be a dangerous member of society.

His last attempt on Emily had crowned his guilt, and he expiated it on a scaffold. Thus, by one of those ordinations of Providence, concealed from human prudence till the hour of completion, Emily, who had been the victim of La Haye, became the executioner of his son, and inflicted on his pride and ambition a pang no suffering could exceed.

His callous heart was yet insensible to repentance. Animated with new fury, he informed the Duke of Lusignan's visit to Lausanne, which, he had flattered himself, no one could reveal, as Vincenza, the benevolent jailer, was the only person in his confidence. But La Haye had spies, who never neglected any information that might be of service to their employer.

By an act of his own authority, he condemned him to chains and a still closer confinement, and Vincenza was deprived of his office.

He then forged a letter from the Duke, addressed to Mademoiselle de Montalte, in which he informed her of the Marquis's situation, and assured her its horrors would daily increase, if she did not consent to marry some other person, and thus put it out of his power to hope any thing from her; that the moment this should take place, he would be liberated, and restored to his rank and fortune; that his destiny now depended on her, and the sentence was left for her to pronounce.

Wavering and wretched, Emily pondered over this letter, and vainly sought counsel and comfort from her friend. So delicate was the point in question, that Caroline knew not how best to direct the influence she possessed.

"Is it in my power to emancipate thee, O thou that my soul idolizes!" she said; "and do I hesitate! Thou for whom I would sacrifice my life! No, Lusignan, you shall at least owe your liberty to me; you shall find that I am at least disinterested!"

Caroline would fain have persuaded her to pause on her resolution, and await the effect of time, which lessens every affliction; but she dreaded the horrors of suspense, and felt that nothing but precipitation could bear her through a trial so severe.

She had hardly perceived that Dorimond had left Lausanne, so entirely were her thoughts absorbed in other considerations. He had never declared his sentiments, though she perhaps was the only person ignorant of the passion she had inspired, which burst irresistibly through every attempt at concealment.

Soon after his departure, the Marquis de Bentivoglio arrived at Lausanne. He was a man turned of sixty, of stature below the middle; his emaciated form, contrasted with the elegance of his apparel, and an attempt at appearing still a man of gallantry, made an impression on the beholder equally disgustful and ludicrous. His complexion, of a saffron hue, and his small dark eyes, which contained an expression of malignity, he vainly endeavoured to conceal, completed his person; and his locks, withered by the hand of time, were supplied by a wig, dressed with the nicest care.

His character might vie with his appearance: jealous, vindictive, cruel; he had broken the heart of a female who had espoused him, at the suggestions of her friends, and he hoped the liberty her death had restored to him would enable him to form a new connection with the sex.

His possessions were large. An Italian by birth, he inherited all the vices of his countrymen, without a single qualification that could make them more supportable.*

In this form he presented himself to Emily, whom he had accidentally seen at mass, and he hesitated not to declare himself her admirer, and a candidate for her hand and heart.

The Chevalier St. Amand was now his only rival, and might justly flatter himself with success; for although Emily could not shew attachment to either, his virtues claimed her esteem, and she treated him with great distinction.

Madame de Meronville herself pressed her to marry: she feared the effect of long confinement on her darling son, and seeing no prospect of their union, she thought the peace of both would be increased by an engagement, in which she might find that happiness which seemed for ever denied her.

On the choice Emily hesitated not. With St. Amand she had a chance of happiness. He was amiable, disinterested, and firmly attached to her; his person and manners might have encouraged the idea that she married from choice, and he might have been a just object of jealousy to Lusignan. This was sufficient to supersede his claims, as she was fully resolved to give him such a rival, as must convince him dire necessity dictated the union she formed; that from her choice she had no hopes but of extreme misery.

Thus resolved, she listened, therefore, to the proposals of Bentivoglio, and, to the utter amazement of all but himself, accepted them.

Caroline saw her agonies, her deep despair, and vainly endeavoured to dissuade her from laying the foundation of long years of misery.

"They cannot be long, my Caroline," would she say; "the period cannot be distant when my sorrows will be entombed with my poor remains. While they endure, I am securing to myself one mitigation, since they are intended as a source of consolation to my ever-loved, ever lamented Lusignan. He will do justice to the generosity of those sentiments which prompt the sacrifice I make. Deprived of him my heart was born to love, all men are alike to me; and, once certain that it is in my power to procure his liberty, I reproach myself every hour for its continuance."

"Tremble," replied Caroline, "for your fate! Bentivoglio, even at the moment when he is endeavouring to recommend himself, betrays a moroseness, a capricious austerity, thoroughly incompatible with connubial happiness. Jealousy, the most baneful of passions, governs him despotically; he cannot even now conceal it, if you address St. Amand, or any person whose superior merits cannot escape him, though he never acknowledges their existence. Think, then, my Emily, how fatal its excess may be, when policy no longer stimulates disguise; when he learns, which, alas, he cannot be long ignorant of, that you accepted his proposals in an hour of despair, and with no other view but that of destroying jealousy in his more favoured rival. Pause, my love, ere it is too late! consider well ere you enter on a state of life fraught with joy or wretchedness. St. Amand offers you a happier prospect: he has generosity to pardon those sentiments you cannot command; to attribute them to the caprice of fortune, and accept your esteem and friendship, in exchange for that more lively passion which cannot twice be felt. If he has not all the charms of Lusignan, he is at least free from the vices of Bentivoglio."

"His merits," replied Emily, "are the only obstacles to his success. He deserves a better fate than that of being united to a woman whose every affection is engrossed by one sole object. Nor was I formed to live in that intermediate state, which lulls the faculties of the soul, and leaves it a prey to inaction: in one extremity I shall live and die, unqualified misery or excess of happiness. Necessity compels me to marry. I am prepared to be wretched. It is for the sake of Lusignan; and yet, perhaps, it will give birth to his severest sorrows. At least by the election I make, I shall prove to him, that his interest alone determined me. Pity me, my Caroline; your esteem I hope ever to merit, but in nothing more than the manner in which I shall conduct myself towards Bentivoglio, when the sacred rites of the church shall have given him a claim to my obedience."

The time insensibly approached that was to decide her fate.

Bentivoglio could not but discern, through her affected composure, an extreme perturbation, a disgust towards him, which he was accustomed to inspire, and which she vainly sought to disguise. He endeavoured to analyse her intentions in accepting him, and attributed them to his rank and fortune, by which he gloried in triumphing over St. Amand, his supposed favoured rival, who left Lausanne as soon as assured by Emily that her determination was unalterable of uniting herself to the Marquis of Bentivoglio.

The eve of that day arrived. She sat down, for the last time, to address Lusignan. She painted her whole soul on the paper, and, having dispatched it, bent all her thoughts to the acquirement of fortitude and tranquillity in the hour which, she knew, must consign her to misery.

The nuptials were solemnized with great magnificence.

Emily, the devoted victim, approached the altar with a wavering step, but a resolute heart. She threw her eyes to Heaven, as though imploring its support, while her tremulous voice pronounced vows her heart could never ratify.

During the ceremony, Caroline shed torrents of tears, but none fell from the burning eyelids of her friend. A composure, the off-spring of despair, supported her, and she appeared collected and unconcerned.

The Marquis, now assured of his victim, resolved to carry her immediately to a Castle, situated in a remote part of the Pyrenees, where no tempter could pursue her steps, and where she would be wholly his.

Lusignan, in his sad retirement, knew not what passed. He had been removed to a dungeon, where there was no chance of escape, and where, apparently, no intelligence could reach him.

Whole days he stood in the attitude of reflection, ruminating on his miseries, and expected their termination with that of his existence.

One day as he was, as usual, profoundly meditating, his reverie was interrupted by a noise at his window, and, looking towards the spot, a letter fell into his cell. He broke the seal with an emotion that almost deprived him of respiration; but cold, inanimate, petrified to insensibility, he stood, when he had perused these lines.

"I am informed of your deplorable situation, dearest Lusignan; I know all you suffer for my sake, and have but one means of restoring you to liberty. Ah! how cruel is the alternative! Arm yourself with courage; imitate my fortitude: the method I am employing for your relief will perhaps complete your misery, but I shall share it: this is my only consolation, the only motive that sustains my breaking heart, and saves me from distraction. I am compelled, by an engagement with another, to administer to your father's resentment, and to quiet his apprehensions of our future union. At this price he grants you your liberty. Cheaply could I think it purchased at the expence of my tranquillity and life, could I with it restore your happiness. I foresee all the calamities that await me: bound in chains, which necessity imposes, and which inclination can alone render supportable; but your prison, your sufferings, are all that can now interest my feelings. How poor, how insignificant, are all other considerations! In a few days I shall become the wife of the Marquis de Bentivoglio. The little knowledge I have of his character announces the horrors to which I am destined; but to you I owe, at least, this sacrifice. This species of fidelity, which must convince you, in forming this sacred engagement, I have no view to happiness—no prospect, but of wretchedness. But you, my Lusignan, sole object of my affections, dearer than ever at the moment I renounce you for ever, try to be happy for my sake, whose only hope is that of restoring your tranquillity.* I feel that I am ungenerous in thus revealing to you the sacrifice your happiness exacts, in betraying the emotions of that heart which beats but in unison with yours. True generosity would have prompted me to conceal the share you have in my marriage; it would have induced me to let you suspect my constancy. I had once formed that design; but, alas, my feeble strength was unequal to the painful effort; I could not support my situation but in the conviction that my memory would not be odious to you; that the remembrance of her you once loved, and who still idolizes you, would at least be favourable to her. Alas! I shall soon be no longer permitted to remember you. It will be my painful, but indispensable duty, to forget that we ever met. Of all my sufferings, this most cruelly afflicts me. You will double them all if you do not sedulously endeavour to avoid seeing or speaking to me. This proof of esteem is the last I exact of you. Cherish that sentiment, it is the only one, with respect to you, I am permitted to retain.—Now, then, farewell, ever esteemed, ever-lamented object of my first choice! It is the last time I shall ever address you; I blush at my want of resolution in thus adding to your woes. Imitate my example; seek consolation in the exercise of your duty; forget that love ever preponderated in your heart; forget all but esteem for your ever devoted

"EMILY."

Lusignan read no further than those fatal words: "by an engagement with another:" they annihilated reason, and deadened his faculties.

He threw himself on his mattrass, and remained for several hours
deprived of all recollection of his misfortunes, but was recalled to
life and misery by the exertions of his keeper, who, though greatly
alarmed at the state in which he found him, was infinitely more terrified at his excess of grief when he recovered. He raved, he tore his
hair, he knocked his head violently against the wall, and exhibited
every symptom of mental derangement.

Inaccessible as this man had hitherto been to the calls of pity, he
could no longer be unmoved at his affliction. He condemned the
rigour exercised by the Duke, and reproached himself for having
been the instrument of his cruelty, execrated La Haye as the minister of vengeance, and on his knees implored pardon for the ill-
treatment Lusignan had received at his hands.

Recalled to reason by this appeal, the Marquis uttered a deep
groan; his soul seemed ready to desert its frail mansion, to burst
from confinement, and hover over her he so tenderly loved.

"Every thing is forgiven you," said he to the jailer, "if you will
release me for a week. I will give my word and honour to return at
the expiration of that term. I will do more: it must one day be in my
power to reward your services—my gratitude shall be boundless."

The emotion visible in his once inexorable keeper had inspired
him with this sudden thought. There was no time to be lost.

The man, in whose breast compassion now for the first time triumphed, moved with his sufferings, and perhaps apprehensive that
Lusignan might one day be avenged, readily consented, but on condition that he should accompany his steps. To this there could be
no objection. But an unavoidable delay arose: horses could not be
procured till the ensuing morning, and, in spite of his impatience,
Lusignan was compelled to submit.

He perused, a thousand times, the fatal letter, and examined the
date. The time Emily mentioned seemed already elapsed; yet he
tried to persuade himself she would seek delays, and sedulously pro-
tract the moment she seemed to dread. He might yet arrive ere the
fatal sacrifice was completed. Ah no! the woman who had fortitude
to form such a resolution, would not seek to impede its accomplishment.

Near as was the period which was to emancipate him, the lingering hours that intervened seemed ages to his anxious mind: one moment might ruin his hopes.

Morning dawned through his narrow casement. The horses arrived; he mounted, and hastened forward, impelled by love, hope, fear, despair, and a thousand commingling passions.

Thought, with unchecked velocity, darted over mountains, precipices, and immeasurable distance: Fain would he have accompanied it, but his less anxious quadruped still lingered far behind, and gave him time for reflection. At one moment, he felt persuaded he had nothing to apprehend.

"The violence of the effort she must make," said he, "will certainly induce her to form pretexts for delay. I will throw myself at her feet, and swear never to rise more if she does not promise to forego her fatal design. Alas! it is perhaps already too late: at this very moment she is perhaps consecrating her vows to another. Pause, cruel Emily! shudder, hated Bentivoglio, my vengeance pursues thee! Dost thou then sacrifice thyself for me, most loved of women? and does that prompt thee to hasten the hour? Ah, why will you judge me by comparison with the rest of mankind! Why will you level your celestial perfection to that of humanity! No: cruel but adored Emily! bereft of you, new prisons will arise wherever I direct my wandering steps! Ah, what is liberty unshared with you!"

From these reflections he was roused by the appearance of a carriage, which advanced rapidly towards them: it stopped, he checked his rapid steed, and beheld his mother.

Dismounting, he entered the vehicle which conveyed her; she pressed him to her heart with affection, but her dejected countenance struck to his soul as she said,—

"My child, I am surprised to meet you here; I was going to release you."

"Ah, then," said Lusignan, "Emily is married!"

Madame de Meronville answered only by her profound silence.

"Then is my misfortune past remedy," continued he; "pitying Heaven, take that life I can no longer support! Cruel father! implacable La Haye! how is thy vengeance glutted!

He sunk into a deep stupor that at once annihilated his sense of misery.

The embraces of his mother recalled him. As she endeavoured to

communicate a ray of hope, his attention, monopolized by one only
subject, had not rested on the mourning garb worn by his mother.

"My child," she said, "your unhappy father is no more;* bury your
resentment for the wrongs you have suffered in that grave which
contains his ashes. Seek not, by your plaints or execrations, to disturb the deep slumber of the dead, or recal his perturbed spirit to
its earthly abode. Raise your thoughts to Heaven, and implore its
blessing for his departed soul."

"My father dead!" replied Lusignan, "and Emily married! Pardon
me, dearest mother, if my agonized soul cannot at once forget its
miseries. Yes, my prayers shall ascend to Heaven in behalf of my
deluded parent, but still the remembrance of his cruelty will survive
when he is long forgotten."

"I cannot give you much hope," said the Duchess, "but there is a
distant possibility that Emily is yet free; I dispatched an express to her,
in hopes to avert the calamity we dread; but there is too much reason
to suppose, ere its arrival she had become the wife of Bentivoglio."

"At the moment," cried Lusignan, "when she might have been
mine! Cruel Emily, your precipitation has ruined us! Let me fly to
her, my mother; let me tear her from his arms! He shall not possess a treasure Heaven designed for me! What are vows to me? The
church has united their hands, nature binds our hearts, in ligaments
too tender, too strong to be broken by human laws!* Yes, I will seek
Bentivoglio, I will compel him to surrender his prize! If he refuses,
this sword shall be sheathed in his bosom! I will fly with Emily to
some sequestered spot, where none shall find her, where nothing
shall penetrate but love, celestial love! Nerved by it this arm shall
guard her, even from the shafts of fortune; hovering over her, the
iron fangs of malice and misfortune shall pierce my breast alone.
The blunted arrow, when it penetrates to her, shall be dipped in the
healing balm of affection! Why do I delay? What spell arrests my
flight? Accuse me not, my Emily—I fly to rescue that angel form
from the wretch that enthrals it!"

As he said these words, he burst the carriage door, and bounded
from it in a fit of frantic agony. He fell prostrate on the pave-
ment; the servants flew to his relief, and raised him to the carriage,
deprived, by the effort he had made, of sense and life. The Duchess
hung over him in mute agony.

When he recovered, the delirium that before pervaded his racked brain subsided into composure and dumb despair. His mother neglected no efforts to console him, as they journeyed towards the Priory.

Arrived there, he vainly entreated her to let him seek Emily.

"Such an attempt, my child," said she, "might render her for ever wretched, and would be a source of grief only to you. You are not master of your passions; you would betray them in the presence of her husband, and give birth to suspicions which must be fatal to her repose. Naturally prone to jealousy, Bentivoglio would yield to all its violence, which wants only an incentive. If reason has no power, let love at least controul you, nor seek, by your imprudence, to heighten the misery of her who devotes herself to obtain your liberty. If she is yet free, my letter will secure her continuing so: if not, no efforts of yours can burst those bonds the church has consecrated. Be persuaded, then, and await the return of my messenger."

With difficulty Lusignan acceded, and when he was sufficiently composed, the Duchess related, that an apoplectic fit had deprived his father of life, and that the quick transition of his soul to immortality had prevented even a late repentance. That a will had appeared, which bequeathed a considerable property to La Haye, in case he survived, and, in failure, to his nephew the Chevalier St. Amand.

The patrimonial estates of Lusignan, now become Duke de Meronville, were so extensive, that the alienation was of no importance; but he considered this donation as the price and remuneration of villany. However, he determined immediately to discharge the bequest, and then banish La Haye for ever from his presence.

The Duchess determined to remain at Belleisle during the season of mourning, and the young Duke agreed to stay there also till news should arrive of Emily.

The day after Mademoiselle de Montalte became the wife of Bentivoglio, as they sat with a numerous company at dinner, a servant brought her a letter. She threw her eye hastily over it, and recognised the well-known characters of Madame de Meronville.

A tremor, which could not be concealed, shook her whole frame as she regarded the black seal that closed it: Perhaps Lusignan was no more; the malice of his enemies might have deprived him of life, or, in a moment of despair, a more impious attempt might have affixed on his memory the stain of suicide.

Whatever should be the contents, she felt unequal to perusing lines traced by his mother, which would awaken recollections fatal to her peace.

Unconscious that the eyes of all were directed to her, she regarded the letter with an expression of profound anguish, and the silent tear fell from her eye.

Bentivoglio, ever alive to suspicion, roused her by enquiring from whom she had heard. Without breaking the wax, she put it in her pocket, and endeavoured to answer, with carelessness, from the Duchess de Meronville.

Here she hoped his interrogatories would cease, and she wished to command resolution enough to conceal her emotion during the repast; but the jealous Marquis insisted on her perusing the contents. In vain she endeavoured to avoid his importunity: her evident reluctance increased his desire of ascertaining whether they were not inimical to his peace.

With a trembling hand and convulsed frame Emily obeyed. The paleness of death overspread her countenance; but, ere she had finished the task assigned her, life receded from her bosom, and she sunk senseless on the floor.

Less anxious to succour her, than to verify his doubts with respect to the mysterious letter, Bentivoglio consigned her to the care of his domestics, while he tore from her hand the paper she eagerly grasped, not doubting but it was the production of a rival.

Undeceived he was in this respect; but what were his emotions when he had read these words!

"Dearest Emily, if it is not now too late, Oh break for ever the odious engagement you are forming! Fly to your more than mother, and bless the arms of her son, who still idolizes you. The obstacle that impedes your union is interred with the Duke de Meronville, who expired yesterday. I have but a moment to assure you of my unalterable affection.

"The agitation of my mind, the palpitation of my heart, communicates itself to my pen, which my trembling hand can with difficulty guide. I sicken with deadly anguish, my sinews relax, while I consider, that the delay of a moment may decide your fate. Ah, generous Emily, how shall I accuse myself, how justify the interested counsel I gave, if, in yielding to it, you should have stamped your existence with misery.

"I am hastening to release Lusignan: how doubly dear would that liberty be he owed to you; but if, alas, you are no longer free, his body only is enfranchised, his soul more deeply enthralled.

"Do not lose a single moment in assuring me of your fate. At the first summons I fly to Lausanne, to sanction by my blessing the union of two hearts formed in one mould, born to vibrate in unison. Adieu, dearest Emily! Ever may I subscribe myself your most affectionate mother,

"ADELAIDE DE MERONVILLE."

This letter the Duchess had sent with one to Caroline, with strict injunctions that it should be delivered only to her, whom she had desired to suppress it, if the dreaded union had previously taken place.

The messenger arriving at her house, and learning that she was at the Marquis de Bentivoglio's, conveyed the letters thither, and delivered them to the porter.

The one addressed to Emily was, in consequence, put into her hand by a cruel error, which at once developed the character of Bentivoglio. He apologized to the company for this interruption to their festivity, and, resuming his seat, affected total unconcern, entertaining his guests with the best grace imaginable.

Caroline had flown to the relief of Emily. By the contents of her own letter, she saw at once the extent of that calamity which had destroyed the senses of her friend, and the fatal consequences she shuddered in considering, knowing the character of Bentivoglio, so tinctured with jealousy, which this incident must inevitably rouse to madness.

When Emily partially recovered, she intuitively pronounced the name of Lusignan; but when her faculties more clearly emerged from the torpor of insensibility, she comprehended at one view the imprudence of her conduct, and the misery to which it might conduce.

Alone with her friend, she poured into her bosom that deluge of sorrow which flowed from her oppressed heart.

How erroneous is the judgment of those who seek by prosecution to destroy the seeds of love. Misfortune ever more closely cements two hearts, which prosperity, by giving a wider range to the passions, might in some degree alienate. Human nature was formed for opposition, ever, by a strange fatality, anxious for enjoyments that seem denied. Adversity had so interwoven the hearts and interests of Lusignan and Emily, that it was no longer in the power of fortune to disunite them.

Emily, when her senses returned, had vainly enquired for her letter, hoping it might be yet time to suppress it, and attribute her fainting to the surprise occasioned by a sudden death; but she soon found that was no longer practicable.

Previous to uniting herself with the Marquis, she had told him, that her esteem and friendship were all she had to bestow with her hand and fortune. This then appeared to satisfy him, but resentment lurked in his breast for the detention of those more tender sentiments he hoped to inspire.

Caroline returned to the saloon to apologize for the non-appearance of her friend, which she accounted for by saying she had received news of the death of a relation. The black seal corroborated this evidence, and the company seemed convinced of its truth.

After their departure, in a private interview with Bentivoglio, she endeavoured to excuse the emotions Emily had betrayed, by telling him she had been affianced early to the Marquis of Lusignan, but that obstacles had occurred to impede their union; that she was now perfectly reconciled to it, and that surprise alone had deprived her of reason.

With these apologies, insignificant as they were, he appeared satisfied, affected to compassionate her feelings, and said, that to obviate such in future, it was his design to remove on the morrow to a Castle of his own in the Pyrenees, where his unwearied endeavours, he had no doubt, would reconcile her to her fortune, and make her look up to him for that happiness he alone could now bestow.

Caroline trembled at this design, and exerted all her influence to divert him from such a project, but she found him inflexible. He said, though sorry to detach her from her friends, he should have the double satisfaction in restoring her to them, when time, which mollifies every pain, and lessens every impression, should temper her now too keen sensibility, and render her less susceptible to past reminiscences, when the warm affections of his heart should claim from her's that return, at least of gratitude, which should make his presence the pinnacle of enjoyment—how happy should he then be to present such a bride to the world.

Caroline judged of his sentiments and intentions very differently, and trembled for the fate of her unhappy friend.

Bentivoglio met Emily with a smile, and seemed desirous of restoring confidence to her mind. Touched by what she thought generosity, her heart expanded to the rights of a husband, and she hoped an unbiassed and open confession of her situation relative to Lusignan would secure her pardon and compassion. She felt that this was the only compensation she could make for her unguarded conduct; and unlimited confidence, she trusted, would ensure the like return.

As briefly, therefore, as the subject would admit, she related the events of her connection with the house of Meronville, and concluded with these words.

"Gratitude for the preference with which you have honoured me, binds me to you by the less ardent, but perhaps more durable, ties of esteem and friendship. I never deceived you; these were all I had in my power, and I trust you will find them sufficient to insure social happiness. I have been taught, in all situations, to pursue the undeviating path of duty: it calls on me to renounce every connection but that I have formed at the altar; you will ever find in me a constant and affectionate wife, and hope the trial you have this day suffered will be the last that can ever disturb your repose, which I henceforward consider as my own."

Emily spoke the genuine sentiments of her heart, and, to a mind capable of one generous emotion, her candour would have borne conviction, and silenced every suggestion of busy imagination.

But every ignoble passion swayed the soul of Bentivoglio. He silently contemned that ingenuousness that he was not formed to imitate, and triumphed at the power the church conferred on him to rule her destiny, secretly meditating revenge for his pretended wrongs.

Of his feelings, however, he was perfect master; a cool, deliberate, unsearchable villain: none of those sensations, which now so powerfully agitated his mind, were suffered to appear above its surface.

He restored to her Madame de Meronville's letter, with permission to answer it, and assumed the semblance of complete satisfaction. He, however, informed her of his design of conveying her to Saint Jago Castle, which he represented as the seat of happiness.

Madame de Bentivoglio acceded to it without difficulty: nothing but absence, she knew, would obliterate the remembrance of scenes, whose recollection could now be only a source of grief. New scenes, new connections, new interests, her present situation opened to her, and from them she hoped much; but whilst she fancied herself engaged only in plans of tranquillity for her own life, Lusignan actuated them all:—careless in effect of what simply regarded herself, she depended on the powerful influence of time and absence to restore him to that peace and happiness, which she would for him have purchased with her existence.

END OF VOL. III.

LUSIGNAN.

CHAP. I.

"Of what avail is fortune unenjoyed,
"Or life in anxious cares employed?"

The brilliant inheritance to which the young Duke de Meronville succeeded, had no charms, no power to turn his attention from the treasure he had lost, the only one, to his pre-occupied mind, worth attainment. Often as the gaze of the surrounding villagers fixed on him, his splendid castle and rich equipage, he would, sighing, envy their more fortunate lot, and repeat to himself—"If these poor rustics would extend their judgment beyond externals—if their glances could penetrate to my care-worn heart, how would they bless their ignorance, and lift their hands in thankfulness to that Almighty Power, which has placed them in a happier sphere! No state is indeed exempt from cares: but the storms of life only hover over their heads, and burst tremendously on ours. The lofty pines, that raise their aspiring heads to the far distant horizon, feel most poignantly the shock of winter's destructive blasts, whilst the modest ivy, that creeps around their bark, receives shelter from the leafless branches, and, as it views the desolation, seems inclined to bless its lowly state. The gorgeous palaces and elevated towers, exposed to the tempest's rage, fall with heavy ruin to the ground—a spectacle to check the pride of man; while the solitary cot scarce feels the shock that spreads such desolation round. Innumerable herbs in safety live upon the mountain's side, while its cloud-clapt eminence yields to the storm that divides it from the sky. Ah, who that could in peace dwell at its base, sheltered from the distant bolts, would seek to reach its elevated summit. Such, happy villager, is thy lot; depending on thy lord for that subsistence which bounds thy wants, the plagues that haunt the rich man's door fly abashed from thy modest dwelling; the snares of ambition, the maze of politics, are unknown to thee—gliding smoothly on the ocean of life, content, the pilot of thy little bark, too wise to seek in unknown climes that happiness thy humble roof affords, blessed in a father's smile, a child's endearing kiss, a weekly holiday, repays six days of toil; whilst he who exhausts the ingenuity of ages to furnish each day some new object, finds satiety in all!"

No answer had arrived from Emily, and various were the conjectures on her silence; at one moment Madam de Meronville hoped she meant to surprise them by her own arrival; at others, she had perhaps left Lausanne. Hope still occupied her mind, but found not entrance into that of her son; fear preponderated, and anxious doubt; his prophetic senses told him all was lost. At length the messenger returned—trembling the Duchess read, while Lusignan, breathless, threw himself back on his chair, dreading to enquire, and discover in his mother's looks the fatal sentence—it was irreversible—the paper dropped from her hand—he hastily seized it, and resolving at once to satisfy his doubts, read thus:—

"All is over, Madam, and my destiny for ever fixed! Fate had but this single stroke to inflict! My agonized soul, perplexed with its various duties, knows not how to address you—for the last time it permits my trembling hand to write the name of Lusignan—dear much-loved name, farewell! Tell him, Madam, if he yet preserves one sentiment of all he once possessed for me, it is my last command—my darling wish, that he should preserve his existence for your sake, and, may I yet say, mine! Tell him I shall strive to be happy, but nothing will so much conduce to it as the certainty that he is so. I have already said too much—let me forget I ever loved—teach him, Madam, to remember me only as the wife of Bentivoglio; for yourself, my affection can never lessen, no, my dearest Madam, it is unalterable; accuse not yourself, fortune only dictated the step I have taken, or rather, that omniscient Being, who best guards our interests; let us then no longer repine, but submit ourselves to him; virtue still remains to us, and in the exercise of it we shall find comfort every where!"

"Here then," cried the Duke, "end my hopes of happiness for ever!" A deep groan succeeded; a responsive sigh issued from the bosom of his mother; both were too deeply absorbed in grief to find utterance for it. The Duchess first recovered, and strove to inspire fortitude in young Meronville; but from that hour he seemed insensible to her tears and caresses. "Yes, sweet Emily," he would say, "at the moment you destroy my happiness, my subject senses still yield to your commands; I yet live, for it is your desire; but mental agony chills the vital current, and soon will have my body inanimate, as are now my faculties; then shall I mingle with my native dust, and it will yet be a crime for thee to shed one tear to my remembrance! Welcome Death, take thy victim—thou can'st level all distinctions, and swallow all afflictions. Impartial Heaven, thou hast ordained a period to all our woes; in one grave are entombed joys, sorrows, riches, poverty; then, Bentivoglio, where is thy triumph? Think not thy beauteous bride shall in another world hover over thee; no, her pure spirit on earth can never mix with thine; but elevated to that blessed abode her ethereal merit calls its home, united to kindred angels, she shall rise superior to earthly ties; then, hated rival, where is thy triumph? In the grave, where is thy superiority? Eloquent, just, and mighty death shall persuade thee, whom none else can convince; if all the world, bowing to thy superficial honours, conceal their contempt for thy sins, death alone shall eject thee; then shalt thou be despised, hated, contemned; all thy far-fetched greatness shall vanish as a dream; pride, cruelty, guilt, and ambition, shall swell thy pompous epitaph. Think not I am a stranger to thee; no, I know thee well, and know how unworthy the treasure thou possessest. Too lovely Emily, thou art indeed immolated! Avenging Heaven protect thee!"

In such rhapsodies he spent the days; whilst his mother, scarcely less afflicted, mourned her inability to lend relief. Mental anguish at length brought on the decay of the body, and a fever ensued, which left him on the verge of eternity. In the violence of delirium he accused his father, mother, and Emily, of conspiring to his ruin; frequently he vowed the destruction of Bentivoglio, and fancying him near, would pierce some inanimate foe with the stroke intended for the bosom of his rival.

To these violent exertions succeeded two days of obstinate silence, during which he refused all sustenance; the third endangered his life. Madam de Meronville, who never quitted his bedside, felt the anguish of mortal despair; her tears, her prayers, and the name of Emily, which she incessantly repeated, seemed at intervals to recall him to life; his soul, taking flight to eternity, seemed arrested by that sound, which would still irradiate with a beam of youthful hope his parting hour.

At the end of a fortnight, severe anxiety gave place to hope in the mind of an affectionate parent. Lusignan began to amend. The talisman which recalled him from the borders of the grave was still successfully employed to accelerate his recovery. A sudden idea appeared to have seized his imagination, and he seemed now resolved to struggle with the violence of that disorder to which he so lately passively yielded.

"If Emily," said he to his mother, "can yet transfer my feelings to her own bosom, she will do justice to the effort I am making; she will be convinced that the pang of parting life is but a momentary agony; and that, in dying for her sake, I should at once have bid adieu to sorrow: but to sustain, through a weight of tedious years, that existence, robbed of every charm that can heighten the burthen, is to condemn oneself to mortal pangs each hour—that sacrifice I make to her, oh, may she never mistake its value!"

In his first lucid intervals he asked for the letter he had received from her in his dungeon. Madame de Meronville had concealed it, but the excess of his affliction made her judge it necessary to restore it. He united it to the portrait he had obtained by a happy device, in the commencement of his attachment to her, and placing them both near his heart, vowed that death itself should never tear them from it. Each day he re-perused it; and those lines which commanded him to live strengthened his resolution of not making any attempt on that existence she had avowed an interest in preserving.

The Duchess submitted to the necessity of yielding at first to his grief, since opposition would only have increased it. To the influence of time she confided the care of restoring him to tranquillity. Finding that while he conversed of Emily, his anguish mellowed into gentle melancholy, which she considered as a prelude to composure, she listened to him with undeviating attention, and opened her bosom to receive his complaints; she cherished the only consolation of which his grief seemed susceptible—the certainty of being beloved by the woman he adored.* This idea calmed his passions, and soothed his afflictions; it furnished an inexpressible balm to the wounds of his mind, and brought him, at length, to a state of resignation.

As he wandered through the woods alone, it frequently occurred to him to seek some solitary habitation, where, with no other companion but his thoughts, he might, secluded from the busy haunts of man, live and die in peace, cherish the remembrance of his once happy days, and breathe in silence his prayers for Emily. From this resolution he was alone deterred by the recollection of his mother; he felt that he was her only consolation, and, sighing, owned that one link still attached him to the world he abhorred. Ah, how frequently did the thought recur of seeking those envied scenes where Emily trod, of endeavouring once more to behold her, to breathe the air her coral lips inhaled; but she had opposed her positive commands to such a project. Yet he was unknown to Bentivoglio; he might, unseen, unsuspected, watch her steps, live on her smile, though bestowed on a rival. Yet how could he ever pardon himself, if such an attempt should be discovered, and call one tear from her eye, one sigh from her bosom; if it should become an incentive to the jealousies of her tyrant, and add a single mortification to those his caprices inflicted? He would then expire at her feet to expiate his crime. He dwelt on the fond idea, which at first seemed only visionary and impracticable; by continued meditation, it seemed feasible, and soon indispensable to his peace. The means were now only to be considered, and he eagerly entered on the execution of a project, which he now considered as his last hope of comfort.

Fearing opposition from the voice of reason, conveyed through the persuasive channel of his mother, he concealed from her his design, and communicated it only to St. Pierre, the faithful domestic who had adhered to him from infancy. This man he dispatched to Lausanne, to learn the abode of the Marquis of Bentivoglio, and after assuring him a thousand times more than his life depended on the success of the present scheme, hastened his departure, and calmly awaited his return.

On his arrival in Switzerland, the place of his nativity, he learnt that the Marquis had conveyed his bride to St. Jago Castle, situate in the Pyrenean mountains, and that a relation of his own, in the service of Bentivoglio, attended them. Having communicated this intelligence to his master, he proposed, by means of his relative, to gain admission to the Castle, and inform himself of Emily's situation, and the best method of procuring Lusignan an opportunity of seeing her, without exciting the suspicious jealousy of her husband.

This project was attended with inconvenience, because it implied delay; but as he could think of none that deserved a preference, he acceded to it, and once more applied himself to beguile the lingering hours that intervened.

In his solitude he was surprised by an unexpected visit from La Haye. This man he could never view without disgust; and how was that sentiment heightened by the obsequious servility of his address, when now he desired to recommend himself to the notice of the young Duke. The melancholy catastrophe of d'Aubignac, and the unsuccessful suit of St. Amand, had proved a complete wreck to his hopes: and although the hand of heaven was manifested in this visitation for the crimes of his guilty soul, he yet seemed to defy the omnipotence of Providence, by shutting his heart from the dictates of repentance, which could alone give him a claim to pardon. To accelerate his designs he had exhausted the resources of villany, and stretched invention almost beyond its power; yet they had all proved abortive, and heaven, by the pangs of disappointment, seemed to give a foretaste in this world of that more ample vengeance it reserved for another. His suit to the Duke was only to be continued in his post of domestic chaplain. Astonishment at his unexampled effrontery stifled every other consideration in the mind of Lusignan, and without deigning to reply, he ordered him to quit his mansion for ever.

The late Duke de Meronville had died very opportunely for La Haye. At the time that he was labouring to procure the lettre de cachet, which confined Lusignan, finding his patron sometimes leaned to clemency, which must have destroyed his purpose, he had thought it adviseable not to remind him too often of the design which was then executing; and as it became necessary for him to affix his name frequently to different documents, La Haye had not hesitated to substitute a forged signature. After the reversing of this order, the regularity of the law required that these signatures should be proved, and attested by the Duke; and commissioners were accordingly appointed to wait on his Grace the earliest day. As La Haye's arts here failed, he was in great perplexity; but one of those fortunate strokes of fate, which sometimes favour the villain, here came to his relief, and Meronville died suddenly, previous to the appointed day which must have developed the enormity of his conduct. Finding that he had no prospect of succeeding with the new Duke, he retired to project new crimes, unconscious that the hour of retribution approached.

Six weeks elapsed in anxious impatience, the seventh, St. Pierre returned, and thus related the events of his absence:—

"It was some time before I could devise any means of procuring admission to the Castle inhabited by Madame de Bentivoglio; at length, some improvements designed by the Marquis presented an opportunity I had almost despaired of obtaining. In a small island opposite the Castle, and appertaining to it, he had resolved to erect a summer-house, on a plan of his own, which, however, no one would undertake to execute. I had an uncle, who followed the trade of an architect, and I engaged him to undertake it, and appoint me his assistant. This device succeeded, and gained me admission to the Castle. I saw Madam de Bentivoglio frequently, and have no doubt she recollected me; for a deep crimson suffused her cheeks, which, in general, want even the animation of health; she appeared languid, and much altered. The Marquis seldom leaves her for a moment; he is said to be much attached to her, but gives no proof but that of excessive jealousy, which, without any provocation, breaks out perpetually in acts of violence and folly; so surprising is its excess, that his own brother, though an inmate of the Castle, is rarely permitted to see her without witnesses. Her life appears the most monotonous and dull that can be conceived. Tormented for ever with the presence of a husband, who has not discernment to perceive her virtues, nor candour to appreciate them, each day is wasted in silence and sorrow; no human being is admitted to interrupt her solitude; time, as it slowly creeps on, brings no change, no comfort to her. The selfish pleasure of occupying her undivided attention compensates with her husband for that confidence, that voluntary homage, her heart would confer on the person who sought to make her happiness his own. Far other are the motives of the Marquis; I have been assured that the persuasions of his brother frequently calm the excesses of his temper, which, nevertheless, render her life a chequered scene of misery!"

"Inhuman villain!" exclaimed Lusignan; "but proceed, St. Pierre, I will endeavour to stifle my indignation! Who is this brother you mention? I knew not that he had one."

"He is a young man," replied St. Pierre, "of whom much is said, and the universal suffrage declares him to be as amiable and virtuous as his brother is the reverse. He appears much attached to his sister-in-law, and omits nothing to soften her afflictions, and render her lot less deplorable; and she seems grateful for his endeavours. I saw her but seldom. Whole days she passes in her apartment, with no other companion but a little dog, of whom she seems very fond."

"Ah, gracious heaven! that little dog," said Lusignan, "was a present of mine in happier days; little did I hope it would ever become necessary to her. Ah, my Emily, let it become my representative; let its faithful attachment remind you of mine! Oh that I could endow it with the gift of speech, that it might incessantly repeat to you, how much, how tenderly I yet love!"

"You would, in so doing, render the Marchioness very unhappy," returned St. Pierre. "Excuse, Sir, the liberty I take in saying, that if you attempt to make yourself known to her, all is over. You must limit your enjoyment to that of seeing her; the most trifling incident would awaken the jealousy of Bentivoglio, and its consequences must be fatal. I will not endeavour to make you cautious, by saying a discovery would endanger your own life, that I know is inconsequential, but her's will be no less exposed. Despotic within his little territories, the Marquis acts unquestioned, and heaven only knows to what excesses jealousy, if fired by any new incentive, might not lead; the risk of your own life would be a feeble motive compared with her repose, which one imprudent step unavoidably destroys. The plan I have concerted for your admission to the Castle is this:—in the pavilion my uncle has lately erected, there are two apartments, the upper one is intended to be painted in Italian landscapes; I undertook to engage a painter, and you are the person. You will then live at St. Jago, and as a wood on the little island is a favourite retreat of Madame de Bentivoglio, you will have the best opportunity of seeing her unobserved yourself. If this plan meets your approbation, we shall set out to-morrow, and in a few days arrive at the Pyrenees."

Lusignan, transported with the prospect of seeing Emily, accepted with joy the menial office assigned him; and telling his mother he was going to spend a short time with a friend in the south, set out at day break the following morning.

What volumes of ideas rushed on his mind, and jarring emotions! He must be presented to the hated Marquis, the tyrant of Emily, the destroyer of his peace. How should he forbear to reproach him?

How conceal the sensations of his soul? How restrain the impetuosity of his feelings? He should meet Madam de Bentivoglio,
his betrothed bride, yet dare only acknowledge her as the wife of
another; he should pursue her steps, perhaps witness a tear shed to
his remembrance. That little dog she surely loved for his sake!

"Ah enviable, but insensible brute, how happy is thy lot!" thought
he; "permitted to attend her steps; to endear thyself by a thousand
caresses; to breathe in her arms, and rest on her bosom!"

He would then seek consolation in the idea of being still dear
to her, and would thank the Marquis for concealing her from that
world, where she would meet as many admirers as beholders, and
perhaps some that might erase his image from her heart. He almost
began to feel a pang of that jealousy which embittered the life of his
rival. When he thought on the brother of the Marquis, St. Pierre
had painted his attachment to her in such glowing colours, and
drawn a portrait so favourable, so fascinating, of him, that he began
to fear this object always near her, always permitted to recommend
himself by a thousand nameless attentions, might, by contrast with
his detested brother, inspire sentiments in her heart, which he considered as exclusively his own. Turning, however, from an idea that
gave him acute pain, he thought only on the approaching happiness
of seeing her; and convinced indeed that a discovery would for ever
ruin her peace of mind, he promised himself and St. Pierre more
circumspection than that faithful domestic had prescribed; and full
of that visionary power, which guides us through life, whose cheering beams still penetrate through every cloud that obscures its radiance, he proceeded on his journey.

CHAP. II.

"Black melancholy sits, and round her throws,
"A death-like silence, and a dread repose;
"Her gloomy presence saddens all the scene,
"Shades every flower, and darkens every green;
"Deepens the murmurs of the falling floods,
"And breathes a browner horror on the woods."

Emily hurried from Lausanne, and scarcely permitted to bestow a parting embrace on the friend of her early years, felt the chill of gloomy presage possess her mind, as she jumped into the carriage, assisted by her husband. He watched each turn of her intelligent countenance, as the rapid steeds conveyed her from the abode of all she loved, with no substitute for lost happiness, but the presence of a man, to whom she had vowed obedience; to whom she would willingly have given her esteem; but whose conduct and manners were little calculated to nurture any sentiments but disgust and aversion. Her knowledge, however, of him was now so contracted, that she judged only from his behaviour on the receipt of Madame de Meronville's letter, and that implied something like the candour of a noble mind. His subsequent conduct in hastening her from Switzerland she attributed to the laudable motive of procuring her, in a diversity of scenes, an opportunity of detaching her mind from ideas that seemed inimical to her peace. Willing, therefore, to testify her gratitude for his intentions, she checked the spontaneous tear, and stifled the rising sigh that offered homage to the dear scenes of infant enjoyment.

Bentivoglio leaned back in the carriage, and seemed occupied in ruminations, that prevented his observing the beauty of the landscapes around. Emily, by forced observations, endeavoured to call his attention to it; but a monosyllable usually bounded his reply; and finding her attempts to engage him in conversation ineffectual, she willingly returned to that silence it had cost her an effort to break.

Their journey, which lasted several days, passed wholly like the first, till, as they reached the summit of an eminence it had cost them

some hours to accomplish, Bentivoglio broke silence, by announc-
ing their arrival at the Castle. Emily started from a reverie in which
she had been long absorbed, and, letting down the glass, uttered
an involuntary exclamation at the luxuriance of the prospect which
presented itself to her wondering eyes. In a valley beneath stood the
Castle, in the construction of which the architect had exhausted his
utmost powers, and one side of it, through the lapse of ages, had
defied the wreck of time. The magnificent ruins of the other side,
which was not equally sheltered by the haughty Pyrenees, formed
a contrast at once terrific and astonishing; its base was laved by the
encroaching waves of the Mediterranean, and the eye, at one view,
seemed to compass the vast expanse and the immeasurable Pyren-
nees; extensive woods, and plains of boundless width, appeared
objects in miniature before these gigantic features of nature; but as
they descended the declivity of the mountain, in which a road had
been hewn to facilitate the approach to the mansion beneath, it
appeared melancholy and cheerless. The dark stones that composed
it, and the antique windows, many of them obscured by strong iron
bars, through which they presented a picture of sublime ancientry, promised little enjoyment, and raised no emotions but those of
wonder, unmingled with a softer sensation. At a moment when the
susceptible mind attunes itself to impressions of sorrow, the most
common incidents convey importance, and are construed into presages of woe. Emily could not have hoped to meet in this isolated
castle a friend to welcome her arrival; yet sadness involved her faculties as she entered the gloomy and spacious halls, which exhibited an awful solitude. While the Marquis gave some orders to his
servants, she relieved her aching heart by yielding to a suffusion of
tears. She threw her deluged eyes round the apartment, and wherever they rested, traces of magnificence appeared. The grotesque
figures on the tapestry, the roof of mosaic fretwork, and the mirrors
which filled the huge pannels, and reflected a thousand times the
various vestiges of antiquity, spoke of former days, and produced a
concatenation of differing ideas.

Solitary was the mansion, more solitary the bosom of Emily; no
friend in whom she could confide her sorrows; no congenial spirit
that could mix with hers. The cold repulsive manners of Bentivoglio
checked her remarks; and frequently, as words trembled on her lips,
a reproachful glance would send them back unuttered to her heart,

and bury all her observations in her overflowing breast. In the wilds of Arabia she would not have been more completely excluded from the converse of her fellow-creatures. For many leagues no human being inhabited the shores of the deep sounding main; and though a few huts scattered on the mountains, and tenanted by the children of penury, offered scope to her benevolent feelings, she was seldom permitted even to perform the gentle offices of charity, lest some tempter should arrest her steps.

Months had elapsed in this manner, when Bentivoglio announced the arrival of his brother, and cautioned her to behave with circumspection towards him. Emily felt no pleasure in hearing that her gloomy solitude was to be interrupted. She concluded that a brother of the Marquis must resemble him, and could, therefore, be no addition to her society; besides, she secretly rejoiced at the rigor of her fate, since that fate had been her choice, at least with a view of rendering an essential service to Lusignan. Frequently her thoughts recurred to him and his beloved mother; but she dared not maintain a correspondence with her, after the specimen her husband had witnessed. With Caroline alone she kept up the pure intercourse of friendship; but Bentivoglio assumed the right of perusing all those letters, which breathed the tender sentiments of that generous attachment, that elevates two hearts linked in its gentle fetters above the level of humanity. His soul was incapable of partaking or appreciating the sweet cordialities of life; and without taking any method of deserving or obtaining her affections, he chose to be so exclusively the master of them, that even her regard for Caroline sometimes excited his jealousy. He pursued her with varying and incessant persecutions. If, yielding to the melancholy which absorbed her soul, she let it appear in his presence, he reproached her with insensibility to his kindness, and uttered the most injurious suspicions. If, by an effort that required all her fortitude, she succeeded in appearing cheerful, he sought to dive into her secret motives, and was ready to conclude some clandestine intercourse had raised her spirits. Ever seeking what it would have been distraction in him to find, he deprived himself of rest, and his guiltless wife of peace.

The day came, and his brother arrived; but Emily's surprise could be equalled only by his, when she beheld the Chevalier Dorimond. Too unaccustomed to disguise ever to employ it, however necessary

it became her situation, Madame de Bentivoglio betrayed an emotion of pleasure, as she acknowledged an old friend in the brother
of her husband. The varying features of Dorimond expressed much
more, when, with a respectful bow, he congratulated her in doubtful accents on her marriage. He had left Lausanne previous to the
arrival of the Marquis, and in the full conviction that Emily would
soon become the bride of Lusignan. Bearing in his heart a passion which deprived him of repose, he had wandered in desultory
researches after that happiness he had left in Switzerland, till he
received an invitation from his brother to spend a short time in the
Pyrenees, with the intelligence that he was lately married, but had
not mentioned the rank or condition of his bride. The Chevalier,
knowing Bentivoglio's disposition, would not have ventured himself
at the Castle but in the certainty that his passion for Emily would
screen his jealousy from all alarms. What then was his astonishment and consternation when he found the woman he adored in
the wife of his brother? Happily the Marquis's attention was all
fixed on Madame de Bentivoglio, or his jealous scrutiny would in
a moment have developed his feelings. The pleasure that uncon-
sciously beamed in the artless features of Emily drew from him a
reproachful glance, which instantly restored their wonted dejection,
and gave Dorimond time to recover.

During the first few days of his residence at St. Jago a kind of
restraint was imposed by him on the violence of his brother, and
Emily's situation was somewhat ameliorated. She had never been
sensible of his attachment, and, therefore, saw no danger in yielding
to the sentiments of real friendship she felt for him.

Dorimond hesitated on what course he should pursue—the most
prudent was to fly, as he had done from Lausanne, since each day
spent in her society added a link to the chain which bound him
to her. On the other hand, he persuaded himself that his desire
of remaining proceeded from the idea that it rendered the melancholy solitude of her life less irksome; but a charm fixed him at the
Castle, which, in defiance of conviction, he could not break. Her
motives for espousing his brother could not be discerned by him.
He saw her melancholy, restless, and perturbed, and knew there was
another cause for it, besides the austerity of Bentivoglio; but why
she should voluntarily have engaged herself to such a man was past
his comprehension. The Marquis, who really loved him more than

any other person, also felt more confidence in him, because he knew
he was attached to some female, and little suspected it to be his
wife; nevertheless he seldom left them together; nor could Dorimond wish it. He feared each interview would betray his passion, and
he knew it would destroy her peace, which he valued infinitely more
than his own.

Each day, however, he found new motives for remaining in the
Pyrenees; he saw that his brother permitted his expostulations, and
frequently was directed by them in his conduct to Emily; and so
truly disinterested were his sentiments, that to procure her remission from a moment's suffering, he could consent to sacrifice his
own happiness for ever. Yet how sweet was his intercourse with her;
how happily did those moments glide he spent in her society. At
first deep sighs and broken sentences almost betrayed him; but by
degrees the fervor of love subsided into the purest sentiments of
esteem and friendship. Oh love, how different are thy effects from
those of friendship; thy ardent fire consumes the heart and destroys
the senses: while friendship's pure flame emits that genial heat, ever
equal, which vivifies without consuming!

Dorimond sometimes talked to her of love, but ascribed it to
some other person. He felt a pleasure in hearing her opinion on
this interesting topic. He had once been attached to another, but in
early youth, and disparity of fortune had disunited them. He one
day took occasion to relate the circumstance to her; she heaved a
deep sigh—

"How cruel is it," she said, "when duty and inclination are at
variance!"

Her eyes were suffused with tears. Dorimond could no longer
doubt the truth of his surmises.

"Her union with my brother," thought he, "is not all that separates us; no, that feeling, that susceptible heart, cannot be a stranger
to the softer passions, and my brother could never give birth to
them in a mind like her's! Happy, envied Lusignan, 'tis you; and
though fortune places a barrier between you, the consciousness of
possessing the invaluable treasure of her heart must pour a cordial
into the bitter cup of affliction—must sweeten its veriest dregs!"

Thankful to Providence, which had bestowed on him the power
to alleviate the sorrow of her he dared not love, Dorimond, by the
noblest efforts of virtue, essayed to conquer his passion, or make it

wholly subservient to her happiness; in this he succeeded, and each day had the satisfaction to find her esteem for him increase.

The time insensibly elapsed. Emily frequently retired with her favourite dog to the little island, divided by the encroachments of the sea from the pleasure grounds adjacent to the Castle. A beautiful wood covered it, except where the little pavilion, lately erected by the Marquis, formed an object picturesque and beautiful when viewed from the opposite windows.

The heat of the day had subsided, and Madame de Bentivoglio, with her frolicsome companion and a book, was rowed over and left on the island. As she passed the pavilion, which she never entered, a groan and deep sigh issuing from the upper room occasioned her to turn her head; but she could see nobody but the artist employed to paint it, who was just retiring from the window, and concluding herself mistaken, continued her walk. Nevertheless the fancied sound momentarily returned upon her ear, and made an indefinable impression on her mind. In vain she sought in the historic page, or in the harmony of poetic numbers, to divert her thoughts; the sigh had penetrated to her heart, and vibrated on her soul.* Had she known whence it sprung, how could she have borne the impression? It issued from the heart of Lusignan!

He had arrived at the Castle some days previous to this, and had in vain hoped to see her till the present hour, when, languid, and sorrowful, caressing her dear Fidelle, she slowly moved along the turf. So great was his emotion at the sight, that he could hardly refrain from throwing himself at her feet, and expiring there; but recollecting that she would suffer for his temerity, he withheld all but an agonizing sigh, which struck upon her heart. Finding it noticed, he immediately retired. When she returned, the shades of night, deepened by the thick surrounding foliage, interrupted his view, and more than usually restless he looked forward to another opportunity of seeing her. It soon presented itself; for on the Sunday following he contrived to place himself in the chapel directly opposite to her, which gave him a full view of her. She was negligently dressed; there was an air of languor and indifference about her so unusual that he could attribute it to only one cause. Her eyes never met his. He felt disappointment, though certain that had she known him he should have received a positive command to depart: nevertheless, when she quitted the chapel, instead of rejoicing in his concealment, he yielded to a degree of agitation and uneasiness even greater than he ever felt before; he did not indeed form the design of speaking to her, but was convinced that should an opportunity offer he had not power to resist it.

He had seen her accompanied by Dorimond, and envied him sincerely the pleasure of attending her. Jealousy almost obtruded itself upon his mind. He remembered to have known him at Luneville. His superior merit, his personal and mental accomplishments, he feared, might, contrasted with the austerity and repulsive manners of the Marquis, have a powerful effect on Emily. He began to suspect a rival. There was a pensive dejection on the fine features of Dorimond. An attention so passionate, so tender, towards his sister-in-law, too much like his own to proceed, he thought, from any other cause; besides, who could live with Emily and not adore her.

Such reflections troubled his repose more cruelly than even the pangs of love. Till this hour he had never presumed to doubt his Emily's fidelity; he had recurred to the certainty of possessing her heart for consolation in his deepest afflictions; it had supported him in a dungeon, when shut out from the light of heaven, and fed with the aliments of a malefactor; it had sustained him in opposition to a father's commands, in resisting a mother's tears; and it had recalled him from the gates of death—to abandon it then was destruction. Like a poor bird deprived of its young, he still hovered near the spot where once his treasure lay, forlorn, desolate, and abandoned. Despair prompted him to a step which must ruin his Emily for ever; in vain reason opposed it; in vain it urged every principle of virtue and equity—how weak is that guardian power compared to love!— he resolved, in defiance of its dictates, to seek an interview with Madame de Bentivoglio; to certify his doubts, and if, indeed, she no longer loved him, exclusively to resign, at her feet, that existence he could no longer support.

The Marquis treated Lusignan with that distant reserve which he could hardly subdue even with his equals, but to inferiors he thought it all that was due, and never condescended to exchange words, but when he had orders to give respecting his work.

Lusignan (whom I shall henceforward call Duke de Meronville) was relieved by this circumstance from much alarm. His profound contempt for his employer might have pierced through all disguise, and the suspicious Bentivoglio might have suspected in the artist a rival, had his superior manner and conversation been permitted to display themselves.

With Dorimond it was otherways—always affable and courteous to all, he frequently discoursed with the Duke, and thought he discovered something distinguished under the disguise of a painter. His features he did not recollect, having seen them only twice, and they were considerably altered by ill-health, a different garb, and the precautions he had taken to conceal them. Notwithstanding the distance fortune seemed to have placed between them, the Chevalier treated him with extreme confidence and familiarity; he discerned in his countenance an air of melancholy, which excited interest in a heart, taught by its own sorrows to respect those of others; but, contrary to the usual bent and candour of his nature, Meronville felt an additional dislike to him for every fresh proof of merit that appeared; it rendered him a more powerful rival, and his heart, corroded by affliction, and poisoned by jealousy, no longer asserted the virtuous energies it once possessed.

His reserve and visible dejection stimulated the curiosity of Dorimond, who sought only to learn his cause of grief, in hopes of being able to alleviate it. Far from suspecting his real situation, the only conjecture he admitted as probable was, that misfortune had reduced him from a more exalted station to the dependent one in which he now appeared. After making various interrogatories respecting his fortune in the most delicate manner possible, he said to him one day—

"The melancholy in which you seem plunged surely proceeds from love; I see its characters indelibly written on your countenance. Think not I am endeavouring to discover your secret from any base or idle motive. If my penetration does not mislead me, you were born to better hopes. Grant me your confidence; I will not abuse it, since my only desire to be informed proceeds from the hope of being able to assist you, for which I would neglect no pains. Misfortune, wherever it bears the name, is entitled to my commiseration, but there is one species which peculiarly claims my interest in its favour."

With a very bad grace Meronville thanked Dorimond for his offers; he confessed, however, that love was the sole cause of his afflictions, to which time alone could bring any relief.

"If that is the case," replied the Chevalier, "there are persons more to be pitied than yourself; I know those who cannot even hope relief from the all-powerful hand of time!"

He said these words with a sigh so profound, that it penetrated to the heart of Meronville; but he waited no reply, hastily quitting the pavilion, where he left the Duke to ponder on his words. They awakened, indeed, a new source of reflections in his mind, they proved to him incontestably, that he was the victim of love, and he doubted not Emily was the object. Yet his observations proved that it was not mutual; he felt his jealousy subsided, and persuaded himself that his esteem for Madame de Bentivoglio lulled his suspicions. He watched still more attentively the motions of Dorimond; he saw him ever attached to her steps, seeking to anticipate her most secret wishes, and looking on her with an expression like his own. No longer fearing a rival, he could even compassionate the sufferings of the Chevalier, and judge of them with the same candor with which he viewed his own, ever employed on the same subject.

He was one day neglectful of his employment, ruminating with his eyes fixed on the vast expanse beneath, when the melodious notes of a lyre issuing from the woods struck on his ear, and vibrated to his heart; the sound was so sweet, so pensive, that it seemed the harmony of the seraphic choir. The Duke stood entranced, afraid of breathing, lest he should lose a single note. It ceased, and a voice, to which his heart was born to vibrate, sung an air, to which he had often, during his residence at Montpelier, listened in rapture. No longer master of himself, he ran down stairs, resolved to discover himself to Emily, the sweet musician of the woods, when, just as he with hasty steps was quitting the pavilion to execute his dangerous enterprize, Dorimond landed on the isle. Disappointed, chagrined, and perturbed, he returned to his occupation. Soon after the door of the apartment opened, and Madame de Bentivoglio, leaning on the arm of Dorimond, entered.

"I know not why," she said, "you wish me to see these improvements; they have, you know, no power to interest me, I am so indifferent, so insensible to the beauties of art; those charming woods I have just left, and the smooth ocean round, suit my taste much better."*

Trembling, Meronville said—

"I flatter myself, Madam, if you will condescend to look at those panels you will find the trouble repaid, as I have been used to delineate Italian landscape."

Struck by the sound of his voice, which she could not mistake, she fixed her eyes on the ground, and without ever raising them to the speaker, said the smell of the paint hurt her, and instantly left the room. Meronville followed her with his eyes, then stood petrified, overwhelmed with grief.

"Ah, gracious heaven," he said, "she no longer loves me! She did not even deign to soothe my anguish by a single look! To demonstrate her perfect indifference, she even withheld reproach! Alas, how have I deserved her scorn, her aversion! 'Tis true, I disobeyed her commands; I came here contrary to her express prohibition; but if love yet predominated in her heart, would she not pardon an error caused by that alone; it is a crime indeed, but it proceeds from excess of passion, from unconquerable affection. Prudence is too cold ever to mingle with love; till the fervor of attachment subsides, we never admit it. No, she has too surely ceased to feel for me. What do I say? She has transferred her heart to another! Oh agony! Oh torture inexpressible! I dare not follow her—reproach her—die by her frown!"

St. Pierre entered the apartment; alarmed at his frantic appearance, he anxiously enquired what had happened—

"Ah, St. Pierre," said he, "never was I wretched before; Emily forsakes me—I am lost, miserable, desperate—she no longer loves me—Heavens, is it possible? I thought her constant, faithful as myself. Fortune, thou art avenged—I complained of thee before; alas, I was then happy—I possessed her heart—this cruel moment robs me of all—what tortures, what pains would I not undergo, to recall that hope which, an hour ago, in the midst of sufferings, filled my heart with soft ineffable delight!"

This rhapsody continued for some time, during which St. Pierre in vain tried to discover what new calamity oppressed his senses. At length he recovered composure to relate the circumstance.

"I see nothing," said St. Pierre, "in all this to occasion the violent agitation you betray. Doubtless, Madame de Bentivoglio is offended at the step you have taken in coming here, a step which endangers her peace, and your life; to punish your rashness she tried to appear indifferent; or, more probably, fearful of betraying herself by a look, she hastened to avert the danger by retiring."

"Ah, no," replied Meronville, "self command belongs not to love; the first movement is that of the heart, it is spontaneous, irresistible. I must see her, I must reproach her, I must convict her of versatility, and then I have no further use for life. Alas! she need not have embittered my last moments. Why did she restore me to liberty? Why did she seek to take me from that prison, which was heaven while illumined by the hope of being loved? No, cruel Emily, I will not survive your affections!"

Dreading that any other person should witness the disorder of his mind, St. Pierre conducted him to bed. He passed the night in fabricating torment for his soul; each new sentiment, each new apprehension destroyed the former one; he condemned his suspicions, he renounced them; but the succeeding impulse revived them all. He reproached himself for wishing Emily to retain a passion it was her duty as well as interest to destroy. He accused himself of selfishness, of loving her more for his own sake than her's.

St. Pierre, who slept in his apartment, was roused by a sudden exclamation—

"Yes, I am resolved I will speak to her—if she loves another it is time I should die! I will see her only to pronounce an eternal farewell! No reproach shall pass these lips—my affliction, my sorrow shall bear testimony to her cruelty; they shall penetrate to that heart which once was mine. She shall learn, that if not permitted to live, I can at least die for her. I will then retire to some solitude, where the cheering beams of hope shall never penetrate; there in eternal seclusion I will await the appointed hour, and prepare to answer the awful, but wished-for summons to eternity!"

The more he reflected on this design, the more was his resolution confirmed. St. Pierre vainly endeavoured, by every argument of sense and reason, to dissuade him from a project so hazardous, and from which no good could result; he continued positive, inexorable. Finding opposition fruitless, this faithful domestic resolved to seek some opportunity that would be attended with least danger. He advised him to attempt seeing her at the time when the two brothers were hunting. Meronville consented to any thing that might assist his design, and solemnly promised to leave the Castle as soon as he should have spoken to her; and to obviate all suspicion, he determined to continue his work as usual, but to talk of leaving it in a few days.

With affected alacrity he resumed his brush. A latent hope, too feeble almost for perception, remained to him, that Emily would perhaps return to seek him in the pavilion, if it was only to command his departure. Every sound he heard, every voice, occasioned a violent palpitation at his heart; an emotion for which there was no name, diffused itself over his whole frame, but issued only in disappointment, which each day renewed, and no opportunity yet presented itself of speaking to Madame de Bentivoglio, always watched by her husband or attended by his brother. He now blamed himself for having discovered himself, which probably prevented her revisiting the island, where he could, with least interruption and danger, have addressed her.

The sight of Meronville had occasioned in the mind of Emily a perturbation that seemed to menace her constitution, and a shivering fit, which succeeded her visit to the pavilion, alarmed her inexpressibly; she knew that her lover, informed of her illness, would, disregarding all suggestions of prudence, discover his anxiety, and reveal his real situation. She trembled for the effect of Bentivoglio's jealousy, less with regard to herself, than the man she still adored, and the more, as each day presented the great and striking contrast between him and her husband. Yet his uncontroulable impetuosity she knew, and proportionably dreaded. She exerted all her strength to avert indisposition, while he remained to witness it, and after revolving in her mind every method of conveying to him her wishes, her commands to depart, she at length rested on the only safe scheme—that of writing, and putting the letter into his hand herself. Yet how to do it was still an almost insurmountable difficulty; she could not reach the pavilion without the assistance of a servant; to return immediately would excite suspicion; and she felt all the danger of remaining alone on the island, after delivering to Meronville an order to quit her for ever. She considered and reconciled all modes of executing her design, but no other presented itself. On this therefore, with tremulous anxiety, she resolved; and one day, when Dorimond was hunting, and her husband engaged in domestic regulations, she took her book, and as she landed, said in an elevated tone of voice to the servant who attended her, that in half an hour he must return to fetch her. This she designed as a warning to Meronville, that the time was short, and there was no opportunity for remonstrating.

With a palpitating heart and unsettled step she wandered a few moments on the turf irresolute, and not able to command strength to enter the pavilion. On a sudden, little Fidelle, who walked by her side, jumping at a fly, which hovered near the sea, plunged into the vast expanse, and unable to cope with the waves, was carried violently towards the opposite shore. Emily gave a piercing shriek at the danger of her faithful companion, and, almost beside herself, regarding not the impractibility of the attempt, plunged after it. Meronville bounded from the window, where he had observed this scene, and catching her robe, rescued her from certain destruction.* Her senses were lost—he lifted her in his arms, and conveyed her to the pavilion, and while he used every means to restore her, bathed the hands he held with impassioned tears. He had saved her life; extatic thought! Fortune, he thought, smiled again, and all her frowns were forgotten. At length Emily opened her eyes—

"Look on me, my love," he cried, "bless me once more with that gracious smile, which can repay me for an age of suffering. You owe your life to me—you can repay the obligation—you save me from death by telling me you pardon me—you yet love me!"

Emily recovered her senses, and with them a conviction of the danger and impropriety of her situation.

"Fly, fly, Duke de Meronville!" she said; "accept my thanks, my eternal gratitude, but fly from me for ever!"

"Would you, Madam, for the last time," replied he, "deprive me of the happiness of addressing you for one moment?"

She attempted to rise—

"Oh, cease, in pity," said she, "if you would not embitter that life you have preserved, and never see me more!"

"This moment, Madam," he rejoined, "is the last that ever I shall either importune or distress you with the sight of a person so odious. I claim no privilege from having been so fortunate as to rescue your life; but one instant I must speak, that passed, I shall fly from you, in solitude bewail the sorrows I have occasioned, and die with grief for the loss of your heart. The happy Chevalier Dorimond, I hope, will feel the value of his triumph, and know better than me how to deserve it!"

Emily, whom surprise and indignation had rendered mute during this speech, could no longer refrain from interrupting him.

"What!" said she, with a look of reproach and disdain, "you

reproach me! you dare suspect me! You forget the sacrifice I made you, for whom——ah, gracious heaven! how have I been deceived!"

These words, uttered in a firm but plaintive tone, struck conviction on the mind of Lusignan, and precipitated him at her feet.

"Pardon, dearest Emily, these injurious suspicions," said he; "no, you are not injured by them, for my heart never avowed their existence! Ah, pardon an excess of love, which betrays my senses—call to mind those happy hours we spent at Luneville and the Abbey— that fatal day which separated us—alas! for ever, and contrast it with the present. Then wonder not, if, bereft of reason, I accuse you, most worshipped woman—but oh, pardon me, lovely Emily, say but you pardon me, and you restore me to life and reason!"

"I pardon every thing," said she, with extreme emotion, "but your remaining here—for your sake I am the most wretched of women; would you make me appear also the most guilty? Ah, it is indeed a crime to let you see my weakness; and every moment that you stay adds culpability to my conduct. Fly then, I conjure you, and fly for ever!"

"I would obey your commands though they struck at my life," said he; "but promise me that you will not hate me—that you will sometimes remember the most affectionate, but ill-fated lover—say that you will not withhold a sigh, a tear to his memory, when he shall have left this world of woe!"

Emily's tears flowed in torrents, and too surely bespoke the feelings of her heart; she raised her dim eyes to heaven—

"Ah, gracious God," said she, "why was I born to be criminal in spite of myself—my treacherous heart betrays my better reason, and leaves me without support. Thou, oh merciful Creator, that knowest my secret thoughts, pardon the errors of weak humanity, and support my sinking virtue. Lusignan," she continued, "(for by that dear name I still remember you) leave me I conjure you; if you value my future peace, my very existence, begone—I tremble, for every moment may bring Bentivoglio here; and what have I not to dread from a jealous husband, justly, alas! but too justly incensed!"

"Fear him not, my Emily," replied the Duke, still at her feet, "while I am here; his sword shall be sheathed in my bosom ere he injures you. Was such a husband designed by heaven for the most faultless of her sex?"

As he pronounced these words the door flew open, and Bentivoglio appeared. He had no sooner discovered the attitude of the disguised painter, than, drawing his sword, he advanced towards Emily, saying—

"Ungrateful woman, thus shall thy perfidy be punished!"

"Not till you have first disarmed me!" cried Meronville, seizing a sword which hung in the apartment.

"Then thou shalt be the first object of my vengeance!" ejaculated the enraged husband. "Traitor, take the reward of thy perfidy!"

He made a violent thrust, and wounded Meronville in the shoulder. Insensible of torture, and careless of existence, the Duke, by a single effort, pierced his adversary, and laid him at his feet.

Life had receded from the bosom of Emily, and relieved her from the terror of her husband, or anxiety for her lover; but her cries on his first appearance soon brought the servants who attended Bentivoglio in the boat; seeing Meronville withdraw his sword from the body of their master, they seized him without resistance, as he leaned in agony over the lifeless Emily. He was conveyed to one of the dungeons of the Castle, while they returned to fetch their master and the Marchioness. Emily, scarcely restored to life, insisted on watching near the bed of her husband, whose wound was instantly dressed, and the surgeon hoped it was not mortal, and only required that he should be kept profoundly still.

Forced to her own apartment, Madame de Bentivoglio hardly recollected the dreadful scene she had witnessed. That Meronville was wounded, and probably imprisoned, first occurred to her. The whole frightful reality soon burst on her imagination, and so horrible it was, that sense enough to bewail it was all that remained to her. A husband, she thought, at that moment expiring, and accusing her infidelity as the cause!—a lover tried for his murder, perishing by the hand of the executioner!—her own spotless reputation exposed, calumniated!—all so dreadful, that she knew not which most to lament. She threw herself on the bed, and, uttering a deep groan, commended her soul to heaven, and supplicated to be released from her misery by instant death. From its confines a gentle tap at the door recalled her. Supposing it to be one of her women, she opened it, but her averted eye met that of Dorimond. He had been out during the whole day, and on his return felt an astonishment that could be equalled only by his affliction on hearing what had happened at the Castle. Indeed the affair, related in different ways by the menials, was so confused that he could not easily develope it; but the painter was a principal actor in it; and he had so often suspected his disguise, that conjecture soon supplied the place of certainty, and he began to fancy the features of Lusignan under the guise of a simple artist. He had been denied admission to his brother, and therefore repaired to the Marchioness, still passionate and deeply concerned for her, to offer his services and mediation, could they be of use. The respectful and timid manner in which he approached her inspired immediate confidence.

"Chevalier," said she, her voice interrupted by convulsive sobs, "can the friendship you have generously expressed for me induce you to rescue from despair an unfortunate, but not criminal, sister?"

"Ah, Madam," interrupted the Chevalier, "how little do you know me, if you can doubt my readiness to assist you with my life. Ah, call it not friendship—a warmer sentiment——But pardon me, Madam, an involuntary impulse dictated my words. Look on me as your friend—suffer me to act as such—permit me to claim your esteem, and command every service it is in my power to lend."

Surprised and concerned at his words, Madame de Bentivoglio knew but one method of proceeding. Certain that he was too generous to take advantage of her situation or betray her confidence, she instantly related her connection with the Duke de Meronville, and all its consequences, without concealing her unconquered attachment to him. After the recital she continued thus:—

"I never wronged the Marquis—previous to our union I opened my heart to him—I told him esteem and friendship were all I had left to bestow. His behaviour, alas! was but little calculated to ensure him these; nevertheless duty prescribed my conduct, and I was regulated by it. The day you led me to the painted chamber, I first recognized in the artist the partner of my soul. My confusion escaped your unsuspicious mind, and ever since I have been seeking an opportunity of delivering to him a letter, to insist on his departure. This fatal morning I landed on the island with that intention, when an accident, alarming at first and baneful in its consequence, brought my husband and Meronville together—you know the result—Shall I seek to justify myself? Alas, chance and cruel destiny are alone to be accused—I was not mistress of my heart—long ere I saw the Marquis it was devoted to another, but I behaved to him as though he had been its first possessor. Was I to blame for bestowing my affections involuntarily on an object truly deserving——"

"Ah, Madam," once more interrupted Dorimond, "I know but too well that we cannot command our affections, nor bestow one's heart only where fortune may design. But continue, Madam. How can I assist you?"

"Alas!" replied Emily, "what I am going to request will put your friendship to a severe test. Your fraternal feelings will induce you to pursue the murderer of your brother. I am going to solicit you to release him!"

Overcome with emotion, she hid her face, and wept abundantly. Dorimond, trembling and breathless, waited the conclusion. At length he broke silence.

"Fortunate Meronville," he cried; "how amply is he repaid by your interest and good opinion!"

"All my weakness is exposed to you," continued the Marchioness, recovering; "I was not mistress of my heart; but I have taken no step the most rigorous duty could condemn, or the purest virtue blush at. Let me conclude, it is in your power alone to save him; confined in a dungeon of the Castle, he is reserved for trial, and I know, that rather than expose me by discovering himself, he will suffer the last torments, and meet, without concern, death itself. Will you deliver him, for my sake? Will you command him to fly for ever?"

"This instant I go," said the generous Chevalier; "no means shall be neglected to ensure his safety, and to convince you of my devotion to your wishes; yet let me add, Meronville is not the only unfortunate man, nor the most worthy of compassion!"

He ended these words with a sigh, and, without daring to raise his eyes from the ground, hastily left the room.

Madame de Bentivoglio now became sensible of what she had never before observed, namely, that Dorimond felt an attachment to her inconsistent with his happiness. Overflowing as was the cup of affliction before, this consideration still added to it; his kindness to her, his virtues and singular merit, interested her so intirely, that she could not see with indifference that he suffered for her sake.

Absorbed in grief, she wasted the midnight hour, devoted by the Chevalier to the escape of Meronville. On quitting her apartment he had retired to his own, to meditate how he might best fulfil her wishes. Involuntarily his own situation recurred to him.

During the recital Emily had made, his emotion had discovered to him the excess of that passion he fancied overcome, or at least subsided into pure friendship. He found himself cruelly undeceived at the moment when it became most necessary to free his heart from an attachment fatal to its repose. He was resolved to liberate Meronville, but doubted whether he ought not himself to shun the fascinating object that enslaved them both. Yet there was a degree of cruelty in abandoning Emily to a jealous husband, irritated by imaginary wrongs, and influenced by the supposed criminality of his wife. After various and desultory meditations, he at length resolved to remain near her, in hopes of calming the indignation of the Marquis, but to avoid her as much as possible, and shun every opportunity for a private interview. To emancipate Meronville was his next care; all his noble and generous propensities were necessary to conduct him through this scene, in which he was to rescue a favoured rival, and confess himself supplanted. To do it in the manner least afflictive, he took a dark lanthorn, and repairing to the cell disguised, he threw open the door, and setting down the lanthorn, exclaimed—

"Fly, Duke de Meronville, the time is precious—a moment's hesitation may ruin you! Fly, you are released by the hand of a *rival!*"

He then hastened back to his apartment, relieved, by the effort he had made, from a weight that pressed on his mind.

Meronville, stretched on the floor, scarcely noticed his intrusion. When first left to himself the imprudence of his conduct overwhelmed him with horror; he saw the dreadful abyss into which he had plunged Emily; the death of her husband he knew must raise suspicions injurious to her reputation. How did he reproach his impetuosity—how execrate his imprudence.

"Yes, my Emily," he cried, "now you must hate me, and I dare not implore your pardon! Oh, how you must lament the hour that first introduced you to my acquaintance and my affections— without that you had been happy, surrounded by admirers— you have attached yourself to one born under happier auspices, formed for your enjoyment—without that you had never married a jealous tyrant—without that your reputation had been spotless as your mind. I caused your first misfortunes, and have now completed them! Oh, my father, could you look down on the sufferings your rigours have entailed on your unhappy son, how would you rue the hour that gave me birth, and made me the victim of hereditary animosity! Oh, my mother, how will you bear my disgrace!—will it not lead you to the grave! Yet perhaps I may save thy immaculate virtue the horror of being suspected, beloved and idolized Emily— my name shall never be known—I will pass for a ruffian—the world shall condemn me as such—your heart will acquit me—your heart is my universe—then welcome fate, spare my love, but wreak all thy vengeance on my guilty head!"

He was ruminating thus when Dorimond set open the door of his dungeon. So fully was he resolved not to abscond, and leave Emily's reputation doubtful, that he would not have noticed his release, had not the word rival struck on his ear, and roused him like an electric shock. He started to find the speaker, but he was fled, and left him to form surmises, and feed on jealousy. Happily the Chevalier recollected that Madame de Bentivoglio had said she was persuaded he would not abandon her but by compulsion, and he resolved to return, lest her wishes should be yet unobeyed. Conquering his reluctance, he entered the cell, and found Meronville resolute to remain there.

"Rise," said he; "I am come by Madame de Bentivoglio's orders to release you; her esteem for me has induced her to conceal nothing relative to you from my knowledge. Alas!" added he, with a sigh, "had she known me thoroughly, perhaps she had judged differently; but no matter, I am resolved to merit her confidence by executing her commands, and rescuing you from danger; yes, I will save you, and save her, if that is possible!"

"Never," cried Meronville; "I remain here to exculpate her— to justify her character; and had I fifty lives to venture, I would still persist in my resolution to the last! I will never make myself known—I will pass for a ruffian, a vile miscreant! I have murdered her peace—that crime surpasses the destruction of a tyrant who oppressed her—I must and will expiate both!"

"Your project," said Dorimond, coolly, "might be executed, if my brother was dead, which I find you conclude; but it is not the case; though dangerously wounded, the surgeon thinks it not mortal. By his behaviour to my sister, you must have observed that he suspected her; you would therefore lose yourself, without rendering her any service. Come," added he, "let us begone; to-day it is in my power to liberate you, to-morrow the hour may be past!"

"And what will become of Madame de Bentivoglio?" exclaimed Meronville. "No, Emily, no, ever dear friend, I cannot leave you in a dilemma where my imprudence has led you, for the sake of preserving an existence I shall justly forfeit for having occasioned you any uneasiness!"

"I have already told you," replied the Chevalier, "that your remaining can only render her situation more deplorable. Your rank cannot long remain a secret; but by absconding you may best conceal it. It is the only method by which you can escape detection, and save Madame de Bentivoglio."

"Well, then," said he, "I will fly, since it is for her interest, and in obedience to her commands. Alas! I hoped to have sacrificed my life to her justification—she denies me that happiness—I am unworthy of it—unworthy of that pity I hoped to inspire, when all other sentiments were extinguished in her bosom—no, she will not permit me even to retain that. Alas! my Emily, recall those halcyon days, when first my heart was yours. Not far from hence we first met—thy lover then—how lost—how wretched now!—entered on life, tutored by hope, pleasure beaming in his countenance—one fatal look brought ages of sorrow—never, never to end! Alas! I appeal to thee in vain, dear mistress of my heart—even now perhaps you expire by my stroke. Pardon me, I hasten to obey your last command—yet how willingly would I remain a prisoner to be near you—but it must not be—lead, Chevalier, I am ready to follow; but oh, protect your sister—her innocence, her misfortunes, must interest your feelings. I know you generous, sincere——remember, I charge you, Emily is innocent, pure as the new born babe!"

"Alas!" said Dorimond, touched by his anguish, "what has already escaped me must convince you her interests are dearer to me than for my repose they should be. Think not my sentiments less warm than your own; there is nothing I would not sacrifice for her—happy if I could only flatter myself, that although I could not obtain her affections, at least she had never loved another; that comfort is denied me; can you compare your sufferings? Insatiable must that man be, whose every wish is not comprised in the possession of such a heart. But come," added he, "each moment is precious—night favours your escape—let us not neglect the opportunity."

Meronville, in attempting to rise, found himself so weak from his undressed wound, that without the assistance of Dorimond it

would have been impracticable. Taking the dark lanthorn they soon
reached the outward court of the Castle; there were lights in several
of the apartments round it; Meronville looked up, in hopes that one
of them might contain his Emily. Suddenly he stopped, and with
an exclamation that startled Dorimond, and threatened to betray
them, fixed his eyes on a window where the Marchioness appeared,
pacing the room in agony and extreme perturbation—

"Oh let me for ever linger here!" said he. "Dear angel, whose
destruction I have been, look on me—let thy benign features fix
on him who adores you! Oh, those tears shed for me, dry them, my
Emily, we shall meet in a better world!"

The noise they made alarmed some person within, and a door
opened, from which two servants issued.

"We are discovered," cried Dorimond, with impatience; "you
would not be guided by me!"

The servants advanced armed. The Chevalier, placing himself
before the supposed culprit, and darkening his lanthorn, said with
a forced laugh—

"It is only me, Bertrand; you need be at no pains to take me."

The man bowed and begged his pardon, saying he had supposed
it was the ruffian who had murdered his master endeavouring to
escape; after which he returned to the Castle. As soon as they were
beyond hearing—

"Now," said the Chevalier, "it is once more in your power to be
free—take my counsel, and restrain the impetuosity of your feelings." They reached the outer court, Dorimond continued, "I have
done but little for you, if I do not conduct you to a place of safety."

Meronville informed him that St. Pierre was at the Castle, and
was devoted wholly to him. The Chevalier then made him promise
to remain where he was, till he fetched St. Pierre. He seated himself
at the foot of a tree, already nearly exhausted by the fatigue.

Dorimond returned to the house, and entering the hall where
some servants were, found St. Pierre; holding out a key, he said—

"You, Sir, belong to the miscreant now confined in the dungeon.
Follow me; you shall dress his wound—he is reserved for a more
public and ignominious death!"

These words he accompanied with a significant glance, which the
sagacious domestic could not mistake. He followed the Chevalier,
who made him secure a horse, and then led him to the place where

he found his master, whom he seated on the horse. Dorimond put a letter into his hand—

"Take this," said he; "a quarter of a league from hence you will find a monastery of Benedictine Friars; the abbot, a man of singular piety and humanity, is my particular friend; he will give you a secure asylum, where you had better remain till the enquiries, which I shall be obliged to make after you, are ceased. It will be long ere the rumour of what has happened at the Castle will penetrate those sacred walls, whence the world and its concerns are for ever excluded. You may confide in Father Anthony, who will never betray you; but once more suffer me to recommend prudence and circumspection; unguarded conduct may ruin my sister and yourself. Go, and God speed you!"

"Wherever I go," said Meronville, "your disinterested kindness shall never be forgotten."

St. Pierre spurred the horse, and took the route to the Monastery, where they soon arrived, and Father Anthony, after reading Dorimond's letter, gave them a sincere welcome, ordered Meronville the best accommodations, and sent a friar, who had studied surgery, to dress his wound, and see that nothing was neglected to forward his recovery. His pallid countenance, and the blood on his clothes, alarmed the good man extremely, who found the wound, at first slight, much envenomed by cold and agitation. He made every necessary application, and searched the hidden stores of art for remedies, which gave him some relief; the most alarming symptom was that of a violent fever. Meronville alone was insensible to his danger; so inconsiderable are the tortures of the body compared with those of the mind.

The faithful St. Pierre watched near his bedside the whole ensuing day and night, lamenting his sufferings.

"You have it in your power to save my life," cried his master. "Disguise yourself—go and learn the fate of Emily—bring me some intelligence, or this horrid suspence annihilates me—lose not a moment—St. Pierre, my life depends on it!"

With tears in his eyes St. Pierre left the apartment to execute this order; and Meronville, once more supported by hope, fell into a tranquil slumber, which brought a temporary oblivion to his sorrows.

CHAP. III.

"Thy hour is past! Thy charms are vain!
"Ill-nature haunts thee with her sallow train;
"Mean jealousy deceives thy listening ear,
"And slander stains thy cheek with many a bitter tear!"

After a sleepless night, Emily repaired early to the couch of her husband. She had been informed by her woman that his wound was not thought mortal, and that his senses were completely restored. She crept near him; he threw on her a look of such pointed indignation and malignity as chilled her very heart; but he spoke not a word. Bathed in tears she hung over him, when Dorimond entered the apartment; Bentivoglio no sooner discovered him, than pointing with a look of ferocity to his wife—

"Deliver me," said he, "from the sight of that perfidious woman, who has dishonoured me; lead her to her apartment, and let it be your care that she does not escape from it!" The Chevalier endeavoured to remonstrate, but he silenced him by adding—"Obey me instantly, or never come again into my presence; I will find another jailor for her, who will have more respect for my rights, and more obedience to my orders!"

Approaching Emily, Dorimond requested to speak with her in her own apartment. She had heard the orders given by her husband.

"Come," said she, "execute the commission given you!"

Her tears seemed to reproach him for his obedience; he hesitated, but dared not justify himself, though a look of ineffable compassion proclaimed the feelings of his heart; and no sooner had she reached her chamber, than pressing the hand he held——

"Pardon, dearest sister," said he, "the cruel necessity which compels me to become your jailor; believe that I accept the office only that I may render your confinement easy. Confound me not, I conjure you, with your persecutor—I who feel your sufferings as though they were my own—I who would give my life for your relief—I shudder whilst I speak, but indeed I fear yours is in danger! My brother's passions are violent—he thinks himself wronged—jeal-

256

ousy never yields to persuasion or conviction—seek some secure retreat—I will engage to have you conducted to it."

"I know not," said Emily, "whether the Marquis may attempt my life; but I know my duty; guilty as I may appear, I never violated it; it prescribes my present conduct, and compels me to remain here; to respect my husband, and never abandon him; if obedience to it costs me existence I shall never repent adhering to it! Alas! with a blemished reputation, a sullied character, life can have no charms; if I cannot avert the stings of calumny, at least I will never deserve them! But dare I enquire? Is Meronville safe?"

"He is, Madam, out of the reach of his enemies, and enviable indeed while you are interested in his safety!"

"I have given you," said the Marchioness, "the greatest proof of my esteem and confidence—I have declared to you all my weakness; alas, would you make me repent it?"

"Never, Madam," rejoined Dorimond. "Ah, pardon my involuntary error; no, it shall be the study of my life to merit your friendship. If I have betrayed sentiments unworthy your honour and my own, from this moment I renounce them; without my participation they took possession of my heart; I could neither prevent it, nor conceal them from you; I will now endeavour to triumph over them—if that fails, at least you shall never be importuned with their existence. I should now quit you for ever, if I did not hope I might be of use to you. I see I have added to your affliction, oh, how shall I pardon myself for so doing?"

"You have indeed afflicted me," said Madame de Bentivoglio, whilst her tears confirmed her assertion; "relentless fortune will even deprive me of the consolation I might have derived from your friendship."

She said no more, but her eyes spoke a language no tongue could express. Dorimond regarded her in silent anguish; his generous nature revolted at the idea of having added to the misfortunes of a person already so overwhelmed with sorrows; her tears had more effect on him than the powerful eloquence of reason; he felt a sudden revolution in his mind.

"No, Madam," he exclaimed, "you shall not be deprived of that friendship you have the goodness to value; I will become worthy of yours, by the efforts I shall make to banish from your recollection the fault into which your charms betrayed me; I will strive by the

purest sentiments of regard to merit your esteem, and its acquirement will form the charm of my existence."

"If my friendship is indeed of value to you," replied the Marchioness, "accept it in its most exalted form, and as a proof of yours try
to reconcile me to your brother; prevail on him to let me watch him
through the day, and in the midnight hour my cares, my attentions,
shall restore him to life. I claim his permission—the task belongs
to his wife—return to him—now, Chevalier, a longer conference
might excite suspicion."

Never had Emily's situation been so comfortless; wherever she
turned her eyes objects of terror and dismay met them; not a ray of
hope appeared; in vain she summoned all her fortitude, and looked
up to him, who alone could extricate her from this labyrinth of
sorrow. In vain she called on her sainted mother; her sullied reputation was the last and greatest of evils. She experienced how necessary it is that the delicate texture of female virtue should be not only
spotless, but free from imputation. The world, ever more ready to
condemn, than seek palliations for an error, rests its judgment too
frequently on appearances—it has no other standard—the secrets
of the heart are impenetrable—the noxious breath of slander compels many a noble and faultless heart to wither in obscurity, and
pine in solitude—the suffrage of conscience is the first thing to be
desired—an unblemished character the next.

When she thought on Meronville, his danger and despair, she
shuddered at the painful recollection of the many calamities their
mutual attachment had created, but resolved to banish his image,
if possible, from her memory; she imposed silence on herself, and
determined never more to let his name pass her lips.

Several days elapsed, and Dorimond returned not to visit her. A
prisoner in her own apartment, she sought to penetrate the cause
of his absence; the most probable was, that he had not been able to
obtain permission for her to attend the Marquis. She sometimes
thought his attachment to her had betrayed itself to Bentivoglio,
and induced him to order his departure; but Gabriella, who still
attended, assured her the Chevalier was seldom out of her husband's room, and gave her a daily report of the progress of his illness, which became almost daily more alarming.

Dorimond found himself much more tranquil after his last interview with Emily; he had promised to conquer every sentiment but

friendship, and he laboured unceasingly to fulfil his engagement. Finding his efforts successful, he returned to her, and far from avoiding her, found in her society each day new motives to strengthen his resolution. His heart sometimes revolted, but reason remained most powerful. Grateful for the struggles Emily saw him make, she gave him additional proofs of esteem and confidence, and, in effect, felt for him every endearing sentiment but that of love.

Entering her apartment earlier than usual one morning, he told her the Marquis was so much worse, that there was no doubt his life was in extreme danger. The news, though expected, affected her sensibly.

"And will he not yet," said she, "permit me to see him? Will he carry his unjust resentment to the grave?"

"I have not been able to prevail on him to admit you," replied the Chevalier; "but let not that afflict you; your duty has been fulfilled in desiring to sooth and tranquillize his last moments. His inveterate anger must console you for his loss, and acquit you of the share you might have had in it."

"Ah, no," said Madame de Bentivoglio, "never shall I feel acquitted. I will confess to you, that had I lost him by any common accident, the event would have been less afflictive to me. His jealousy has embittered my days; but it proceeded from excess of love, and I surely owed him gratitude even for that. I fear not his resentment, nor the ill-treatment and persecutions to which his recovery might expose me; I only dread his dying in the false conviction that I have wronged him; if he lives I may prove my innocence, and obtain his pardon—that is all I desire."

Emily seemed to have reached the climax of her fate; each footstep, each noise she heard, made her shudder, and expect to hear her husband had expired; nevertheless, after being for a considerable time on the verge of eternity he began to recover, and although he still obstinately refused to see her, he yet enquired for her with apparent solicitude. Dorimond seconded her entreaties with all his influence, but in vain; Bentivoglio persisted in denying her request.

Perpetual anxiety had supported Emily through these trials, and prevented her dwelling too long on the same object; but the restoration of the Marquis's health having removed a dreadful weight from her mind, left her at leisure to ponder on woes to come; and his extreme obduracy menacing her future peace, oppressed her heart, and transferred his indisposition to her. She fell dangerously ill, and once more hoped the end of her sufferings approached. Bentivoglio now appeared affected by her condition, and consented, at the earnest solicitations of his brother, to visit her apartment, as soon as the surgeon permitted him to quit his own. Her languid features revived when he entered; she extended her hand, which he coldly received.

"I thank you for this condescension," she faintly said; "I had hardly dared to hope it; I cannot crave your pardon, for indeed I never offended you—my last wish was to convince you of my innocence. If you do not suspect me of every vice, you will acquit me of perjury, now that on a bed from which I shall never rise but to appear before my Creator, I solemnly swear I never was unfaithful, I never wronged you; the truth of this I call Almighty God to witness, and pray, that according to my sincerity or falshood I may be judged in the day of retribution!"

The Marquis appeared satisfied with what she said, and the physician requested she might be kept quiet. They all retired. Relieved by the opportunity she had had of endeavouring to justify herself, and by the hopes that her husband's visit was a prelude to future comfort, she began from that hour to amend. Youth is a powerful assistant to medicine, and co-operates strongly with the physician's art. Emily saw that her husband was free from danger—free from resentment, she hoped, and free from doubt she wished to make him. Fervently she vowed, if life was restored her, to devote it to her justification and his happiness; and Dorimond, whose anxiety had been boundless, saw with delight her daily amendment, and approaching convalescence. Whenever he was with his brother he talked of her alone, and watched each turn of countenance to see if it conveyed some hope or fear to his mind.

After his first interview with Madame de Bentivoglio, nothing could induce him to renew it, though she earnestly requested it. Dorimond excused his obstinacy to her by saying the physician had forbidden it. One day, however, he resolved to make a last effort to interest him in her favour, and make him accede to her wishes. He entered his closet with this design, and found him perusing a letter.

"Chevalier," said he, folding it up, "affairs of great importance summon me to Rome; my presence is necessary there, but as my health will not permit me to take the journey, I cannot do better than depute you. I shall feel much indebted by your compliance, as the business is important. My horses, servants, and equipage, are ordered, and at your command. The affair is urgent, let no time be lost; but if you wish to oblige me, set out immediately."

Dorimond hesitated a moment on this proposal; the thought of leaving his sister-in-law, before her recovery was ascertained, was to him a cruel necessity; and he felt an unaccountable reluctance to leave the Castle ere his mediation had restored peace there; yet early deprived of his parents, and younger by thirty years than the Marquis, the latter had been to him a father, and as such he was used to consider him: besides, he could assign no good reason for a refusal. Bentivoglio saw him change colour, and enquired why he hesitated. The Chevalier had no alternative but compliance; he resolved to set out, but thought this concession gave him an additional right to plead the cause of Emily.

"I am at your devotion, brother," said he, "and will commence my journey without delay; but suffer me once more to implore your clemency in favour of a wife, who is unfortunate, but not criminal, and who desires only to prove the truth of my assertion by devoting her life to you. Consider her youth, her beauty, and I may say her virtue; they give her claims to your pardon and affection. Let me not quit you without the hope that at my return I shall find you restored to confidence and conjugal felicity. You seem moved— the tear starts in your eye—ah, do not seek to repress the generous emotions of pity, which ennoble our nature and assimilate it to perfection. Your wife is innocent—she merits your esteem—restore it to her, and you restore her to life!"

"I am but too much inclined," resumed the Marquis, "to be moved by your entreaties; I only dread my own weakness, which may induce me to forget my wrongs; in this breast they shall gladly be buried if she can prove her innocence. I loved her once with an affection unequalled by any other, and that sentiment is too profound to be wholly eradicated; but time and her future conduct can alone restore the confidence I once placed in her virtue, and efface the remembrance of what is passed."

Dorimond dared not enter into a discussion of his supposed injuries, lest it should revive his anger.

"Will you permit me," said he, "to tell my sister what you say, and to communicate my hopes to her? The healing balm will accelerate her recovery, and give her an earlier opportunity of demonstrating her gratitude."

"That I leave to your discretion," resumed the Marquis; "you are informed of my sentiments, and I wish not to conceal them."

The Chevalier then received his instructions relative to the affair that called him to Rome; it was a law-suit which had existed for upwards of twenty years.

The Marquis had a younger brother, to whom the Castle of St. Jago, which he now inhabited, had been bequeathed; but the testator dying only a few weeks prior to the death of the legatee, the will arrived at Paris, where the latter resided, two days subsequent to his demise. Bentivoglio, as heir to his brother, had taken possession of the estate, and retained it, notwithstanding the remonstrances of the testator's relations, who contended that Henry being dead before he had acquired this bequest, it returned to the family. This Bentivoglio could not deny, but excused his usurpation by saying he held it in trust for a child left by his brother, but which had been conveyed from his presence, and he had not been able to discover those who concealed it. In the meantime he took no pains on the subject, and the law-suit continued. It was now on the eve of termination, and this was the business he entrusted to Dorimond. Previous to his departure the Chevalier repaired to the apartment of his sister-in-law, and repeated to her the hopes he had conceived. With joy she subscribed to them.

"I have no hopes," said she, "of being happy with the Marquis, but I shall have fulfilled my duty, and that is sufficient."

Nevertheless she lamented deeply the absence of Dorimond, and he no less regretted it, assuring her, however, it could not exceed a month, and that his impatience would curtail it as much as possible. He took an affectionate leave; her tears and anguish seemed to say how doubtful it was that they should ever meet more.

Dorimond, in departing, secured to himself the consolation of hearing of her, by confiding in one of the head servants, who promised to inform him of every thing that passed, and of her health, as he was connected with Gabriella, her favourite woman.

After taking these precautions, which appeared sufficient, he took the road to Italy.

CHAP. IV.

"To bless mankind with tides of flowing wealth,
"With power to grace them, or to crown with health,
"Our little lot denies—but heaven decrees
"To all the gift of ministering ease;
"The gentle offices of patient love,
"Beyond all flattery, and all price above;
"The mild forbearance of another's fault,
"The taunting word suppress'd as soon as thought;
"On these heaven bid the bliss of life depend,
"And crush'd ill-fortune when it made a friend."

Meronville, after he had dispatched St. Pierre to the Castle, waited impatiently his return. How tedious did the interval appear? How slow was the progress of time? It elapsed, however, and the faithful domestic, at the end of a week, appeared. He had been delayed by the difficulty of procuring access without incurring suspicion; but the relation he had in the Marquis's service at length satisfied his curiosity, and he learned that Bentivoglio was dangerously ill, Emily inconsolable, and that Dorimond pretended to seek diligently for the supposed murderer.

This intelligence was ill calculated to calm his senses, or accelerate his recovery; so deep was its impression that reason often yielded to the violence of affliction, and he became perfectly insane. In his lucid intervals he knew not what to hope, what to wish, or pray for. Death would bring relief to him; but his life seemed due to the exculpation of Madame de Bentivoglio. So cruel was his destiny, so fatal every new event, that he knew not where to turn for comfort.

The venerable Friar, whom misfortune had made his friend, seemed like a guardian angel sent to save him from despair; he neglected no office of kindness, or patient love, to sooth the acute feelings of sorrow that overwhelmed him; he moderated and calmed his passions. At first he sought not to console him, but merely to testify his sympathy in afflictions, past his skill to alleviate. He represented this world as it is—a scene of trial, and pointed for comfort to the skies. He listened with exemplary patience to the complaints of Meronville, though hourly repeated. His grief, thus shared, became more supportable.

Father Anthony became so necessary to him, that if he was absent a few hours, the Duke again relapsed into stupor and inertion. He was a man who had been much in the world, and one of the few who retire to a cloister from a pure, though mistaken motive of religion. If ever the supine indolence of a monastic life merits applause in a sex formed for the active duties of life, it is when embraced with views like his; he thought his sacred character gave him new opportunities to extend his benevolence, and administer comfort to the children of misery.

In Meronville he found a fit object for the exercise of Christian charity; he listened to him, he participated his sorrows; he shed tears at the unbidden relation of his misfortunes, and echoed sighs to those which seemed to rend his bosom. Never was more true and generous piety.

Finding his efforts succeed, he ventured to inform him of the transactions at the Castle. Bentivoglio was at length recovered—every thing appeared profoundly still—the Marchioness, though in a delicate state of health, was in no danger; her solitude was greater than ever; and retirement seemed the effect of choice rather than compulsion.

These particulars only Father Anthony thought it prudent to relate, and he hoped they would contribute to restore the sinking spirits and decaying health of his hearer. When he found him in some degree tranquillized, he told him, that unwilling as he was to lose a guest for whom he had so much esteem, yet he began to wish his departure, as the Convent, though on the confines of France, was, as well as St. Jago Castle, in the dominions of Spain, and consequently within the jurisdiction of the inquisition; that the Marquis, a man unbounded in resentment, was absolute within his little territories; and that should his retreat be discovered, the charge of murder, whether actual or intentional, would enable Bentivoglio to force him from the sanctuary he had chosen; that it would not be in his power to defend him against the agents of that horrid tribunal, which governed Spain; and that once within the inquisition, he would never more be heard of, or suffered to escape.

Alarming as this account was, which Meronville knew to be accurate, he could not prevail on himself to quit an asylum so near his Emily, of whom he could daily hear news. This was the only charm that attached him to existence, and but for it all situations were indifferent.

He was as yet not in a condition to remove. A slow fever still remained, and the wound in his shoulder was unclosed; the least irritation increased his pain; and so agitated was his mind, that every time the door opened he changed colour, and seemed to expect some dreadful intelligence.

He was in this situation, when one day the pious Friar, who constantly attended him, appeared more than usually dejected; as he repeated his diurnal narrative, the tear frequently started in his eye; his sighs were more frequent than those of Meronville; an evident agitation pervaded his mind; compassion in the gentlest and most exalted form sat on his brow.

Tremulously alive to every appearance of sorrow, and rendered doubly susceptible by his own misfortunes, Meronville eagerly enquired what disturbed him. Father Anthony evaded the question, but seemed in his answers striving to prepare him for some new calamity, when St. Pierre entered the apartment, and approaching his bed, informed him the Chevalier Dorimond was in the Monastery, and that he had just seen him.

Meronville cast a penetrating look on the Friar. Sorrow overspread his mild features, and seemed to imply some dreadful secret.

"Ah, gracious heaven!" cried the Duke, "Dorimond here, and you have not informed me of his arrival! Ah, this mystery convinces me a more fatal event has happened! Speak, in mercy tell me! Why this silence? Oh, my prophetic soul trembles within me! Where is Emily? What have they done to her? Heavens, you weep! Relieve me, I conjure you, from this cruel incertitude—tell me she is no more, and suffer me to expire at the sound! But oh, relieve me from the horrors of suspence!"

"Would to heaven I could for ever leave you in them!" said Anthony, the pious tear trembling on his aged cheek. "Alas, my son, has not misfortune yet weaned your heart from worldly considerations? Has it not taught you that the death of the virtuous is the commencement of eternal joy. And can you lament that her you most love is translated to the heaven where you will one day join her?"

"Ah, God!" said Meronville; "it is then indeed true! Bentivoglio has sacrificed her to his cruel resentment! Inhuman villain! But no, 'tis I am merciless—'tis I plunged a poniard in her faultless bosom— but for me she would yet live—her presence would gladden these dreary scenes! Then farewell hope—welcome despair—fix thy abode in this breast—here—here! Feed on my entrails—corrode my heart—it defies thy power! Emily is dead!—never shall I see her more!—never shall her lucid smile chase sorrow from my mind— never shall that gentle voice recall me from death—pour balm into my wounded soul! No, those eyes are for ever closed! What remains of the beloved of my soul, but an inanimate corpse? Fortune, can'st thou torture that? No, thy power extends not beyond the grave, relentless fiend! Didst thou, my Emily, in thy latest hour curse the wretch that ruined thee? But wait, he will attend thee to the confines of a distant unknown universe—he follows thee—Emily, dearest Emily, art thou gone? Art thou dead? Dead, did I say? no, thy pure spirit lives in heaven! But hast thou left this world, and left me in it? Why do I pause? Why delay to follow thee? No, I will live to expiate my guilt—to find a living tomb—the stroke of death would be too merciful, too mild!"

He started from the bed. The effort he made opened the wound but lately closed; torrents of blood issued from it, and deprived him of sense and life. Conveyed to the bed, a long lethargy made those who surrounded him think his prayers were heard, and he was gone to join his Emily. After some hours however, signs of life returned.

Father Anthony, apprehensive he might make some attempt on his existence, which seemed to depend on a thread, enjoined St. Pierre to keep him in view, and not leave the apartment till his despair should subside.

His grief now took a different turn; he preserved a mournful silence; he shed not a tear, but formed the irrevocable design of retiring to some sequestered spot, where he might enjoy the luxury of uninterrupted sorrow. Every thing that he conceived might add to his affliction, he cherished with frantic pleasure. It was then Father Anthony called forth all the aids of religion, and poured its salutary balm into his wounded soul—its mild precepts, how sooth- ing to the lacerated bosom! The sacred truths he taught reaped new effulgence as they passed his lips.

Having wrought, he hoped, some composure in the mind of the suffering invalid, he at length consented to his request of seeing

Dorimond. He brought him in the morning to his apartment. The meeting was painful to both; a profound silence prevailed for some time; they regarded each other in mute agony, as though seeking in their mutual sorrows reciprocal relief.

Meronville seemed calm; it was the torpor of despair. Dorimond, emasculated by affliction, shed a woman's tears. He sat by the bed-side. Meronville at length broke silence.

"You are too generous, Sir," said he, "to visit a wretch who has caused you so much affliction. That my sufferings exceed yours is no palliation; you must still hate, and feel abhorrence at a sight that reminds you of such cruel scenes!"

"No," said Dorimond; "hatred is a stranger to my bosom; and had it ever existed with respect to you, your present sorrows would change it to compassion. Fatal indeed has been your attachment to the loveliest of her sex; and discretion has not always guided your steps; but an error so severely punished merits no reproach."

"Since you commiserate my misfortunes," replied the Duke, "let me supplicate you not to conceal any thing from my knowledge that relates to Madame de Bentivoglio. It is perhaps your interest to let me know whether she has died the victim of jealousy or in the course of nature. Fear not to increase my affliction; that can never happen; misery is at its summit, you can only alleviate it; then tell me, I implore you, all."

"I shall augment your grief and my own," said Dorimond with a sigh, "but no matter, I yield to your request. In my narrative you will find that you are not alone unfortunate. To relate minutely all you wish I must make some mention of myself. You will excuse the ego-tism that may perhaps appear; it is an effect of the desire I have to satisfy your curiosity. Melancholy is the detail. Alas, from the hour I first knew Madame de Bentivoglio, my heart has taken an active share in all that concerned her; I had been attached to her long ere my more fortunate brother obtained the gift of her hand, and had designed, previous to your last visit at Lausanne, to offer myself to her. I witnessed your reception, though you was too much engaged to notice me. Deprived of all hopes by the joy Emily betrayed at sight of you, I quitted her dangerous society, and heard of her no more till summoned by the Marquis to St. Jago. My astonishment and dismay were inexpressible, when I found her the wife of a man I thought unworthy of her. I knew she had a multitude of admirers and pretenders to her hand, who had all the advantages of rank and fortune possessed by my brother, with persons and manners infinitely better assorted to her own. Her motive for preferring him was past my comprehension. I have since learned that an excess of refinement dictated her choice, which she was resolved should not give umbrage to the man who held her heart."

"Ah, heavens!" said Meronville, "I was that fortunate being, now more superlatively wretched!" A deep groan concluded his ejaculation.

"Yes," continued Dorimond, "you possessed her best affections. Heavens, what a fund of tenderness towards you did I not afterwards discover! It is still my astonishment, that certain of such a treasure, you could desire any other blessing, or take the chance of losing it by venturing on a scheme that must offend a mind so delicately susceptible to all its duties!"

"You can form a more accurate judgment," replied the Duke, "of the felicity of such a possession, than the consequent, and almost inseparable cares attached to it; the more inestimable it was, the greater was my anxiety in the prospect of losing any part of it; and surely my fears were not unfounded, since the rights of a husband were opposed to my perhaps stronger, but necessary subordinate claims.

"Obliged to content myself with her friendship," continued Dorimond, "I strove to include every sentiment in that; but fearing the inefficacy of such an attempt, I would have shunned her for ever, had not my presence seemed necessary to moderate the transports and impetuosity of my brother. Her sweetness, her gentleness, appeared more than ever conspicuous as her husband put them hourly to new trials. An expression which one day escaped her, convinced me she was indeed attached to another—'It is a cruel necessity,' said she, 'which compels us to sacrifice inclination to duty!'—I called to mind her love of solitude, her aversion to all those amusements so attractive at her age. Her extreme melancholy, which I had attributed to the ill-treatment of my brother, now appeared to have another cause—I saw you in them all—what melancholy reflections presented themselves to my mind! Warmly attached to the wife of another—sensible of all her charms, I saw them sacrificed to a man incapable of appreciating their value; and I saw her sinking under her sorrows. If, thought I, she had ever loved, her friendship would have satisfied my every wish; my attachment, though hopeless, would not have wanted a charm; but convinced that she feels a warmer sentiment towards another, her friendship is no longer valuable. Determined to conquer this illegitimate passion, I entered my brother's apartment to bid him adieu, and leave the Castle for ever. Madame de Bentivoglio was there; she looked on me, and all my resolutions fled. At this crisis you arrived; your disguise prevented my recollecting you; but there was something in your manners which convinced me you were born for a different situation. I testified friendship for you, I endeavoured to obtain your confidence; your reserve and coldness repulsed me; but I wished to prevail on you to take the portrait of my sister; for, not withstanding all the illusions of love, I was still resolved to quit her, but wished to carry her portrait to another clime. You soon convinced me I had nothing to hope, for in spite of all my advances you seemed to regard me with aversion——"

"Pardon my want of generosity," interrupted Meronville; "I thought you a rival, and that influenced my conduct; but my heart ever did justice to your condescension and kindness."

"The fatal day on which you wounded my brother," continued the Chevalier, "I was gone to seek a more accommodating artist. I will not describe to you my surprise and affliction, it is more easily conceived. Compelled by Bentivoglio to become the jailor of his wife, I conducted her to her own apartment, but offered to assist her escape. She resolutely refused, but put my fortitude to the test, by requiring me to release my rival. The manner in which I succeeded you need not be informed. In spite of her misfortunes and present disastrous situation, I saw that she dwelt with pleasure on what you had done for her; she confessed she knew you when I led her to the painted chamber; and that she had written to command your departure, and was seeking an opportunity of delivering her letter, when a fatal accident betrayed you. What passed afterwards you already know. My brother, scarcely recovered, sent me to Rome on the subject of a law-suit. With extreme regret I quitted Madame de Bentivoglio at a time when she was hardly convalescent, but left to a servant the charge of transmitting to me every thing that passed. Notwithstanding this precaution, I was so melancholy that my heart seemed to forebode we should never meet more. The law-suit was nearly terminated, when I received a letter from the servant, stating

that soon after my departure the Marquis had dismissed all his servants, except an old man and his wife; that even Gabriella, Emily's
favourite woman, had vainly solicited to remain with her mistress,
yet an invalid. This information gave me the most lively inquietude;
I shuddered as I perused the letter, and wondered to what fate my
unhappy sister was reserved. Without considering that my commission was but half executed, I set out post, and travelling with
a speed which appeared to myself incredible, I arrived within two
days journey of St. Jago. Rumour here conveyed to me the fatal
intelligence, that the Marchioness had expired, and a tenant of my
brother's I met on the road assured me he had attended the funeral.
Her delicate state of health when I left her, and the lengths to
which I feared my brother's passions might lead him, left no room
to doubt the truth of this report. I reproached myself a thousand
times for having deserted her, thus exposed to scenes she had not
strength to support. But a letter next day reached me from the Marquis; he mentioned the death of his wife in terms of such piercing
sorrow, that I fully acquitted him of having any share in it. He said
her repentance and amiability had conquered his resentment, and
stifled every sentiment but that of love; that he was on the eve of
receiving her to his bosom, when death deprived him of every hope.
A malignant fever had seized her when but half recovered from her
late indisposition, and carried her off in five days. He had watched
near her couch, he had endeavoured to recall her to life by his passionate and tender exclamations; but her hour was come; she had,
however, died easy, and assured him she died innocent. Oppressed
with anguish, I continued my route: I passed the Castle, and paused
a moment to view those scenes once animated by the presence of
my beloved sister; the woods seemed to have acquired a darker hue;
the lofty battlements appeared in more awful gloom; the birds had
forgotten their notes; the wind roared; the waves of ocean beat
tremendously against the walls of the edifice, which defied their
power. My heart was in unison with the dreary scene;* I could not
prevail on myself to enter the mansion, deprived of its only charm. I
continued my route, and arrived here. Father Anthony was with my
brother, he told me he was plunged in the deepest melancholy, and
refused to see any person. Informed of my arrival, he sent me word
it was not in his power to bear my presence in his afflicted state. I
was not sorry to hear it. To inhabit again the place where I have

often seen the unfortunate Emily, would hourly remind me of her, and furnish new subjects of grief; and I could not, if invited, have refused my society to divert the gloom of solitude in my brother's melancholy situation. Death appears to have revived my former sentiments—alas! I fear love is as much mingled in my regrets as friendship. Pardon, oh most angelic woman a passion which can no longer dishonour you! Look from that heaven you inhabit, and pity my sorrows! Accept a monument in this heart still yours, and believe, that while it continues to beat, it beats for you! During my residence here," concluded Dorimond, "I have learnt that my brother's suit is terminated against him. The Castle and property are adjudged to the infant of my late brother, if it still lives; and in default, to the relations of the testator. I am charged to make enquiries after my niece; but it is two-and-twenty years since my brother died, and I have but little hopes of success, as I have no clue to my researches; considering myself, however, as bound to make them, I shall set out for Paris, and after that enter the army in the service of my country. I may find repose from sorrow, or that death I am ready to encounter!"

Dorimond ceased.

Meronville had, during his relation, shed tears, and heaved profound sighs; but towards the end relapsed into torpor and mute anguish.

The Chevalier left the room, followed by the venerable Friar, whose compassionate nature could not endure the sight of misery, superior to consolation, and for which there was no remedy.

Left to himself, the Duke soon resolved on the course he should pursue. While Emily lived he had thought of retiring to some secret abode, where the world should never penetrate; but now that he was deprived of her for ever, no alternative offered.

The conversations he had had, during his confinement, with Father Anthony, had taught him to shudder at the idea of suicide, that last and most unpardonable of human crimes. Compelled, therefore, to endure the burthen of existence till it should please the Almighty disposer of events to take him to himself, he resolved to deposit it in some quiet retreat, where the offices of religion, he hoped, might eventually banish love from his apostate heart.

CHAP. V.

"Oh thou, with whom my heart was wont to share
"From reason's dawn each pleasure and each care!
"With whom, alas! I fondly hop'd to know
"The humble walks of happiness below;
"If thy blest nature now unites above
"An angel's pity with a sister's love,
"Still o'er my life preserve a mild controul,
"Correct my views, and elevate my soul."*

The desire of executing his project of seclusion, hastened the recovery of Meronville's health. After a long confinement his strength began to renervate, and he took the air daily in the gardens of the Monastery. His wound was entirely closed, and he was in a situation to be removed in a short time.

Before he quitted the world for ever, he was desirous of visiting the tomb which contained his heart, and the ashes of Emily. They were deposited in the chapel belonging to St. Jago, and there was no means of gaining admittance without the knowledge and concurrence of the Marquis. He mentioned his wishes to the benevolent Anthony, who, fearful of the consequences, endeavoured to dissuade him.

His remonstrances were vain. Callous to the voice of reason, Meronville persisted, and the Friar promised to procure him admission. He solicited Bentivoglio to permit himself and another monk to pray over the tomb of the deceased Marchioness on a day of peculiar solemnity in their convent.

The Marquis, not knowing how to refuse, consented, and Anthony provided his disconsolate guest with a monastic habit, and after recommending prudence to him in the strongest terms for the sake of both, accompanied him to the chapel.

He unlocked the door, and again fastened it after them to exclude intruders. The sacred sanctuary was still hung with black. A monument raised in the side aisle guided the footsteps of Meronville. Anthony left him to meditate near it, and retired to the altar to pour forth prayers for him. The Duke knelt over the inanimate marble, which enshrined the no less inanimate form on which he once fondly doated; his sighs, tears, and groans echoed through the asylums of the long forgotten dead.

"And is this all, my Emily, all that remains of that angelic form, the remembrance of which still gives life to him that adored thee? Are those eyes for ever closed, whose mild effulgence pictured the benevolence of a faultless heart? Shall that heavenly smile for ever cease which taught misfortune to forget its sting, and was ever ready to cheer the afflicted? Ah, if thou livest indeed in a world more worthy of thee, let thy gentle precepts descend to guide my steps; teach me like thee to unite cheerfulness with devotion, activity with resignation; teach me like thee, whose blameless wishes submitted to their God, to meet the changes time and chance present. Grant me thy peace and purity of mind. But what do I say?—ah, gracious heaven! 'tis I have murdered thee! Pardon me, gentle spirit, I go to mourn for ever, and pray for that hour when my soul shall reunite with thine! Yet wherefore, deluded mortal, mourn? Cannot this spectacle repress thy grief? Behold all that remains of what once was beauty, grace, loveliness! Shall not the happiest and the most wretched here find rest? Shall not he who dwells in splendid palaces, and feasts the live long day, here be levelled with the child of penury that haunts his door? Can cares that so soon must end so deeply affect short-sighted mortals? I think I see thee, adored Emily, rising from thy tomb to reprove my sorrows! Dead or living thou still shalt guide my destiny! Farewell, my plaints no more shall rouse thy peaceful ashes! Farewell, farewell!"

He still knelt near the insensible monument, on which his tears fell, when Father Anthony approached, and warned him to depart. Thrice he kissed the inanimate marble, and with a sigh that seemed issuing from his soul, he followed his venerable guide.

Arrived at the Monastery, he turned all his thoughts towards the execution of his design of speedily retiring. Fearful that the project should meet opposition if he disclosed it, he gave not a distant hint to any person of his plans.

Calling St. Pierre, he gave him every thing of value that he had with him, reserving only the letter and portrait of Emily, with sufficient money for his journey. He wrote an affectionate letter to his mother, containing a detail of all that had happened to him, and an eternal adieu. He prayed that her blessing might follow his unknown steps, and asked pardon for leaving her. The light, he said, was odious to him, that he should retire to some cell, where it might never penetrate: he added, he thought it his duty to spare her the sight of a wretch no longer worthy her affection, or capable of returning it; and concluded by intreating her not to make any fruitless perquisitions to discover him, as he never should be found. He recommended to her the faithful St. Pierre, by whom he dispatched this letter, telling him he would wait his return at the Monastery.

Having seen him depart, the following day he took leave of Father Anthony. The good man shed tears, and recommended him to providence. His professions of eternal regard hardly called forth any return from Meronville, who, having lost his Emily, had no sentiments but for her—no tears but to shed at her remembrance.

The Friar would accept of no reward; the consciousness of having performed a good action fully repaid it, and he found in the Convent all that was necessary to his comfort.

"Heaven bless you," said he, as Meronville quitted the Monastery, "restore your peace, and take you to itself! Remember, my son, there is an early period to your woes, and a bright inheritance above for the patient sufferer below!"

The great gate closed, and Meronville found himself on the wide world, no guide to mark his toilsome road; no friend to share his griefs; no hope to illumine his path!

The Abbey of La Trappe he designed as the boundary of his journey; it was situated on the confines of Perche, in Normandy. To arrive at it he must traverse the kingdom. Finding himself unequal to perform it as a pedestrian, he mounted a horse, and travelling night and day, he soon reached it.

The Monks of La Trappe had been long celebrated for the austerity of their lives, and sanctity of their manners. During several ages it had existed, and undisturbed by the civil wars that desolated France, or the many irruptions of the English on the coast near which it stood. Time, which in its progress destroys all, seemed to have respected this ancient sanctuary.*

As Meronville approached it a religious awe took possession of his soul; nature seemed to have formed the scene for the asylum of penitence, when false shame drove it from the world. It is surrounded with woods, hills, and rivulets, which render it nearly inaccessible and impervious to the traveller's eye. The air is damp and unwholsome, thickened by perpetual and impenetrable fogs; a profound and solemn silence reigns, which seems to have existed from the creation of time! What a field is here presented to the hypochondriac!—what food for melancholy!

Meronville felt his heart in perfect unison with the scene; a sort of pious terror penetrated his soul; he stood for a moment in the attitude of contemplation; the mournful cypress and the weeping willow, their leaves agitated by the breeze, to which terrified imagination and his ill-boding mind ascribed a horrid murmur and a prophetic sound, covered the valley beneath. A long and hollow but unvarying murmur met his ear, caused by the passage of a thick stream over the broken stones in its bed. These traces convinced him he had reached the long-sought port, where his sorrows should find rest.

He descended the mountain on which he stood, and after traversing vast and wild heaths, and pursuing his route through hedges and rugged paths, winding into innumerable mazes, he on a sudden thought he discovered a new and unknown land. The abode of modest devotion revealed itself in majestic austerity.

He arrived at the outward court; over the portal was a statue of St. Bernard.* The inner court contained marks of the most prolific vegetation; here was every thing necessary for the subsistence of the community, which relieved them from the necessity of ever mixing with the world, or holding intercourse with any person out of the Convent.

Meronville arrived there at the hour of the tenebres.* He entered the chapel; it was lighted by a single lamp, placed in the midst, whose dim and solemn light increased the awful horror of the place. About sixty monks were assembled; their long visages and dark clothing exactly corresponded with the scene without; they continued an hour in prayer, sometimes kneeling, sometimes prostrating themselves before a crucifix, or the images of saints; then, with one voice they chanted the praises of their Creator. A profound silence succeeded, after which each kissing the consecrated shrine, retired to their daily employment, saying to Meronville as they passed, "*Memento mori!*"* the only salutation they are permitted.

As silence is one of their fundamental vows, the Abbot only is allowed to address a stranger; he approached, and enquired Meronville's business. He told him it was his wish to be admitted a member of the holy community.

"Have you well considered," said the Monk, "the austerity of that life our laws prescribe? Listen whilst I relate the duties our habit imposes:—a year of trial is allowed you, after which you are admitted amongst us. If restraint and perpetual mortifications does not alter your resolutions, you are excluded for ever from the converse of man; debarred for ever from the intercourse of friendship; condemned to perpetual silence; fed on herbs, or the coarsest viands; deprived of liberty; and of every luxury, as well as recreation; confined here during life; and interred here at your death! My son, do not these rigors shake your resolves?"

"Far otherwise, holy Father," replied the Duke, "they increase my desire to become a member of your society. I mean to consecrate my life to God, and no austerities can terrify me! Cannot you dispense with the year of trial, and receive my vows to-morrow?"

"That is not in my power," replied the Abbot; "but your noviciate commences now. I will order you a habit; but remember, you are never more to be indulged in the liberty of speech."

Meronville bowed. He was furnished with the monastic habiliments, and led to a cell; he passed the night in it, on a bed of straw, and without sheets, and was informed he must never undress.

Next day the Abbot began to initiate him in his diurnal occupations, which through the year never varied. They rose at three in the morning to perform matins. Each day they dug part of their graves, to remind them of mortality. The hours not employed in prayer, were devoted to the cultivation of the earth and household affairs, as no woman ever entered the walls; and as all here were equal, all by turns performed the most menial offices. *Memento mori* was the morning salutation, after which not a word was permitted to disturb their inviolable silence.

In these austerities Meronville rejoiced. More apparently pious, more rigid than the oldest inhabitant, the Abbot took his melancholy, his profound despair as a proof of zeal, which he could not sufficiently admire. Yet to the altar he carried a heart but half devoted to its maker. Emily still lived there; her image triumphant contended with its God, and Meronville, consecrated to heaven, was still the slave of love.

Nevertheless the year elapsed, and he was admitted to perform his vows. With perfect composure he approached the altar, and renounced for ever the world and its concerns.

Each day as he continued to dig that grave which was to inter his weight of misery, he took from his bosom the portrait of Emily, and bathed it with tears.

One day a messenger arrived at the Convent, to request one of the monks would attend the last moments of a poor sinner, just expiring in a neighbouring cottage. The Abbot selected Meronville for that purpose, and gave him, as was usual on these occasions, power to receive the confession of the dying man, and to speak comfort to him.

He entered on his office, and conducted by the messenger, arrived at a small cottage, where, on a wretched mattrass, lay a man in the agonies of death. Meronville had his face nearly covered with his cowl; he drew near the bed. The sick man, requesting every person might leave the room, received the crucifix from his hand, and joined with him in devout prayer.

"Father," said he in a faint voice, but one which struck horribly on the ear of Meronville, "you see before you the vilest of sinners! Through a long life I have practised every horrid crime, which the hour of death only concludes! Is there mercy in heaven for such a wretch? Shall murder, fraud, forgery, be forgiven there?"

"What presumptuous mortal," replied the Friar, "shall dare to limit the mercy of heaven——"

"Hear my confession," continued the expiring sinner; "I have set father against son! I have by forged signatures convinced the Duke de Meronville that his son conspired against him! I have ruined a lovely and innocent woman, to whom that son was attached!"—A hollow groan from the Monk here interrupted him.—"You shudder, holy Father; but I have more to confess—my guilt will congeal the blood in your veins! My forgery, on the eve of being discovered, I had no means to avert the danger that threatened, but by the death of my patron——oh, my agonized soul, desert not yet thy mansion—wait while I disclose the load of guilt that overwhelms thee! But hark, what sound was that? Oh God, thy thunder rolls!—thy lightnings will consume me!—no, 'tis the torch of hell that waves around the murderer's bed!—foul demon, thou callest thine accomplice—nay, tear me not so—my strength fails—are not those hell's dreary confines? Are not those horrid spectres issued from it? Now

you have me!—now I go! Oh God, I dare not call on thee!"—He hid
his face under the bed clothes with horrid groans. Meronville had
instantly recollected the hated voice of La Haye; he endeavoured to
subdue his indignation by fervent prayer, but his limbs shook, his
tongue refused its office. The dying miscreant in a few moments
recovered, and continued to speak—"Unsuspicious the Duke slept,
unconscious that an asp so venomous was near—a subtle poison
poured into his ear made that sleep eternal!—Oh God, I sent him
to a world of retribution with all his sins unexpiated—but pardon
may be found for him—the accumulated weight of guilt rests on my
perjured soul! The deluded female, in whose cot I now lay, fell early
a victim to my designs, which the sacred character of religion I had
assumed prevented her suspecting. Two sons she brought me; to
enrich these I have not shuddered at the worst of crimes! Heaven's
vengeance is not so tardy as might appear: conscience embittered
every enjoyment in my most successful moments; but one of my
sons, taught guilt by me, died on the scaffold—venerable Monk,
thou never wert a father, else wouldst thou know a parent's pangs
when his crimes are visited on his child! Methinks I should die more
easy, could the Marquis of Lusignan, whom I pursued with cause-
less, but inveterate hate, see his injuries avenged by the agonies of
parting life—of a soul on the verge of eternity—that dreadful eternity to the unpardoned sinner! One other victim haunts my mind,
and kindles flames around me—Madame de Bentivoglio———"

Here Meronville's groans could no longer be suppressed; he
threw himself almost expiring on a chair.

"Thou," continued La Haye, "who art used to hear the confes-
sions of sinners, art petrified with the accumulated horrors I disclose;
yet listen, Father—my hour approaches—I cannot die unabsolved
at least by you. Emily de Montalte was her name; she early loved
the Marquis. After various persecutions, I forged a letter from his
father, stating that he was confined in chains, and that he could only
be liberated the day she became the wife of another. One of my sons
then courted her alliance; I hoped he would succeed; but driven to
despair, she chose a wretch formed to torture her existence; one
whom jealousy fired to madness. Yet unsatisfied, I fed this jaundiced
passion by anonymous letters, warning him that a favoured rival was
near his wife!———"

Ere La Haye could finish this sentence his eye balls flashed; he almost started from the bed at sight of a fancy-wrought spectre—a convulsion seized him—he expired with such dreadful groans as brought the affrighted household into the room. They found the Monk extended on the floor, hardly less lifeless than the corpse near which he lay—they soon restored him, and he requested a private interview with the female owner of the house. Trembling she approached him, and related her connection with the deceased. Her sincere repentance made it an easy task for him to console her. She further informed him that La Haye, in attempting to carry Emily from Luneville, had been wounded in the leg; that it was long ere he could return to Paris, because his age made a cure more difficult; that it had never been wholly cured, and that a late fall from his horse, near her cottage, had opened it afresh, and brought him to the grave.

Meronville, dreadfully shocked, and desirous of returning to the Convent, hastily assembled, as was usual, the family round him, and after praying over the deceased, delivered this short exhortation—

"Let this dreadful example now before you, teach us that guilt, however apparently successful, ever meets its just reward from the omnipotent disposer of events; let it convince us that fraud, though concealed from all others, is open to him from whom nothing can be kept secret; and that vengeance, though delayed, pursues the sinner with unerring certainty. Remember, my friends, this awful lesson—remember the dying agonies of this wretched sufferer, and lift your hearts to heaven in supplications for his soul, now appearing before the dreadful tribunal of an avenging and offended God!"*

He ceased, and with perturbed steps returned to shut himself in his cell, and weep anew those sorrows this incident had so painfully recalled.

CHAP. VI.

"A solitary blessing few can find;
"Our joys with those we love are intertwin'd,
"And he whose helpful tenderness removes
"Th' obstructing thorn that wounds the breast he loves,
"Smooths not another's rugged path alone,
"But scatters roses to adorn his own!"

In leaving the Monastery of St. Benedict, Dorimond had, pursuant to his design, arrived at Paris, and made it his duty to discover the heiress of a brother he but faintly recollected, as he was only ten years of age when he died, and they had never lived together. His mind was so wholly employed in this interesting research, that he, at times, forgot his own sufferings; nevertheless disappointment succeeded every ray of hope that partially disclosed itself.

The persons who inhabited the house once tenanted by his brother, had purchased it of an old woman, and could not tell whether she yet lived, as her age must be very great, if the debt of nature was yet unpaid.

Finding all his attempts abortive, he resolved to visit Caroline Dorville, for whom he had a sincere regard, in Switzerland; to relate to her what he knew of her deceased friend, Madame de Bentivoglio; to weep with her those sorrows death had concluded, and then enlist in the service of his country.

Nine months had elapsed when he set out for this purpose. One day, absorbed in meditations and versatile reflections, he wandered, unconscious of the progress of time, or the night shades which already prevailed, and concealed in gloom the distant prospects; nor did he recollect his situation, till a flash of lightning darting across, frightened his timid horse, and made it set off with extreme rapidity, stopping only where the road became almost obstructed by thick interwoven trees and brambles. Dorimond then found himself in the midst of a forest, through which he could discern no passage that seemed likely to lead to a human abode. Loud claps of thunder rent the clouds, which appeared ready to burst over his head; and the frequent and successive flashes of lightning illumined

the forest, and discovered to him the solitary awfulness of his situation. Unused to fear, the sensations he now felt resembled more
religious terror, caused by the sense of an omnipotent Deity,* than
that phantom of the mind which weakens the influence of reason,
and makes us very cowards.

Recommending himself to providence, he sat down at the foot
of a tree, sheltered by its branches from the rain which now fell in
torrents. The desultory storm at length subsided, and the murky
clouds recovering from the shock, assumed the grey garb of evening. One by one, innumerable stars twinkled in the horizon, and
our benighted traveller began to hope he might reach the skirts of
the forest, where, probably, some woodman's cot would shelter him
from the weather.*

After much labour, he at length found his attempts to extricate
his horse perfectly vain; he therefore resolved to tie it to a tree, and
endeavour to penetrate through brambles and thickets alone. To
his unspeakable joy, he soon discerned a glimmering light, which
seemed a vestige of some human recess; he advanced towards it, and
it led him to a cottage, at the door of which he stopped, and knocking, a voice from within enquired his business.

"A benighted traveller," he cried, "entreats your charity to shelter
him from the inclement sky."

He heard several female voices within, debating on the safety of
admitting him; at last they seemed decided by the observation of
one, who said it was but a sorry night to sleep abroad, and providence always rewarded a charitable act.

The door was then opened, and he entered a neat cottage, distinguished only by extreme cleanliness. An old woman sat in the
corner spinning, two younger ones were knitting, while the fourth
opened the door, and welcomed him with a modest curtsey.

He related to them the accident which had brought him there,
and was assured he might in safety pass the night under their roof.
Whilst he spoke the old woman several times rubbed and adjusted
her spectacles, fixing her eyes on him with surprise and curiosity.
When the Chevalier was seated, she continued to look on him, and
at length exclaimed—

"By St. Gertrude,* I never saw so striking a likeness—the figure,
the voice, and those bright eyes—since my poor master died, I never
saw any like them before!"

Dorimond smiled at her observation, and enquired to whom he was so resemblant.

" 'Tis a long story," said the old woman, "and you must be hungry. Isabella, try if you cannot bring the gentleman something to eat?"

Isabella obeyed; she roasted some potatoes by the embers on the hearth, and with some oatmeal made a delicious cake. The Chevalier thought he had never made so exquisite a repast.

"How old are you, my good mother?" said he.

"Fourscore and five years," replied she, "and, thank God, hale and well. It will be twenty-three years come next Martlemas, that my poor master died—God bless his soul!—'Annette,' says he to me, the day before he died, 'Annette, I shall die younger than you, and you must take care of my poor wife and daughter, and talk to them about me when I am gone far away!'—Alack-a-day, would he were still here—there are few like him left behind—you will wonder, Sir, what made me think of him; but if I may be so bold to say it, you are as like him as two drops of water—he was not much younger than you when he died!"

"What was his name, good woman?" asked Dorimond.

"His name was Montfort, his christian name Henry—how he loved my dear mistress, and how she loved him! Oh that sad day when he died—I shall never forget it!" The tear stood in her eye, and gently trickled down her furrowed cheek, whilst with the garrulity natural to age, she continued—"That sweet babe that I used to call mine—heaven only knows what chance may have befel it—it was the image of both father and mother, and, I dare say, as good as them—old Annette she loved too—oh if I could but see her once before I die—but I ask each traveller that comes this way, and nobody knows about her!"

"Is her mother also dead?" enquired the Chevalier, whose curiosity was more than commonly excited.

The old woman shook her head.

"There's a sad tale there!—nobody can tell where she is! If you will take time to read it, I will fetch you some papers, that will tell you how it happened; it makes me very unhappy that I cannot find my little Cony, and give them to her; for they of right belong to her; and if I should die, nobody will take care of old Annette's paper treasure—and a treasure I assure you it is, as you shall see!"

She rose with these words. Isabella enquired if she should fetch them—

"No, no, child," said she; "I have strength enough left to fetch them, and I do not like any body to touch them but me!"

So saying, she hobbled to another room, and soon returned with a casket, which she carefully opened, and as she displayed its contents said:—

"I have read this so often that it is almost worn out, and quite dirty; but I would not have it copied, because it's the hand writing of my dear mistress, and worth ten copies!"

A picture dropped from it as she put it into his hand; she picked it up, and kissing it, looked first at Dorimond, then at the painting, and each time with new surprise.

"Look," said she to Isabella; "did you ever see a greater likeness? Look at those eyes! My poor master looked sorrowful, just as the gentleman does!"

Isabella assented.

Dorimond requested to see it. She presented him a portrait, containing the heads of a male and female—he started, exclaiming—

"Heavens! what a resemblance!"

"There," cried the old woman, "you see I told you the likeness was striking; the gentleman sees it himself!"

"It is the female, so like a friend of mine," replied Dorimond, "which surprised me. Was this your mistress?"

"Yes, and a dear precious soul she was!"

"Her christian name?" said Dorimond.

"Was," replied the old woman, "Adelaide!"

"Heavens, what a wonderful coincidence!" cried the Chevalier. "Henry and Adelaide! But are you certain his name was Montfort?"

"Certain, indeed," replied the old woman; " 'tis a name I shall never forget!"

Dorimond turned the miniature a thousand ways; the glass at the back had been loosened by a fall, and came out in his hand; a small paper appeared beneath it.

"Oh, St. Gertrude," cried Annette, "it is broken! I had rather have given worlds than it should have received any injury—let me put it away, or worse may happen; and what would Miss Caroline say if I should ever find her?"

"What is this paper at the back of it?" said the Chevalier. "Have you examined it?"

"Not for worlds!" said Annette. "It's only belonging to the picture—don't touch it, you will spoil it!"

"Assure yourself, good woman," replied Dorimond, "I feel too much interested in this miniature to injure it; but this paper cannot belong to it!"

After much opposition, Annette consented; it was a thin paper, carefully folded, and when removed, discovered a plating of hair. The Chevalier unfolding it, found some lines within, containing these words:—

"The portraits of Henry Dorimond and Adelaide his wife, intended as a present to their daughter, when she shall learn that the name of Montfort was only assumed, when misfortunes, and the persecutions of her uncle, obliged her unhappy parents to degrade their rank, and become simple roturiers!"

The Chevalier fell back in his chair; Annette terrified called for water.

"'Tis nothing, good mother," said he, "only surprise—I shall soon recover—your lost master was my brother!"

The old woman became frantic with joy.

"Then you know where my dear mistress is? But no," continued she, with evident disappointment, "you cannot be his brother; though like him to be sure you are; he had but one brother, and a cruel wretch he was—the Marquis of something; I forgot his name, for I never tried to remember it. He used my poor master sadly; and he was older than him, and you are only about his age when he died; so it cannot be!"

"I was very young, and you perhaps never saw me," replied the Chevalier; "it is nevertheless true! But I will retire, and read this manuscript, and then I shall know more. To-morrow we will talk about it."

Annette lighted him to his room, and left him with a thousand charges to take care of her treasure.

Dorimond shed abundance of tears as he perused the manuscript, which contained an account of the misfortunes of his brother, written by his wife, who survived him.

Day-light surprised him ere he had concluded, and brought with it old Annette, who had not slept a wink, so fully were her thoughts employed.

"Good mother," said Dorimond, wiping a tear from his cheek, "your master was certainly my brother, and if you can but tell me where his daughter is, you will render her and me an essential service!"

"Would to Heaven I could!" said Annette; "but I will tell you how I missed her:—A good lady, the Duchess of Meronville, I think, came one day and took her, and said how she would provide for her, and bring her up; and the house my poor master lived in she gave me. I was so sorry to part with my child, that I never thought about the portrait, or the manuscript, which, to be sure, was her's by good rights; so I let her go without them; and sometime after when I called at the Duchess's, she was gone to the country, and nobody could tell me where Miss Caroline was gone; so I did not like to trust them out of my hand, and I kept them. Soon after, being poor, I thought of this cottage, my deceased husband left me, and thinks I, if I sell this house, I can live comfortable in the forest all my life, with a little spinning, though I was loth to leave the house where my master died; yet God would have it. So I came here, and took my grandchildren to live with me; and I am so old that I never could go back to Paris, so I never could hear of my young mistress, only the Marquis (I have forgot his name) sent me word she was dead; but I never believed him, though mayhap he had her killed!"

Dorimond pondered on this intelligence. The circumstance of Henry's having changed his name, he thought, might induce Bentivoglio to hope the inheritance of St. Jago would come to him, if he could persuade the old woman, who he supposed knew her real name, that she was dead. In effect, the Marquis had so concluded, having first assured himself that Madame de Meronville knew her only as the daughter of Montfort. So much time had elapsed that he himself knew not whether she still lived; and as he had for twenty years quietly possessed her property, he had taken no pains to discover her.

A variety of conjectures, compounded of hopes and fears, now filled the mind of Dorimond. After an infinity of entreaties, he prevailed upon Annette to lend him the miniature, which he was resolved to carry to the Duchess de Meronville, the only person who could give him information on the subject. For this purpose he must retrace his footsteps, and return to Paris, where she probably resided. Having sought his horse, which he left in the forest, he eagerly mounted. With blessings the old woman attended him to the road, and prayed to heaven for his success, and speedy return.

The Chevalier was soon introduced to the Duchess; and having enquired for Caroline Montfort, received from her a confirmation of what the likeness in the portrait had made him suspect, namely, that she was now the wife of Dorville.

Overjoyed beyond expression, he related the circumstance that occasioned his present enquiries; and after gratefully acknowledging her kindness in preserving her from those evils which had brought his brother to the grave, set out with undiminished speed for Switzerland.

It will be remembered, that at the time Annette received her casket, one also arrived, addressed to Madame de Meronville; this contained a duplicate of the manuscript, from which Caroline learned the sad adventures of her parents, and was still in her possession.

Dorimond first informed Dorville of the property to which his wife was heiress, and then by degrees explained it to her. Nothing could exceed her surprise and joy to find herself so nearly allied to a man she so highly respected; but it recalled the remembrance of her lost parents, and drew from her eye the tear of filial affection.

Dorville and his friend set out for Italy, and soon established her claims to the disputed property. The Chevalier, entirely alienated from the Marquis, by his treatment of Henry, went with them to take possession of St. Jago; he found his brother dangerously ill, and the surprise and consternation caused by the discovery of his niece, hastened his death, and he expired execrating Dorimond, who succeeded to his title and estate.

Caroline for some time could think and talk only of her lost Emily, whose tomb she frequently visited. The Chevalier was particularly reminded of her by every scene in the Castle, where once she lived, and which could only be rendered supportable by her society.

He led Caroline to her apartment; many of the things she wore were scattered about the room; her lyre lay unstrung; there was an awful solemnity in the chamber, hung with black, which proclaimed it the chamber of death!

To the wood, her once favourite retreat, she often wandered, and sought the ill-omened pavillion which occasioned her death;

it was neglected, like the rest of the Castle. The implements for painting Meronville had left, were untouched, and the half-finished figure reminded them of the scene that happened on the last day he worked there. Painful yet soft were the recollections these circumstances brought—invaluable are the treasures of memory, they continue when the persons and scenes which created them are long past—how sweet to age is the remembrance of unblemished youth!—when every pleasure dies, and the torpid faculties are no longer sensible of present enjoyment, memory still remains—its joys ever estimable, ever new!

Contiguous to the pleasure grounds of the Castle was a rock that overhung the sea; it was high, and commanded on all sides a distant and extensive prospect. Caroline frequently sat on its extremest verge, contemplating the great expanse, which ever brought pleasing reminiscences since the hour when Dorville was restored to her wishes; she almost fancied she could discern the far distant coast of Africa, where he had been so long a prisoner.

One day as she was slowly descending its craggy sides, a moan, like that of human misery, struck on her ear; she listened; the sound was repeated, and seemed to issue from within the rock. Returning to the Castle, she communicated what she had heard, and summoned old Bertrand, the servant of the late Marquis, who had resided above twenty years at St. Jago, to know if it was possible any cavities in the rock should inclose a human being.* Bertrand, surprised at this unexpected interrogatory, stammered, but answered in the negative, affirming that rooks and owls often sheltered there, and their notes resembled those of human plaints.

Caroline, but half satisfied, returned the following day. The dismal sound, more frequently repeated, interested her feelings past forbearance, and hastily summoning Dorville and Dorimond, convinced them her apprehensions were not merely ideal. A strict search was made, but no entrance could be discovered, and they left it disappointed and uneasy.

So deep was the impression made on Caroline, that she could not rest by night or day, and in spite of the endeavours of Dorville to sooth her distress, or ridicule her dejection, a pensive melancholy seized her, and she was never happy but when returning to the sound which so powerfully awakened her feelings. He had in vain interrogated Bertrand, who could alone throw any light on the subject; he persisted in his first assertion, that the cries were those of night birds, or sea fowl.

One night Caroline, wakeful and disturbed, heard about midnight the sound of oars, apparently near the shore; she arose, and looking from the window, saw by the light of the moon a small boat approaching, with two men, whilst one from the shore beckoned them to advance; a confused idea, incapable of form, made her shriek, and awaken Dorville, and having shewn him what occasioned her terror, he hastily dressed himself, and calling his servants, determined to dive into the apparent mystery. Caroline in the meantime watched the motions of the men below, and was almost convinced Bertrand was one. The boat had several times made towards the shore, and been driven from it, when she saw them throw a cable on shore, which being caught by the man in waiting, then he pulled them to the coast, and fastening it, they leaped on land.

Dorville having enjoined his astonished menials' silence, reached the spot unobserved, and drew near enough to hear these words:—

"We shall soon be over," said one; "the tide and wind are for us; I thought we should never have got here! Remember all our toils, Signor Bertrand, and the reward you promised us!"

"Rely on that," replied a voice; "only be silent, and follow me!— You must gag her, for women make a confounded screaming; she has contrived to make herself heard, even when she was safe within the rock—so now I dare say she will try to be heard still more—but come on lads, I warrant three of us can master her!"

They then tied a rope to a kind of ring in the ground, and heaving violently, pulled up a trap door, and descended a little staircase. Dorville, trembling with rage and eagerness, ordered his servants to be in readiness when they should return. The screams of a female preceded it, but in a moment she was silenced, and they advanced. As they issued forth, Dorville fell upon them with a drawn sabre; he seized the first, the other two, letting their fair burthen fall, ran to the boat, and in a moment disappeared, their light vessel only skimming the surface of the waves.

Dorville charging some of his train with the care of the ruffian they had secured, flew with the rest to the relief of the lady, whom they found deprived of sense. Conveying her to the Castle, every means was used for her recovery, but terror each time she opened her eyes deprived her anew of life.

Caroline, who with her maids now descended, requested they might be left alone, as seeing so many men, whom she could only suppose were the ruffians from whom they had rescued her, prevented her recovery. This precaution had the desired effect; the lady, seeing only females, whose sympathetic looks proclaimed them friends, at length assumed courage to enquire where she was. Caroline assured her she had nothing to fear, and that she was in a place of perfect security. She then ordered her maids to convey her to an apartment, where repose might restore her, and retired herself, not indeed to rest, but to reflect on this extraordinary occurrence.

In the morning she hastened to the chamber of the stranger, while Dorville and the new Marquis of Bentivoglio repaired to the dungeon to interrogate Bertrand, who was the miscreant they had there confined.

The lady was already risen, and was traversing her room. Caroline was struck with her appearance; she was tall, and might once have had symmetry in her now emaciated form, but so thin that there were no remains of due proportion. Her face exhibited the outline of decayed beauty; her large dark eyes were deeply sunk in the projecting cheek bones, which almost concealed them; her livid complection deprived them of all animation. She had an aquiline nose, and was slightly marked with the small-pox.

The benevolent features of Caroline, as she kindly enquired how she had passed the night, appeared to surprise, no less than all the objects around; she answered that she was very well, and had slept better than she had done some time; but complained that the light, to which she had been long unused, hurt the visual optic, and inflicted much pain.

"Tell me, Madam," said she, "wherefore have I been removed, and why, after so many years' confinement, I am again permitted to revisit that light from which I thought myself for ever excluded? Perhaps I must be subjected to fresh persecutions, and the tranquillity of my cave was thought too much indulgence! Alas! my faded beauty can no longer raise emotions in that heart, callous to all but self-enjoyment! Your courteous behaviour, Madam, and the voice of pity, which long has been a stranger to my ear, induce me to hope protection. Will you permit me to enquire by what fortunate chance I again behold a human being, who seems indeed to have the feelings of humanity?"

Caroline related to her the death of Bentivoglio, and the accident by which her retreat had been discovered, intreating in her turn to know by what fatal chance she had been confined in the rock.

The stranger raised her eyes, suffused with tears, to heaven frequently during this recital, and when it concluded, fervently exclaimed:—

"So inscrutable are thy ways, Almighty God—thou hast heard my prayers, kind heaven—now receive my soul! Since you desire to hear my melancholy story, Madam," continued she, "I will not conceal it, though fearful of wounding your sensibility by a recital, which will make your gentle nature shudder—to shew you how depraved is the heart of man, is perhaps to rob your existence of all enjoyment; but I hope there are few like him, who is now answering at the great tribunal of justice for my unmerited fate! He had a brother once—ah heavens! a pattern of every virtue that can adorn humanity—his reward, oh God, is with thee!"

Caroline, without knowing why, felt so interested whilst she spoke, that her tears fell, and she threw herself into her arms; there was something in her tone of voice that penetrated to her soul. She at length found utterance, and enquired her name.

"Adelaide Dorimond!" was the answer.

"Ah my beloved, my long lost mother, is it indeed you?" cried Caroline, passionately embracing her.

"My Child," faintly said the stranger, "is it my Caroline, once the image of her adored father?"

"No common interest," said Caroline, "led me to that spot where villany concealed my dearest tie on earth! Yes, my mother, look on your child, and oh do not refuse to acknowledge her!"

Adelaide pressed her to her heart.*

"Yes, it is my Caroline!—that sound of voice so like the one to which my heart was born to vibrate, tells me I am not mistaken! —I asked of heaven but once to fold thee in these arms—it has heard my prayer—I die in peace!"

Various emotions had so exhausted her feeble frame, that Caroline feared she had only found a parent, more acutely to feel her loss. She was immediately put to bed, and the room ordered to be profoundly still.

Dorville had already guessed the truth; he had interrogated Bertrand, who, full of contrition, spoke thus:—

"Guilty as I must appear, I fear, Sir, it will be impossible for me to persuade you, that I have suffered by the rigors I was compelled to inflict on a helpless female; but hear my whole confession, and then judge of my cruel state. I was born of poor parents, and about thirty years ago condemned, for the trifling crime of once attending a Huguenot meeting, to spend my life at the galleys.* In this dreadful slavery I had continued for some years, when one day I was accosted by a gentleman, who asked if I desired to be liberated; I eagerly assured him it was my most ardent wish. Then, said he—'It depends on yourself—I want a person on whose fidelity I can rely; he must be ready to execute my orders, without considering what they may be. If you are such a man, I engage to procure your liberty!'—I paused a moment—of what nature is the service you require, Sir? said I; if my conscience does not oppose it, you may command me.—'Conscience,' said he with a smile, 'is generally very compliant to galley slaves;* and I shall not require you to commit murder. Let me have no more questions—take a solemn oath to do whatever I order, provided it is short of murder, or deny me and remain a slave!'—I hesitated. My parents had brought me up with strict principles, and taught me to shun evil; and I was moreover, Sir, a rigid Catholic. My only design in attending the Huguenot meeting was to ridicule its tenets, and dearly I paid for the recreation. Conscience, therefore, forbid me to take an oath of obedience to commands whose import I could not guess. I made an effort, and rejected the proposal. Nevertheless, the idea of liberty once raised in my mind, made my situation yet more irksome; and as each day seemed to make our task-master more rigid, I began to repent the sacrifice I had made to conscience, when, in about a week, the gentleman returned, and found me employed in the severest toils. He shook his head as he passed, and my dejected look inspiring him with hopes that I should be more tractable, he ventured to try once more. Liberty with all its joys he offered, and shewed, on the other hand, all the horrors of the vilest slavery! I long doubted, but yielded at length. I took the oath prescribed, and in a few days was liberated by the Marquis of Bentivoglio. He carried me to Paris, where for some time no service was required which could make me regret the exchange I had made. At length, he one day told me to be in readiness for an important action, and above all to remember my oath, which he had caused to be renewed in the presence of a priest.

At midnight he summoned me to attend, with another man since dead, and conducted us to a small house in the suburbs of Paris; here we were ordered to secure the lady now in your possession, and secrete her for some months in the Marquis's hotel, after which, this Castle falling to him by inheritance, I conducted her here, and have ever since strictly guarded her! My heart frequently bled at her sorrows; and melted by her tears, I remonstrated, but my master with a stern look reminded me of my indissoluble engagement. He frequently left the Castle for months, and left only me. At length on his death-bed he charged me to feed her as usual till she died; never to discover her abode to any person, and should any body suspect it, to send for a boat, and conveying her to the shores of Spain, put her into the power of the inquisition as an heretic! I intreated him vainly to relent, and suffer her to be released; I pleaded that at his death my engagement ceased, and I was at liberty to break it. Though I could not obtain his consent, I resolved to consult my confessor, and stating the circumstance as well as I could without betraying the secret, was assured by him that an oath was sacred till the death of both dissolved it.* I now thought myself obliged to obey, and accordingly was preparing to execute his last orders, when you, Sir, happily prevented me! If this cannot excuse my guilt, I hope you will think it some palliation. My life indeed, I value not, for clogged by this fatal oath, it has long been a burthen. Another fruit of it still weighs heavy on my mind—but time and accident must also reveal this!"

Dorville was hastening to his wife with this communication, when informed by her that she had discovered her long lost mother. The joy of all was for a time abated by the ill state of the poor prisoner, whose extreme surprise at her liberation, and happy meeting with her child, threatened to prove fatal. At length, however, she recovered, and never was social happiness more complete, though it was long ere Adelaide, whom misfortune had so cruelly subdued, could feel that composure requisite to domestic comfort.

Caroline, the image of her once loved Henry, and her sweet babe, in time supplied to her the loss of every other tie; and though she could never entirely conquer the habitual melancholy that pervaded her mind, despair entirely subsided into pensive serenity and grateful resignation to that Providence which had so eminently protected her.

She related to Caroline, that on the dreadful night when her husband deprived himself of existence, while she was weeping over her, and expecting the return of Annette, two ruffians entered, of whom Bertrand was one, and conveyed her lifeless to the hated Marquis.

"In the state I was then in," continued Adelaide, "I thought myself callous to every suffering, till I beheld the detested wretch who had ruined my Henry. I had still strength to abhor him and his hateful purpose of seduction! He triumphed over my misfortunes with the most indignant pleasure, and boasted his power to compel what I refused! Kind heaven had not entirely deserted me—it brought, by a most unforeseen expedient, relief to my woes, and delivered me from those hated persecutions, more dreadful far than death! I began to grow ill after I had been at his hotel about a month, during which he confined his indignities to reproaches and menaces, without attempting to use violence, which he reserved till it should be impossible for me to be rescued, of which at Paris there was always danger. In the first symptoms of my indisposition, fearing that death might deliver me from his power, he made a concession, which he expected to produce an instantaneous effect; this was permitting me to write an account of my life to Annette, for the use of my child, stipulating, however, that he should peruse it, to be assured that it contained no latent hint of my situation. I was indefatigable in the task; and fearing that any accident should befall one manuscript, I wrote two, addressing one to my angelic protectress the Dutchess de Meronville. My pleasing employment had prevented me marking the progress of a disorder which rapidly increased, and soon discovered itself to be the small-pox. Bentivoglio now felt all the terrors of guilt on the eve of publicity. To leave me without assistance in so malignant a distemper, was to consign me to destruction, yet to call in a physician would give me an opportunity of disclosing the coercion he exercised. In this perplexity he assigned me a monk, who had superficially studied medicine, but whose chief recommendation was unlimited devotion to the will of his employer. This man I endeavoured frequently to move by entreaties and unfeigned tears, but ineffectually. He treated my disease with so little judgment that it became to all appearance mortal—how frequently have I since wished it had been so! Just Heaven, pardon the frailty of human nature, which presumed to arraign thy decrees by means infinitely various—thy will is accomplished, and I was reserved for future, but certain mercy! I was in so bad state that my body appeared a mass of horrid putrefaction, when Bentivoglio came one day to see me. He had never been attached to any thing but a few personal charms with which nature had endowed me. His passion now changed into unconquerable disgust, when he beheld that lump of clay, whose form had once charmed him, a striking emblem of human corruption! Though out of danger, I was for a considerable time a spectacle of horror to every beholder.* He seldom visited me, when he did it was to heap reproaches on my head.—'Ungrateful woman!' would he say, 'once I thought you worthy of my bed—you then rejected those proposals, too honourable far!—now your disgusting loathsome form extinguishes my love!—but think not to escape—you are yet a fit object for revenge! Confined in a dungeon, your days shall be consumed in repenting that haughtiness which denied my wishes! Shall your poisoned Henry rise to your relief? Shall he visit you in that living tomb which I give you as the jointure his love has left? Weep, wretched woman, your orphan child, for never again shall it know a mother's fondness, or a father's smile!'—This mention of my lost husband awakened all my tenderness; he saw the effect it had, and cruelly enjoyed it! I yet returned thanks to God who had delivered me from his love; confinement, chains, and tortures, were nothing to that! Conveyed here, I was confined in the dungeon where you found me. Deprived of light, of hope, of every thing which could beguile the slow progress of decrepid time, I yet felt comparatively easy in being relieved from the sensual attachment of the monster who had ruined my Henry! For my child I had no fears, for she was protected by the Duchess de Meronville. For a considerable time the Marquis brought me daily food, but never uttered a syllable; at length he returned no more, and Bertrand assumed his office. You know the rest; but I must request pardon for that man who acted himself under the influence of compulsion; for whenever he had an opportunity he rendered my confinement less dreadful by the loan of books, lights, and other comforts!"

When Madame Dorimond had ceased to speak, a long silence succeeded, Dorville and Caroline being unwilling, by expressing their detestation for the late Marquis, to wound the susceptible mind of his successor, whose virtues exceeded the vices of his brother. He was fully sensible of the enormity of the conduct of one so nearly allied to him, and proportionally lamented it. The happiness, however, of the young couple, and the restoration of Madame Dorimond was the fruit of his exertions. In tracing and establishing Caroline's rights to St. Jago, he felt rewarded by this for an age of sorrow, and almost forgot in their felicity that he could not partake it.

Old Annette was brought to the Castle, and passed her few remaining days there.

Bertrand, at the request of Adelaide, was pardoned, and lived to repent his errors.

CHAP. VII.

"Maître des passions! toi, qui forma mon âme,
"Ne peux tu dans mon sein étouffer cette flamme.
"Me vaincre, anéantir, ces traits persecuteurs,
"Qui, chaque jour, hélas! plus cher, plus enchanteurs,
"Reviennent de mes sens égarer la foiblesse?
"De cercueil entouré, je parle de tendresse!"*

The wretched Meronville, with accumulated grief, had, on returning from the cottage, thrown himself at the foot of the altar to implore the aid of Heaven. The Abbot, a man of real piety, had frequently observed his unconquerable despair, and thought it his duty to enquire its cause, and offer the consolation of religion; he followed him to the chapel, and after observing for some time his tears and agony, he called him by the name he had assumed in the fraternity. The Duke rose, and prostrated himself, as was usual, before the Superior.

"Rise!" said he; "my heart, sensible to your sorrows, invites you to repose them there. Your deep despair and gloomy sadness, visible to the whole community, are offensive to religion. I might exert my authority, point out your duty, and my rights; but I hate the appearance of virtue too severe; behold in me only a friend, a father, and a man born to compassionate the sorrows of humanity! No, religion does not prescribe rigor—it is not merciless—always open to the wretched, it offers its salutary aid to all who seek it! In a world, the abode of crimes and injustice, it is the only support of those whom Fortune oppresses! Is not mercy the attribute of the deity? and would not God less merciful, be less adorable? Oh, my son, repose your troubles in my bosom, and suffer me to offer comfort! Two years are elapsed, since, led by Heaven itself, you sought here a refuge from the storms of adversity in this sacred asylum, separated by God from the world! You bear sorrows, which should be banished from the retreat of religion—innocence of mind and virtuous peace reign here—you do not enjoy them—your affliction betrays itself—you sigh, you weep!—pour forth your agonies in my breast—the burthen shared becomes less weighty! For your sake, I relax the severity of our laws, I permit you to break the solemn silence they impose—I repeat it to you, genuine piety is not austere, it opens a sanctuary for all the wretched—humanity and mercy adorn its shrine!"

"To that shrine, my father," said Meronville, "I drag an unconquerable weight of woe."

"What crime," resumed the Abbot, "contaminates your soul? Conceal it not—religion has no secrets—whatever may be your guilt, remorse expiates it in the eyes of a merciful Saviour, whose lightning is extinguished by a single repentant tear! Crimes, which human justice punishes, are pardoned here!"

"Such guilt," replied the Duke, "never polluted my soul—one crime only I have committed!—it is irreparable! What am I going to tell you, oh my father! and what a place have we chosen to speak of love! In these walls, consecrated by the death of many a sainted Monk, and sacred alone to religion, may I then recall the world and its delusions, its false grandeur and fugitive joys? You command it; receive then my confession, and supplicate my Creator to extinguish that flame which destroys his image in my subject soul!"

Meronville then related the history of his misfortunes to Father Francis, who was deeply affected, and could hardly permit him to conclude ere he exclaimed—

"Heavens, what a link of woes! To what storms is the life of man exposed!—the world how full of tempests!—how subject to continual wrecks!—Fragile mortals, like reeds before the wind, bend, totter, and sink!—Oh Providence supreme, Almighty God! by what unknown paths dost thou conduct humanity to the destined port!"

"Driven to excess," continued Meronville, "I sought this solitude—you received me—I knelt at the foot of the altar—my prayers mingled with your's—but Emily was still the divinity I adored!—I summoned reason to my aid, but found it a feeble support, for I was yet guided by that impotent and barren philosophy, which brings no relief, and whose sophistries only irritate our wounds! In grief my days begin and end! the rising sun witnesses my tears, and its declining rays leave them undried! Towards religion my eyes are raised, and enlightened reason views it with transport; but my heart is yet unsubdued; a guilty flame still burns within it; one seducing object pursues my steps, even to yon grave, which I prepare to receive my ashes! Oh, my father, assist me to conquer it, and point my hopes to heaven!"

"It is not I, my son," said the holy man, "a frail mortal like yourself, that can succour you—to Heaven alone you must apply—it will assist you to subdue this tyrant passion! Defended by it, you have nothing to fear—continue your efforts—it is only after a combat that we gather the laurels of victory! You are not the only one, who, in this solitude, groans under a weight of affliction! Brother Ambrose is no less the victim of it—he was admitted the day you were professed—his year of novitiate is now expired—I was prepared to bind him in holy chains—but the hand of death is on him—at the foot of the altar he groans, and seems to attend your steps as though sensible that you are brothers in affliction!"

"Frequently I have observed him," replied Meronville; "the iron hand of adversity oppresses his soul—my grave is sometimes bathed with his tears—an involuntary impulse prompts me to inquire the cause of his grief, but, submissive to our laws, I preserve silence."

The Abbot was then called away, and the Duke found himself partially relieved by the disclosure he had made. He left the chapel, and hastened to the grave, which he was condemned each day to enlarge. It was in the midst of a wood; as he approached it, he met Brother Ambrose, and saluted him with "*Memento mori!*" The Monk, without reply, continued his solemn pace. Meronville reached the grave, he saw his coffin bedewed with tears, and began to dig.

"Oh earth!" he said, "sole refuge of the miserable, soon shall my dust return to thee!—there shall my sorrows find rest!—in that little space shall be entombed a weight of anguish!—all shall there be forgotten—even hope—even despair—ah, even love! What do I say? I yet live—I yet burn—I bow to Heaven—but Emily alone I adore! Pardon me, gracious Heaven!—let this be my last sigh—let me for the last time look on that portrait, which, in spite of my vows, recalls me to the world—let me throw it from me—but no, it entwines about my heart, and death, only death, can detach it!"

He drew the portrait from his bosom, and bathed it with tears. A piercing shriek roused him; he turned, and saw the unfortunate Ambrose supporting himself against a tree. He advanced towards him; he made a sign for him to retreat. Meronville, forgetting his vows, entreated him to indulge his sorrows by communicating them. He shook his head, and retired, crying—

"Ah, Duke de Meronville!"

Astonishment arrested his steps; his rank was unknown in the Monastery; he had carefully concealed it. Who then could have penetrated the secret? A trouble and confusion, new to him, added now to his melancholy. Ambrose pursued his steps, and he felt an unaccountable interest in being near him; nevertheless he was daily and evidently verging towards the tomb. Compelled by the rigid rules of the order to continue his usual occupations, he performed them with the languor of ill-health and decaying nature. No physicians were ever admitted; nor were any remedies suffered but in the extremity, when they usually came too late. Ambrose was obliged to rise at three in the morning, to read, pray, and work, like the rest. To accept broth or any relief would have been thought disgraceful. Even when he could no longer support himself, he repaired to matins and vespers, leaning on the arm of one of the fraternity. Meronville was always foremost to assist him, and would willingly have kept for him the midnight vigils when it was his turn to watch.

One day he was accosted by the Abbot, who told him a stranger wished for an interview with one of the community.

"Some sinner," said he, "conducted perhaps by Heaven, demands a conference with me! To this sacred ministry I was early called, and am ignorant of the ways of a world from which I am excluded—more enlightened by the torch of affliction and experience, you must possess the benevolent means of healing the wounded heart, and combatting the senses! Go then, point out that God who ever watches over us—shew him as he is—just, but merciful! Convince the stranger by your own experience—prove to him the danger, the trouble, the tortures of uncontrouled passions! I permit you to speak—to sympathize with the unfortunate, share their sorrows, and administer relief, are the first duties imposed by Heaven—go, and fulfil them! Speak to the stranger, while at the altar you offer incense and tears for frail mortality!

Meronville obeyed, and sought the intruder, though little inclined to the converse of any being who inhabited the world.

He started as the stranger entered, retreated a few steps, and seemed unable to support himself, for he beheld the rival he had once dreaded—the Chevalier Dorimond!* An involuntary exclamation betrayed him. Dorimond recognised him—

"Heavens, is it possible?" he cried, "the Duke de Meronville!"

"Titles," replied the Duke, "are banished from these abodes—pride here is deprived of its ornaments! But Oh, say what has brought you here? have you news of Emily? Alas, I wander—she is no more! Is her tyrant husband satisfied? Do her ashes rest in peace? Impious mortal! darest thou violate this sacred sanctuary, and let thy thoughts rove to a world thou hast abandoned? Pardon, great God, my weakness!"

"Heavens," cried Dorimond, "it is Meronville himself!"

"Himself indeed!" said the Duke, "who, to conquer an ill-fated and hopeless passion, sought these sacred solitudes, resolved to live and die in them! But how are they profaned by sighs and tears devoted to a mortal! Concealed from nature itself—in the midst of remorse, prayers, and tears, a guilty flame still burns within me—corrodes my reason, and tears me from my God! But say, Chevalier, what brought you hither?"

"My brother," replied the Marquis, "is dead, and Emily still lives!"

"Lives!" repeated Meronville, "did you say lives? Oh complete my guilt—speak of her—nourish the flame in this bosom—make me a wretch indeed! But no, banish her from my remembrance—name her not—I will not listen!——Yet tell me, how was she restored? Is she happy? Is peace an inmate of her bosom? Does she sometimes think of me? Are her charms——alas! how am I betrayed by this guilty passion! Religion lends its aid, but I refuse it! My arm is raised against the Power Supreme—the voice of Heaven is stilled, is stifled in the name of Emily! Yes, I know it, I offend thee, oh God—I resist thy orders! Begone, Dorimond, let me forget her!"

"Alas!" replied he, "I suffer no less than you! But hear me: Bentivoglio, enraged with his wife's supposed infidelity, confined her, after my departure, in a dungeon, near to one in which another victim of his was entombed!* By an extraordinary accident the latter was discovered; she had heard Emily's groans, and directed us to seek her. We found her, and restored her to liberty—her husband was no more—she thought herself permitted to pronounce your name! The Duchess de Meronville, mourning your loss, was at St. Jago—she could give no tidings of your retreat. I saw that Emily, pining at your lot, enjoyed not the happiness of being freed from a tyrant husband—I undertook to seek you, though without communicating my design. During a whole twelvemonth I have traversed France in vain. Judging that you had chosen some Monastery as an asylum, I passed none without enquiry. My researches were almost ended, when chance led me here. Are your vows yet unpronounced? Are you yet free?"

Meronville threw himself on the ground.

"Great God! am I sufficiently wretched? Is thy vengeance satisfied? Emily is free—I am for ever enchained! But for these fatal bonds I might be now at her feet, calling her the arbitress of my destiny, pouring forth my soul in effusions of love! Begone, cruel Dorimond! fly for ever! Why did you tear the bandage from my eyes? Why not leave me in blissful ignorance? Are you come to render my tortures more infernal—to alienate me still more from my God? Such designs are worthy a rival!"

"Is it possible?" cried the Marquis. "Are these sacred fetters—"

"Eternal!" exclaimed the Duke; "death alone can break them, and each day they must now become more insupportable! What have I to hope but the termination of a life, long consumed by remorse and endless sorrows? But what does a dreadful futurity offer to a soul, which, while it is consecrated to God, worships a mortal? I see nothing beyond the grave but an avenging arm, ready to strike, to punish my impiety—in this horrid gulph my senses are lost! She is free—I love her—I adore her—heaven and honour, in vain you oppose the flame it rekindles—Afresh from every opposition, I tell my passion to the morning sun, and repeat it in the midnight hour!"

"Meronville, you may yet be restored to her!" said Dorimond; "take my habit, give me your's—the world has no charms for me —fly to Emily—I shall be happy here—religion will have more power over my mind, because freedom gives me no hopes! Do not hesitate—the invariable silence preserved here will prevent the cheat being discovered. What say you, Meronville?"

"The cloud of death overwhelms me!" said he in a solemn tone. "Shall I break these sacred vows? or, can I erase them from the register of heaven? Yet were not my oaths of tenderness, of fidelity to Emily, first enrolled there? Are they not equally binding? Is man a slave fettered by heaven? Is that merciful God who created us, who is the benefactor of our race, whom we are taught to love, is he an implacable tyrant that can behold with pleasure the envenomed shaft that pierces our heart? Were we designed by him for a living tomb? Can my tears sooth his jealous fury? or my torments add to his glory and greatness? Would it be rendering him a worthy homage, to consume my days in hated hopeless slavery? No, I resume my rights—these chains are the work of man—feeble humanity was formed for liberty—our sins and frailties already load us with fetters—we have no right to increase the burden—no, it is an impious design, condemned by Heaven! Vows, oaths, chains, farewell! you are all forgotten—I fly to thee, my Emily!"

A groan here interrupted his rhapsody. He started to see whence it issued. Brother Ambrose was kneeling at the base of the altar.

"Heavens!" said Meronville, "why does that sound penetrate my inmost soul?"

Ambrose rose, lifted his hands to heaven, then disappeared.

The bell tolled—the fraternity were summoned to the refectory—the Marquis promised to return, and Meronville to consider his proposal, and they parted.

Meronville repaired to the chapel, where the Marquis was to meet him. He stood for some time reflecting, surrounded with graves and images of death.

"What am I going to do?" said he, "and to what crimes does love lead me? To blaspheme my Creator—to outrage the Deity—to defy his omnipotence—to mock the Divinity, by breaking my sacred chains!—If that vain phantom which deludes mortals, and which the world calls honour—if that which is no virtue, but only the semblance of it, bound a frivolous promise, should I not blush to break it? When now religion and the host of heaven sanctioned vows directed to God himself, I am ready to betray them, to sacrifice them to profane love! But no, if God indeed was offended by this flame, would not he extinguish it? Shades of departed saints, leave your sacred receptacles, and come to my relief—I see you looking on me, trembling for my apostacy! The gulph of eternity is open—horrid spectres rise—oh, save me, Heaven!"

He concealed his face, and remained some time in prayer; as he rose, a phantom stood erect before him; a hollow voice addressed him—

"What are you about to do? Pause, presumptuous mortal! Heaven extends its arms to receive you, and you fly from it! Those chains that bind you, are the work of God—think not to escape the vengeance due to perjury! Hear your sentence—if you leave these walls, hell opens to receive you! Tremble!—The demon asks his prey—heaven abandons you—you are lost to all eternity!"

It vanished. He fell on his knees.

"It must be so! great God, receive me! Yes, I will banish that image I adore—which shares my heart, and disputes its empire with thee! Thy warning shall not be vain—I will forget her—I will die here!"

As he pronounced these words, Dorimond returned.

"Now, Meronville," said he, "is the moment—do not hesitate—fly to secure your own happiness and that of Emily! At this holy shrine I accept the vows you resign, and am ready to confirm them by new ones!"

"Generous rival!" cried Meronville; "no, 'tis you must go! Seek my first, my only love, and tell her it is my wish, my last prayer, that to you her affections be transferred! You will make her happy—you will teach her to forget me! But fly instantly—I fear my own weakness—it may again betray me into doubt! Do not try to shake my resolves—a warning from heaven has made them immutable! Go to Emily; for the last time I pronounce that darling name, tell her Heaven has made me its own! I go to pray for her! Alas! the dear idea of her my soul worships will, till my latest hour, mingle in the fondest vibrations of my heart!"

"Let me persuade you," interrupted Dorimond, "to——"

"Avaunt!" cried the Duke, "I must not hear you! Know you not that no eloquence is so persuasive as that which prompts us to what we earnestly desire? But just restored to myself, reconciled to my Creator, you would again plunge me into that gulph from which I only now emerge! No, Emily, your lover will die worthy of you!"

Deep and successive groans interrupted him; he started, and looked around to see whence they issued, but could discover no person.

"From the depth of the silent tomb," said he, "those sounds arose! My guilt awakens the spirits of the long-forgotten dead, and causes tumults in the solemn sepulchres of departed saints!"

Dorimond himself felt awed; the tenebrose gloom of the place, and the lugubrious sound vibrating on his ear, struck to his soul, and taking a melancholy farewell of Meronville, he retired with a determination of instantly returning to Emily.

Meronville, hourly more wretched himself, yet could not help feeling for Brother Ambrose, whose unshared sorrows seemed precipitating him to an early tomb. A sentiment, to which he could attach no name, took possession of his heart, and deeply impressed it for that unfortunate recluse. After the loss of Emily, he had thought it impossible that any affliction could touch his soul; yet he seemed to participate every tear, every sigh, that wrung the bosom of the poor Monk. How frequently does the too susceptible mind suffer more than the pangs of mortality, and how feeble is the aid reason lends to subjugate the more powerful feelings! Immersed within walls where repose and tranquillity appeared to have fixed their peaceful abode, he sought repose in vain; his own sensitive heart supplied sorrows with prolific abundance. Ambrose seemed to avoid him at the moment he pursued him. Frequently he found him with his spade in his hand, digging at his grave; he would quit it hastily when Meronville appeared, and the handle was ever bedewed with new-fallen tears.

The Duke at length mentioned the circumstance to the Abbot, who informed him Ambrose, after frequently postponing the day of his profession, had at length fixed it for that day se'nnight. He added, that previous to administering the vows, it was his design to interrogate him on the subject of his profound anguish, and the predilection he seemed to have for always pursuing the steps of Meronville.

Each day made the latter more interested in his fate. On the eve of that day, when he was to be irrevocably admitted a member of the sacred community, the Duke had a vision, which, in spite of reason, made an impression on his mind that almost deprived him of sense. The evening had been spent in preparations for the ensuing solemnity; he retired to rest, and fell into a slumber so profound that it resembled the sleep of death! His perturbed imagination wandering into an infinitude of wild horrors, at length led him to a vast and dreary plain. The sky was dense and dark; it opened at intervals, and dreadful lightnings burst forth, succeeded by claps of thunder, that appeared to shake the universe. Trembling, he fleeted across the plain, but sought shelter in vain; the fury of the storm pursued him, and destruction hovered in the blast. Screech-owls and birds of prey, terrified, fell lifeless to the ground; the sable raven only fixed on him, and took shelter under his habit.* After long wandering, he darted into a wood, whose trees, the growth of ages, spread their umbrageous branches, and appeared to offer a secure retreat; but scarce had he entered it, than a scene no less dreadful than that which he had escaped presented itself. He was impelled forward by an invisible power, acting in defiance of his will. He found himself in an extensive cemetery. Innumerable spectres rose to view: some even in death retained the traces of native ferocity; others exhibited that pensive melancholy which told of mortal sorrows. These wandered amidst the tombs, echoing groans to those which issued from the sepulchres below. Confused noises filled the air, and seemed repeated by numerous and distant echoes. Antique monuments and ruins of mausoleums, once formed to receive the remains of departed magnificence, were spread around. To the eye, the ear, the heart, and all the subject senses, death in every horrid shape presented itself. Still as Meronville stretched the optic nerve to compass this vast and terrific scene, its limits seemed to extend; he could have fancied it the common sepulchre of the universe.* Whilst he was contemplating in mournful affright each object, which equally claimed his attention, though none could fix it, a groan so deep, so piercing, burst from a tomb, as seemed prophetic of some dread apparition. A torch, whose dim and blue light increased the awful horror of the place, first appeared. The whole cemetery was instantly involved in obscurity. A phantom rose, bearing the torch; it shrieked, and wore a female form, but clad in deep mourning. As it advanced towards Meronville, he cried—"Emily!" and flew to clasp it in his arms; but while he thought to press at his throbbing heart that form so dear, it burst from him, and became that of Brother Ambrose. His mantle opened, his heart displayed itself enveloped in flames, which seemed every moment rekindled. He vanished by degrees, and as he sunk into the grave, assumed again the semblance of Emily, who, in a solemn tone, addressed him thus—

"Cruel lover! am I not sufficiently wretched? do you desire to increase my torments? Behold these flames—they consume my days—happy if they could expiate the crime of that guilty passion which attends me to another world! Repent! it is yet time—let your tears and prayers, addressed to heaven, obtain redemption for two souls united in one error! Follow me—I wait for you—I go to prepare for you!"

It vanished. The tomb closed with a sound so hollow that it shook the concave of heaven, and the earth was convulsed.*

Meronville trembled and awoke. He rose from his humble couch, and paced his little cell. Fancy or reality again conveyed the sound of deep lament to his ear; he listened, rubbed his eyes, and was convinced that he was now awake, and concluded that the sighs and groans penetrated through the thin partition which divided his from the adjoining cell. Yet wherefore should they so deeply interest him? Why call forth that sympathetic tear reserved only for Emily? His heart palpitated; he meditated entering the cell to enquire whence that grief sprung, which in accents so plaintive communicated itself to his heart.

When the bell rung for matins he heard a voice exclaim—

"Ah, that sound announces the return of morn!—but day-light to me is as the darkest night! When next the sun's refulgent orb shall rise to bless the universe, I shall be——oh God! let me not think how much more closely I shall be united to misery! Supreme Creator, ah deign to listen to my prayer, ere I pronounce those vows my heart rejects—take my immortal soul to thee, and let my perishable body unite with its parent dust! Destroy that flame which kindles at a mortal name, and substitute the pure love of thy divinity! Yes, I am heard at this moment—I feel thy vivifying spirit within—my soul recognises, loves, and blesses its God!"

Meronville suspended his respiration, fearful of losing one of those accents, which, he doubted not, flowed from the lips of the Monk who was that day to be received into the fraternity. He entered the chapel and looked for Ambrose—he was there, reclining on the arm of the infirmary keeper. The Duke, whilst others raised their eyes to heaven, fixed his on the mournful recluse, whose weakness and debility announced approaching dissolution. The vision he had seen preyed on his mind, and was so correspondent with the words he had heard in the neighbouring cell, that he dreaded the event.

Ten in the morning was the hour fixed for the ceremony of

profession. The monks all assembled in the chapel, and prayed to God to consecrate the vows he was about to about to receive. Only Brother Ambrose was absent. The deep-toned organ sounded through the long aisles its solemn notes in unison with the place. The monks raised their voices, and chanted to the praises of their Almighty Creator. The infirmary keeper by a sign called the Abbot away. The friars, whose thoughts, elevated to sublime subjects, were lost in divine contemplations, did not observe his departure; but Meronville fancied every casual circumstance connected with Brother Ambrose, and shuddered at his fate.

In a few moments the melodious notes of the organ ceased, and were succeeded by the hollow discordant sound of the death bell; it tolled with awful solemnity, and chilled the heart of Meronville. In a moment the fraternity were mute, and ventured to look on each other with surprise and horror. The Abbot at length returned. He prostrated himself before the cross; then broke silence—

"Death," said he, "lays his hand on one of us! Brother Ambrose touches at that dreadful hour, which delivers us to the sentence of an incorruptible judge! Man by nature is criminal. Let us unite our voices, and raise them to the eternal throne of mercy! Let fervent prayer ascend to Heaven for his sins. Devotion, and resignation to the Almighty will, opens the way to the blessed abodes prepared for penitents! Prayer lends its aid to the tears of repentance, delivers us from infernal snares, suspends the stroke of heavenly vengeance, extinguishes its lightnings, disarms an offended God, and claims redemption for our souls! For Brother Ambrose let us now implore the aid of providence, that, triumphing over mortal weakness, he may receive the sacred fire of hope, drink of the cup of mortality without bitterness, and that his soul in peace, rejecting worldly ties, may rush with ecstacy into the presence of its Creator!"

Two Monks now entered, one bearing an urn filled with ashes, the other a truss of straw. They spread them on the ground to form a sort of bed. Ambrose then appeared, supported on each side, and feebly dragged himself towards the bed of ashes, on which he was soon stretched, and Father Francis resumed his speech.

"At the request of the dying Brother I have relaxed the severity of our laws, and permitted him to speak ere he dies—he wishes to reveal a secret, which he says may edify those that he leaves in this world of trial! All you, who, though now inhabiting this sacred

asylum, were once members of the world, who have witnessed the
death of heroes, or persons called virtuous, approach now, and
behold the end of a Christian! Speak, Brother, we await your secret!"

"You permit me, Father?" said the dying recluse. "The unfortunate Ambrose may, animated by celestial transports, reveal a secret,
which will render God more visible, more revered in this his chosen
sanctuary. His arm, by ways unknown, has led me from the confines
of hell to the sweet anchorage of heavenly hope! Let my lips, O
God, by a supernatural effort, afford a shining proof of thy glory,
reanimate my expiring voice, suspend my fleeting breath, that I may
declare thy wondrous works! Virtuous recluses! you thought my zeal,
my piety, sincere; worthy of the rank to which you raised me—you
thought that faith and religion led me to your sacred shrine—but
'tis time to undeceive you!—Behold in me the sad victim of sensibility—behold *a woman!*"—A general groan interrupted her.—
"Yes," she continued, "a woman who has lived for man—but dies
for God!—a guilty miserable woman, who calls on religion to assist
her end!"—She lifted her cowl, which had concealed her features.—
"Look on me, Meronville! Listen, and recognize her who took love
for her guide—her who misled you——"

"Ah, heavens, my Emily!" cried the Duke, throwing himself on
the ground by her; "here will I also die!—one tomb shall receive us!"

"Meronville, if I am still dear to you, cease to offend heaven by
unavailing regrets—God chastens but to shew his love! Rise and
listen; our sorrows have brought reproach on this holy fraternity—we owe to it a great example of repentance! Behold," said
she, addressing the superior, "the fatal object of an impious worship! Yes, I loved him too much, too well—jealous heaven was
betrayed, forgotten! For the sake of this lover I espoused a man I
detested! God pronounced his malediction on a union formed with
such views! My cruel husband*——But pardon, oh God! can I call
that cruelty which was the instrument of your vengeance!—By his
death released from bondage, I flew to enquire for Meronville—
his mother long mourned his absence—we mingled our tears and
regrets. By the rugged path of misfortune heaven frequently leads
us to itself, and opens our hearts to God; but mine rejected his
image—Meronville alone filled it—at his name it beat—he returned
incessantly to my mind—reason, honour, all were forgotten!—I left
his mother, and taking a male habit, caused a report of my death to

be spread—I sought my lover throughout the kingdom—a friend of his lived not far from hence—I stopped to gaze on the gloomy scene around, and the sound of the organ drew me to the chapel—I entered—heavens at what a moment! Amid the united voices that sung the praises of God, I recognised one that would have recalled me from the grave, and I too soon discovered that he was at that moment pronouncing vows that decided his fate and mine for ever! Here, holy Father, we discover the hand of Providence. Impelled by a motive too strong for resistance, and which conquered even love itself, I entered this temple, led by God himself. At the sound of that voice, to which my delighted ear had been so long accustomed, I fancied myself deluded by a dream. I drew near, and all doubt was removed! Notwithstanding the ravage time and affliction had made on those features, I discerned through the furrows of adversity the object of an eternal flame, so dear, so seducing—the master of my soul—I made an exclamation, compounded of horror, joy, surprise, and love. Your devotions were too profound to be easily interrupted, and I escaped detection. But ah, gracious God! what were my emotions? every opposing passion by turns agitated my bosom, already cruelly lacerated by suffering! I enquired, and learned that Meronville had indeed that day made his profession. Far from blessing the Almighty, who had called him to this holy ministry, I blasphemed his name, accused him of injustice, of rigour, partiality, and every failing that belongs only to humanity! Great God, thou didst not punish my impieties, but employed misfortune to attract me to thyself! I formed the presumptuous design of detaching from its Maker a soul that appeared full of divine love—I resolved to become the rival of my God!"

"Avenging God," cried Meronville, "is thy jealousy appeased?"

"Return thanks to that power," continued Emily, "that spares us now! Shall we augment the number of ungrateful creatures?—we who have been rescued by him from a dreadful precipice, and led by ways, inscrutable to man, to the path of salvation! After such various and infinite cares, I at length found the object of my researches— my aching eyes once more rested on his loved image—but oh, grief inexpressible! torture inconceivable to a heart burning with love— he was lost to me for ever! I, once his sole idol, was sacrificed to my God! Oh thou to whom my reproaches ascended, thou didst not send thy lightning to consume me; no, this detested passion was made subservient to your designs, and proved a magnet to attract me to thy altar! What ties, alas! attached me to this spot?—twenty times I abandoned these walls, and as often returned. How could I leave a scene so dear, which became my heaven, since he I only loved, lived and must die here? The air he inhaled, I might also respire—I should be near him—I should see him, if fatal silence prevented my telling him to what excess he was adored—if I must suppress my sighs, and conceal the ardent fire that consumed me, at least I might ease his labours, pursue his steps, and in death be united with him! Such were the sentiments that led me here; I nourished in my breast these culpable designs, when you, Father, received me into this sacred community. In vain you sought to terrify me by an account of the austerities of a monastic life. Meronville had chosen it, and nothing could alarm me. My eagerness appeared to you the effect of holy fervor—God only can penetrate the deep disguise of human perfidy! You permitted me to try the chain; I extended my arms to receive it, for it was worn by Meronville! What a heart did you admit, oh Father! all its disorders must now be developed! Ah wretch, ever at the altar's foot, you believed me the servant of God—but no, I was the slave of man—to man my homage was offered—to man my sacrilegious vows were paid! Oh God, a man was your rival—your conqueror! Ah, what do I say! Meronville was the only deity I acknowledged! The companion of his steps, certain that here our melancholy career must terminate, that near his my ashes would rest, at his side I groaned, I lamented, and in the sole pleasure of loving, without hope or return, I fancied myself happy! Could the most virtuous ardour have been stronger? I did not even observe that a gloomy languor, overspreading my life, faded the blossom of youth; nevertheless I was verging towards the grave. In that grave which my hands had dug, I sat and deplored not my sad destiny, I grieved only that in the tomb I could no longer adore Meronville! But 'twas in that spot, chosen for the deposit of his ashes, that my tears abundantly flowed—'twas there my anguish became mortal! Yet, solicitous to ease his labours, I forgot my languour and weakness; the spade he resigned, I took and bathed with scalding tears! But a few weeks ago, when the hand of death oppressed me, I tried to resume it; but my heart betrayed the design, and the fatal instrument eluded my grasp. You will be surprised that with so much weakness, and governed by the wildest

transports of love, a woman could triumph over the powerful suggestions of her heart, and not discover herself to the tyrant of her
soul! Ah, think not 'twas virtue or religion withheld me; no, it still
was love, and the fear of troubling that repose he appeared to enjoy.
I thought that the God I now revere had attached him by the purest
devotion to his own worship. His tears, his deep sighs, I thought
the happy fruits of religion. Confining myself to the pleasure of
seeing and hearing him, great God, how frequently did my steps,
my voice, my too tender heart, seem ready to betray me! But I loved
him too sincerely—I concealed that flame, which, fostering in my
bosom, consumed my vitals, and taught me to die! How prolix is
the historian of love! Pardon me, Father, my end approaches! A few
weeks ago, led by the arm of God, I entered the wood; my trembling
steps guided me to the tomb of Meronville; he was bedewing it with
tears—he left it—I dragged my feeble body to the spot, and in my
dying bosom tried to reap those precious tears! My feelings could
be now no longer controuled; in vain love itself opposed them, for
love to love was opposed. I determined to be convinced of the cause
of his grief—I drew near—I heard him pronounce my name—I
looked—ah, gracious God support me—I saw his tears fall on my
portrait! My heart deserted its mansion, quivered on my lips, and
pronounced his name!—life fled from my bosom, and left me expiring!—the heavy, but cold stroke of death, has ever since been there!"

Meronville now rose, and seemed hastening away.

"Where are you going?" said she.

"To seek," said he wildly, "some assistance to deliver me from
woes past endurance!—from the burthen of life!—from an existence which thy vengeance, oh God, pursues!—to pierce this bosom
with a thousand strokes!"

"Meronville, you once loved me!" said Emily.

"Loved you!" repeated he, "ah, to an excess of distraction I still
adore you!"

"Then stay," said Emily, "and learn remorse from me—my life has
been your destruction, let my death be the instrument of salvation!
You know my guilt, now learn its chastisement! Yielding at last to
the sovereign hand that ruled my destiny, I returned from the gates
of death. With opened eyes I saw the heavy hand of God weighing
on my lover, punishing him of whom I was the guilty accomplice!
What do I say?—the crime was only mine! Eternal Justice, pardon

him, and let me only suffer! Oh Meronville, too dear, too wretched mortal! I asked of God to take my life for your sake!—he has heard my prayer, and even now grants my petition! My tenderness, purified by his aid, conjures you to repent, to expiate our mutual errors, by restoring to him that heart I once possessed! Oh ever dear, ever loved friend, I entreat you not to mourn my death; no, let those tears fall only for my life! Ah, let your heart, since it must be so, forget me, banish my image, and make place for God!—obey his voice—submit to his will!—Say, will you by this promise ease my last moments?"

"Oh Emily!" cried he.

"Disdain not the hand that offers to guide you," replied Emily; "let religion henceforth supply to you the place of every thing you have lost; and promise me——"

"I promise every thing!" cried he with energy; "to live, to die for you!"

Emily drew back the hand he passionately grasped.

"Leave me!" said she. "I still dread, oh God, this flame, which death only can extinguish!"—Addressing the fraternity, she continued,—"Oh ye, whom I no longer dare call my brethren, unite for me your regrets, your prayers—I was denied your virtues—I knew how to respect them! Tremble all you that listen; these are the effects of the passions, the fatal illusions of sensibility!* One more request may I offer? Father, may I hope that when the hour appointed by heaven is come, when the lifeless form of him I love shall be inanimate as mine, our ashes shall unite? our cold remains be deposited in one tomb? Alas! is this my last wish? And do my dying accents speak of love? is my latest breath exerted to pronounce thy name? my parting sigh heaved to thy remembrance? thy idea mingled in the last vibration of my heart? Farewell! no more will I return to thee! But oh, remember, my spirit, even after death, shall linger on the verge of eternity, and wait to unite with thine!"*

Life fast receded from her bosom; her eyes closed; the bell ceased to toll; her spirit had flown to heaven!

FINIS.

NOTES

(p. 1) *Kings of the Carlovingian race:* the Carlovingians (or Carolingians), a powerful Frankish noble family, gained increasing power in the late 7th century, and in 751 a Carolingian, Pepin the Short, was crowned King of the Franks, founding a dynasty that persisted until it was displaced in most principalities in 888. The greatest Carolingian monarch was Charlemagne, crowned by Pope Leo III at Rome in 800.

those civil wars, in the reign of Charles the Ninth: The reign of Charles IX (1550-1574), who ruled France from 1560 until his death, was dominated by a series of religious wars between Huguenot and Catholic factions associated with aristocratic houses: from 1562 to 1563, from 1567 to 1570, and from 1572, the Huguenots finally being granted substantial freedoms and rights by the Edict of Nantes in 1598, although hostilities did not altogether cease then.

the celebrated Admiral Coligni: Gaspard de Coligny (1519-1572) held the office of Admiral of France, and was a Huguenot leader who demanded religious toleration and other reforms. When the religious wars began in 1562, he took up arms reluctantly and was always ready to negotiate. After the Peace of Saint-Germain in 1570, he became quite influential with the young Charles IX, and was particularly hated by the Catholic Henri, Duke of Guise, who accused Coligny of being responsible for the assassination of his father, François de Guise, during the siege of Orléans in 1562. Coligny was murdered by a servant of the Duke of Guise on the night of the St. Bartholomew's Day massacre in August 1572, a subject treated by Baculard d'Arnaud in his play, *Coligny; ou, La Saint Barthélemi, tragédie* (1750).

(p. 2) *the Grand Constableship:* an extremely powerful position at this time. As the Lieutenant-General of the King, the Grand Constable outranked all the nobles and was second-in-command only to the King. He was Commander-in-Chief of the army, and responsible for its finances, military justice and chivalry.

Poltrot: Jean de Poltrot (c. 1537-1563) a fanatical Huguenot nobleman of Angoumois, who murdered François, Duke of Guise. He was tried, tortured, and sentenced to a dreadful death.

(p. 3) *Marquis de Lusignan:* Lusignan is named for a noble family with whom many legends are associated and who held what was at one time the largest castle in France, near Poitiers. The Lusignan family, as lords and kings, feature greatly in stories about the Crusades in the East from the 12th to 15th centuries. Early in Vol. I, Ch. VII of *Lusignan* the author has Lusignan survey weapons and armour at Luneville Castle that bear "the insignia of the Crusades." The old Christian father of Voltaire's heroine Zaïre, in his tragedy of that name, is also called "Lusignan," and is mentioned by Baculard d'Arnaud, in his *Discours Préliminaire* to *Les Amans Malheureux, ou Le Comte de Comminge* (1764) La Haye (Paris): L'Esclapart, 1765, p. 10.

(p. 7) *Carthusian Monastery*: The Carthusian Order is a Roman Catholic religious order of enclosed monastics which takes its name from the Chartreuse Mountains in the French Alps. As the order has neither abbots nor abbeys, the author is not accurate in later calling the monastery "the Abbey of Semur," or referring to Lusignan's uncle as the "Superior" and "Abbot of Semur". In Claudine-Alexandrine de Tencin's *Memoirs of the Count of Comminge* (London: G. Kearsley, 1774), pp. 14-15, the Abbot of Rouillon acquaints the family "that the titles of the estate, on which the law-suit depended, [are] lodged in the archives of his abbey, where the deeds of [their] own family had been concealed during the confusion of the civil wars." This abbot has no further role in de Tencin's narrative.

Montpelier: Montpellier, on the Mediterranean in the south of France, is described by John Armstrong in *The Art of Preserving Health*, Book I ("Air"), l. 196, as "pure Montpelier." The air of "Montpelier" is also said to "afford relief" to the ailing in health by La Luc's physician in Ann Radcliffe's *The Romance of the Forest*, edited by Chloe Chard (Oxford: Oxford University Press, 1998), p. 291. The proximity of the St. Clément spring, which had enabled the construction of many elaborate fountains in the town, was no doubt another facet of Montpellier's reputation for a wholesome and recuperative climate for the frail, sick and invalided. The purpose and atmosphere of such spa towns also encouraged sociability and the formation of friendships.

(p. 8) *fête champêtre*: Fr., an outdoor entertainment or sumptuous garden party.

the Medicean Venus: The Hellenistic life-size size marble sculpture depicting Aphrodite, the Greek goddess of love, which became known via the publication in 1648 of its existence in the Medici collection in the Villa Medici in Florence. It is still housed in Florence, in the Uffizi Gallery. In the 18th century, it was a popular referent for ideal female beauty; for example, the same image is used erotically by Matthew Lewis early in Chapter I of *The Monk*.

(p. 10) *affaire d'honneur*: Fr., a matter of honour, especially a duel.

(p. 11) *He now congratulated himself . . . Abbaye of Semur*: Lusignan's motive for adopting an alias is the same as that of de Tencin's Comminge, whose father had thought it expedient for him to assume the title of the Marquis of Longville, "the better to escape suspicion at the abbey where the Marchioness of Lussan had many relations". However, without Lusignan's rejection of aggrandizement, Comminge continues to go under his assumed name only "because it would have been requisite to have appeared with a grander retinue to support the dignity of the house of Comminge" (*Memoirs*, op. cit., pp. 16-20).

epigraph: from Hoole's 1772 translation in heroic couplets.

(p. 16) *I would chiefly guard you against the errors of sensibility, and a too fervid imagination:* Madame de Clarival's warning to Emily of the dangers of sensibility is a reworking of the deathbed warnings of St. Aubert to Emily in Radcliffe's *The Mysteries of Udolpho*, edited with an introduction and notes by Jacqueline Howard, vol. I, pp. 78-79:

> Above all, my dear Emily, [. . .] do not indulge in the pride of fine feeling, the romantic error of amiable minds. Those, who really possess sensibility, ought early be taught, that it is a dangerous quality, which is continually extracting the excess of misery, or delight, from every surrounding circumstance.

(p. 18) *a confidential servant of his father's . . . to inform La Haye . . . to his disadvantage* : de Tencin's Comminge (op. cit., p. 40) also realizes too late that his father has had a servant spy on him during his stay at The Wells. The servant reports on all his activities, including his duel with the Chevalier St. Odin over Adélaïde's bracelet, and paints the Marchioness of Lussan and her daughter "as artful designing women" who know his true identity.

(p. 19) *partial Time seemed to have extended his wide pinions, and to have flown with unusual swiftness*: Descriptive of Lusignan's consciousness, this is the first of the author's metaphors regarding Time, which are similar to those of Ann Radcliffe in her poetry. For example, in "A Second View of the Seven Mountains'"(*Posthumous Works*, op. cit., vol. IV, p. 184.), Radcliffe addresses the mountains with the lines: "For of a grander world ye seemed the dawn/ Rising beyond where Time's tired wing can go." A number of variations on the trope occur in *Lusignan*. In vol. II, p. 94, as Lusignan awaits his wedding day: "The appointed week rapidly elapsed, though Time, in the ideas of Lusignan, had borrowed leaden pinions." Again, in vol. III, p. 112, when Lusignan is incarcerated at Belleisle Priory, and anticipating pen, ink and paper with which to write to his Emily, the narrator says of Lusignan that, "occupied with this idea, time seemed divested of its leaden pinions." Cf. also Ann Radcliffe, *The Italian*, edited with an introduction and notes by Robert Miles (Harmondsworth: Penguin Books) p. 32: "[Vivaldi] had received permission to wait upon Signora Bianchi on a future day, but till that day should arrive, time appeared motionless.'"

(p. 22) *He collected the papers, and committed them to the flames*: de Tencin's Comminge destroys the documents immediately after receiving his father's letter, not after the revelation of his identity to Adélaïde.

(p. 28) *Obedience is no longer a virtue when confined to those points in which inclination and duty happily unite*: Emily appears to be influenced anachronistically by Kantian moral philosophy here. See Immanuel Kant, *Grundelung zur Metaphysik der Sitten* (1785), *Groundwork of the Metaphysics of Morals*, translated and edited by Mary Gregor (Cambridge: Cambridge University Press, 1998), p. 12: "It is just then that the worth of character comes out, which is moral and incomparably the highest, namely that he is beneficent not from inclination, but from duty." Cf. Adélaïde's spoken words to Comminge in de Tencin (op. cit., p. 56): "My utmost endeavours . . . shall be exerted to make my inclinations conformable to my duty; but I feel, that I shall be most miserable, if duty should oblige me to renounce you."

(p. 30) *Henry of Navarre . . . Henry IVth's bodyguards:* Son of Jeanne d'Albret, Queen of Navarre, and Antoine de Bourbon, Henry was King of Navarre from 1572 to 1610.

(p. 31) *a roturier*: Fr., a commoner.

(p. 34) *intendant*: Fr., steward; manager of estate.

(p. 43) *it brought to his recollection former days, and "tales of other times"; many of these arms bore the insignia of the Crusades*: "tales of other times" is a quotation from the poems of Ossian, famously explicated by Hugh Blair in his *A Critical Dissertation on the Poems of Ossian* (London: T. Becket and Paul A. De Hondt, 1753), p. 15: "His words," says he, "came only by halves to our ears; they were dark as the tales of other times, before the light of the song arose." The old tales which Lusignan recollects here are no doubt old Provençal tales about knights and chivalry during the Crusades, such as the one Ludovico reads in Vol. IV, Ch. VI of *The Mysteries of Udolpho* (op. cit., pp. 517; 520-525), and which Radcliffe reworks in an English setting in *Gaston de Blondeville.*

(p. 44) *a vast and distant prospect . . . a cottage in that happy land*: In content, sentiment, and diction this passage bears a striking similarity to the following lines written by Ann Radcliffe in her poem "On the Isle of Wight", possibly composed during her first visit there in 1798. See *Gaston de Blondeville or, The Court of Henry III Keeping Festival in Ardenne, A Romance*, half title, *The Posthumous Works of Mrs. Radcliffe*, 4 vols. (London: Henry Colburn, 1826, vol. IV, pp. 221-222:

> Oh! for a cottage on the shady brow
> Of this green Island, where the Channel flows
> With less tumultuous wave, and sends abroad
> The many sails of England to the world,
> And beareth to his home the mariner
> Who shouts to see the light blue hills, that rise
> [. . .]
> Oh! for a cottage on the breezy cliff,
> That points the crescent of thy harbour, Cowes!
> And bears the raptured glance o'er seas and shores—
> A boundless prospect. . . .

(p. 53) *The voice issuing from the cavity still vibrated on her ear*: In common with Ann Radcliffe in all of her romances, the author's poetic descriptions of the protagonists' intensities of sensory perception, feeling and remembrance draw frequently on David Hartley's neuropsychological theory of vibrations and association, as presented in his influential *Observations on Man, his Frame, his Duty, and his Expectations,* 2 vols. [1749] (New York: Garland Pub., 1971), Vol. I, pp. 5-114. For examples in Radcliffe, see, *The Mysteries of Udolpho,* op. cit., Vol. IV, Ch. VI, p. 519; *The Italian,* op. cit., Vol. I, Ch. I, p. 11.

She pressed her repeater; it was three o'clock: This is anachronistic. The repeater watch, invented for determination of the time in the dark, was patented by Daniel Quare in England in 1687, although an English cleric, Edward Barlow, had also invented one in 1676. Madame de Meronville appears to have a simple repeater that, on pressing the button, chimes only the hours.

(p. 56) *La Haye, who fortunately for himself, held familiar converse with the spirits of darkness ... the letter addressed to Lusignan:* At one level, this intrusive narratorial comment supplementing Madame de Meronville's rational explanation of the mysterious events in the gallery seems an oddly teasing and ironic reflection on both her (and our) presumption of the "the explained supernatural" in regard to these events. However, as La Haye's supposed resort to the services of "spirits of darkness" or "aerial beings", is not distinctly developed, and it remains an isolated reference in the novel, it could be that the author-narrator is simply using a mock heroic irony to indicate La Haye's depths of criminality in feigning the supernatural. The use of "could have" also implies a certain speculativeness, or limit to the narrator's knowledge, without suggesting unreliability. Such narratorial speculation is evident on occasion in Ann Radcliffe's novels, for example regarding the testimony of Du Bosse in *The Romance of the Forest,* op. cit., p. 334: "It is probable that Du Bosse, in this instance, gave a false account of his motive, since if he was really guilty of an intention so atrocious as that of murder, he would naturally endeavour to conceal it. However this might be...."

(p. 57) *she had read some romances, which taught her that love was the business of life:* An anachronistically mischievous reference to the most famous and scandalous "new romance" of the 18th century, Jean-Jacques Rousseau's *Julie, ou la nouvelle Héloïse,* first published under a different title in Amsterdam in 1761. In an early letter, Julie tells her lover, St. Preux, that "love will be the major business of our lives". See Jean-Jacques Rousseau, *Julie, or The New Heloise: Letters of Two Lovers Who Live in a Small Town at the Foot of the Alps, The Collected Writings of Rousseau,* vol. 6, translated and annotated by Philip Stewart and Jean Vaché (Hanover and London: University Press of New England, 1997), p. 89. The author may have read William Kenrick's English translation of the novel, under the simple title, *Eloisa,* which was reissued fifteen or more times in England between 1761 and 1810.

(p. 58) *Amadis the Gaul:* the hero of *Amadis de Gaula,* a Spanish or Portuguese "old romance" of knight-errantry originating at the turn of the

14th century, and written by Garcia de Montalvo in the form published in the early 16th century. As a knight-lover, Amadis is handsome, courteous, gentle, and ever faithful to his Oriana, heiress to the throne of Great Britain, though her father opposes their marriage. Following their illicit consummation of their love (on one occasion only), Oriana gives birth to a son. *Amadis* was translated into French by Herberay des Essarts in 1540, and into English by Anthony Munday in approx. 1590. It was one of the chivalric tomes held back from the burning of Quixote's romances by the priest and barber in Cervantes' *Don Quixote*. However, it still had currency throughout the 18th century as is evidenced by Handel's adaptation of it in his opera, *Amadigi di Gaula* (1715), J. C. Bach's opera, *Amadis de Gaule* of 1779, and Southey's abridged *Amadis of Gaul* of 1803.

lettre de cachet: A sealed letter from the King of France ordering the governor of the Bastille to imprison the person named; hence in modern parlance any arbitrary warrant for arrest. According to the laws of the time, d'Aubignac could be convicted of rape and receive the death penalty if he were to elope with Eugenia, not withstanding her consent and connivance.

(p. 59) *epigraph*: *Jerusalem Delivered*: *An Heroic Poem* translated from the Italian of Torquato Tasso by John Hoole, 2 vols. (London: Printed for R. & J. Dodsley et al., 1764), IX, 435-40; vol. I, p. 219. "With triple light he blazes, Three in One!" in the original. Given *Lusignan*'s heavy reliance on the workings of Providence, the lines that follow these are also germane to the novel's religious underpinning: "Beneath his footstep, Fate and Nature stand, / And Time and Motion wait his dread command." Tasso was one of Ann Radcliffe's favourite poets, mentioned in her novels, though not quoted, for example, in *The Italian*, Ellena is given a volume of Tasso by the nun Olivia.

Montalte Abbey ... nearly at the entrance of St. Michael's Bay: Montalte Abbey is the author's invention. It seems to be situated on the eastern tip of the Cherbourg Peninsula, and to be inspired by the famous Benedictine Abbey of Mont Saint-Michel founded in the 8th century by St. Aubert, Bishop of Avranches, and built on an 80-metre-high islet of outcropping granite inside the flat bay of Mont Saint-Michel, a dangerous tidal basin. In the 13th century, the King of France, Philippe II Auguste, financed the Gothic reconstruction of the abbey following its partial destruction during his wars against the English occupiers. This Gothic extension is known as La Merveille (the Marvel) and is the most architecturally impressive part of the site.

the Casquets: Les Casquets, a group of rocks 13 km northwest of Alderney and part of an underwater sandstone ridge. Over the centuries there have been numerous wrecks on these islets due to fierce tides reaching 6-7 knots on springs and a lack of landmarks in the area.

(p. 60) *the celebrated Rollo*: A legendary Viking leader, and subject of a

17th century play by Fletcher, Johnson, Chapman and Massinger, Rollo invaded the area of northern France now known as Normandy. In 911 his forces were defeated, but King Charles the Simple decided to grant Rollo the coastal lands he occupied on condition he defend the country against other invading Vikings. In the Treaty of Saint-Clair-sur-Epte, Rollo pledged feudal allegiance to Charles and converted to Christianity. In return, the king granted Rollo upper Normandy, and the titular rulership of Normandy, where Rollo made restitution for the plunder of the Abbey of Saint-Michel. His statue can be seen in the city of Rouen.

that narrow channel which separates the island from the coast, and called the Race of Alderney: Alderney, the most northerly of the Channel Islands, and the only one actually in the English Channel, is part of the Bailiwick of Guernsey, a British Crown dependency. Closest of the Channel Islands to both France and the United Kingdom, it is separated from the Cherbourg Peninsula by the dangerous Race of Alderney (*Le Raz Blanchard*), notorious for its extremely strong currents and rough seas.

(p. 63) *Reason is given as an antidote to the passions, and if listened to is all-sufficient*: the view of Jean-François Senault, whose *L'usage des passions* (*The Use of Passions*) of 1641 was translated into English by Henry Carey, Earl of Monmouth, and published in 1671. By the late eighteenth century this view had been widely discredited.

(p. 68) *which his Esculapius . . . effect of the damps*: also spelt "Aesculapius," the name of the Greek and Roman god of medicine, healing arts and rejuvenation. Consistent with those of John Armstrong in *The Art of Preserving Health*, the diagnoses and remedies of Monsieur Le Saxe in *Lusignan* are always sensitive to his patient's emotional as well as physical well-being. In a recent edition of Armstrong's poem, Adam Budd notes that Esculapius was "a distinguished physician of antiquity celebrated for bringing speculative and theoretical knowledge to medical practice," and that he favoured non-invasive medical treatments, including bathing and adjusted diet, consistent with those of John Armstrong. See Adam Budd, *John Armstrong's* The Art of Preserving Health: *Eighteenth Century Sensibility in Practice* (Surrey, England: Ashgate Publishing Ltd., 2011), p. 85, n.98.

(p. 72) *Besançon*: a large town in eastern France near the border with Switzerland.

(p. 78) *A lettre de cachet would be more eligible*: Until the end of the *ancien régime* such arbitrary warrants were in fact used on occasion by fathers to persuade recalcitrant sons to agree to their father's wishes in respect to marriage. See Anne Jacobsen Schutte, *By Force and Fear: Taking and Breaking Monastic Vows in Early Modern Europe* (Ithaca and London: Cornell University Press, 2011), pp. 53-55; James F. Traer, *Marriage and the Family in Eighteenth-Century France* (Ithaca and London: Cornell University Press, 1980), pp. 137-141.

the more northern shores . . . neighbourhood of the sea: a reference to the rocky coastline of Picardy which is marked by high, white chalk cliffs, similar to those of England's Dover.

(p. 81) *something like prognostic*: a presentiment of what would occur.

(p. 82) *surtout*: overcoat.

(p. 86) *Algerine corsair*: ship of pirates or privateers who operated from the port of Algiers. Pirates from such North African coastal ports, or "the Barbary Coast" as it was called in England, were active from the 16th to the early 19th centuries, especially in the Western Mediterranean. Their main purpose was to capture young, strong Christians for the Islamic slave market in Northern Africa and the Middle East.

(p. 90) *cruse*: small earthen vessel for drinking.

(p. 94) *Nature had implanted in their untutored minds such sentiments of true benevolence and humanity . . . station*: The attribution of uncorrupted morality and genuine happiness to those who maintain a simple existence close to Nature is a tenet of sentimentalism deriving from the mid-eighteenth-century writings of Jean-Jacques Rousseau.

(p. 98) *civilized Barbarians*: The idea that "savages", uncorrupted by Europeans and their culture, were noble children of Nature is usually attributed to Rousseau's *Discourse on the Moral Effects of the Arts and Sciences* (1750) and *The Discourse on Inequality* (1754), but by 1800 this notion had permeated much eighteenth-century writing.

(p. 101) *She threw her eyes to Heaven . . . an all-protecting, though invisible, Power reigned there*: The author has imbued the supplicating Yaratilda with a species of "natural religion", as she exhibits the sort of expansive love for the universe, a "reasonable enthusiasm", that some philosophers, such as Shaftesbury, held to be the essence of "natural religion". David Hartley also argued that humans could "infer the existence and attributes of God", along with "their relation and duty to him, from the mere consideration of natural phenomena". See David Hartley, *Observations on Man, his Frame, his Duty, and Expectations*, 2 vols. (Bath and London: S. Richardson, 1749) Vol. II, pp. 10-11, 49. Emily St. Aubert (*The Mysteries of Udolpho*, op. cit., p. 310), has a similar love to Yaratilda of the planets, though her interest in them is informed by her father's scientific teachings.

(p. 102) *epigraph*: From Edward Young, "Love of Fame, The Universal Passion," in *Seven Characteristical Satires*. See *The Works of the Author of The Night Thoughts in Four Volumes, Revised and Corrected by Himself*, (London: A. Millar, 1747), Vol. I, p. 87.

(p. 107) *It is the spot . . . the scene of my infant joys, my earliest and best delights . . . some sweet remembrance*: Cf. the very similar description of Emily St. Aubert's fond memories of her childhood home, La Vallée, and her father, in *The Mysteries of Udolpho* (op. cit., Vol. IV, Ch. XI, pp. 556-7):

With the melancholy she experienced on the review of a place which had
been the residence of her parents, and the scene of her earliest delight, was
mingled, after the first shock had subsided, a tender and undescribable
pleasure. [...] as she walked beneath the groves, which her father had
planted, and where she had so often sauntered in affectionate conversation with him, his countenance, his smile, even the accents of his voice,
returned with exactness to her fancy, and her heart melted to the tender
recollections.

(p. 108) *the merry Lavolta*: "La volta" or "volte" (the French definite article
has been telescoped into the Italian noun in the English term): a quick
three-in-a-measure dance which, as its name suggests, involves turning
around. It was especially popular in England in the sixteenth century, but
banned from the French court during the reign of Louis XIII in the early
17th century because of its perceived lack of decorum, as the man had to
lift his female dancing partner into the air.

(p. 114) *"Sublimer happiness... No!"*: these lines, written by the now forgotten Scottish poet, James Graeme (1765-1811), constitute the final stanza of
his "Elegy XLIII to Mira", and were singled out for quotation in a biographical preface on Graeme by Robert Anderson in the latter's *The Works
of the British Poets, with Prefaces, Biographical and Critical* (London: John
& Arthur Arch, 1795), p. 422. The stanza was also reproduced as part of an
excerpt from Anderson's preface in a review called "Dr. Anderson's Edition
of the British Poets" in *The Monthly Review*, xxviii (Sept. 1798), p. 20. The
lines thus had some currency when *Lusignan* was published. Given the
recurrence of their theme in *Lusignan*, Anderson's commentary, for which
the stanza served as illustration, is also of interest:

> To his [Graeme's] sincerity is also owing, that the character of his elegies
> is but little diversified, presenting chiefly... a series of pathetic compari-
> sons of the pretensions of birth and wealth, with the happiness and secu-
> rity of humble fortune, in which preference is constantly ascribed to the
> latter, and the rights of sensibility asserted with persuasive energy (ibid).

(p. 115) *Emily... shed torrents of tears at their approaching separation*: Like
the female friendships of Radcliffe's heroines, such as Adeline with Clara
in *The Romance of the Forest* and Ellena with Olivia in *The Italian*, Emily's
friendship with Caroline exhibits features which go beyond the treatment
of such relationships by other writers of Gothic romances and novels at
this time.

(p. 130) *the Duke's Avocat and Homme d'Affaires*: his advocate or legal con-
sultant, and business or financial manager.

(p. 131) *St. Jerome*: a learned biblical scholar who lived from 340? to 420,
and was renowned for his forthright assertions of what he perceived as
truth.

(p. 135) *He was too bigotted... to render his consent unnecessary*: while the

Duke's blindly intolerant adherence to Catholicism is coextensive with his acceptance of the counsel and priestly intercession of La Haye whose falsity and hypocrisy he fails to recognise, he obviously does know and believe independently that, should Emily and Lusignan marry clandestinely without his consent, their marriage would be recognised by the Roman Catholic Church as valid. See Anne Jacobsen Schutte, *By Force and Fear*, p. 53.

She ... counted the beadroll: Among Catholic priests the beadroll referred to the list of people for whom prayers were to be offered. It seems likely that Emily was praying in turn for each of her loved ones, rather than that she was was moving through the rosary bead based sequences of Marian devotions.

(p. 143) *my Lord's Maître d'Hôtel*: the Duke's majordomo or chief of house; the highest official in his household.

(p. 145) *a postern gate*: a secondary gate in the castle's curtain wall. Such castle gates were often in a concealed location, allowing occupants to come and go unnoticed.

(p. 148) *infuse into my mind that fortitude, the best gift of Heaven*: Fortitude is listed as one of the seven gifts of the Holy Spirit—blessings given to human souls—to which there exist many scattered biblical references, but which are most clearly brought together by the 13th century Dominican theologian St. Thomas Aquinas in his *Summa Theologica*. However, Emily's supplication here for fortitude and virtue contains echoes of John Armstrong's *The Art of Preserving Health*, op. cit., Book IV, ("The Passions") ll. 284-285: "Virtue, the strength and beauty of the soul, / is the best gift of Heaven. . . ."

(p. 149) *"My hour is come ... Adieu! Remember thy father!"*: Like the ghost's opening affirmation of his identity, his words of farewell to Emily at the onset of dawn are reminiscent of those in Shakespeare's *Hamlet*, I. v. 2, 9, 91.

Vice was engraved in shining characters on his forehead: Emily's dream vision, of a hideous phantom in the form of La Haye, recalls the gigantic, swarthy "monster", with "Pride! Lust! Inhumanity!" inscribed on his forehead, that appears to Lorenzo in a dream in Matthew Lewis's *The Monk*, op. cit., pp. 27-28.

(p. 151) *Her fixed eye ... insensible as marble*: Clinically, Emily's symptoms are those of stupor brought on by shock or trauma. Cf. the similar temporary stupor experienced by the highly-strung Emily St. Aubert in *The Mysteries of Udolpho* (op. cit., Vol. III, Ch. I, p. 331-332) which occurs after Emily has escaped abduction, and also seen a bloodied corpse which she believes to be that of her aunt.

(p. 154) *Where is my mother? Send her to me,—I hate strangers*: Cf. Emily St. Aubert's similar Ophelia-like lack of recognition of Montoni and her reference to her deceased father in *The Mysteries of Udolpho*, op. cit., Vol. III, Ch. I, p. 332.

pardon my sins . . . she looked an angel: Emily's assertion of a conflict between worldly, romantic love and love of God foreshadows the d'Arnaudian theme of Lusignan's final chapter. The description of Emily's angelic appearance here also recalls that of the saintly nun, Cordelia, (also inspired by de Tencin's Adélaïde) who raises her eyes to heaven and dies in "a fine devotional glow" in Ann Radcliffe's *A Sicilian Romance*, edited with notes and an introduction by Alison Milbank (Oxford: Oxford University Press, 1993), pp. 118, 136

(p. 155) *A reunion with those we love . . . in the realms of bliss*: Cf. Pastor La Luc's statement in Radcliffe's *The Romance of the Forest* (op. cit., Ch. XVIII, p. 274): "One of our brightest hopes of a future state [. . .] is that we shall meet again those whom we have loved on earth."

if after death we are permitted to communicate with terrestrial beings, I will still watch over him, and, as a guardian angel, protect him!: Cf. in *The Mysteries of Udolpho* (op. cit., Vol. I, Ch. VI, pp. 66-67) the ailing St. Aubert's fervent hope that "we shall be permitted to look down on those we have left on earth . . . that disembodied spirits watch over the friends they have loved".

(p. 157) *Belleisle Priory . . . situated in the Cevenni Mountains*: The name of the priory appears to be fictitious. However, Belleisle (Belle Île) itself, just off the Brittany coast, was in the news in 1800 due to an abortive British naval expedition to seize the strongly held small island. The Cévennes, a remote and wild chain of rocky hills, plateaus and valleys in south-central France, part of the Massif Central, and to the west of the Rhone Valley, were controlled in earlier centuries by monastic orders such as the Benedictines and Cistercians, who built numerous abbeys there. After the Reformation, its peasant inhabitants, the *cévenois*, were mostly Huguenots, and were brutally persecuted by the French Monarchy. In Vol. I, Caroline, in telling her story to Emily, mentions Madame de Meronville's sojourn of some months at "an estate in the Cevannes" (*sic*).

(p. 158) *Emily felt as though she was actually restored to life, and Madame de Clarival and the Duchess could hardly persuade themselves it was her*: Ann Radcliffe's journal for Sept. 25, 1798, (Talfourd, op. cit., p. 32) reveals her interest in this subject when she criticises an altar piece of Lazarus rising from the dead both for the depiction of Lazarus's death-like face and the lack of appropriate astonishment and wonder in the faces of the spectators.

(p. 164) *epigraph*: "*Hark! the death-bell sounds!*": perhaps an adaptation of "Hark how the solemn Death-bell's sound" from the opening line of R. H., (possibly Richard Hurd) "Verses on hearing of the Death of Gray the Poet" published in *Scots Magazine*, 33 (September 1771), 484.

(p. 170) *In the presence of his keeper he had several times written to his father, but had received no answer*: Unless this refers to earlier letters Lusignan wrote to his father while confined at Luneville Castle, it is one of the novel's minor inconsistencies.

(p. 172) *a thousand ideal phantoms haunted her imagination*: imaginary, not real or actual phantoms. Cf. Radcliffe's use of the phrase "ideal terrors" in *The Mysteries of Udolpho*, op. cit., Vol. II, Ch. 6, p. 242.

(p. 173) *She threw herself on the clay-cold corpse, . . . to retire to her own apartment*: This passage is a reworking of La Voisin's discovery of Emily St. Aubert "lying senseless across the foot of the bed, near which stood her father's coffin" in *The Mysteries of Udolpho*. Moreover, the overall narration of the death of the saintly Countess and Emily's demonstration of grief over her corpse follows a similar pattern to that of the death of St. Aubert in Radcliffe's romance. For example, like Madame de Clarival in *Lusignan*, before St. Aubert expires, he speaks to Emily "with the tenderness of a father [. . .] dignified by the pious solemnity of a saint", of his faith in a future existence. Again, Emily de Montalte's presentiment of the death of her mother, and her "imaginary terrors", parallel Emily St. Aubert's "superstitious dread", "sublime devotion and awe", and "uneasy dreams". Notably, Emily de Montalte does not exhibit quite the same ongoing obsession with her parent's corpse, nor the accompanying enervation of Emily St. Aubert, but instead, through prayer, recovers Armstrong's "dignity of mind" before, like her namesake, retiring to the Convent of St. Clair. Cf. *The Mysteries of Udolpho*, op. cit., Vol. I, Ch. VII, pp. 75-81.

(p. 175) *Bretanny*: Brittany (Fr. *Bretagne*). Historically Celtic and Catholic in culture, it is located on a peninsula in north-west France that extends about 150 miles into the Atlantic Ocean, separating the English Channel to the north from the Bay of Biscay to the south. It is bordered by Lower Normandy to the north-east, and the Western Loire to the east. It became a province of the Kingdom of France in 1532.

(p. 176) *firelock*: a musket with a gun-lock in which sparks were produced to ignite the priming.

(p. 182) *Very early in life he designed me for the cloister . . . property might revert to my brother*: The nun's story of parental tyranny is similar to that which the nun Cornelia tells Julia at the Abbey of St. Augustin in Ann Radcliffe's *A Sicilian Romance*, op. cit., pp. 118-119. Such tales of the forced consignment of young European women (and men) by parents to Catholic religious houses were not merely the mythical stereotypes of Protestant ideology, but had a factual foundation in real life. This is attested by the many petitions from 1668 to 1793, of almost one thousand women and men who sought release from their vows, and have been documented from the Vatican Archive by Anne Jacobsen Schutte.

(p. 183) *The organ swelled a solemn peal*: Ann Radcliffe uses this exact description in relation to a procession of monks into Furness Abbey in her

Journey Made in the Summer of 1794 (Dublin: Wogan, et al., 1795) p. 490.

the lamps burnt pale . . . to view the sacrifice I made: Cf. Alexander Pope's "Eloisa to Abelard", ll. 111-114: As with cold lips I kiss'd the sacred veil, / The shrines all trembled and the lamps grew pale: / Heaven scarce believed the conquest it survey'd, / And saints with wonder heard the vows I made.

(p. 185) *How is it that memory fondly dwells on scenes of such exquisite grief?*: a link to the chapter's epigraph from Samuel Rogers's *The Pleasures of Memory*. Rogers comments in his "Analysis of the Second Part" that "events, the most distressing in their immediate consequences, are often cherished in remembrance with a degree of enthusiasm". Such was his poem's popularity that Rogers's friend Robert Merry published a companion poem, *The Pains of Memory* (London: G.G. and J. Robinson, 1796). Merry's theme, the pain that memory can bring to old age, is illustrated by a series of scenes, one of which also features a nun "doom'd to long involuntary pray'r".

(p. 189) *epigraph:* From Edward Young's *The Revenge*, II.i. The words are spoken by Don Carlos. The original reads "And he who knows not that, was born for nothing."

(p. 191) *legal prostitution*: a phrase used (but not coined) by Mary Wollstonecraft to describe marriage for support in *A Vindication of the Rights of Woman with Strictures on Political and Moral Subjects* (Boston: Thomas and Andrews, 1792; repr. edn. New York & London: Garland Publishing Inc., 1974), p. 259. Although Wollstonecraft did not write about free love in *A Vindication*, she shared the ideal with Gilbert Imlay, by whom she had a daughter, but who defected from the relationship, leading to her attempted suicide.

Why should we . . . invented for the use of fools?: With his sophistical denigration of "honour"and "the prejudices of custom" as "error", d'Aubignac's anachronistic discourse is of a piece with the Gallic primitivist arguments and practices of the hedonistic Marquis de Montalt in *The Romance of the Forest*, op. cit., pp. 159-164, 222. In the view of Edmund Burke, Jean-Jacques Rousseau was responsible for the fashionableness of such views in eighteenth-century France. In 1791 he attacked Rousseau's *La Nouvelle Héloïse* for "perverting morality," and teaching Frenchmen "to love after the fashion of philosophers, [. . .] a love without gallantry". By its "false sympathies", the novel endeavoured to "subvert those principles of domestic trust and fidelity, which form the discipline of social life". Edmund Burke, "Letter to a Member of the National Assembly," in *Reflections on the Revolution in France*, edited and with an introduction by L. G. Mitchell (Oxford: Oxford University Press, 1993), pp. 274-275.

(p. 192) *nobody who has not, like me, experienced it, can form an adequate idea of the sufferings of these miserable beings*: Here the author gives the nun's cautionary tale a contemporary resonance regarding prostitution in London. Cf. Mary Wollstonecraft, *A Vindication of the Rights of Woman*, op. cit., pp. 127-128, 215. In her novel *The Wrongs of Woman: or, Maria, A Fragment* (1798), Wollstonecraft also has Maria's warder, Jemima, describe her own rape and abandonment by a former employer, and the subsequent "debasing misery" of her life as a prostitute amidst the vice of the metropolis.

(p. 194) *the Suffragan Bishop*: in the Roman Catholic Church, the bishop at the head of a diocese, and having jurisdiction over clergy in his see.

my sufferings may furnish a useful lesson to the inconsiderate multitude . . . has reached maturity: Throughout the nun's story, the distinction between the repentant and spiritually evolved Julia, as adult narrator, and her former, youthful self, focalized as weak, deluded, and morally culpable has been clear. However, this concluding, reflexive statement about her tale's "moral utility" makes the author-narrator's didactic purpose unmistakable. In this respect, Julia's cautionary story may well be the author's pointed response to Hannah More's trenchant criticism, in her *Strictures of the Modern System of Female Education*, 2 vols. (London: Cadell & Davies, 1799; repr. edn. New York: Garland, 1974), Vol. I, p. 32, of the 'pernicious' influence of novels, which following Rousseau have diffused "destructive politics, deplorable profligacy, and impudent infidelity", and do not paint "an innocent woman ruined, repenting, and restored; but with far more mischievous refinement, . . . annihilate the value of chastity".

(p. 197) *a violent concussion of the vehicle . . . overturned the carriage*: This event marks a return of the plot to a temporary alignment with de Tencin's classically structured *Comminge*, albeit the incident of the overturned carriage occurs very early in her novel, when Adélaïde and Madame de Lussan are *en route* home from The Wells. While no villain is involved, Comminge, like Lusignan, fortuitously arrives on the scene as rescuer.

(p. 200) *epigraph*: Thomas Gray, "Ode on a Distant Prospect of Eton College," ll. 11-14. This epigraph, signalling Emily's return to her childhood home in the Valais, is also used by Ann Radcliffe to herald the return of Emily St. Aubert to her childhood home, La Vallée, in *The Mysteries of Udolpho*, op. cit., Vol. IV, Ch. XI, p. 556.

(p. 201) *Monte-Sancto*: Holy Mount is in Turkey, but in this context it is a fictional place in south-western France.

(p. 202) *The groups of peasants . . . despotism was banished from their abodes*: The idyllic description of Emily's approach to her childhood home draws on St. Preux's description of the Valais in Rousseau's *New Heloise* (op. cit., pp. 65-68). St. Preux writes of the "simplicity" and "equanimity" of the enchanting inhabitants of the upper Valais, and of "that peaceful tranquillity that makes them happy through freedom from pain rather than taste for pleasures". He also praises the beauty of the young women, and the elegance of their dress. Historically, the Valais had been a republic since 1628, with a Catholic Bishop in power, until Napoleon invaded the area and created the *République du Valais* in March 1798. Then, on May 1 of that year, it had become part of the Helvetic Republic and still remained so when *Lusignan* was published. It became independent of France again in 1813.

She pleased herself with throwing from the windows pieces of money: Emily's throwing of coins to the children seems a jarring and contradictory note in this scene, but may take its cue from the observations of St. Preux (ibid., pp. 65-66) regarding the contrasting practices, in respect to money, between the inhabitants of the upper and lower Valais.

(p. 212) *His character might vie with his appearance ... An Italian by birth, he inherited all the vices of his countrymen*: Bentivoglio is conceived in the tradition of the vengeful Italian villains of Jacobean and Shakepearean tragedy. Cf. de Tencin's brushstroke description of the corresponding character, the Marquis de Benavides, in *Comminge*, op. cit., p. 85-86: "Benavides' person is odious to a degree, which his meanness of spirit and capricious humour have rendered more despicable."

(p. 215) *In a few days I shall become the wife of the Marquis de Bentivoglio ... of restoring your tranquillity*: Cf. the similar letter written by de Tencin's Adélaïde in *Comminge*, op. cit., p. 73: "In a few days I shall be the wife of the Marquis of Benavides. That which I know of his character, tells me what I am to undergo. But at least I owe you this mark of fidelity, that I can from my engagement foresee nothing but misery. You, on the contrary, endeavour to be happy. Your ease and tranquillity will be my only consolation."

(p. 218) *your unhappy father is no more*: Although the close alignment of the plot of *Lusignan* with that of *Comminge* continues with Lusignan's reaction to Emily's letter and his release by his keeper from imprisonment for a week, when Comminge meets his mother on the road, she informs him not that his father is dead, but that Adélaïde is already married.

What are vows to me? ... nature binds our hearts, in ligaments too tender, too strong to be broken by human laws!: In rejecting vows, Lusignan here appeals to the transcendental nature of love as explored in medieval tales of passion, a love which does not require vows imposed on the lovers by custom or required of them by church law. His questioning of the marriage vow is thus different from the libertine desire and rejection of marriage exhibited by d'Aubignac.

(p. 228) *she listened to him with undeviating attention . . . the woman he adored*: While Comminge's mother also uses this tactic to soothe her son, in addition she gives a detailed explanation of her own face-to-face role in persuading Adélaïde to marry, and of the similar pressure imposed on

Adélaïde by her father, as well as Adélaïde's own motive in choosing the "odious" Bentivoglio from among her suitors. Comminge says of the effect of this knowledge, "Although my melancholy was excessive, it yet had that inexpressible sweetness of being beloved." Cf. de Tencin, op. cit., pp. 83-87.

(p. 239) *the sound momentarily returned upon her ear ... and vibrated on her soul*: Neither the sigh, nor the island, nor the pavilion with its wood and adjacent sea is found in *Comminge*. From the window of a room in which he is painting, Comminge simply sees Adélaïde walking in the garden with her little dog, Fidele (de Tencin, op. cit., p. 96). The author of *Lusignan*, like Ann Radcliffe in all of her romances, uses forms of the verb "vibrate" to describe sense impressions which generate moments of heightened or intense awareness, for example, the weak English king's climactic recognition of the truth in *Gaston de Blondeville*, op. cit., p. 196).

(p. 242) *I am so indifferent, so insensible to the beauties of art; those charming woods ... suit my taste much better*: Cf. Emily St. Aubert's loss of enthusiasm for drawing and sublime writing during her time of sorrow at the castle of Udolpho in *The Mysteries of Udolpho* (op. cit., Vol. II, Ch. VI, p. 235).

(p. 246) *rescued her from certain destruction*: The incident concerning the dog and its owner, and the subsequent dramatic rescue, does not occur in de Tencin's *Comminge*; nor does Adélaïde attempt to contact Comminge; rather, he waits for an opportunity when the Marquis de Benavides and his brother, the Chevalier d'Orfanne, are separately otherwise occupied, and then catches Adélaïde alone as she enters her apartment (cf. de Tencin, op. cit., pp. 107-108). Interestingly, in her journal entry for July 23, 1800, Ann Radcliffe describes her "favourite dog", Chance, pursuing wheatears (little birds) that were flying up from the shore beneath Beachy Head, and that she was "almost frightened" by her solitude before the raging ocean and vastness of the scene (Talfourd, op. cit., p. 41).

(p. 270) *the woods seemed to have acquired a darker hue ... My heart was in unison with the dreary scene*: Like Ann Radcliffe, the author-narrator uses for atmospheric effect the device of describing solemn or threatening scenes as "in unison" or "in correspondence" with the feelings of a main character.

(p. 272) *epigraph*: Samuel Rogers, *The Pleasures of Memory*, ll. 406-413. In the original, "a sister's love" is "a brother's love".

(p. 274) *During several ages it had existed, undisturbed by the civil wars ... ancient sanctuary*: Historically, this is not entirely accurate. In the course of the Hundred Years War between France and England, on account of La Trappe's geographical situation, it became a prey to troops on at least two occasions, and after reconstruction in the sixteenth century, like all the other monasteries, it had the misfortune to be given to a series of absentee abbots "*in commendam*".

(p. 275) *a statue of St. Bernard*: St. Bernard of Clairvaux (1090-1153) of the

Order of Citeaux, was founder of one hundred and sixty-three monasteries
in different parts of Europe. Canonized in 1174, he was the first Cistercian
monk placed on the calendar of saints.

the tenebres: *ténèbres*, more correctly, *tenebræ* (Lat. "darkness"), the ecclesiastical name given to the office of Matins and Lauds of the following day,
formerly sung on the evenings of the Wednesday, Thursday and Friday of
Holy Week.

"Memento mori!": Lat. "Remember your mortality!" The author has appropriated this supposed sole customary greeting of the monks from
d'Arnaud's *Les Amans Malheureux*. According to *The Catholic Encyclopedia*,
Trappist monks do not salute one another by the "memento mori". On
meeting each other they salute by an inclination of the head.

(p. 279) *now appearing before the dreadful tribunal of an avenging and
offended God!"*: The strong, Old Testament language here may draw on
the first stanza of Francis Quarles's Emblem to Job 14.13: "O whither shall
I fly? What path untrod / Shall I seek out to 'scape the flaming rod / Of
my offended, of my angry God?" Ann Radcliffe quotes stanza 6 of this
emblem as epigraph to Ch. XIII of *The Romance of the Forest*, op. cit., p.
199. See Frances Quarles, *The Complete Works in Prose and Verse* edited by
Alexander B. Grosart, 3 vols. (Hildesheim: Georg Olms, 1971), Bk. III, no.
XII, pp. 75-76.

(p. 281) *frequent and successive flashes of lightning illumined the forest . . . religious terror, caused by the sense of an omnipresent Deity*: Cf. Ann Radcliffe's
description of her religious awe and fear during storm in her journal entry
for for Autumn, 1801 (Talfourd, op. cit., pp. 52-53), such that she is relieved
to hear cheerful voices from another room:

> After dark, a storm, with thunder and lightning; listened to the strong,
> steady force of the wind and waves below. The thunder rolled and burst
> at intervals . . . This display of the elements was the grandest scene I ever
> beheld; a token of God directing his world. What particularly struck me
> was the appearance of irresistible power, which the deep monotonous
> sound of the wind and surge conveyed.

*the skirts of the forest, where, probably, some woodman's cot would shelter him
from the weather*: Cf. Radcliffe's journal entry for autumn 1800, regarding
a very thick forest. On this occasion she appears to have spent a fortnight
at a beach house at Little Hampton by herself, returning via Haslemere
(Talfourd, op. cit., p. 44):

> Have never seen such wild woody mountains before in England; they
> resemble the forests of Wetteravia more than any I have seen [. . .] com-
> fortable cottages lies snug beneath noble trees . . . among the huge timber
> felled on the ground, the Woodman's implements and the thatched hovel.

By St. Gertrude: a German Benedictine nun, mystic and theologian (1256-

ca. 1302), said to have the gift of miracles and prophecy. She was never formally canonized, but received equipotent canonization. Her feast day, November 16, was declared in the year 1677 by Pope Clement XII.

(p. 287) *the sound . . . seemed to issue from the rock . . . should inclose a human being*: regarding Ann Radcliffe's fascination with the notion of apparently human sounds issuing from a craggy rock in the neighbourhood of Steephill, Isle of Wight, one of her favourite areas, see her journal entry for Oct 15, 1811 (Talfourd, op. cit., p. 80): "Some of the shattered masses give most clear echoes . . . we stood before one . . . it seemed as if a living spirit was in the rock, so loud, so near, so exact!"

(p. 290) *Adelaide pressed her to her heart*: Cf. Julia's reunion with her "pale and emaciated" mother, Louisa, whom Julia had thought dead, in Ann Radcliffe's *A Sicilian Romance* (op. cit., pp. 174-183), and that of Ellena with her supposedly dead mother, Olivia, in *The Italian* (op. cit., pp. 435-437).

(p. 291) *"I was . . . condemned, for the trifling crime of attending a Huguenot meeting, to spend my life in the galleys"*: After the revocation in 1685 of the Edict of Nantes by Louis XIV, the grandson of Henry IV, Protestantism again became illegal in France. Huguenots were actively persecuted and thrown into dungeons. Seeking to enlarge his fleet, Louis XIV also ordered the courts to sentence prisoners to the galleys as frequently as possible. The conditions and ill treatment of galley slaves were notorious; hence it was a much feared sentence. The author may have read Jean Marteilhes' *Memoirs*, in which he described his unjust sentence in 1700 and ten years in the galleys in France. His shocking exposure of the evils of the system was translated by Oliver Goldsmith under the pseudonym of "James Willington", and published in England in 1758. See *The Memoirs of a Protestant Condemned to the Gallies of France for his Religion*, with an introduction by Austin Dobson, 2 vols. (London: J. M. Dent & Co., 1895).

(p. 291) *"Conscience," said he with a smile, "is generally very compliant to galley slaves"*: Marteilhes (ibid., pp. 100-112) describes how, in contrast to some of the other galley slaves, he and his Huguenot comrades resisted the efforts of unscrupulous Jesuit priests at Marseilles to have them publicly abjure their religion in return for their freedom.

(p. 292) *was assured by him that an oath was sacred till the death of both dissolved it*: The author again uses the ploy of having a Catholic believe that a promissory oath is binding. However, for Catholics, such an oath then and now entails the obligation of fulfilling it only if what is promised, and the possibility of its execution, are lawful. In this case, they obviously are not lawful. Given Bentivoglio's power in his domain, Bertrand would nevertheless have had to suffer the consequences imposed by his master for not fulfilling his oath.

(p. 294) *I was for a considerable time a spectacle of horror to every beholder*: In the nature of this disease, the masses of pustules covering her face and body would have started to leak and deflate after about a fortnight, transforming into scabs which would eventually have flaked off, leaving depigmented scars, or "pock holes" that in turn would have taken considerable time to fade.

(p. 295) *epigraph*: Baculard d'Arnaud, *Les Amans Malheureux, ou Le Comte de Comminge*, I.i. 7-12:

> O master of passions! Thou, who shaped my soul,
> Can you not stifle this flame in my breast,
> Conquer, annihilate in me, these persecuting features,
> Which, alas! by the day dearer, more enchanting,
> Return to madden the weakness of my senses?
> Surrounded by coffins, I speak of tenderness!

The last two lines are as follows in the 1764 edition. Translations mine:

> Reviennent à mes yeux se remontrer sans cesse?
> Dans ce lieu de terreur je parle de tendresse!
> Returning to my eyes, show themselves without ceasing?
> In this place of terror, I speak of tenderness!

(p. 299) *for he beheld the rival he once dreaded—Chevalier Dorimond*: In *Les Amans Malheureux*, d'Orvigni is recognised immediately by Comminge/Fr. Arsene as the virtuous brother of Adélaïde's perfidious husband but not as the rival who had freed him from imprisonment at the Chateau, following his near fatal wounding of Adélaïde's husband, the Comte d'Ermansay.

(p. 300) *near to one in which another victim of his was entombed!*: In her *Memoirs*, Madame de Genlis describes having heard in 1776, from the Prince of Palestrina, the story of the incarceration of his daughter, the Duchess of Cerifalco, in an underground cave for nine years by her jealous husband before she was eventually released. See Stéphanie-Félicité de Genlis, *Memoirs of Genlis, Illustrative of the Eighteenth and Nineteenth Centuries. Written by Herself*, 8 vols. (London: Henry Colburn, 1825), Vol. III, p. 35. Genlis used this as the basis for her "Histoire de la duchesse de C***". See Mary Trouille, "Buried Alive: Genlis's Gothic Tale of Marital Violence in 'Histoire de la duchesse de C***'", *Studies on Voltaire and the Eighteenth Century*, 2005, 12:77-114. Like Radcliffe, the author of *Lusignan* may have been influenced by de Genlis's tale, which was embedded in the latter's 1782 epistolary novel, *Adèle et Théodore ou Lettres sur l'éducation*, first published in English in 1783.

(p. 304) *a vast and dreary plain . . . screech owls and birds of prey . . . under his habit*: Taking a cue from the terrible storm with its supernatural occurrences in Shakespeare's *Julius Caesar*, I. iii. 3-77, the author here expands d'Arnaud's "gloomy desert" to a scene of Gothic sublimity. Frère Arsene/Comminge's account of his dream to D'Orvigni occurs in thirty-four lines, bringing Act III Scene I of *Les Amans Malheureux* to a dramatic close.

To the eye, the ear, the heart, and all subject senses, death in every horrid shape presented itself. . . *he could have fancied it the common sepulchre of the universe*: cf. D'Arnaud's similar images, op. cit., V. i, p. 75: "On eût dit que ces bords, de la nature entière, / Du monde enfin étoient l'éternel cimetière. / Tout à l'oreille, aux yeux, au cœur, à tous les sens; / Portoit l'affreuse mort & ses traits déchirants.

(p. 305) *Whilst he was contemplating* . . . *and the earth was convulsed*: Details of this Gothic nightmare encounter differ from those in *Les Amans Malheureux*. For example, Comminge does not immediately identify the vision as a phantom, but as a woman in garments of mourning: ". . . une femme égarée & tremblante; / En vêtements de deuil, les bras levés au Ciel, / Dans les pleurs, succombant sous en trouble mortel." The torch he sees is also not borne by the woman; nor is it blue. In the darkness it is simply there, and "sanglante". Nor is the co-extensive identity of Adélaïde and Euthime immediately made explicit. When Comminge falls on his knees to embrace Adélaïde, he is terrified to find he has encircled "une plaintive tombe". Only as he draws back from this tomb does a menacing spectre arise in the habit of Euthime and uncover to Comminge a heart being devoured in flames, an image to him more terrifying than death itself. The spectre, lamenting in a dolorous voice its cruel destiny of misfortune, calls on him to stop, and to contemplate, as "a monument of celestial vengeance", those flames kindled by heaven to expiate errors of criminal tendency. It further commands him to repent, as there is still time, and to repair his offences. Concluding with an abrupt, "You see Adélaïde . . . I await you", the apparition then drops and vanishes into the night-dark tomb, accompanied by a thunderclap and roar from Inferno (ibid., pp. 75-76).

(p. 307) *For the sake of this lover I espoused a man I detested* . . . *cruel husband*: In de Tencin (op. cit., pp. 165-166), Adélaïde, who does not expose Comminge as her lover, is even more spirited about her profanation of the marriage vow/sacrament: "Even in the choice of husband, I sought only to give proof of the extravagance of my passion: and he who could inspire hate alone, was to obviate my lover's jealousy to all unworthily preferred. But it was the will of the Almighty, that a marriage thus contracted with views so criminal, should be an uninterrupted source of misery."

(p. 311) *Tremble all you that listen* . . . *the effects of the passions, the fatal illusions of sensibility*: Ambrose/Emily's admonitory words are similar to those of the dying Sister Agnes in *The Mysteries of Udolpho*, op. cit., vol. IV, pp. 541, 607. In *Les Amans Malheureux* (V. vi., p. 100) this injunction is addressed specifically to the still yearning d'Orvigni, who is present to the end.

"Farewell! no more will I return to thee!. . . *wait to unite with thine!"*: Cf. the brevity of d'Arnaud, ibid., p. 101: "Mon Pere [*sic*] . . . approchez-vous . . . Dieu . . . Comminge . . . Je meurs."

Appendix: Sources of the Chapter Epigraphs

VOLUME I

CHAP.

1 Thomas Gray, "Elegy Written in a Country Churchyard," ll. 33-36.
2 *Paradise Lost*, Bk. VIII, ll. 488-489.
3 Torquato Tasso, *Jerusalem Delivered: An Heroic Poem*, Bk. IV, ll. 663-666.
4 Mary Robinson, "Lines to Him Who Will Understand Them," ll. 21-24.
5 John Milton, *Paradise Lost*, Bk. V, ll. 153-155.
6 Robert Merry, *The Pains of Memory*, ll. 391-396.
7 Mary Robinson, "Ode on Adversity," ll. 11-14.
8 Torquato Tasso, *Jerusalem Delivered*, ll. 435-440.

VOLUME II

CHAP.

1 Sir Richard Fanshawe's translation of Giovanni Battista Guarini's *Il Pastor Fido*, III. i. 2091-2094.
2 Torquato Tasso, *Jerusalem Delivered*, Bk. III, ll. 25-32.
3 John Armstrong, *The Art of Preserving Health*, Bk. IV, ll. 147-153.
4 Edward Young, *Love of Fame, The Universal Passion, in Seven Characteristi-*
5 *cal Satires*, Satire I.
Samuel Rogers, "To a Friend on His Marriage," ll. 13-16.
6 William Shakespeare, *The Tragedy of Othello, the Moor of Venice*, III. ii. 116-120.
7 William Shakespeare, *Hamlet*, I. iv. 46-48.
8 William Shakespeare, *The Tragedy of Othello, the Moor of Venice*, I. iii. 160

VOLUME III

CHAP.

1 Alexander Pope, "Elegy to the Memory of an Unfortunate Lady," ll. 1-2.
2 John Armstrong, *The Art of Preserving Health*, Bk. IV, 281-284.
4 Samuel Rogers, *The Pleasures of Memory*, II. 27-32.
5 Edward Young, *The Revenge. A Tragedy in Five Acts*. II.i.
6 Thomas Gray, "Ode on a Distant Prospect of Eton College," ll. 11-14.
7 Robert Merry, *The Pains of Memory*, ll. 385-390.

VOLUME IV

CHAP.

1   Leonard Welsted, "The Invitation," ll. 23-24.

2   Alexander Pope, "Eloisa to Abelard" ll. 165-170.

3   Mary Robinson, "Ode to Beauty," ll. 13-16.

4   Hannah More, "Sensibility: An Epistle to the Honourable Mrs. Boscawen," ll. 301-311.

6   Hannah More "Sensibility: A Poetical Epistle to the Hon. Mrs. Boscawen," ll. 321-326.